More Than a Millionaire
by Emilie Rose

Only one woman held Ryan's attention – Nicole Hightower.

Ryan shouldn't find her attractive. She wasn't his type. He liked his women curvy and soothing. Nicole bordered on too slender and restless. Yet when Nicole's aqua eyes turned his way, she hit him with another megavolt jolt of awareness. He couldn't prevent the unwelcome gut-jarring reaction each time their gazes met.

He didn't want a relationship with her other than a contractual surrogate one. If all went according to his plan, she'd have his kid, hand it over and get out of his life. He didn't want her underfoot and interfering. He didn't need the drama.

Still, she tempted him. And the chemistry between them sizzled hot enough to make him want to engage in a short-term affair. What consequences would there be? After all, she was already having his baby.

The Untamed Sheikh
by Tessa Radley

"Don't look at me like that. I'm not going to hurt you."

Megan's gaze dropped to her phone gripped high in Shafir's strong dark hand. Nothing about this situation reassured her. "I'm supposed to believe that?"

The frantic vibration of her phone diverted her attention. Her messages had come through despite the limo's path through the remote desert. Not a minute too soon! Disregarding his power, his size, Megan dived across his lap, intent on claiming back the phone – her phone, damn it.

Hard thighs of rock-like solidity beneath the elegant trousers were the first warning that she had made a colossal mistake. She jerked her gaze upwards.

Oh, no.

Bare inches separated their faces. Megan was aware of muscle shifting under her. He surrounded her. And he was big – much bigger than she'd realised.

Her breath came in ragged fits – yet he didn't appear to be breathing at all. She gulped in air, but her pounding heart she could do nothing about.

MORE THAN A MILLIONAIRE

BY

EMILIE ROSE

THE UNTAMED SHEIKH

BY

TESSA RADLEY

MILLS & BOON

Published in Great Britain 2010
Harlequin Mills & Boon Limited,
Eton House, 18-24 Paradise Road, Richmond, Surrey TW9 1SR

ISBN: 978 0 263 88178 3

51-0910

Harlequin Mills & Boon policy is to use papers that are natural, renewable and recyclable products and made from wood grown in sustainable forests. The logging and manufacturing processes conform to the legal environmental regulations of the country of origin.

Printed and bound in Spain
by Litografia Rosés S.A., Barcelona

MORE THAN A MILLIONAIRE

BY
EMILIE ROSE

Dear Reader,

I'm a firm believer that everything happens for a reason. When I was bored out of my skull and picked up a magazine last year, I had no idea one article on aviation management companies would launch an entire series ofstories for me. And I had no idea that what I read would give my sons and I so much fun stuff to do together – something we really needed. Thanks to this research and my two oldest sons' passion for flying, I've had a load of new experiences this year, including No. 2 Son flying me to lunch (wow!).

For Nicole Hightower, one devastating mistake leads to her finding the man – none other than Ryan Patrick – and the family she was meant to have. Here's hoping that happenstance brings you new discoveries that brighten your days and the courage to seize the moment.

Happy reading!

Emilie Rose

Bestselling Desire™ author and RITA® Award finalist **Emilie Rose** lives in her native North Carolina with her four sons and two adopted mutts. Writing is her third (and hopefully her last) career. She's managed a medical office and run a home day care, neither of which offers half as much satisfaction as plotting happy endings. Her hobbies include gardening and cooking (especially cheesecake). She's a rabid country music fan because she can find an entire book in almost any song. She is currently working her way through her own "bucket list" which includes learning to ride a Harley.

Visit her website at www.emilierose.com. Letters can be mailed to PO Box 20145, Raleigh, NC 27619, USA or e-mail EmilieRoseC@aol.com.

JBR, you light up the room (and me)
with nothing more than a smile.

No matter what happens, my time with you
has truly been a gift I will never regret.

One

"Define *unfortunate incident,*" Ryan Patrick ordered the director of the Lakeview Fertility Clinic from the visitor's side of the ornate walnut desk.

The director's leather chair creaked, revealing each nervous shift of the man's body. "One of our trainees neglected to cross-reference the lot number on your sample. He only checked the names and those were reversed. I want to assure you, Mr. Patrick, this is an unusual circumstance. We have many checks and balances in place to—"

"What does this mean? To me. Specifically," Ryan cut in impatiently. He unclenched his fingers from the arms of the chair, but it was hard to relax when the man in front of him looked like he was about to have a heart attack at any second.

The director inhaled a long, deep breath. "Your contribution was given to the wrong woman."

Ryan's abdominal muscles tensed. That would only be a problem if—

"Her pregnancy was confirmed two weeks ago," the director added.

Problem. One that jeopardized Ryan's goal of proving to his father that he'd settled down and was ready to take over the reins of the Patrick architectural dynasty. But Ryan was a master troubleshooter. He wouldn't have climbed this far up the ladder of success if he'd thrown in the towel at every obstacle.

Too bad his father couldn't see that.

"Two weeks ago? Why am I just now being informed? And what about my surrogate, the woman I hired?"

"We discovered the situation yesterday when she came in for her appointment. She wasn't inseminated since at your insistence we only had the one vial."

They'd only had one vial because with the reputation of this place he'd expected them to get it right the first time.

"And you're certain this other woman is pregnant with *my* child?"

"Yes, sir."

Ryan tamped down his frustration. Once he'd decided to take the surrogate route he'd spent months interviewing to find the right candidate—one with looks, brains and good genetics. One who wouldn't get emotionally attached to the baby she hosted in her womb for nine months and change her mind about handing over his child.

And now the wrong woman was carrying his baby.

"Who is she?"

"I'm not at liberty to release that information, sir."

Ryan exploded to his feet. "You're not at liberty to tell me who's carrying *my* child?"

"Yes. Confidentiality—"

Ryan intended to get the information one way or the other. He braced his fists on the desk and leaned forward. "Don't make me bring a platoon of lawyers in here. Not only will that be financially costly for you, the negative publicity will knock you right off the list of top fertility clinics in the country. This is my kid, and I have the right to know who and where its mother is and whether she's qualified for the job. I want *everything* you have on her."

The director's face flushed dark red. "Mr. Patrick, I'm sure you understand the privacy of Lakeview's business—"

"I want her name and contact information now. Otherwise my legal team will be all over you like a bad rash before lunch."

The man stiffened and swallowed then fumbled with a folder on his desk. "I'm sure that won't be necessary. Ms. High—our other client seems like a reasonable, understanding woman. Once I explain the situation to her—"

"I'll handle it. You've screwed up enough. You can cover up your mistake with words like *incident, circumstance* and *situation,* but the truth is you've committed malpractice and negligence."

Sweat beaded beneath the man's receding hairline. Ryan eyed him without blinking. Once the man paled, Ryan knew he'd get what he wanted without the aggravation of lawyers. Good. He did not want his father to catch wind of this disaster.

"*Ahem.* I'll get you the information, sir."

Ryan settled back in the chair when the director hustled out. Next on his agenda: find this woman and convince her to give him his baby—the way the surrogate he'd chosen had agreed to.

She would be the best aunt her baby could have.

And it would be enough. It had to be.

Nicole Hightower rubbed one hand over her unsettled stomach and reached for a cracker with the other. She was finally going to have Patrick's baby.

And Beth's.

Her fingers spasmed around the stylus of her PDA at the reminder that her dream wasn't going exactly as she'd once planned.

She shoved the bland whole-wheat cracker into her mouth and tried to focus on the calendar in front of her. She needed to schedule the client's pilot, crew and plane maintenance for the next three months. She usually loved keeping her customers happy and their travel stress-free, but today her private life kept distracting her from the workload on her desk.

Relinquishing her baby would be hard, but she could handle it because she would be not only a godmother, but also a hands-on aunt. Her sister had promised, and Beth kept her promises. Nicole had always been able to count on her big sister—even at the times when she hadn't been able to count on their parents. Carrying a child for Beth was the least Nicole could do.

And since her sister would continue to work at Hightower Aviation Management and bring the baby to work every day, Nicole looked forward to going down the hall to the on-site day care and visiting her—*Beth's*—baby during lunch. Even from her desk she'd be able to observe her b— niece or nephew. She clicked on an icon on her computer screen and a live feed from the company nursery filled her monitor. The caregivers bustled around, tending to the adorable children of HAMC's employees.

The intercom buzzed jarring her from her tangled thoughts. She quickly broke the nursery link. "Yes?"

"There's a Ryan Patrick here to see you."

Nicole smiled over her assistant's mistake. "You mean Patrick Ryan."

"No, I don't. I'm not talking about your brother-in-law," Lea whispered. "I'm talking about the gorgeous black-haired, blue-eyed, towering hunk of manhood standing in the reception area. His business card says he's the VP at Patrick Architectural Designs. That's one of Knoxville's most prestigious firms, in case you didn't know. Are we expanding again?"

"As far as I know Hightower Aviation isn't planning to build any new structures." But then her oldest brother, Trent, the CEO, didn't tell her everything. As the youngest Hightower offspring until recently, Nicole was often kept out of the loop.

She double-checked her calendar to make sure she hadn't forgotten an appointment and found no one scheduled for another hour. Then, because she didn't like to go into a meeting unprepared, she typed Patrick Architectural Designs into her Internet search engine. A series of links popped up on her screen. She chose the one that looked the most useful, clicked and scanned the Web page. There were no pictures of the man in question, only of buildings designed by his company and a brief company history. Impressive. They'd been around awhile.

"Patrick Architectural is a commercial firm with projects across the continent," she said into the intercom. "Do you think Mr. Patrick might be a potential client?"

Although normally new clients came to her through the sales department *after* they'd purchased, leased or bought shares in an aircraft.

His name was an interesting coincidence, though.

"I prefer my fantasy to your logic," Lea quipped.

"You always have, Lea. Bring him back."

"Yes, ma'am."

Nicole brushed the crumbs from her silk blouse and into the trash can then slid the sleeve of crackers into her drawer. She rose just as Lea tapped on her door and pushed it open.

The man striding into her office like he owned the place was everything her assistant had said and more. Lea hadn't mentioned her visitor's short hair had a curl that he couldn't quite subdue or that his shoulders filled out his navy suit jacket like a tailor's dream above a flat stomach, lean hips and long legs. And his eyes weren't just blue; they were an amazingly intense shade of cobalt. Those eyes assessed her now as he would a Learjet he was considering purchasing.

Nicole fought the urge to check her neckline and the corners of her mouth for more crumbs.

"Nicole Hightower?"

Even his voice had a deep and slightly rough sexual fantasy quality. Not that she ever fantasized about clients. That would be totally unprofessional.

And too much like her mother.

She walked around the corner of her desk and extended her arm. "Yes. How can I help you, Mr. Patrick?"

His handshake was warm and firm and electrified.

Giving up caffeine must be having unforeseen side effects on her system. Why else would she experience a faux espresso buzz on contact? She broke the connection as quickly as courtesy allowed.

His intense gaze shifted to Lea and conveyed something that made the redhead snap to attention. "I'll just…go now."

Surprised, Nicole watched her usually unflappable assistant hustle out the door and close it behind her.

Nicole reappraised the man in front of her. Besides tall,

dark and gorgeous, he had some kind of magical talent. She'd have to figure out what trick he'd used to make Lea leave without saying a word.

Lea wasn't only an employee. She was also a friend and sometimes the line between friend and supervisor blurred—like when Lea had voiced her vehement disapproval of Nicole's decision to become a surrogate for her sister and brother-in-law. But that was because Lea knew how Nicole felt about her sister's husband. They'd been college roommates when Nicole had fallen head over heels in love with Patrick. And Lea had been there to help pick up the pieces after Patrick had eloped with Nicole's sister Beth.

Lea was convinced that the entire "baby debacle," as she referred to it, was going to blow up in Nicole's face now that she was pregnant.

"Please sit down, Mr. Patrick, and tell me what I can do for you today."

Nicole felt his gaze on her the entire way around her desk as she returned to her seat. Pregnancy had made her breasts larger. She hoped it hadn't done the same to her behind. Not that she cared what he thought of her butt.

After she sank into her seat he lowered himself into the chair across from her desk. The old-fashioned courtesy surprised her. Fewer and fewer men practiced it these days—especially among the megarich she dealt with through work.

"Congratulations on your pregnancy."

His words stunned her. She hadn't told anyone except Beth, Patrick and Lea. The parents-to-be had the right to know, and Lea had caught Nicole heaving a couple of times and guessed. The rest of their friends and family would find out Saturday when Beth and Patrick made the official announcement at the family's Labor Day picnic. Nicole suspected most people who knew her would be a little freaked out by her decision.

"Thank you. What brings you to Hightower Aviation today?"

"You're carrying my child."

His statement knocked her back in her chair. She must have misheard.

"Excuse me?" The words sounded more like a wheeze, but that was because she couldn't seem to make her lungs work.

"The fertility clinic made a mistake and inseminated you with my sperm instead of your intended donor's."

Head reeling, she grasped the edge of her desk. "That's not possible."

Her visitor reached into his suit coat, extracted an envelope and extended it toward her. When she didn't—couldn't—take it from him he tossed it on her blotter. It slid across the smooth surface and stopped within easy reach. She eyed it like she would a big, hairy, jumping spider.

"The clinic director has written a letter explaining the situation. In summation, my name is Ryan Patrick. Your intended donor's name is Patrick Ryan. The lot numbers weren't checked and you were given the wrong sperm because some moron neglected to notice a comma."

Horror raced through her, making her heart pound and her extremities tingle. "No. You're wrong."

He had to be.

"Read it."

She stared at the envelope. Afraid to open it. Afraid not to. But she couldn't prove him wrong if she didn't open the thing. Her hands shook as she reached for it.

The tearing of the seal and the rustle of paper as she unfolded the page sounded unnaturally loud even above the pounding of her pulse in her ears. The letter bore the Lakeview logo at the top and the director's signature on the bottom. She forced herself to read through the document.

Words jumped out at her. *Unfortunate error... Donor mix-up... Apologize profusely...* The alarm in her chest and her brain expanded with each line, making it difficult to breathe and think. She read the letter a second time, but the bad news didn't get any better, and she hadn't misinterpreted.

Unless this letter was a hideously tasteless joke, she was carrying Ryan Patrick's baby. Not Patrick Ryan's, the man she had loved since her junior year of college. The man who'd married her sister.

Please, God, let this be a joke.

"This is not funny."

Her visitor didn't crack a smile. "Medical malpractice usually isn't."

She had hoped her sister had developed a sudden sick sense of humor. His stoic expression said otherwise. Pressing a hand over her churning stomach, she dropped the page. "There must be some mistake."

"Yes. Lakeview Fertility Clinic made it. You're carrying my child as a result."

"That can't be right."

"I wish that were true."

She stared at the letter while her overloaded mind struggled to process the information and the possible repercussions. For herself. For Beth and Patrick. For the man in front of her. But it was too much to take in.

What now? What if the baby really wasn't Patrick's?

She struggled to find her professional demeanor, and the best way to do that was to focus on his problem instead of hers. "I'm sorry. This must be very difficult for you and your wife."

"There is no wife."

"Girlfriend, then."

"No girlfriend, either."

That confused her completely. "I'm afraid I'm not following."

"I'll be a single parent."

"That's not unusual for a woman, but isn't it a little out of the norm for a man? Couldn't you just get married?"

"I've been married, and I don't ever intend to do so again."

There had to be a story behind that bitter tone. But she didn't care to hear it at the moment. She had enough of a mess on her hands. *If* his story was true. She sincerely hoped he was deranged. A psycho in her office would be much easier to handle than the situation described in the letter. One call to security would fix everything. But this…

He extracted a second envelope and placed it in front of her. "I'm prepared to offer you the same financial and medical support I offered the surrogate I'd hired."

Taken aback, she blinked. "You hired a surrogate?"

Why would a guy who looked like him need to pay someone to have his baby? Women should be lining up around the block and begging for the privilege.

"A well-qualified, carefully screened surrogate."

She bristled at his implication that she might be less than qualified to carry his child. For the second time this morning she forced herself to read something she didn't want to and picked up the contract.

Shocked, she looked up from the document that had

her name typed in all the appropriate places. "You want to *buy* my baby?"

Duh. That's what surrogacy is, Nicole. But seeing it in black and white rattled her.

"It's a service contract. You provide a product and a service. I pay you for your time and the use of your body," he replied as coolly as if they were haggling over the price of an airplane.

A product? Revulsion slammed her chest a split second before an unexpected surge of possessiveness swelled within her. She wrapped her arms around her middle. Until now she'd been ready to hand over her baby to Beth and Patrick. With dignity. Without a fight. But she'd be damned if she'd *sell* it to this stranger.

"You are out of your mind, Mr. Patrick."

"It's my child."

"It's mine, too. My egg. My body. My time."

"My terms are quite generous."

She tossed the document back at him. He made no effort to catch it. The pages fluttered to the desk. "I don't care about your terms. Go back to your surrogate."

"And forget I've already fathered one child?"

"Yes. You have no emotional investment here and no financial obligation. You can have another baby much easier than I can. I will carry this child for nine months. Your contribution only took seconds."

"You're only eight weeks pregnant. You haven't had time to bond."

Her mouth dropped open. She snapped it closed. "Spoken like a man who doesn't have a clue. You have no idea what you're talking about."

She'd begun bonding from the first moment she'd noticed her taste buds had gone crazy—just days after conception and even before the positive pregnancy test. She remembered the exact moment she'd realized she was pregnant with Patrick's baby.

According to *him* it wasn't Patrick's baby.

He might be wrong. Please, please let him be wrong.

"I'm sorry. I'm not going to believe your story without proof."

"You have it." He indicated the letter by dipping his chin.

"This is not enough." She'd go through the clinic's records personally, if need be. And if that didn't work…there was always DNA testing. How soon could that be done? And was it safe for the baby? She jotted down the questions to ask her doctor.

Her visitor's jawline hardened. "You're only twenty-eight. You have time to have other children."

Unlikely, since her heart was already taken. "You're not exactly ancient."

"I'm thirty-five."

"Women have a shorter window of opportunity for reproducing than men. You can keep fathering children for another fifty years."

His lips thinned in irritation. "I want a child now, and I'm not walking away and leaving the door open for you to sue me for child support."

The jerk's personality did not improve with exposure. Usually she could find something to like about even the most difficult person. Not so here. Other than his physical packaging which was prime.

She took a deep breath and reminded herself that any problem could be solved with patience, politeness and perseverance. Her three *P*'s never let her down.

"I would never do that, Mr. Patrick. I don't want or expect anything from you."

His eyebrows lowered. "You expect me to take the word of a stranger?"

She was too busy reeling over the possibility that she might be carrying a stranger's baby to care what he thought.

"I'm not interested in your money, and I'm willing to have my attorney draft a document stating that fact and relieving you of all responsibility."

"That would be useless. You'd have eighteen years to change your mind."

She wanted to smack him. "Mr. Patrick, I couldn't give you this child even if I wanted to—which I don't."

She pressed her fingertips to her stomach and gathered the words that had become her mantra since she'd committed to this plan. "This baby is not mine. I'm carrying it for my sister and brother-in-law."

Who might not want the baby if it wasn't Patrick's.

Oh my God.

Panic tightened her chest. A cold sweat seeped through her pores. What was she going to do? She certainly wasn't handing her baby to this knuckle-dragging Neanderthal who acted as if giving up her child would be as easy as giving a panhandler the change from her pocket.

"You're acting as a surrogate for someone else?"

His clipped words interrupted her chaotic thoughts. "Yes. Patrick Ryan is my brother-in-law."

"How much is he paying you?"

Appalled, she reared back. "Nothing. This is a gift."

"I'm offering a hundred thousand, plus expenses. You're going to give up the kid. Why not to me? You can have his kid next year."

His cavalier attitude winded her. "I'm not a broodmare."

She'd geared herself up to do this once. She didn't think she could handle giving a baby away a second time.

"I'll make it worth your while."

"No, thank you. I gave my word." For once she wanted to come through for Beth instead of having Beth make all the sacrifices for her. She owed her sister a huge debt.

And she wanted to give Patrick something Beth couldn't.

Not nice, Nicole.

"Tell her you changed your mind. If the egg is yours, then the child is in no way hers or her husband's."

She flinched and wished he'd quit reminding her of that.

Adrenaline surged through her veins. If the baby wasn't Patrick's then it was *hers.*

Hers and the Neanderthal's.

"I signed a contract," she said more to herself than to him. So where did that leave her? Was the contract even valid if the baby wasn't Patrick's?

"Contracts can be broken."

She needed to talk to her lawyer before tackling the legalities. "You don't understand. I will be this child's aunt. I'll see it almost every day. I'll get to watch him or her grow up and be a part of its life. I'll still be family."

She hated the anxiety sharpening her voice. The idea had sounded so much better before her pregnancy had been confirmed. "Go back to your surrogate."

"You're carrying my firstborn and firstborn Patricks have taken over the family firm for three generations."

"What if my child doesn't want to be an architect?"

One dark eyebrow hiked. "Why wouldn't he?"

"Because I don't have an artistic bone in my body and he or *she* might take after me."

"Or he might take after me and be damned good at it. Don't turn this into a legal battle, Ms. Hightower."

His threat was clear. The muscles of her spine went rigid

and her heart thumped even harder. Her arms tightened protectively around her middle. They'd done that a lot since he'd walked in. "This is my baby."

"Is it, if you've already signed away your rights? As the child's biological father I probably have more rights to it than you do."

Fear slithered down her spine. She was very afraid that what he said might be true, but she wasn't giving up without a fight. She glared at him, silently telling him to bring it on. The stiffening of his features told her he'd received her message loud and clear. He stood and towered over her.

She rose to meet him at his level, but still had to tilt her head back. How tall was he, anyway? Well over six feet.

"This discussion is over, Mr. Patrick, until I talk to my attorney."

"Do that. Mine will be calling you. But be warned, Ms. Hightower, I always get what I want, and I will be a father to my child. Make it easy on yourself, accept that and don't prolong this."

He turned on his heel, flung open her door and stalked out of her office, sucking all the oxygen with him as he went.

Sapped of strength, but conversely filled with an energizing surplus of adrenaline, Nicole sank into her chair. She had to do something to stop him. Because if Ryan Patrick had his way she would be giving up far more than the right to mother her baby. She might never see her child again. And that was not going to happen.

Two

Apparently it didn't matter which side of the desk Nicole sat on. Today was her day to receive bad news.

She stared in dismay at the woman in front of her. "You're saying he's correct. Ryan Patrick has more right to my baby than I do?"

While her attorney's smile and brown eyes were sympathetic, they didn't offer much encouragement. "I'm sorry, Nicole. The clinic confirmed his story. There was a mix-up. Biologically, this is his child unless DNA testing proves otherwise."

"But my doctor said I couldn't do prenatal DNA testing without significant risk to the baby. So that's out of the question." Nicole had called her in a panic the minute Ryan Patrick left her office. "I don't think I can stand seven more months of uncertainty."

"I understand. And it really isn't necessary since the lot

number of Ryan Patrick's…contribution was found written on your record. Too bad the technician didn't double-check it beforehand."

She was carrying a stranger's baby.

Not Patrick's.

Disappointment and helpless frustration filled her with an antsy urge to climb out of her skin. "Is the contract even valid since the baby isn't Patrick's?"

"The wording states you're providing them with a child, and that you have no intention of claiming that child. It doesn't specify paternity. The agreement is pretty ironclad. They used all the right phrases to protect themselves in case you changed your mind, and since we didn't think that would be an issue, I didn't strike or amend the clause."

A heavy weight settled on Nicole's chest. "I don't want Ryan Patrick to get custody. If he does, I may never see my baby again. At least Beth promised me I could be a hands-on aunt."

"But you didn't get that promise in writing, so it wouldn't hold up in court. I wish I could say the chances of Mr. Patrick winning at least partial custody were slim, but they're not.

"This isn't your fight, Nicole, unless you elect to try and revoke your surrogacy contract which I can tell you will be a tough and expensive battle. If you choose that route you'll fight your sister and her husband first, and then the winner of your battle will fight the baby's father."

A lose-lose proposition. "Breaking the contract would destroy my relationship with my family. I won't do that. My family is too important to me."

Her attorney nodded. "Then your first order of business is to talk to Beth and Patrick. Tell them what you've discovered. Make sure they still want to adopt this child. Their decision determines your next action."

The idea of confronting Beth and Patrick and the fear of what they'd say made her queasy. Her dream of having Patrick's baby had become a nightmare. Or had it? She'd given up long ago on ever having children of her own.

"If Beth and Patrick no longer want this baby, can I keep it?"

"Your odds of winning either way are not good. The day you signed the waiver to relinquish to your sister and brother-in-law you knowingly entered into this agreement with no intention of parenting this child. Precedents in Texas and California have granted custody to the father in similar situations."

That was not what she wanted to hear. But even if she could keep her baby, what did she know about good parenting? Her parents certainly hadn't set an example to emulate. They'd been gone more than they'd been at home, and when they'd been at home they both tended to be self-centered. Not a pretty picture despite the united front they presented to the world.

"In the meantime," her attorney continued, "I'll pursue legal action against the clinic. Besides their negligence, they've violated so many rules and regulations by releasing your personal information to Mr. Patrick without following proper legal channels that the courts and several regulatory agencies will be occupied for a long time."

"I…I suppose that has to be done to prevent the clinic doing this to someone else. I'll talk to Beth and Patrick this afternoon." Until then she had no idea where she stood.

And that was one conversation she dreaded more than anything she'd ever had to do in her life except for smiling through congratulating the man she loved on marrying her sister.

"Nicole, I'd like to caution you to be civil to Mr. Patrick.

In my thirty years of experience I've learned the more contentious the fight becomes, the uglier and more expensive it gets. People forget about doing what's right and start fighting to win at all costs."

Nicole had a sinking feeling Ryan Patrick didn't like losing, and he could afford to fight a lot longer than she could.

Beth and Patrick's silence spoke volumes as did the look they exchanged.

Nicole's stomach cramped with tension while she waited for their response to her bad news. She dampened her dry lips. "So the baby is still yours…if you want it."

Beth gave her a patient smile. "Of course we want the baby, Nicole. The child is yours and therefore related to us."

Relief loosened the knots in Nicole's muscles.

"Beth, a legal battle could be expensive," Patrick pointed out with his usual pragmatism.

"This baby is a Hightower, dear," Beth countered. "We can't let that man break up our family."

Beth and Patrick shared another long, speaking glance, and a teensy twinge of jealousy pricked Nicole. In the three months she and Patrick had dated before she'd brought him home to meet her parents and siblings she and he had never shared that type of silent communication.

But Beth and Patrick had been married for a long time, Nicole reminded herself. They'd had time to develop those skills. If things had gone differently, if Nicole and Patrick had married as she'd once believed they would, then they would have been the ones with that special bond. Wouldn't they?

But Patrick had preferred her sister, and Nicole wanted

him to be happy—even if it wasn't with her. He was one of a kind and the only man who'd ever win her heart. She wasn't like her mother who flitted from one affair to the next searching for some fantasy that didn't exist.

"Beth," Patrick protested.

"Nicole is doing this oh-so-generous thing for me—for *us*—to repay me for looking after her when we were growing up. How could I refuse such a selfless gift? And we do want a baby more than anything, don't we?"

"Right. More than anything."

Did Patrick's tone sound a little bitter and resentful? No. He was just shaken and disappointed by Nicole's news. He'd wanted to be a father and now he wasn't…biologically, anyway. And if he was on edge it was only because he and Beth had been trying to conceive for more than three years. The doctors couldn't find anything wrong with either of them and didn't have a clue to the cause of Beth's unexplained infertility.

Thank God Nicole had conceived on the first try. Otherwise—

You'd have come to your senses.

Lea's nagging voice echoed in Nicole's head. She squelched it. Her assistant didn't understand how much Beth had sacrificed for Nicole to have a regular childhood. Beth had forfeited dates, the prom, going to college among other things to play substitute mom while their globe-trotting parents gallivanted frequently and parented sporadically.

Carrying a child for Beth was the least Nicole could do.

"This could get expensive," Patrick persisted. "You know how much we're already spending on—"

"On getting ready for the baby," Beth replied with a tight smile. "Yes, darling, I know. But Nicole doesn't need to worry about that. She needs someone to take care of her little problem, and taking care of problems is what I do best." Beth turned to Nicole. "Don't worry yourself. Big sister will handle everything. Just like I've always done."

Nicole stifled a wince. Yes, there had been dozens of incidents when Beth had covered for Nicole—none of which Nicole was proud of these days. But somehow Nicole didn't feel as confident in her sister's abilities this time. She wasn't sure that even the mighty Beth could deter Ryan Patrick from his goal.

Her baby would be happy here, Nicole assured herself as she lugged a mountain of insulated food containers past a black Corvette convertible and up Beth's concrete sidewalk between rows of blooming dianthus, begonias and hostas.

Beth and Patrick had bought the large two-story traditional brick home with the lush emerald lawn and white picket fenced backyard with a large family in mind. On any given weekend morning children laughed and played in the neighborhood, riding their bicycles in the cul-de-sac. What more could any child want?

And what more could any woman want for her child?

You've made the right decision. All you have to do is keep Ryan Patrick from upsetting your plan.

The smell of roasting meat filled the air, made her mouth water and thankfully, distracted her from her negative thoughts. She'd been running since her feet hit the floor at five this morning, and she'd barely had time to eat a granola bar for breakfast and swallow her prenatal vitamins.

Letting herself in Beth's side door the way she always did, Nicole checked the kitchen. Empty. That was odd since there was so much to do before the guests arrived at noon. Beth and Patrick were probably getting dressed.

Nicole deposited the food she'd prepared for the party on the counter then put the cold items in the fridge and the warm items in the oven on low heat.

Next on the agenda, the backyard. She stepped onto the stoop, scanned the fenced area and smiled. The weather on this first weekend in September couldn't be more perfect for a picnic. The sun was out, but the expected afternoon high temperature wouldn't be too hot or too cool. This close to autumn it was difficult to anticipate what Knoxville's weather would be when planning weeks or months in advance as she always did.

The additional tables she'd rented had been delivered and set up on the grass. The party supply company had draped the tables with red-and-white checkered cloths and decorated each with a potted blooming red or white geranium as Nicole had instructed. Everything looked bright and cheerful, the perfect place to announce the family would be growing.

A lanky apron- and ball cap–wearing man stood by the massive grill on the edge of the large flagstone patio.

"Good morning," she called out as she approached him. "I'm Nicole Hightower."

He nodded and shook her hand. "Bill Smith. Your rent-a-chef. Great day for a pig pickin'."

"Yes. Do you have everything you need, Bill?"

"Yes, ma'am. Pig's 'bout done. I just put on the chicken. Veggie skewers will go on in a few minutes."

Her stomach rumbled in anticipation, but she had too much to do to get ready for the others' arrivals to take time for a snack. "Excellent. Please help yourself to a soda or iced tea, and don't hesitate to ask me for anything you need."

"Thank you."

She lifted a lid on a nearby cooler and found it filled with ice and canned sodas and bottled water as requested. The second cooler revealed more ice and beer—the varieties her brothers preferred and a couple of magnums of champagne. Perfect. She'd definitely use this party company again. Letting someone else do the grunt work was far better than making Patrick and Beth get up at the crack of dawn to attend to the tasks or racing over here to do it herself.

Beth hated planning events. That's why Nicole always landed the job, and she didn't mind because making sure things ran smoothly was sort of an obsession with her. Now more than ever. She brushed a hand over her belly.

The family picnic was a Labor Day weekend tradition—one she'd started herself after Beth and Patrick had married. If anything needed to run smoothly, today's event did. For the most part her family members got along well, but this year they'd have not only the stress of Nicole's pregnancy news to contend with, but also the pressure of the newest Hightower—a younger half sister none of them had known about until a month ago when she'd shown up on their doorstep and their mother had insisted she be given a job at Hightower Aviation.

Having a living, breathing reminder that her mother was a bit…um, free with her affection had been unsettling to say the least. In the past everyone including their father had pretended not to notice Jacqueline Hightower's indiscretions, and no one talked about her affairs. It would be hard to ignore the situation with her mother's love child at the family gathering. And how had her mother hidden a daughter for twenty-five years, anyway?

Nicole headed back to the house. From the kitchen she followed the sound of Beth's voice toward the living room.

Her sister's tone wasn't the one she used when talking to Patrick. Some of the nonfamily party guests must have arrived early. Probably the owner of the convertible.

"The child is not yours." The deep voice stopped Nicole in her tracks in the foyer.

Ryan Patrick was *here.* Talking to Beth.

"The baby is Nicole's," Beth replied.

"Sweetheart," Patrick interjected in that gentle, patient tone of his that Nicole adored. "You do understand that Mr. Patrick is offering us a lot of money to accommodate him."

Nicole's mouth dried and panic caused her heart to gallop. That devious bastard was trying to bribe her sister and brother-in-law into giving up her baby.

If he brainwashed Beth and Patrick, he could cut Nicole out of the child's life altogether. She wasn't going to let that happen.

She rushed into the room. "How dare you go behind my back?"

Ryan slowly unfolded from the leather wingback chair. His cobalt eyes locked with hers. "I'm going to the ones who have the power to make a decision—the right decision to allow this child to live with his natural father."

She couldn't help noticing the way his charcoal suit, pale blue shirt and crimson tie accentuated his good looks and athletic frame. But pretty is as pretty does, or so one of their many nannies had always said. And what Ryan Patrick was doing was downright ugly.

"I told you, you're not getting this baby."

He shoved the lapels of his suit coat aside and planted his hands on his lean hips. "If you've consulted your attorney, then you know that you don't have any say in the matter."

Unless she went to war with her family. And even then her chances were slim. She glanced at Beth and Patrick and hugged her churning middle. She couldn't start a family feud. Her mother had wreaked enough havoc on them all over the years.

Patience, politeness and perseverance. Her motto echoed in her head. Every problem had a solution. All she had to do was find it. In the meantime, she'd have to be nice to the jerk if she wanted any chance of wringing a positive outcome from this situation. She hated sucking up to blowhards, but she'd mastered the skill.

"Could I speak with you outside a moment?" she said through a smile stretched so tightly her checks hurt.

Ryan gestured toward the door.

Trying to ignore the delicious tang of his cologne, she accompanied him to the center hall then led the way to the back door. He reached past her to open it for her. She marched across the backyard, heading toward the gazebo in the back corner of the lot with Ryan close on her heels. Too close.

Inside the jasmine-draped structure she put as much distance between them as the shelter would permit before facing him. How could she make him see reason?

"Do you have any brothers and sisters, Ryan?" His name felt awkward on her tongue. But she couldn't keep calling him Mr. Patrick. Each time she said his last name she thought of the man inside the house—the man whose baby she should be carrying.

"No."

So much for appealing to his family nature. He didn't have one. "Then you can't possibly understand how important it is for me to have this child for my sister."

"That's irrelevant. It's not her kid. It's mine."

She couldn't argue with facts. She took a calming breath and tried a different tactic. "She has been yearning for a baby for years, and she'll love this one as if it were hers. How much experience do you have with children?"

"I'll learn what I need to know."

The stubborn blockhead. She had to find a way to convince him that the baby would be better off with Beth and Patrick. But how? The answer was almost too easy. She smiled.

"As you can see from the setup, we're having a party in a few minutes. It will be mostly family with a few friends and neighbors thrown into the mix. Please join us."

His eyes narrowed. "Why?"

"So you can see what a great life Beth and Patrick can give this baby. The child will be surrounded by a loving family. He or she will have aunts and uncles and soon, cousins. My sister-in-law is expecting to deliver just a few months before me."

"You won't change my mind."

Maybe not. But it was a risk she had to take if she wanted to be a part of her baby's life. "All I ask is that you keep an open mind and see what you're determined to deny this child. Join us, Ryan…unless you're allergic to good food and good company."

He stiffened at her implied challenge and accepted her dare with a slight dip of his chin. But his drilling stare warned her he wasn't going to make this easy for her. For the next four hours she would have her work cut out for her in convincing him to change his mind.

Her baby's future and her role in it depended on her success in making Ryan Patrick agree to go away empty-handed.

Forty people milled about Beth and Patrick Ryan's backyard. But only one held Ryan's attention. Nicole Hightower.

He shouldn't find her attractive. She wasn't his type. He liked his women curvy and soothing. Nicole bordered on too slender and restless. Not only could she not stand still for more than thirty seconds, but also her lean build didn't include the matronly "breeding hips" he'd chosen for his surrogate. Yet he had no problem imagining her nursing a baby at the small, but firm-looking breasts outlined by her sundress.

Not a thought he needed to entertain since that would not happen with his child. His child would be bottle-fed by a nanny from day one.

Nicole's aqua eyes turned his way, hitting him with another megavolt jolt of awareness. She'd nailed him with a similar glance several times this afternoon, and he couldn't prevent the unwelcome gut-jarring reaction each time their gazes met.

He didn't want a relationship with her other than a contractual one. If all went according to his plan, she'd have his kid, hand it over and get out of his life. He didn't want her underfoot and interfering. He didn't need the drama.

Nicole indicated his beer with a slight nod. He shook his head. Drinking to excess didn't mix well with sexual attraction unless he intended to end up in bed with the object of his attention. He'd done that often enough in the past couple of decades to push his father into concocting the stupid stipulation that Ryan prove his stability and maturity if he wanted to take over the reins of Patrick Architectural upon his father's retirement next summer. If Ryan failed, his father had threatened to sell the firm. That made ignoring the chemistry between him and Nicole imperative because another short-term affair—no matter how hot it might burn before it fizzled out—wouldn't help his cause.

A breeze lifted Nicole's long hair away from her face. He preferred the wavy caramel-colored strands loose and swishing between her shoulder blades instead of twisted up on her head the way they had been the day he'd confronted her at her office.

Not that his preferences counted.

Genetically, she should produce a good-looking kid. She was more attractive than the surrogate he'd hired. Her face was fine-boned and full-lipped, her smile quick and frequent—except when she looked at him. Then the stretch of her lips was slow and forced as if having him here were a pain in the rear.

Another thing he'd noticed this afternoon, Nicole was a toucher. Every time someone got close enough, she reached out and brushed a hand over their arm or shoulder or kissed a cheek. That's why he'd kept his distance. He didn't want a repeat of the zap she'd delivered with that first handshake the day they'd met. Chemistry was great. Unless it was unwanted. Then it was nothing but trouble.

He scanned the yard, passing over each of the Hightowers. He'd bet Nicole would look exactly like her mother in forty years. She possessed the same slender build, same features. Behavior-wise, other than the high energy level, Mamma Hightower was the opposite of her daughter. Whereas Nicole was friendly, but reserved, her mother was flirtatious, gregarious and sexually aware of every move she made in that way well-maintained wealthy older women exhibited when they'd been the type to bring men to their knees in their younger days.

Nicole's father, a silent loner who nursed his imported beer in the shade of a tall oak tree, only spoke to those who sought him out. Her older twin brothers looked identical, but one was a player and the other appeared to be an unhappily married man with an eye that often strayed from his pregnant wife to the female guests.

Ryan's gaze skimmed over neighbors and other company until it landed on Beth and Patrick Ryan huddled in the corner of the patio. They were arguing. Again. Ryan had caught several heated exchanges between them during the past three hours.

Nicole might believe this was the perfect setup for raising a child, but Ryan sensed trouble in this suburban, cookie-cutter paradise. The tension between the couple was palpable from fifty feet away, and it had been even more obvious when he'd presented his offer before the party. Just one more reason to make damned sure he got full custody. He didn't want his kid to be a bone of contention in an ugly divorce the way he'd been. And he'd bet his Corvette, his boat and his motorcycle the Ryans would land in divorce court sooner than later.

Beth reminded him of his mother. She wore the same self-suffering martyr attitude his mother had pulled in the years after she'd packed up a ten-year-old Ryan and moved away from her husband. Millicent Patrick had spent the next eight years using Ryan as a weapon against his father and bitching about his father's mistress—work.

Her complaints had fallen on deaf ears. A love of architecture was something he and his father had had in common even back when Ryan had been a snot-nosed kid. For as far back as he could remember, Ryan had spent hours beside his father's drafting table asking questions, begging to be allowed to "help." His father had always indulged him until the separation after which he'd had little time for his only son.

Work was the only mistress he and his father respected or committed to for the long haul. Women couldn't be trusted or counted on. A lesson he'd learned the hard way compliments of his ex-wife, the lying, cheating bitch.

His gaze shifted to the youngest Hightower. She interested him because as much as she resembled her mother and Nicole, she didn't fit in. The roar of her Harley splitting the silence of the neighborhood had been his first clue. Like him, she was an outsider here. Not even Nicole's frequent attempts at drawing her sister into the crowd could breach the gap between her and the rest of the siblings. And Nicole seemed to be the only one making an effort to include her sister.

The Hightower in question looked up, caught his eye and headed in his direction. Her black leather boots and jeans-covered legs crossed the lawn with a long stride. In the past the rebel in her would have called to the rebel in him. But for some reason, her wild side didn't twitch his interest today.

She stopped in front of him. "You don't look like one of Beth's snooty neighbors."

Ryan smiled. He'd made the same assumption about the guests' attitudes. He offered his hand. "Ryan Patrick and, no, I don't live in the area."

Her eyebrows rose when she heard his name, but she didn't comment. Her handshake was firm and brief with no sparks despite her resemblance to her sister. "Lauren Lynch."

She looked enough like Nicole that he would have sworn they were closely related. "You're not a Hightower?"

"Jacqueline is my mother, but William isn't my father. My father died a couple of months ago. And before you strain your brain trying to unravel that long, boring story, my mother had an affair with a Hightower Aviation pilot. I'm the byproduct. She delivered me, left me with my dad and returned to her husband and other children like a good little wife."

That explained the tension between Lauren and the Hightower siblings. "I'm sorry for your loss."

She shrugged. "Thanks. Losing my dad was hard, but his passing gave me the opportunity to meet a family I didn't know I had. So what brings you here? Are you a Hightower Aviation client?"

He wasn't ready to reveal the truth. "Not yet, but I'm considering contracting the company."

Access to a plane would make his life easier since he traveled the country on a regular basis. He definitely wanted to contract one of the Hightowers. But not for flying.

"Married?" Lauren asked.

He gave her credit for being direct. "Not anymore. You?"

"No way. Never have been. Probably never will be. Do you have any children?"

"Not yet."

Lauren glanced down at her beer bottle then back up at him through lashes as long and thick as her sister's. "Can I give you a hint?"

About what? "Sure."

"Nicole's probably the most decent one in the bunch. Maybe even the only decent Hightower. But she's going to be a hard nut to crack because… Well, she just is. I'll let you figure out the whys. Stick with her. She's worth it."

Were all women born with a matchmaking gene?

"What makes you think I'm interested in Nicole?"

Lauren grinned and sipped her beer. "Could be the way you've been watching her all afternoon."

Guilty. But how else was he going to learn about the mother of his child? He searched for her. Nicole had joined her sister and brother-in-law and was currently engaged in a hushed but animated conversation. Nicole covered her belly with one hand. Her gaze bounced over the crowd and landed on Ryan. He didn't know what her sister had said to upset her, but the distress on her face was clear. Adrenaline shot through his system.

"Go ahead," Lauren prompted.

"Go ahead and what?"

"Ride to her rescue. You know you want to."

Smart girl. "Is Nicole the type to need rescuing?"

Lauren grimaced. "Let's just say if I were her, I would have told this bunch of leeches to go to hell a long time ago. But she's the one deputized to maintain the peace."

Lauren was full of interesting factoids. One of these days he'd buy her dinner and pick her brain. "Nice meeting you, Lauren."

"You, too, Ryan. And good luck."

He wasn't going to need luck. He had the law on his side.

His feet carried him across the grass to the trio. "Problem?"

Beth shook her head and gave him a disingenuous smile—the only kind he'd seen from her to date. "We've decided against announcing Nicole's pregnancy today."

He liked the sound of that. The longer they delayed, the more time he'd have to prepare for the possibility of the entire Hightower clan siding against him. The extra time would give him time to plot a new strategy.

But why would the decision to keep the news under wraps upset Nicole? He searched her face, but didn't find his answer.

Little did she know, she'd done him a favor by showing him the dissension amongst the Hightowers, and she'd given him ammunition toward suing for sole custody.

He needed to divide and conquer the trio wanting a piece of his kid, starting with the weakest link.

Nicole's brother-in-law, the greedy bastard.

Three

"Ryan Patrick is here for your lunch appointment."

Lea's announcement made Nicole's already stretched nerves snarl. Her fingers spasmed on the keyboard, filling the document on her monitor with a spew of gibberish.

She punched the intercom button. "We don't have a lunch appointment."

"Yes, you do. He called and I scheduled it."

She wanted to strangle her assistant. "What does he want?"

"There's only one way to find out." The smirk in Lea's voice came through the speaker loud and clear.

Nicole saved her work, closed the file and rose. She'd fix the gibberish later. She wasn't capable now. "Send him in. But Lea, don't make any more surprise appointments for me. And stop matchmaking. Your record proves you suck at it."

Over the past few years Lea had made a determined effort to find the man who could make Nicole forget Patrick. Her friend couldn't accept that such a man didn't exist.

Unlike Nicole's fickle mother who changed her lovers as often as she touched up her manicure, Nicole would only love once in her lifetime. She'd rather be alone than with the wrong man—or a series of them. And she was very careful not to let herself board that crazy lust-love-crash roller coaster. Whenever she realized she was in line for that ride she stepped aside. No more heartache for her.

Moments later her door swung inward and Ryan filled the opening. He wore a black suit with a white shirt and a cobalt tie that matched his eyes. Her stomach fluttered.

Who would her child take after? Him or her?

The man would make beautiful babies.

Never mind. Looks don't matter. A healthy baby is all you're after.

"Nicole." He nodded his dark head in a greeting and his eyes raked over her, making her very conscious of how her raspberry-pink V-neck, wraparound dress clung to her pregnancy swollen breasts. "Ready?"

His low-pitched voice scraped over her nerve endings like an emery board, leaving her feeling raw and exposed and strangely out of sorts.

"Why are you here, Ryan?"

He pushed the door closed between him and Lea. "Because I'd like to know something about the woman carrying my child besides the sparse raw data in the clinic's file. I imagine you have questions concerning my health and history, too."

Now that he mentioned it, she did. With Patrick she hadn't needed to ask because she'd already known everything about him.

Do this for Beth and for the baby you're carrying for her.

What was it the old cliché said? Keep your friends close and your enemies closer. Ryan Patrick qualified as the latter. He definitely threatened all she held dear. And the only way she could learn more about him was by spending time with him.

"I can give you a couple of hours."

"That's all we'll need."

She grabbed her purse and crossed the room. He opened the door as she approached and pressed his hand to her waist to guide her through as she passed by him. Every cell in her body snapped to attention startling her so much she bumped the door frame.

He caught her upper arm and steadied her, his fingers branding a circle around her biceps. "Careful."

Their gazes met. Her heart stuttered. Why did *he* have to have this effect on her? The man was an arrogant ass.

You're carrying his baby. Of course you're going to have a reaction to him.

Nicole shook off his hold.

Lea grinned unrepentantly. "Have a great lunch. Don't rush back. I have everything under control."

Nicole frowned at her assistant. "I'll be back in time for my next appointment."

"Your two o'clock postponed until four. I can reschedule him until tomorrow, if you'd like."

Nicole glared a warning. "Don't you dare."

"Well, take it easy. You have plenty of time."

Not what she needed Ryan to hear when she wanted an excuse to cut lunch short. But she bit back her reservations and accompanied him outside to his Corvette. He opened the door for her. She avoided his touch and slid into the leather seat.

He climbed into the driver's side, making the luxurious sports car feel crowded. His scent filled her nostrils and his nearness addled her nerves.

"Why did your sister failing to announce your pregnancy upset you?" he asked as he started the car.

Give the man points for being perceptive. But her feelings were none of his business. "It didn't."

He cut her a hard look before pulling onto the road. "I don't like or respect liars."

She gasped, gritted her teeth and focused on her three *P's*. *Patience, politeness, perseverance.* "I like things to go according to schedule. Beth changed the schedule at the last minute. That's all. No big deal."

But it was. A week ago Beth had been ecstatic about the upcoming announcement and ready to blurt out the news at any second. Waiting until the party had driven her up the wall, but she'd claimed she wanted the announcement to be memorable. So why had her sister suddenly developed cold feet? Was she having doubts about adopting this baby now that she knew it wasn't her husband's? Or maybe Patrick was the one with doubts.

Nicole caught herself examining Ryan's cleanly chiseled profile and the soft line of his lips. She felt the stirrings of something deep inside her abdomen and clamped down on the unwelcome feelings. She was not attracted to him. She was merely curious to know if her—*Beth's* baby would inherit those great genes.

She turned away from his face to look out the window. He drove through downtown, past the university and toward Volunteer Landing, a riverfront section of the Tennessee River flanked by a park, restaurants, pricey condos and the sprawling hospital complex. On summer weekends tourists and locals filled the concrete stands along the water to watch the water ski and wakeboard competitions. It had been ages since she'd taken the time to attend one of the events.

But instead of parking at the Landing, he crossed the Henley Street Bridge and turned into an exclusive gated condominium complex. A guard waved him through the entrance. The tall, modern waterfront structure had expansive windows and long cantilevered porches. This wasn't a commercial property.

A parade of prickles marched up her spine. "Where are we going?"

"My place."

Too private. Too personal. Too…everything. "I don't think that's a good idea."

He parked in the ground level area beneath the condos beside a wicked-looking black motorcycle and turned off the engine. Both his and the motorcycle's parking spaces were labeled 10A.

"Would you prefer to discuss our unusual situation across the river at Calhoun's or Ruth's Chris where we might be overheard?"

As much as she liked both restaurants, he'd made a good point. "Um…no. The motorcycle is yours?"

"Yes."

That made him a risk-taker. Not good parent material.

A vision of him straddling the machine and dressed in black leather flashed in her head. The confines of the car suddenly felt stuffy. She shoved open the door, climbed out and let the breeze blowing off the water cool her hot skin.

He led her toward a bank of elevators. Her heels rapped out a beat on the concrete almost as rapidly as her heart knocked in her chest. Inside the elevator he punched the button for the top floor, and the brushed steel cubicle shot upward quickly and noiselessly.

The doors opened onto a spacious atrium-style foyer with a modern peaked glass ceiling similar to the pyramid shapes at the Louvre. Natural light flooded the plant-filled space, and a fountain gurgled in the center. Four doors opened off opposite sides of the octagonal area.

"This is nice." Too modern for her traditional tastes, but still attractive with its curved teak benches and pebbled pathways.

"Thanks. I designed the building."

Extremely pricey waterfront real estate. Penthouse level. Her worry multiplied as she filed the information away. Neither she nor Beth and Patrick could afford the kind of lengthy legal brawl Ryan apparently could. Not that any of them were hurting for cash, but they weren't in league with someone who could afford multimillion-dollar accommodations.

Ryan unlocked a door on the river side of the building and gestured for her to precede him. Dreading the hour to come, she gathered her courage and entered Ryan Patrick's domain.

His entry opened directly into a huge living area with a wall of floor-to-ceiling windows. Dark slate floors gleamed beneath her feet. The stone might be beautiful, but it would be hard and cold and hazardous for a child learning to crawl or walk. The urban industrial upscale furnishings would also be problematic with their sharp brushed steel edges and glass table tops.

She crossed to the window and looked down. A wave of vertigo hit her, and she staggered back to assess Ryan's space from a safer distance away from the glass. Outside to her left a stark, Plexiglas-railed patio jutted from the dining area beside her to the far end of the building. The modern stone sculptures, plant holders and glass-and-steel dining set couldn't keep the slab from looking like a giant diving platform from which you could tumble right over the edge.

The condo suited him perfectly. Dark. Edgy. Cold. Dangerous.

Taking tiny, careful steps she forced herself to return to the window and a clear view of World's Fair Park with its Sunsphere. The Tennessee River drifted lazily past ten stories below. Volunteer Landing stretched along the opposite bank with its broad walkway and manmade water features. The tourist paddle boat, a favorite for weddings, clung to the shore upstream.

In front of Ryan's complex on this side of the river a long boat dock floated parallel to the tiny green space. Watercraft of assorted sizes filled the slips.

"Is one of those yours, too?" She pointed to the boats.

"Third from the right."

She knew enough about water sports from her brothers' exploits to recognize the long, low boat had been built for speed.

Ryan's place was a mother's nightmare. Add in his expensive and risky toys and the possibility of her child growing up here scared her witless. "Your home isn't suitable for children."

"Why?"

She startled at his nearness and spun to find him standing only inches away—far too close. She hadn't heard him cross the room. She sidestepped to put a few feet between them.

"Besides the fact that you apparently have a death wish with your need-for-speed toys?"

His muscles tensed. "I'm careful."

She rolled her eyes at the ridiculous statement. "There's no fencing to keep a child from falling off the dock and into the murky water, and there isn't nearly enough grass for a child to run and play. Children need playgrounds and yards."

"City kids around the world manage without acre lots."

"Are there any other children in this building?"

His jaw shifted. He shrugged. "I don't know."

"A child needs playmates. Beth and Patrick's place is better suited."

His intense blue gaze held hers. "Forget your sister and her husband for a moment. This lunch is about you and me."

Her pulse stuttered. "How so?"

He advanced a step. She retreated one. "I've been tested for HIV and every other sexually transmitted disease and I'm clean. Have you been tested?"

Startled by his blunt question, she flinched. "No. There was no need."

"You're a virgin?"

Her cheeks burned. "Of course not. I'm twenty-eight."

But she was careful. More careful than anyone knew. Because she didn't want to end up like her mother.

"I required testing from my other surrogate candidates. I'll set up an appointment for you."

Appalled, she sputtered. "You'll do no such thing. I'm not one of your candidates."

"No. You're the woman carrying my child. That makes a clean bill of health even more critical. Get tested voluntarily or I'll get a court order."

She snapped her gaping mouth closed. "You can't do that."

"I've already spoken to my attorney. I can. This is my kid. I have a vested interest in his welfare."

Nicole wanted to slap her hands over her ears, but she refrained. "Stop saying that. Your contribution was an accident.

You weren't there. You had nothing to do with it. And if the clinic hadn't broken the law and given you my confidential information then you wouldn't even know my name."

"Irrelevant. I know who you are, and I'm not going away. Do us both a favor and don't make our lawyers rich." He turned, releasing her from the tension of his total concentration, removed his suit coat and tossed it over the back of a minimalist leather chair.

She took the opportunity to move away from him. He made her uncomfortable. Why? She had no idea. She dealt with powerful men on a daily basis—men who were in-her-face obnoxious and demanding. She easily kept her cool with them. It wasn't as easy with Ryan.

Because he's threatening your—Beth's—*baby. That makes it personal.*

He faced her again, unbuttoned his cuffs then started rolling up his sleeves. "Do you smoke?"

The slow revelation of a tanned, muscled forearm riveted her attention. "No."

"Drink alcohol?"

"Occasionally. But not at all now that I'm expecting."

"Have you had more than five sexual partners?"

Offended, she stiffened. "That is none of your business. Take me back to my office. Now."

He finished rolling up his second sleeve and parked his hands on those lean hips. "These are standard questions from the fertility clinic questionnaire which they neglected to have you complete. You have the right to ask the same questions of me. And you should."

As rude and insulting as he'd been, he was also correct and fair-minded. She hated that a virtual stranger had the right to pry into her personal business. But what if he ended up sharing custody of this child with Beth and

Patrick? She—*correction*—Beth and Patrick needed to know everything about him.

"The clinic doesn't accept donations from or inseminate HIV-positive clients. If you'd done your research, you would know that."

"They also claim they don't make mistakes."

Point to Ryan. She sighed. "I've had less than five partners. You?"

"More than five. But I've been careful. Are you seeing anyone now?"

"No." This was worse than a blind date. "Are you? Is there a woman who'll have problems with my pregnancy?"

"No."

"A man?"

His venomous look should have dropped her on the spot, but she had to ask since his solo quest for a child was an unusual one.

His blue eyes scanned her body, leaving a ripple of sensation in their wake. "Do you have any habits that might aversely affect my child's well-being?"

"I never would have agreed to carry this child for Beth if I did, and I don't take any drugs except for the prenatal vitamins."

"Good. Let's eat." He walked away.

"I'd rather go back to work." Or even as far away as Alaska to get away from him.

"You need to eat for yourself and the baby," he called over his shoulder.

Unfortunately, he was right again. Rather than wait for him in his austere living room, she followed him into a spacious kitchen with stone countertops, glass-front upper cabinets and top-of-the-line stainless steel appliances. As much as he'd already unsettled her stomach with his intrusive questions, she doubted she'd be able to swallow a bite.

He pulled a casserole dish from the top of the double oven. A delicious tomato-and-garlic scent filled the air. Her stomach growled in anticipation. "You assumed a lot by preparing a meal before I agreed to go out with you."

"We both have the kid's best interest at heart, and from what I've read about you, you're intelligent enough to know we need to have this discussion. Take a seat and help yourself. It's vegetable lasagna."

He had no idea how close she'd come to refusing his "invitation." She crossed to the glass-topped iron table. He set the rectangular dish on a trivet in the center then returned to pull a loaf of bread from the bottom oven. He sliced the bread, tossed the slices into a basket and brought the basket to the table.

She could get used to a man who was good in the kitchen.

Oh no you won't.

Next he retrieved a bowl of marinated green beans with grape tomatoes and a pitcher of iced tea from the refrigerator and placed them in the middle of the table, then he sat across from her and filled their glasses.

Nicole's stomach did one of those weird things it had been doing a lot lately. In a split second it went from not remotely interested in food to ravenous. She loaded her plate and as soon as Ryan had done the same, she dug into the lasagna. The tangy, sauce made her eyes roll back in pleasure, and the thick chunks of eggplant and mushroom tasted better than anything she'd eaten in ages.

She ate for several minutes before looking up and finding his gaze on her. Embarrassed by her unladylike appetite, she paused with her fork halfway to her mouth—the mouth his eyes had focused on. "You know how to cook?"

"My grandmother made sure I learned."

She'd always envied her friends whose men enjoyed sharing the kitchen with them. But that kind of domestic bliss wasn't on her agenda. "This is very good."

"Thank you." He watched her tuck a tomato between her lips and something changed in his eyes. Something that caused her stomach muscles to tense and her pulse to flutter.

She fought off the sensation and concentrated on the things she didn't like about him. His bossiness. His risky hobbies. His determination to deprive her of her child.

"Despite your domestic skills, between your motorcycle and your boat and from what I've read about you, you're nowhere near responsible enough to raise a child."

"You shouldn't believe what you read in the gossip columns."

How could she ignore what her Google search had revealed? Look at him. What woman wouldn't want him? Except her, that is. He was smart, successful and wealthy. Hadn't her brothers proven that men constantly bombarded with women tended to be selfish and far from good father material?

"Do you or do you not trade in your women more often than most people charge their cell-phone batteries? A child needs security and stability."

"I haven't been involved in a long-term relationship lately, if that's what you're asking. Have you?"

"My love life is none of your business."

"It is if your habits could endanger my kid's health."

Her mouth opened and closed like a goldfish, but she couldn't manage to dredge up a blistering comeback. Once again, as ugly as his comment might have been, his concern was valid. "That isn't an issue."

"I want a copy of your medical records and to attend every doctor's appointment with you."

She bit her tongue. Pain stabbed her mouth. "What?"

"You'll need to transfer your records to the obstetrical practice I've chosen."

"Are you out of your mind? You can't make those decisions for me."

"I want to track his development. And this obstetrical group is the best in the region."

She shoved her plate aside. "First of all, *he* might be a *she.* Second, I have my own doctor. I've been seeing her for years, and I'm not changing. You can't make me."

He weighed her words as if debating arguing. "Is he or she board certified?"

"Of course. I wouldn't go to a hack—especially now. I'll have my doctor fax you a report after each visit."

"Not good enough. I want to be able to address questions as they arise and see the ultrasound scans."

Any child would be lucky to have a parent so interested. If only hers had been, but her father had been too busy with his gambling buddies.

"I'll check with my doctor, but I think she'll agree to meet with you. I also want to make sure Beth and Patrick are comfortable with your intrusion."

Not that either of them had attended her appointments thus far. Their absence had surprised Nicole. But maybe the obstetrical appointments were painful reminders of Beth's inability to conceive.

"They'll have to deal with it. Get used to it, Nicole. I will be a part of this child's life with or without your voluntary consent. And I won't be parked in the waiting room at the doctor's office. I'll be right by your side during every examination."

Four

Ryan's audacity astounded Nicole. He was backing her into a corner, and she really didn't like it.

She could feel her muscles tensing, her heart pounding and her hands trembling. She silently chanted her three *P*'s. Her mantra didn't have its usual calming effect. The urge to tell him to go to hell nearly overcame her good manners, but volatile reactions never solved a problem. They only exacerbated the situation, and alienating him was the last thing she needed to do.

"You can't impose on my private doctor's appointments."

"Would you like to bet on that? Your exams are also my child's exams. I have the right to make sure you're following doctor's orders and not endangering my kid."

She crumpled the cloth napkin in her lap and her toes curled in her shoes. "I would never do that!"

It took everything Nicole had to rein in her temper. For Patrick and Beth's sake, for her baby's sake, she had to find a solution—a peaceable solution. She excelled at finding ways to make the impossible happen at work. Wasn't she known as the go-to girl? But compromise ideas were scarce now.

She'd learned that whenever a problem was this complex it helped to break it down into manageable increments and address each component separately. She needed time and distance away from Ryan to get her thoughts in line.

Carefully pushing her chair back from the table, she took a deep breath and then rose to her feet. "Thank you for lunch, but I'd like to leave now."

He stood more slowly. "You haven't finished your lunch."

"I don't think I can eat another bite. Morning sickness." More like man sickness.

"It's not morning."

"The baby doesn't wear a Rolex." Ryan did—an expensive gold model like her father had gambled away at a casino. She remembered the screaming match that had ensued when her mother found out.

"I'll drive you."

She dropped her napkin beside her plate. "I'd rather call a taxi."

"We haven't finished our discussion."

She couldn't possibly remain polite in his company. "There's no need. Please have your physician fax your health records to my office."

"Mine?" His dark eyebrows winged upward.

"Yes. Yours. As you pointed out, I—we have every right to know if this baby will inherit something from you that might affect the pregnancy or delivery."

"I told you I was healthy."

"And you expect me to take the word of a stranger?" She threw his words back at him, and then smothered a wince.

That wasn't nice, Nicole.

But maybe if he realized how ridiculously intrusive he was being then he'd back off.

"I'll take care of it. But I'm not calling a cab for you. I brought you. I'll take you back." His inflexible tone and rock-hard jaw warned her arguing would be a waste of time.

Some battles weren't worth fighting. As long as she won the war—and she would win—she could concede this one. "Fine. Lead the way."

"Before you go, I have one more request."

Her insides snarled into a tense knot at the calculating glint in his baby blues. Her control was already teetering on the edge. One teensy shove and she'd lose her temper.

"If you find my home unsuitable, then help me find another one."

She blinked and swallowed, not liking the direction of his thinking. "Why would I do that? And why would you want me to?"

"Because we both want my child to be raised in a safe environment."

My child. The words raised her hackles, her temperature and her heart rate each time he said them. But at the same time, she couldn't help but be impressed that he cared enough to make the effort to provide a better environment. "A real-estate agent would be more knowledgeable."

"Without a doubt. I'll engage one to find the houses, but she won't have a personal stake in my decision. You might as well know I intend to sue for sole custody, but worse case scenario, I'll end up sharing with Beth and Patrick.

Either way, I'm looking for a safe place, and I know you have a vested interest in my selection."

He'd certainly laid his cards on the table. And while part of her respected him for his honesty, the other hated knowing his strategy.

Her lawyer had confirmed the courts would be unlikely to deny him some form of connection. If the worst case scenario he mentioned came about, the child's welfare came first. And she'd rather her child live anywhere than here in a place where his or her safety would always be at risk.

"I'll help you find a house. But don't believe for one minute that equates to me accepting the inevitability of you as a parent to my—*this* baby. You are not parent material."

One corner of his mouth quirked up with stomach-flipping, breath-catching effect. "Guess I'll have to prove you wrong."

"Is that your latest floozy?" Harlan Patrick spit the question from the opposite side of Ryan's desk.

Ryan glanced at the photo lying on the top of the open file he'd composed on Hightower Aviation. He'd printed the professional shot of Nicole from the Hightower Web page. The photographer hadn't managed to catch the fire in her aquamarine eyes or the golden glints in her light brown hair.

He wasn't ready to share his surrogacy plan with his father yet or discuss how it had gone wrong. "I don't sleep with every woman I meet."

His father snorted in disbelief. He'd always believed the worst of his son—probably because until recently Ryan had given him reason to. Ryan had spent a lot of time acting obnoxious as a kid hoping his mother would get sick of his shenanigans and send him back to his father, but his strategy hadn't worked. By the time he'd gone off to college the rebel pattern had become a habit.

But his partying and rebelling days were over. And while he would never deliberately deceive anyone, he wasn't above letting his father's tendency to jump to conclusions work in his favor for once.

Nicole Hightower was exactly the kind of woman his father wanted him to marry. Ryan had no intentions of marrying anyone, but if his father saw him and Nicole together and believed there might be a long-term relationship in Ryan's future, then he wasn't going to correct him. At least not now. There would be ample time for that later—after his father handed over the presidency of Patrick Architectural.

"Her name is Nicole Hightower. She's a client services manager for Hightower Aviation Management Corporation." He removed Nicole's picture from the file, laid it to the side of his blotter and passed the folder to his father. "We should consider fractional ownership or leasing a plane from HAMC."

"Why? So you can have another damned expensive toy? My God, Ryan, you risk your neck with no thought to who will take over Patrick Architectural if you kill yourself."

The repetitive lecture that had launched Ryan's current campaign set his teeth on edge.

"You already have a thirty-thousand-dollar motorcycle and a sixty-thousand-dollar boat. What next? A five-million-dollar plane? And I suppose you want to get your pilot's license, too."

Ryan bit back his irritation. "I don't want or need a pilot's license. Hightower maintains and staffs the plane. Patrick Architectural flies associates all over the country on a last-minute basis, and we pay a premium for those tickets. Hightower guarantees that if we contract their services we could have our plane and their pilot on the runway within four hours or less."

"Pretentious waste of money."

"They'd fly us directly to our destination without connecting flights, layovers, limited flight schedules and other inconveniences. They can even land the jets at smaller airports when there isn't a large hub near our destination."

"The costs of owning a plane would be prohibitive." His father dismissed the idea without even looking at the data. Typical.

"Not necessarily. I've talked to a Hightower representative. There are a variety of options. We can buy a plane outright, lease or even buy a specified number of flight hours per month or year in a pay-as-you-go program. The best deal is fractional ownership which means we'd only buy a one-eighth to one-sixteenth share, but a plane would always be available to us. When the size of our team required it, we'd be able to request a smaller or larger aircraft.

"The company makes it work for us. Their motto is Comfort, Convenience and Time Savings. From what I've heard, they deliver that promise."

He rolled to his feet, circled the desk and tapped the folder in his father's hands. "Turn to the chart on page six. Take a look at the data I asked Cindy to compile."

God bless his assistant's fascination with tracking the most ludicrous factoids.

He waited until his father did as asked. "This graph catalogs how much time our employees have lost over the past year on layovers, flight delays, inconvenient connector flights and last-minute cancellations or reroutings. They're on the clock during that lost travel time. There's your waste of money. Averaged out, our total travel expense comes close to covering the monthly cost for fractional ownership, but without the added benefit of a tax write-off and convenience. Access to our own plane would allow us to expand globally."

His father's gaze sharpened as the idea took root and the automatic rejection to any idea Ryan presented faded. Harlan ran a finger down the sheet as he perused the data a second time.

Ryan shoved his hands in his pockets and walked to the window overlooking downtown Knoxville. "The packet includes Hightower Aviation's brochure. Read the documentation and you'll see that a plane could be an expedient asset for us. If we set up the aircraft as a mobile office complete with wireless Internet and a fax machine, we could work midair and-or meet with clients on the way to a site. A bedroom suite containing a full bath is also available so we can fly overnight and arrive rested and ready to work first thing in the morning—negating the additional expense of a hotel room. An airplane is not a frivolous waste of money."

"And the girl?"

His father wasn't stupid. Ryan had known he wouldn't be so easily distracted. He faced his father, who also happened to be his mentor and sometimes his enemy. "As our client services representative Nicole would be our main contact. When we need to travel we'd call her directly and tell her our requirements—right down to which meals we'd want served on the flight. It's her job to make it happen."

"You think she'd be assigned to us?"

"I'm told she's the best they have. We would make her part of any deal we strike."

His father tapped the edge of the folder on Ryan's desk. "I'll give it a look, but I doubt it's feasible."

Another wave of irritation washed over Ryan. "If it weren't feasible, I wouldn't have presented the idea to you."

"We'll see."

Ryan smothered his frustration. History had shown his father would do everything he could to prove Ryan's idea a bad one. Only when he couldn't, would he come around.

Ryan looked forward to the day his father retired, leaving Ryan as president of Patrick Architectural. But first he had to prove he could handle the job, or his father would sell the firm his great-grandfather had started right out from under him.

Days like today convinced Nicole she was doing the right thing. She sank onto her sofa and pried her pumps off her swollen feet Saturday afternoon with a smile on her face.

Seeing Beth's excitement as they raced around Knoxville shopping the baby goods sales filled Nicole with a sense of purpose and rightness. This would work out. All she had to do was keep the fly out of the ointment. The fly being Ryan Patrick.

Thinking of him made her smile fade. The three days without seeing or hearing from him had been good and relaxing. She'd even forgotten about him several times. For a few minutes.

Exhaustion slammed her suddenly from out of nowhere. During the past month her morning sickness had been minimal and manageable, but she hadn't been able to eliminate the fatigue. When it hit, it hit hard and fast. Yawning, she stretched out on the cushions and pulled a floral woven throw over her legs.

She was floating in that hazy just-before-sleep stage when her doorbell rang. Forcing open her eyes, she blinked at the cuckoo clock on the wall until her eyes focused on the hands. Beth had dropped her off barely ten minutes ago. Her sister must have forgotten something.

Nicole levered her body upright, trudged barefoot to the front door of her town house and yanked it open. Instead of Beth, Ryan Patrick stood on her welcome mat—a most unwelcome sight. Surprise knocked her back a step, and her warm and fuzzy good mood evaporated instantly.

Her lack of shoes gave him the height advantage. She had to tip her head way back to look at him. He looked gorgeous in a black polo shirt with his bright blue eyes and an afternoon beard shadowing his angular jaw.

"How did you get my home address?"

"Your clinic file." His thorough head-to-toe inspection made her yearn to smooth her hair and check her makeup which was ridiculous considering she didn't care what he thought of her appearance.

How dare he invade her personal space? Antagonism prickled over her. She tried to rein it in. Tried and failed miserably. She could feel her face getting hotter. "Did you need something so urgently you couldn't call?"

"I called and left a message. You didn't reply. I don't have your cell-phone number."

And he never would. "I've been out all morning and just returned home. I haven't checked my machine yet. What do you want?"

Ooh. That hadn't sounded friendly. *Tamp the hostility, Nicole.*

"We have an appointment to look at a couple of houses this afternoon."

"We?"

"You agreed to help me search."

So she had. But today? She needed time to prepare for

his company and time to concoct excuses to avoid him. "And if I'm busy this afternoon?"

"Are you?"

She'd love a nap, but admitting weakness to the enemy was never good strategy. Times like this made her miss the caffeine she'd given up for her pregnancy. She needed a jolt to put up with Ryan. "Nothing that can't wait."

"Grab whatever you need and let's go."

Resigned to a few miserable hours, she put on her shoes, scooped up her purse and followed him out the door with a serious lack of enthusiasm weighting her steps. She'd rather spend her day staked to an ant hill than beside him in his Corvette.

His absolute certainty that he'd win custody of her baby unsettled her and made her doubt her ability to do her job. Her job was to give Beth and Patrick the family they yearned for.

He negotiated his way out of downtown and headed east on the interstate before glancing in her direction. "You left the house early this morning. I called at eight."

She wasn't in the mood for chitchat, but the situation demanded she keep things civil. When she caught herself studying the way his khaki pants clung to his long, muscular thighs she quickly transferred her attention to the rolling hills outside the windshield.

"There was an early-bird sale across town. Beth and I were shopping for baby things. She gets teary-eyed and chokes up when she handles the tiny clothes. I bet you don't do that."

A beat of silence passed. "I thought pregnant women were supposed to be the emotional ones."

"Maybe she's having sympathy pains. Studies show that some husbands have sympathy morning sickness. Apparently adoptive mothers-to-be can, too. Beth and I were always close." Sometimes too close. Sometimes she'd wondered if Beth were living vicariously through her, because her sister preferred to stay at home and read or watch movies then hear about Nicole's adventures later.

"If men appear to share morning sickness it's only because watching their wives heave makes them want to do the same."

She struggled with the juvenile urge to stick out her tongue at him. She knew Beth shared her roller-coaster emotional swings—swings which had grown worse for both of them since Ryan had exploded into their lives two weeks ago—because she'd witnessed a few wild fluctuations. "You are a cynic."

"Not a cynic. A realist. I see things for what they are."

And he was bitter, too, from the sounds of it. "What do you know about pregnant women?"

"I spent nine months with my ex-wife."

Shock stilled her breath. That implied he had fathered a child before. "You said firstborn Patricks always took over the family firm. Why isn't this child?"

"She wasn't mine." The hard, flat words opened a Pandora's box of questions.

"I'm not following. She was your wife's child but not yours?"

A nerve twitched in his clenched jaw. "Yes. The neighborhood is a mile ahead on your left."

She'd spotted the signs for several Douglas Lake housing developments a few miles back, but location didn't interest her at the moment. His evasion did.

"We've proven you're fertile, so she obviously didn't need to use donor sperm. Was she involved with someone before you? No, wait. You said you were with her for the full nine months. You're going to have to explain that."

He sliced a quick, hard glance her way. "And if I said it's none of your business?"

"I'd remind you you're the one who told me to ask questions about your sexual history."

He pursed his lips and blew out a slow breath. "My girlfriend was screwing my best friend. I was too blind to see it. When the pregnancy test turned up positive she swore the baby was mine. I married her. Turns out she lied."

Poor guy. From the sounds of it, like her father he'd been wronged by the woman he loved. But unlike her father, Ryan hadn't hung around for more of the same bad medicine. But then everyone knew her father only stayed because the money came from her mother's side of the family, and her mother owned the lion's share of Hightower Aviation.

"I'm sorry. How long ago was that?"

"Fourteen years."

"Were you involved in her pregnancy before you found out?"

"Every damned day. Through every doctor's appointment, every time she hugged the toilet and every midnight craving."

No wonder he was such a jerk now. Betrayal could make you bitter—if you chose to let it. She'd chosen not to. Just as she'd chosen not to let sympathy soften her dislike of him.

"How did you find out? Did your wife eventually tell you?"

"Hell no. My best friend was African-American. Let's just say my beautiful blond wife's daughter was the spitting image of her daddy."

Ouch. So he'd lost a wife, a best friend and a child at the same time. Triple whammy. "Have you kept in touch with them?"

"Why would I?"

Typical male. "Is she happier with him than she was with you?"

"How the hell would I know? And why would I care?"

"If you truly love someone, then you want them to be happy—even if it's not with you." That's what she wished for Patrick.

Ryan looked at her as if she'd lost her mind. "That's bull."

"We choose whether to look on the positive or negative side of a situation."

"You're a real Pollyanna, aren't you?"

Her spine stiffened. Was he laughing at her? "Because I focus on what I have instead of what I don't have?"

Shaking his head, he turned the car into a new and exclusive waterfront community, went a few blocks then drove up a winding driveway through thick evergreen trees. The property had to be several acres. A beautiful two-story house with a wraparound porch came into view, but even before he stopped the car by the three-car garage Nicole knew the place would never work.

A multitude of objections gathered on her tongue, but "No," was all her quickly tiring brain could manage.

"You haven't even seen the place."

She smothered the yawn she couldn't hold back. "All I need to see is the steep drop-off to the lake. If you tripped, you'd roll like a snowball going down a ski slope. Don't get me wrong, Ryan, the house is gorgeous and it's a lovely neighborhood, but there's no way to make that yard safe for a toddler to run and play in."

He scanned the property again as if verifying her words.

"Wait here." He climbed from the car and greeted the suit-clad woman climbing from a minivan bearing a local real estate agent's sign on the door. After speaking with her he returned to the Corvette.

Resting his forearm on the steering wheel, he twisted in his seat to face her. "The next house is waterfront, too. Should we even bother to look at it?"

"You like your water, don't you?"

"I used to row and wakeboard competitively in college."

Why didn't that surprise her? He had the wide shoulders and thick biceps either of those sports would develop. One of those big arms drew her attention now. She'd bet the fingers of both her hands together couldn't circle the width. For a split second she wondered what he'd look like wearing nothing but swim trunks. Shaking her head, she banished the image of his lean, tanned frame.

Why did his physique fascinate her?

Because your child carries half his DNA and might inherit some of those attractive traits.

Satisfied with her answer she met his gaze. "Water is a hazard. But if you can fence it off, then maybe it would work. I guess this means you're not going to give up your dangerous toys just because you're about to become a father."

His eyes narrowed. "No."

She gave him credit for his honesty—even though she knew she'd recommend Beth to use it against him in the custody battle. But Ryan had a lot to learn if he thought a baby wouldn't change his life. She wasn't even keeping the child, and pregnancy had completely changed hers. She wasn't sure her life would ever return to normal.

Five

Ryan couldn't remember the last time a woman had fallen asleep on him without the prelude of mind-blowing sex. The sleep part had always been his cue to slip out and avoid the postmortem. Leaving wasn't an option now.

Waiting for the red light to change, he silently drummed his fingers on the steering wheel and let his gaze skim over Nicole's face. Her thick lashes couldn't conceal the lavender circles beneath her eyes. According to her clinic file she was about ten weeks pregnant, in her first trimester.

Jeanette had slept a lot, too, during those early weeks. She'd missed enough classes to flunk out of college. His ex had also complained incessantly about her lack of energy, her nausea and her frequent need to pee—as if each irritation had been Ryan's fault. She'd wanted to be waited on hand and foot and played every sympathy card in the deck. Love-struck sucker that he'd been he'd fallen for her act. His mother's manipulative attitude should have made him immune to those kinds of tricks, but the old "Love is blind" adage had certainly applied to him.

Nicole, on the other hand, hadn't said a word about her condition. She hadn't even complained about being hungry. She'd simply pulled a snack and a bottle of water from her tote bag. And then twenty minutes ago in the middle of discussing the pros and cons of the house they'd toured she'd trailed off midsentence. He'd looked over and found her slumped sideway in her seat asleep.

The tilted position caused her V-neck top to gape, revealing the swell of her pale breasts. That distracting sight combined with her soft, parted lips had hit him with a grenade of hunger.

The urge to stroke a silky lock of hair from her cheek was about as welcome as a severe case of poison ivy. He shook off the feeling and focused on their earlier conversation. She was right about the water hazard. He couldn't be sure any nanny he hired would be diligent enough to never let the kid out of sight. That was one reason he appreciated Nicole's perspective. While he'd examined the structural integrity of the house she studied the practical aspects. Teamwork.

He checked his watch. He'd driven around for the past twenty minutes to let Nicole sleep, but now it was time to implement phase two of his plan. The light changed. He accelerated and turned toward the restaurant where he knew his father would be meeting his golf buddies later for the obligatory after-eighteen-holes cocktails.

After he snagged a parking space he killed the engine. As soon as the car fell silent Nicole's lids fluttered open. She sat up quickly, scanned her surroundings and touched her chin as if checking for drool. He found the insecure gesture oddly endearing. His lips twitched.

Those eyes hit him like laser beams, and he felt the heat and the pull deep in his gut. He took a mental giant step backward. The need to test the softness of her lips was damned hard to resist. If she weren't carrying his child, he'd act on this attraction, but the pregnancy was a complication. That didn't mean he wasn't tempted. He just had better sense. Having an affair plus sharing a child with her meant a continuing connection. He wasn't going there. This kid would be his and his alone, not leverage between parents. Once he had custody of the child he didn't intend to see her again.

Nicole smoothed her hair. "I'm sorry. I must have drifted off. Why are we here?"

"I made dinner reservations."

She blinked. "You're assuming I'll eat with you."

Her less than enthusiastic response took a bite out of his ego. He wasn't used to women refusing his company.

"I'm assuming you're hungry. Other than the squirrel food you pulled out of your purse over an hour ago, you've had nothing to eat all afternoon. In my experience pregnant women need to eat regularly."

"Dried fruit is a healthy snack."

"It wasn't substantial enough to keep a rodent going. Did you have other plans tonight?"

She glanced at the steak house, inhaled deeply and licked her lips. No doubt the aroma of grilling beef emanating from the premises made her mouth water as it did his. That was the only reason his mouth dampened. His reaction had nothing to do with the slow glide of her pink tongue. "No."

"Then let's eat. You can give me a list of things the

agent needs to look for in the next house." He climbed from the vehicle and came around to her side. He reached her just in time to see her swing those long legs out the door. Her thigh and calf muscles flexed beneath the hem of her above-the-knee-length dress as she rose. She had great muscle tone, but she was lean like a distance biker or a runner.

He offered a hand which she ignored. Point taken. She didn't want this to feel like a date any more than he did. And while part of him respected the boundaries she marked, another part of him wanted an excuse for contact. But that would be flirting with danger. Not smart.

As he escorted her to the entrance he placed his palm at the base of her spine. Her startled jump let him know his touch wasn't welcome, and the tingle rising up his arm warned him that he danced on a hazardous edge.

Inside the darkened pub-style interior he gave the hostess his name. She led him and Nicole toward the table for two he'd requested. His gaze drifted past Nicole's slender waist to her slim hips in the burgundy dress. No one would guess her condition if she didn't tell them, and he was counting on her not volunteering the information in the next hour.

The waitress took their drink and appetizer orders and left them a basket of rolls. Nicole immediately selected a piece of bread, split it open and slathered butter on the steaming center. The hot yeasty smell reached across the table.

Her blissful expression as she tore off small pieces and tucked them between her lips made it look as if the bread were the most delicious thing she'd ever put in her mouth. For some reason that made him think of sex. Would she look the same when she took a man inside her?

He reached for his iced water, but clenching the cold glass didn't distract him. The woman was getting to him—probably a combination of knowing he couldn't have her and his recent celibacy. Since he'd begun his surrogate search he hadn't had time for a relationship. All the energy he hadn't devoted to his job had been expended on reaching his goal.

"You've shot down two houses. Do you have any suggestions for where to look next?"

"North Knoxville is nice."

Near her sister's suburban cookie-cutter neighborhood. Decent area, but a little too stifling for his tastes. "If I had time I'd design and build a house."

"Why don't you?"

He hoped the kid had her eyes. The color reminded him of the Caribbean waters off the bow of the sailing yacht he'd cruised on last summer. "Six months isn't long enough to do it right."

"If you used your surrogate you'd have more time."

The statement surprised a chuckle out of him. Persistent, wasn't she? He gave her credit for trying. "She's been paid for her time and released from her contract."

"I'm sure you could get her back if you wanted—"

"I don't."

She abandoned the last bite of bread. "Ryan, it would be easier for everyone if you let this go."

"The easy way isn't always the right way. And time is an issue. I want a baby before next summer." Before his father retired.

The front door swung open. His father and his buddies walked in right on time. Dear old Dad had a habit of scanning any room to search for potential connections. Ryan always did the same, but he hoped he was more subtle. As expected, his father spotted them and broke away from his group to stride in Ryan's direction.

He stopped by the table and, ignoring Ryan, offered his hand to Nicole with as much polish as a politician. "We haven't met. I'm Harlan Patrick. You're Nicole Hightower."

Nicole blinked and sent a quick questioning glance Ryan's way before pasting on a professional smile. "Yes. You're Ryan's father?"

She couldn't miss the resemblance. His father might be six inches shorter and twenty pounds heavier, but otherwise, they looked a lot alike. Same hair. Same eyes. Same profile. The Patrick Irish genes were strong.

"That's right. Ryan, you didn't tell me you were dining here tonight. You could have joined us."

"Nicole and I have business to discuss."

Ryan had chosen this table specifically because there wasn't any space for his father and his cronies to pull up another and join them. Nicole didn't seem like the type to blurt her condition to a stranger before she'd informed the rest of her family, but he didn't want to risk the news of her pregnancy slipping out and shocking the ultraconservative golfers—particularly his father who would definitely find fault with Ryan's method of providing an heir. After the fact was soon enough.

"Would you like to join us in the bar for a drink?" His father addressed Nicole.

"Nicole doesn't drink." Not while she was carrying his kid.

His father shot him a scowl. "I'd like to hear more about Hightower Aviation. Patrick Architectural is considering engaging your services."

He noted his father didn't give him credit for the idea. He caught another flash of panic in Nicole's eyes. A pleat formed between her eyebrows before she turned back to his father. "I'm sure HAMC could meet your needs, but our sales department can answer your questions better than I can."

She dug in her purse, extracted a business card and pen and scribbled something on the back. "This is my brother Brent's direct line. Why don't you give him a call?"

Brent. The one who was probably cheating on his wife. After three minutes of his company at the picnic Ryan didn't like or trust the guy, and he didn't want him anywhere near his kid.

He took the card before his father could. "I've already spoken to one of your sales reps, Nicole, and given my father his card and a current brochure."

Nicole met his gaze. The color leeched from her face and a trapped look entered her eyes. "You didn't mention you'd been thinking of contracting our services."

"I've been investigating the possibility, and as I said, I've spoken to one of your salesmen. The idea is financially viable for us." He turned to his father. "Dad, if you'll excuse us?"

For some reason he was tired of sharing Nicole's company. The downward twitch of his father's lip told Ryan he didn't like being invited to leave, but after a moment Harlan nodded. "I'll talk to you later, Ryan. Nice meeting you, Ms. Hightower."

"You, too, sir." Her worry-filled eyes turned on Ryan as soon as his father was out of hearing range. "Why are you doing this?"

"This?"

"Intruding into my life."

"You have something I want. I'll stop at nothing to get it." And in this instance, winning was everything.

* * *

Darkness had fallen by the time Ryan paid the tab for dinner and escorted her from the steak house, increasing the sense of entrapment choking Nicole as they drove toward her home.

Ryan was crowding her and she didn't like it. Her nails bit into her palms in the shadowy confines of his luxury sports car. "There are other airline management companies, you know. I could recommend a good one."

Ryan cut her a look, his face illuminated by the dashboard lights. "I've done my research. Hightower is the best. You have the largest staff and offer the widest selection of aircraft. HAMC has three global operating centers and a higher safety rating than any of your competitors. You provide services 24/7/365 on four hours' notice. The other companies can't compete."

All facts straight from the HAMC brochure, but hearing them from Ryan's lips turned the Cajun chicken pasta she'd eaten to lead in her stomach. If she couldn't talk him out of contracting HAMC, she'd be seeing him more often and that wasn't a good thing unless it gave her a link to her baby. But she'd prefer to get rid of that complication by getting rid of Ryan Patrick.

"Your Web page doesn't list any international projects. That makes one of the smaller companies more feasible and less expensive for you."

"Logistically it didn't make sense for us to accept overseas jobs in the past because we do a lot of hands-on consulting after a project has begun. If we contract Hightower Aviation, we won't have to turn them down in the future."

Panic swelled inside her at the certainty in his voice. With any other man his confidence would have been attractive, but not so here. "Bigger isn't always better."

He kept his gaze on the road, but the amusement crinkling the corners of his eyes and carving a groove in his cheek told her he knew she was trying to run him off. “I’m surprised HAMC is still a privately owned company. Some corporate giant should have overtaken you by now.”

She shrugged her stiff shoulders and realized he couldn’t see the gesture. “Several have tried. My brother Trent is determined to prevent that from happening.”

“You’re financially strong and have a low debt to asset ratio. The odds are in your favor.”

Her mouth went dry. “You’ve been checking up on us.”

“I’d study any company I intended to indebt Patrick Architectural a million plus dollars with over a five-year period.”

Five years of seeing Ryan on a regular basis. She gulped.

She shouldn’t be surprised by his diligence. From what she’d seen he wasn’t stupid, just misguided and stubborn about the baby issue. “Still, a long-term commitment to a plane is a huge expense and a risky move in the current economic environment. You should be very, very sure before you contract our services.”

“I’m sure—especially now that I’ll have a child to rush home to. Less time on the road means more time with my kid.”

The road to her personal hell was paved with his good intentions.

Her heart sank as she realized she might not be able to dissuade him from the custody battle.

He turned the car into her condo complex and parked in her driveway. She instantly reached for the door handle. “Thanks for dinner. But please call me before setting any more appointments to see houses. I do have other obligations.”

"What could be more important than providing a safe home for this child?"

Nothing. She hated that he was right. She shoved open the door, bailed out and headed up the walk. The quiet thump of his soles echoing the rapid tap of her heels told her she hadn't escaped him. He followed her up the shallow stairs to her front door and crowded onto her tiny porch.

Her hanging baskets of petunias filled the humid evening air with their sweet smell, but they couldn't completely mask the subtle citrus tang of his cologne. It took her three tries to get the key into the lock. She twisted hard and fast and opened her door. Determined to get rid of him ASAP, she quickly stepped inside and turned abruptly to say goodbye. She collided with Ryan who had decided to follow her into her foyer despite the lack of invitation. The impact punched the air from her lungs and knocked her off balance.

Ryan grabbed her elbows to steady her. His pelvis, the length of his thighs and his chest pressed hers, scorching her. Her stomach did a funny flip-flop thing, then a spark of awareness flickered to life.

Nicole stared into his bright blue eyes, watching as Ryan's pupils expanded and his lips parted. The burn in her abdomen intensified and spread, warming and weighting her limbs. She couldn't get enough air through her nose and had to gulp deep breaths which only increased the pressure of his chest to her breast.

Back away, Nicole.

But she couldn't. Her muscles mutinied, refusing to take orders from her mind.

His gaze drifted to her mouth and panic pulsed through

her. Surely he wasn't going to— His hands tightened and his head lowered, slowing down her brain. Transfixed she watched him come closer. Her heart raced and her breath hitched.

"Ryan, don't—"

His mouth smothered her protest. His lips were surprisingly soft, but at the same time commanding and hungry, plying hers with an expertise she couldn't help appreciating. She lifted her arms up to push him away, but her bullheaded fingers dug into his rock hard biceps and held on instead of shoving. Her muscles contracted, pulling him closer instead of pushing him away.

A shiver rippled through her like waves radiating from a stone thrown into a pond. His tongue stroked a molten trail across her bottom lip then penetrated, found hers and circled. A rush of desire shocked her, making her skin flush and her abdomen tighten.

She fought the heat spreading through her, and yet she couldn't dam the seeping awareness or make herself move away. How could she respond so intensely to Ryan—or any man for that matter—with the way she felt about Patrick? A sound meant to be a protest but sounding more like a moan slipped from her mouth into his, echoing in his low growl.

Ryan eased back incrementally, his grip loosening and the warmth of his body slowly leaving hers until only their lips clung. And then those, too, parted.

Gasping for air, Nicole pressed her fingers to her mouth and tried not to pant. "You shouldn't have done that."

"Agreed." His low, rough tone scraped over her exposed nerves like short nails on bare skin.

She hugged her arms around her middle and fought to stop the tremors that racked her. No man's kiss had ever rocked her that intensely. Not even Patrick's. She staggered back in her tiny foyer until her heels hit the bottom stair.

Why had Ryan's kiss packed such a punch? She searched her brain for a logical explanation for her illogical reaction and grasped on to the first idea that came to her.

"We're just drawn to each other because of our crazy situation. You're not my type. I don't want you."

His gaze dropped to her breasts. She didn't have to look down to know what he saw. Her nipples tingled, telling her they were tight and very likely tenting her blouse and contradicting her words. Damn her out-of-control hormones.

She'd read some pregnant women often craved sex, but she hadn't expected to experience the phenomenon. While she liked sex, it had never been one of those things she couldn't live without.

Ryan brushed her cheek with a fingertip. The simple touch hit her like a crackling power line. "I don't want to want you, either, Nicole, but I find you very attractive."

Hearing the gravelly words only exacerbated the needy spasms of her internal muscles. She dodged out of reach on unsteady legs, stopping in the archway leading to her den. "Please don't say that or do that again."

He held her gaze without blinking. "I'm not making promises I'm not sure I can keep."

Her breath shuddered out, pounded out of her chest by her hammering heart. "You need to go."

"I'll call you when the real estate agent locates the next house."

She wanted to scream at him to never call again.

But she couldn't. Beth and Patrick were counting on her to keep the peace. Somehow, some way, she would not let them down.

* * *

"Way to go," Trent said as he entered Nicole's office Monday afternoon.

Her brother wasn't the type to offer approval unless something really big had happened.

"What are you talking about?"

"Patrick Architectural just bought fractional ownership in a Cessna Citation X. They listed you as the referral."

Not what she wanted to hear. But she'd been warned.

The Citation was the fastest midsize jet HAMC offered. She gave Ryan credit for going top-of-the-line. Her attention fell to the client file in Trent's hand. His arm lifted, extending across her desk and offering a burgundy-and-gold folder. The color combination signified a contract for the highest level of service HAMC provided.

Déjà vu. Another document she didn't want to read.

"They've requested you as their client aircraft manager."

Her stomach plunged as if she'd just parachuted from a plane—something she'd never do again because she hadn't enjoyed the being-out-of-control sensation. "Trent, my casebook is full. Please assign them another CAM."

"Not an option." His clipped tone warned her not to argue, but that wasn't going to stop her. Not this time. She had too much to lose.

"I really can't handle another client without my performance suffering on the ones I already have."

"I doubt that will be a problem, but if you're concerned we'll shift some of your other customers to someone else."

"No. I don't want to give up any of my people. They're like family." And like every family, hers had some eccentrics who required special handling.

His eyebrows dived toward his nose. "Tough. This deal was contingent on your acceptance."

She had to talk to Beth and get her sister to announce the pregnancy to the family. Until she did, Nicole couldn't explain to her brother why she had to refuse Patrick Architectural. How could she work with someone when she was about to become embroiled in a nasty custody battle over the baby she carried with him? But until then…

"C'mon, Trent, I never argue and never refuse an assignment—not even the most difficult cases that others have dumped. You know that. So the fact that I'm asking for a break now tells you I need it."

His face didn't soften one iota. "Let Becky know who you're handing over by the end of the day."

"You're pawning me off on your assistant? Trent—"

"Familiarize yourself with the file. Your first meeting with your new client is Friday afternoon, two o'clock."

"But—"

"There are no buts, Nicole. It's a done deal. Patrick Architectural is yours." He dropped the file on her desk, pivoted and stalked out.

Case closed. Nobody won an argument with her big brother—especially when he was locked in stubborn mode.

Nicole flopped back in her office chair and stared at the ceiling. This could not happen. And it had nothing to do with that kiss. Nothing. Absolutely, positively nothing.

Her lips tingled as if she could feel Ryan's kiss again, and that stirred up a termites' swarm in her belly. And termites left nothing but destruction in their path. She was very, very afraid Ryan might kiss her again, and that she'd do something stupid like her mother and act on that lust.

No, she wouldn't. The kiss had been a fluke, a combination of out-of-control pregnancy hormones and the strange tie she had with him as the father of her baby. That's all. She was certain of it.

Well…mostly certain.

She could call Ryan and plead conflict of interest, but she suspected her arguments would fall on deaf ears. He was tightening the screws and he'd show no mercy. That meant she had to talk to Beth. Now. She bolted to her feet, and ignoring a slight wave of dizziness, charged out of her office.

"Hey, where are you going?" Lea called out. "You have Tri-Tech in ten minutes."

Ten minutes. Normally she'd be at her desk reviewing the file ten minutes before a meeting. She couldn't today.

"Are you okay?"

"I have to talk to Beth. I should be back, but if I'm not, make sure Ronnie gets his coffee with cream and three spoons of sugar, and a raspberry jelly donut."

As the CAM in charge of each owner's service team she knew her client's preferences as well as she knew her own.

"Got it, boss." Lea snapped a smart-aleck salute.

Nicole didn't want to wait for the elevator or risk running into Ronnie coming up and have to return to her office before talking to her sister. She headed for the stairs and jogged down three flights. She was slightly winded and perspiration dampened her skin by the time she knocked on Beth's open door.

With the phone to her ear, Beth held up one finger, pointed at the visitor chair and turned away. But Nicole couldn't possibly sit still. She checked her watch. Eight minutes. She'd never been late for an appointment before and didn't want to start now. She prided herself on promptness.

What felt like an eon later but was actually only two

minutes—she knew because she counted off the seconds—Beth cradled the receiver and faced her. "What's up?"

"We have to tell the family about the baby."

Beth stiffened. "Not yet."

"Beth, Ryan Patrick's company just contracted us and demanded me as their CAM. I can't do it. You and I know why, but I can't tell Trent the reason I must be excused until you let the family in on our little secret."

Beth bit her bottom lip, shifted in her seat and shook her head. "I'm not ready."

"What do you mean, you're not ready? I'll be showing soon."

Tense, silent seconds passed. "Nicole, Patrick and I are…having problems."

Nicole's heart stuttered. She knew they argued. "Every marriage has rough spots."

"This is bigger than that."

Her pulse fluttered. In the first few years of Beth and Patrick's marriage, Nicole had selfishly wished for Patrick to realize he'd married the wrong sister. But that wasn't what she wanted or needed now. If Beth and Patrick separated with Ryan circling like a shark, the custody issue would only get more complicated, and Ryan would stand a better chance of winning.

"Is it because the baby's not his?"

Beth adjusted the pens on her desk. "That's part of it."

A fresh wave of panic hit. What would she do if they decided not to adopt her baby? Ryan would win and she might never see her child again.

"You'll work it out, Beth. You've always worked it out before. You guys are perfect for each other. Remember?" She heard the desperate edge to her voice.

"This time is different."

"I'll help. I'll talk to Patrick. I'll do whatever you need me to do, but you guys have to stay together. You love each other." The irony of begging for the man who possessed her heart to stay married to another woman didn't escape her.

"Nicole, sometimes love is not enough. And the timing for the announcement is all wrong."

"You've known for five weeks."

"Give me a little more time," Beth said with a tight smile. "And then everything will be settled."

Nicole pressed a hand over the little life causing so much upheaval and felt the extra firmness beneath the skin. "I don't have more time. And you know we're having the ultrasound Wednesday. You're going to want to share the pictures. The doctor even said she'd make a video of the baby for us."

"Patrick and I will have to watch the video later. I'm not ready to share the news."

Surprise rocked her back on her heels. "*Later?* You're not coming to the appointment?"

Beth made a show of checking her calendar. "I can't get away."

Nicole couldn't remember Beth ever lying to her before. Lying *for* her, sure. Many times. But she knew from the look in her sister's eyes Beth was telling a whopper this time. Beth was HAMC's publicist and there were no urgent marketing campaigns going on now. September was traditionally a slow month, and Beth's office was practically a tomb. It had been no big deal when Patrick and Beth had skipped the earlier routine appointments, but this time they'd get their first look at their future son or daughter.

Pain made Nicole look down. She'd dug nails so deeply

into her palms she'd broken a fingernail at the quick. Blood filled the tiny crack. That was going to hurt for a while.

But not as long as losing her baby would.

Her thoughts swirled like leaves in a windstorm. Needing to collect herself, she checked her watch and realized she was out of time. Panic rose within her.

"Beth. Please reconsider. I can't keep Ryan on my client roster."

"I'm sorry, Nicole, but we can't make the announcement yet. Maybe in a few weeks."

A few weeks. Two weeks ago Beth had barely been able to contain the news, then at the picnic she'd begged for a few more days. And now she was delaying *weeks?*

Nicole had a bad feeling about the whole situation. Something was really, really wrong, and until she knew what it was, she couldn't fix it.

"Beth, I need your help."

"This isn't high school anymore, Nicole. It's not as simple as lying for you like I did when you skipped class or picking you up when your date dumped you on the side of the road because you refused to put out, or forging Mom's signature on a note home from your teacher. Handle your own damned problems for once and quit screaming for me."

Stunned speechless by Beth's vehemence, Nicole fisted her cold fingers by her side. She was on her own and she had no idea how to handle the disaster that had become her life.

Six

The back of Nicole's neck prickled late Wednesday morning. On alert, she swiveled her office chair away from her side desk. Ryan leaned against the doorjamb and observed her through narrowed eyes. Her heart slammed against her rib cage.

"Ryan Patrick to see you," Lea chirped from beside him.

Nicole cut her assistant a dry look and caught the matchmaking glint in her eyes. "I can see that."

Lea grinned unrepentantly and shrugged. "Sorry, I was stuck on the phone and I waved him through. I knew you were only finishing the pilot scheduling chart."

How long had Ryan been watching her? Had she done anything obnoxious?

"Thank you, Lea." Nicole didn't want to talk to him, but while she could get away with refusing personal visits at work, she couldn't refuse to see a client, and she didn't know in which capacity he'd come today. Judging from his tailored gray suit he'd come from work. He looked handsome, successful and rich like so many of the other HAMC clients, but her reaction to him was far from her usual business-only response. He had a way of looking at her that made her feel jumpy, jittery, tongue-tied and feminine.

Pressing suddenly damp palms to her skirt, she rose. "Good morning, Ryan. I wasn't expecting you until Friday."

It took a conscious effort to keep her gaze from drifting to his mouth, but that didn't keep her lips from warming at the memory of a kiss she couldn't seem to erase no matter how hard she tried.

"The agent has two houses lined up on this side of town. Ride over with me during your lunch hour."

An order. Not an invitation. His timing couldn't be worse.

Lea practically jumped for joy. "You're looking at houses together?"

Nicole winced. "I'm helping Ryan find a place for himself."

Lea's face fell. "Oh, I thought maybe you two—"

"Lea, don't you have supplies to order for an overseas flight?"

Behind Ryan's back Lea stuck out her tongue. Nicole ignored her and glanced at her watch. "If you'd called, I would have told you I can't go with you. I already have something scheduled, and I have to leave in a moment."

Ryan had insisted on being present at each doctor's appointment. Should she tell him where she was going?

No.

And then she remembered Lea knew. But Lea didn't know the baby was Ryan's. Nicole hadn't dropped that bomb yet. But surely her assistant wouldn't—

"I want to see the ultrasound video of the little tadpole when you get back," Lea said. "You said the doctor was going to record it on a CD, right?"

Nicole's body went cold. She simultaneously wanted to dive beneath her desk and strangle Lea. She prayed Ryan wouldn't understand the remark. "We'll discuss that *later.*"

Ryan straightened and his alert blue gaze probed hers. "You have a doctor's appointment today?"

So much for keeping secrets. She swallowed. "Yes."

"You didn't tell me."

"No."

Out of the corner of her eye she caught Lea's frown as if her assistant had finally picked up on the undercurrents. "Lea, please excuse us."

Lea didn't move. Ryan cut her a look and she backed out of the room. He shut the door in her face. "I told you I expected to be included in any doctor's visits."

"My attorney says I don't have to let you into my private appointments. You're entitled to the doctor's notes pertaining to the baby and that's it."

Without moving a muscle, his demeanor changed completely. He suddenly looked dark, dangerous and fierce, his eyes glinting like ice chips and his face rigid. Not the kind of guy you'd want to meet in a dark alley.

"You don't want to start a war with me, Nicole." The quietly uttered words packed more punch than if he'd shouted them.

No, she didn't want to fight with him and not only because her attorney had cautioned Nicole against causing unnecessary friction. Okay, she might as well admit that if not for the baby, she'd enjoy Ryan's company. He was smart, attractive and ambitious—all the things she enjoyed in a date. But none of that mattered since she wasn't looking for a relationship.

She licked her dry lips. "I'll burn you a copy of the ultrasound video."

"Not good enough. I want to be there where I can ask questions."

While she understood his request and admired his dedication to his child, she suspected she'd be an emotional wreck during and after this appointment. Agreeing to have a child and give it away was one thing. Actually seeing the baby growing inside her and knowing it was a part of her and yet it wasn't hers was another. She didn't want Ryan to witness any potential meltdown she might have.

She shook her head. "I'm sorry. I really need to do this alone."

"Not an option."

That made twice this week she'd heard that phrase. She liked it even less this time. "Ryan—"

"I'm coming with you."

"What about the houses?"

"I'll postpone our appointment."

She could object to him shadowing her, call her lawyer and put the legal wheels in motion to stop Ryan from butting in, but as her attorney had pointed out, a nationally acclaimed fertility clinic's mix-up between two prominent Knoxville families was the kind of fodder tabloids loved to exploit. She'd lose credibility with her clients if that happened. And considering her family didn't even know about the pregnancy yet, exposure through the media wasn't a path Nicole wanted to take. Besides, hadn't her mother's affairs garnered enough bad publicity for Hightower Aviation?

The alarm on her cell phone chimed. If she didn't leave

now she'd be late for her appointment. Being late or taking legal action meant rescheduling, and she didn't want to wait even one more day to see her—*Beth's* baby. She shut off the alarm.

Letting Ryan accompany her was the most expedient choice. Even if she hated it. She sighed in defeat. "You can follow me to the medical complex in your car."

"And give you the chance to lose me in traffic? No. We'll ride together." He withdrew his key ring from his pocket.

Her hackles rose. He might have her backed into a corner, but that didn't mean she had to go down without a fight. "I'm driving."

With a shrug he pocketed his keys and opened the door then extended his arm, palm up, to indicate she lead the way. Nicole snatched her purse out of the drawer and marched ahead. His palm pressed her lower back and her pulse jumped. She wished he'd quit doing that—at least until she could numb herself to his touch.

Thank goodness Lea was on the phone, but her eyes rounded as she took in Nicole leaving with Ryan and the familiar placement of his hand. There would be questions later, and eventually Nicole would have to figure out how much she was going to share. Right now she was too rattled to worry about it.

She led the way to her car. Ryan folded himself into the passenger seat. "Nice ride."

Her pearl-white Cadillac SRX Crossover was both comfortable and roomy. "I have to taxi clients and their luggage around sometimes. As you may have guessed, we deal with high-end clientele. A luxurious vehicle is a necessity."

He turned off her stereo, silencing the soothing flute concerto playing quietly in the background. "Are Beth and Patrick meeting us at the doctor's?"

Ryan didn't need to know about the dissension between Beth and Patrick. Nicole pointed the car toward the medical complex and tried to come up with an answer that wouldn't lead to more questions. She couldn't. "No."

"Aren't they interested in the kid?"

"Yes. But they're…today's not a good day."

His lips and eyes narrowed. "For either of them?"

"No. They'll watch the video."

Ryan's presence overpowered the interior of her car. She'd never felt this cramped even with four clients packed inside and had never been as conscious of anyone's scent as she was the subtle hint of his cologne.

Her gaze strayed to the tanned, long-fingered hands resting on his thighs. How would those hands feel on her skin? Her stomach swooped at the taboo question. She shut down that line of thinking…or tried to, but her out-of-whack hormones wouldn't let her.

"Ryan, I can't be your CAM. It's a conflict of interest."

"One your brother assured me you'd make work."

"You told him about the baby?" Her voice squeaked.

"No. I told him we were…acquainted. He drew his own conclusions."

"You mean he thinks we're lovers." She shot him an exasperated look. "Torturing me is not going to make this go any smoother."

"I'm not torturing you. I'm going after what's mine."

"I keep telling you. The baby isn't yours except by a genetic link. You have no more connection to it than any other sperm donor does to his offspring."

"I have a legal connection. That's what matters."

She wasn't going to win this war of words. The brick office building came into view. Every muscle in her body snapped taut. The ultrasound was going to be hard. Part of her ached to see the life growing inside her. Part of her dreaded it. She parked, but her hands couldn't seem to release the steering wheel.

"Nicole?"

"We're here," she said in as cheerful a voice as she could muster. When his frown deepened she wanted the stupid, unnecessary words back, but she couldn't unsay them, so she met Ryan's gaze and tried to emit a calm vibe. From his serious expression she'd guess she received a D minus for her effort.

"Is this your first ultrasound?"

Her fingers remained clenched. Her knuckles looked blanched in the sunlight. "Yes."

"Let's do it." He shoved open his door, exited the car and came around to open her door. When she didn't get out, he crouched down to meet her at eye level. "The scan won't hurt you or the baby. You have nothing to worry about."

Surprise jerked her eyes to his. *He* was comforting *her?* "I know it won't hurt."

He offered a hand. "Come on. Let's go see what we've made."

She almost liked him at that moment.

She willed her muscles to loosen and accepted his assistance. His warm fingers closed around hers and tugged her from the car. She found the contact calming which was exactly why she pulled free. She couldn't afford to lean on him or to trust him. Her legs quivered with each step as she accompanied him to the building, and her voice shook as she gave the receptionist her name.

She sat in a vinyl chair beside Ryan and scanned the room. Several women smiled at him then at her as if they believed them to be a happy, expectant couple. She wanted to correct them. But she didn't. She noted the rounded tummies of the moms-to-be. That would be her in a matter of months. On the other side of the room a tiny baby slept in a carrier beside a woman who looked both exhausted and exhilarated.

That would not be her. When she came for her postpartum checkup she would be alone. And empty. Her baby wouldn't be hers anymore.

It's not yours now.

Her chest ached and her throat tightened. An urge to run raced through her, and a choked sound bubbled from her throat. She tried to cover it by faking a cough.

Ryan's hand covered hers on the armrest. Startled, she lifted her gaze and found understanding in his eyes. Her breath caught. How could he possibly know how much this hurt? She shifted her hand to her lap. She didn't want to share her misery with him. It left her feeling exposed and vulnerable.

"Nicole?" a pink-scrub-clad woman called from the door to the treatment rooms. Nicole bolted to her feet and raced away from the unwanted connection she felt with him.

Ryan shadowed her steps.

"Who do we have with us today?" the woman asked with a sunny smile.

"Ryan Patrick, the baby's father," Ryan said before Nicole could find the words to explain their convoluted relationship.

"You're going to see your little one today," Ms. Cheerful said as she waved Nicole onto the scale. "But first… Let's see how Mommy is doing."

Mommy. Nicole's throat closed up. No, she wouldn't be a mommy.

The nurse noted Nicole's weight and took her blood

pressure. "Any problems? Are you keeping food down okay? Having regular bowel movements?"

Nicole's cheeks burned. Including Ryan in such a personal conversation seemed…invasive. "I'm fine. Everything's fine."

"Dad and I will wait for you in room four. You head off to the lab."

Dad.

Nicole's gaze jerked to Ryan's. He looked a little shell-shocked. Good. She shouldn't be the only one suffering here.

She ducked into the lab and let the technician do her thing, wondering all the while what Ryan was telling the nurse. Nicole headed to the exam room as soon as she could.

"First babies are always the most exciting," the nurse was saying as Nicole entered. "And it's early, but you might possibly get a peek at the sex today. Do you want to know?"

"No," Nicole blurted.

"Yes," Ryan answered simultaneously.

The nurse chuckled. "I'll warn the doctor we have a difference of opinion."

Understatement of the year.

As far as Nicole was concerned, the less she knew about the baby the less she'd bond with it before she had to relinquish.

The nurse laid a folded pink paper sheet on the table. "Dr. Lewis will be right in. Strip off the skirt, sweetie, and cover your lower half with this."

Nicole froze. The nurse left before she could protest. Nicole's breath burned in her chest and her heart thundered like stampeding horses as she slowly lifted her gaze to Ryan's. She couldn't help cringing when she remembered the underwear she'd put on today. The scrap of black lace was practically nonexistent, but the woman at the appointment desk last time had suggested Nicole go tiny or bare for the ultrasound.

Ryan did not need to see her in her underwear.

She gulped then she noticed the curtain tucked out of the way in the corner. A yank sent it sailing along the track on the ceiling, separating her from those intrusive blue eyes. But even though she couldn't see him, she knew he was there on the other side of the thin floral fabric. Her hands shook so badly she could barely unfasten her skirt. She was beginning to think she'd have to ask for help in manipulating the button at her lower back when it popped free.

With a sigh of relief she checked to be sure the curtain was still in place, stepped out of the garment and draped it over a chair. She snatched up the pink sheet, unfolded it and wrapped it around her lower half. The protective paper sheet covering the vinyl made a god-awful racket as she climbed on the exam table and sat. She double- and then triple-checked to make sure she had everything concealed that could be hidden from Ryan's prying eyes.

The door to the hall opened. "Well hello," the doctor's voice greeted Ryan. "And you are?"

"Ryan Patrick. The baby's father."

"I'm Debbie Lewis, Nicole's OB. Nicole didn't tell me you'd be joining us today."

"I'll be here for every appointment."

Ryan's answer made Nicole shudder. She gave her doctor points for taking Ryan's presence in stride. Debbie knew the basic situation, but she didn't let on that having Ryan here was anything out of the ordinary.

Debbie peeked around the edge of the curtain. "Hello, Nicole. Are you ready for this?"

No. "Yes."

Debbie whipped the curtain back to the corner. "Lay back."

Nicole did as asked, the paper crinkling noisily. But she couldn't care less about the paper beneath her. She was more concerned with anchoring the slipping pink sheet, and Ryan standing a few feet away and watching her every move.

"Lift your top for me," Debbie instructed.

Nicole focused on a seam in the wallpaper and hiked her camisole and sweater to her rib cage. She thought she heard Ryan inhale, but she was probably wrong. Cool air brushed her stomach from the air-conditioning gusting through the overhead vent.

The doctor tucked the pink sheet into the lace band of Nicole's panties then palpated her abdomen. After she took a few measurements and wrote them down she picked up a tube. "First we'll listen for the heartbeat with the Doppler. Brace yourself. The gel is cold."

Nicole winced when the chilly goo hit her skin. Determined to pretend Ryan wasn't there, she focused on the mobile spinning slowly above her. But she knew he was watching, looking at her pale who-has-time-to-tan? belly. She felt completely naked and exposed. But strangely, it wasn't a creepy feeling. An odd awareness crept over her, quickening her pulse, warming her skin and tightening her nipples. She wanted to cover them, but couldn't without being obvious.

Excitement about the baby. That's all it is. You're about to hear and see the life growing inside you. It has nothing to do with Ryan.

The OB slid the small handheld instrument across Nicole's stomach just above her bikini line. The speaker emitted what first sounded like white noise then morphed into a rhythmic swishing pattern.

"That's your baby's heartbeat."

Nicole couldn't breathe. Against her will her gaze slid to Ryan's face. His brilliant blue stare focused on her stomach, and his throat worked as if he'd swallowed. His emotional response multiplied hers. Tears burned her throat and eyes.

Her baby's heartbeat.

No. Not yours.

Beth's. And Patrick's.

And Ryan's.

She was the only one left out of this equation.

Seven

His baby.

It took one hundred percent of Ryan's concentration to force air into his deflated lungs.

The doctor pulled the device from Nicole's smooth ivory skin. He caught a glimpse of a sliver of black lace and brown curls a shade darker than the silky honey-toned hair on her head before the doctor adjusted the paper-thin pink sheet. Ryan clenched his teeth tighter. Nicole's toes curled, drawing his attention to her toenails which she'd painted a dusky shade of peach. The one-two punch of shock and arousal nearly knocked him off his feet. He sank into the visitor chair.

"The heart rate is approximately one hundred-sixty beats per minute. For a fetus at this stage it's in the normal range." The doctor wrote in the chart. Ryan struggled to pull himself together while she tugged a boxy apparatus with a TV screen on it from the corner and played with the knobs.

She squirted more clear gel on Nicole's belly and Nicole flinched. Goose bumps lifted her flesh. Ryan's fingers itched to test the texture, to warm her with his hands.

The doc followed the same procedure she'd used with the previous instrument, scrolling it below Nicole's navel until a ghostly image appeared on the screen.

"Here's our baby," she said.

The hairs on the back of Ryan's neck rose. He'd done this before, seen a baby he'd thought was his via ultrasound. He'd held Jeanette's hand, shared the excitement with her and soaked up every detail while planning to be the best parent he could possibly be. Only that opportunity and his heart had been ripped away from him.

Ryan tried to pull back, but he couldn't look away. He tried to maintain an objective attitude and keep his emotions out of the mix. This time he had three people determined to take this kid from him.

The doctor pointed to a lopsided circle that contracted and expanded like a fuzzy strobe light. "That's the heart."

His body went numb. His thoughts raced. He'd paddled the Yukon, parachuted from a plane, sailed the Bermuda Triangle and raced his Agusta motorcycle through the hairpin turns of Tail of the Dragon, but none of those feats gave him half the adrenaline rush of seeing that white, chalky form and that little pulsing blob.

The doctor shifted her cursor and clicked on the image. "This is the head. I'm going to take a few measurements. Right now your baby is only a few inches long, but the basic skeletal parts are recognizable. Can you see them?"

He could, but he couldn't find his voice. A nod was all he could manage. Ryan saw eyes, a nose, a little chin, and his throat closed up. The doctor pointed out the spine, the arms and legs and electronically measured each.

The chalky figure moved its hand and suddenly the picture in front of him became all too real. A little person with knees, elbows, fingers and toes.

His kid. *His.*

"Does the baby look healthy?" He sounded as if he had laryngitis.

"We can't see everything with ultrasound, but what I can see looks exactly the way it should."

The words didn't alleviate his gut-twisting tension. He told himself this was no different than construction. He was used to seeing sketches and blueprints of buildings yet to be built. Feeling the excitement and anticipation of pulling a project together and watching it develop from the ground up was nothing new. But he experienced that rush tenfold now along with a heart-pounding, lung-crushing shot of fear. In a few months this finished product would be his responsibility. But a child wasn't something he could make adjustments to if the wiring or plumbing didn't work out as expected.

A weird feeling crept over him. It was as if this event was happening to someone else or he was sitting in front of a Discovery Channel TV program. Detached, but engrossed. Awed. Mesmerized. This wasn't just a game of one-upmanship anymore or a case of winning or losing. This was life or death. And that little life was his responsibility. His. He'd do anything to protect it.

In theory, having an heir to insure his father would entrust the family firm to him had been a good plan. The reality of being held accountable for that child's well-being scared the crap out of him.

He pried his gaze from the shadowy image and looked

at Nicole. Equal parts wonder and agony chased across her face, but the tears streaming from her eyes and dampening the pillow under her head as she stared at the screen without blinking hit him like a falling I beam.

He'd completely misread her. He'd believed having this baby for her sister and walking away was going to be easy for her. Wrong. Judging by the pain on her face she might well change her mind and refuse to relinquish.

He'd have to alter his strategy, because Nicole's greedy brother-in-law wasn't the weakest link. Nicole was. She was the one who could snatch his child from him at the last possible second—just like Jeanette had before.

If he wanted this baby, then Nicole Hightower was the one he had to work on, the one he had to win over.

To do that he needed to get closer to her. He had to get into her head so he could anticipate her next move and be prepared to counter it.

He wasn't losing another baby.

Nicole hurried from the building, running from her thoughts, running from her doubts and trying to escape the pain tearing her apart. Maternal instincts she hadn't known she possessed surged though her, making her desperate to flee her current situation.

How was she going to keep her promise to Beth and Patrick?

Unless they pulled out of the contract, she had to or she'd turn her family against her. Hurting Beth meant incurring the entire family's wrath. Beth might be her older sister, but she was also the acting matriarch of the family because their mother had abdicated that position a long time ago. At fifty-eight Jacqueline Hightower was little more than a figurehead president of the HAMC board of directors who wanted what she wanted and more often than not managed to get it.

Nicole knew giving Beth and Patrick the baby they'd wanted for so long was the right thing to do. She knew deep in her heart somewhere that once the stress of being denied the child they'd craved passed they'd be happy again.

But knowing that didn't lessen the ache in her chest.

You'll get past your doubts. Today was just a shock, that's all.

Ryan caught her elbow outside the doctor's office and pulled her to a stop yards short of her car. Despite the sun overhead, she was so cold she couldn't stop shivering. His hands buffed her biceps, warming her cold flesh through her sweater. She wished he'd quit touching her. The contact confused her.

Correction. Her reaction to his touch confused her.

Her shivering lessened. His hands stilled, squeezed in silent support that made her eyes burn with the few tears she hadn't shed all over the exam table. This was so much harder than she'd thought it would be. She struggled to mask the hurricane of emotions churning inside her before she lifted her face to his.

"Hand over the keys, Nicole." His voice was soft, gentle, and yet still commanding. His eyes held both sympathy and understanding. And then she remembered. He, too, knew how it felt to lose a child. He'd already been down the road she was about to travel. "You're in no shape to drive."

How astute of him to notice. She considered arguing, but she didn't have the energy. And he was right. She had no business behind the wheel at the moment. Uncurling her fist, she offered the keys. His short nails scraped her palm as he scooped her key ring from her hand, and a flaming arrow of energy shot up her arm and crash-landed in the pit of her stomach.

How did he do that? How did this man she barely knew affect her on such a visceral level? And when she was already an emotional wasteland? It couldn't be anything but the baby they shared. Her body must somehow recognize him as the father of her child on a primitive level.

He gently thumbed away a fresh tear then helped her into the car as if she were fragile, and circled to the driver's side.

No doubt about it, Ryan Patrick puzzled her. He was understanding and yet ruthless. He opened doors, held chairs, seated her before seating himself and did a multitude of other gestures you usually only saw from an older generation. And yet he went to a fertility clinic and hired a surrogate to have his baby.

The contradiction between his old-fashioned courtesies and his modern science choices intrigued her. And the emotional response to the baby that he hadn't been able to hide had shaken her conviction that he'd be a bad father. He'd been as enthralled by the image on the screen as she had. At that moment he'd become more than the man who wanted to take her baby. He'd become the father of the child she carried, someone with a valid emotional stake in the outcome of her pregnancy, someone with something precious to lose.

Someone like her.

But how could someone who always chased thrills be a good parent? Her parents were perfect examples. They'd traveled the globe, always searching for their next good time. Her mother chose men, her father casinos. And they'd left their children at home in the care of nannies. There had been some good, loving nannies who Nicole had hated to see go, but the majority had been there for the paycheck and even a child could feel the difference. Nicole had learned early on not to bond with someone who might leave unexpectedly.

Ryan slid into the driver's seat and turned the key. "What time is your next appointment?"

"I don't have any official appointments this afternoon. I'm working on scheduling and client special requests." She'd deliberately allowed for emotional recovery time after her doctor's visit and chasing down obscure items seemed like a good way to keep her mind from straying along forbidden paths. "Why?"

"We're having lunch before I take you back to work."

She'd planned to eat before returning to the office, but not with him. She needed solitude to get her head together. "That's really not necessary."

"We both need the decompression time. We'll also pick up your prescription."

Hadn't he heard a word she said? "I can do that myself."

"I want to make sure you have it, and I intend to help you with your medical expenses."

Why? Because he genuinely wanted to help? Or because helping would give him leverage? "Thank you, but no."

"Are Beth and Patrick covering your medical bills?"

Another sore subject. "No. This is my gift to them. My health insurance covers almost everything."

"What kind of deal is that? You're making all the concessions."

"That's the way I want it." Beth had told her finances had been severely stretched by years' worth of failed fertility treatments.

"I don't want you cutting corners. I'm helping. Deal with it."

She did not need his bossy attitude right now. She needed peace and quiet and time to think. The emotional appointment had drained her. Exhaustion made her head and shoulders heavy and her patience short. A tension headache nagged at her nape.

"Are you going to show up each morning to make sure I take the iron tablets along with my prenatal vitamins, too?"

Oops. So much for patience, politeness and perseverance. Sarcasm wasn't a good choice if she wanted to keep this on a friendly footing as her attorney had suggested.

"Do I need to?"

She didn't doubt he would for one minute. "I would never do anything to endanger my child."

"Our child. Yours and mine." His possessive tone sent a wave of goose bumps rolling across her skin. "Admit it, Nicole. After seeing the scan you don't want to give your sister and brother-in-law this baby."

The truth of his statement punched the air from her lungs. How had he known what she'd been unwilling to admit even to herself? Ryan read her too easily.

"What I want is irrelevant. I gave my word and signed a contract. The baby will be better off with two parents."

"Two parents who bicker incessantly?"

She smothered a wince. She'd hoped he'd missed that at the barbecue. "It's a high-stress time for Beth and Patrick. They've been trying to get pregnant for years. They love each other. It's just a little hard to see that right now. Once the baby arrives everything will be fine again."

"You don't honestly believe that?" His tone said he didn't.

After her conversation with Beth she wasn't as certain as she'd once been. Ryan didn't need to know that. "Yes, I do."

Ryan scowled harder. "It's better to be with a single parent who wants you than stuck between two who use you as a weapon against the other. I lived that life. My kid won't."

Sympathy and empathy she didn't want to feel for him invaded her like a rising tide. When her parents had fought she'd either taken cover or looked for a way to distract them. Distracting them more often than not meant she'd ended up in trouble—trouble Beth had had to fix when their parents had thrown their hands up in disgust. But at least it had stopped their fighting.

"I'm sorry, Ryan."

He shrugged. "I survived."

He turned into the closest restaurant driveway and pulled up to the drive-through speaker, cutting off her questions. Without asking her preference, he ordered a variety of foods. When they reached the window he handed her the massive bag. The mouthwatering aromas of fried chicken, barbecue, Brunswick stew and peach cobbler filled the car as he headed toward downtown, and at the moment she craved every fat-laden, Southern cooking calorie of those comfort foods.

Leaning back in her seat, she closed her eyes and held on to the hot bag. She'd counted ten fingers and ten toes on that black-and-white screen, and seeing those little digits wiggle had reached right out and grabbed her heart with crushing force.

How would she survive giving away her baby?

She didn't protest when Ryan drove into his condo complex, but she bolted upright in her seat when he bypassed the building and pulled up to the dock. "Why are we here?"

"We're going to take a short boat ride and picnic."

Her uneasiness increased. "I don't think that's a good idea."

"Do you get motion sickness?"

That was the least of her worries. She didn't want to run the risk of another one of those misguided kisses when she hadn't been able to erase the first one from her mind. She was already vulnerable and that spark of attraction each time their fingers touched made it clear the earlier chemistry hadn't been a fluke.

Ryan made her feel things she shouldn't and didn't want to experience ever again. Things she didn't want to believe she was capable of feeling for any man other than Patrick. If she could experience that attraction for other men that would mean that there was some of her mother in her, and she didn't want to be like her fickle, promiscuous mother.

"I don't get seasick, but I can't waste a day on the river."

"Racing across the water with the wind in your hair will blow away the stress. The bike does the same thing on the road, but I'm not putting you on a motorcycle when you're pregnant."

Her older brothers had taught her to never admit weakness unless you wanted it to be used against you. "Who says I'm stressed? And just for the record, I don't want to ride your death rocket."

Ryan hit her with a lowered eyebrow look. "Riding a bike is only dangerous if you're careless. I'm not."

The conviction in his eyes told her he believed what he said.

He climbed from the car and paused beside the open door to remove his suit coat and toss it into the backseat. One tanned hand reached for his tie, loosening the knot and pulling the silk free. He released the cuffs of his shirt and then unbuttoned the placket.

Nicole shouldn't have been hypnotized by his actions,

but she couldn't look away. Nor could she force herself into motion. For pity's sake, he wasn't going to get naked, but his movements were every bit as erotic as a slow striptease, and the show sent a surge of energy through her like she'd never before experienced.

Her exhaustion vanished, and tension fisted beneath her navel as he peeled off the dress shirt to reveal a snug white T-shirt underneath. The cotton molded his muscular chest and his pectorals as he braced himself on the roof with one arm and leaned in to lay his shirt and tie on top of his coat. Shadows of the dark whorls of his chest hair and the tiny beads of his nipples showed through the thin fabric.

Should she play it safe and insist he take her back to the office, or could she count on her usual aplomb to get her through this meal? Her stomach rumbled, giving her an answer—just not the one she wanted. She didn't want to spend time with him, but she'd be wise to take advantage of the opportunity she'd been presented, learn everything she could about him and find any weaknesses Beth and Patrick might use against him in a custody battle.

Resigned to her fate, she shoved open her door and hauled herself and the food out of the car before he reached her side. He took the bag from her.

"You'll be more comfortable without the sweater."

She glanced down at the black silk tie-waist cardigan she'd thrown over her burgundy camisole this morning when there'd been a slight chill in the air. The sun shone down from a blue cloudless sky, warming her skin, and a gentle breeze teased her hair, tugging strands free from her clip and blowing them across her face. She smoothed her hair back but bits slipped free again. It was a beautiful day, one of the few warm ones left before fall's frost nipped the air. Why not enjoy it?

She removed her sweater and dropped it on the car seat. Ryan pivoted and strode down the sidewalk toward the bobbing boats, his long, athletic stride eating up the distance.

Determined to eat quickly and get back to work, she followed him. He boarded a fast-looking white boat with a red racing stripe, set down the bag and then turned and held out his hand. "Pass me your shoes."

Second thoughts about spending the next hour on the water with him intruded, but she nonetheless removed her high-heeled pumps and gave them to him. He tucked her shoes in a side cubbyhole and once more offered assistance. "Come aboard."

Touching him again was a bad idea, but slipping might hurt the baby. She reluctantly laid her palm in his. Her body instantly responded with unwelcome enthusiasm to his heat and strength, and she had to fight the knee-jerk reaction to yank away. The boat rocked beneath her feet, but Ryan held her steady.

He pointed to the seat curving around the back of the craft. "Sit and relax. I'll get us underway."

She was too wound up to sit and there wasn't enough room to pace, so she stood, her toes digging into the short, thick, red carpet. But as she watched him move about the boat she couldn't help wondering if her child would inherit his athletic grace, his power. Would he or she grow up learning Ryan's old-fashioned courtly gestures?

Not if Patrick raises him.

The words dive-bombed her brain like an annoying mosquito. She swatted them away. Patrick was the best father for her child. He was gentle and kind and patient, an intellectual with a love for learning. If he never opened doors or held chairs for her or her sister, it was because he was a modern man who treated women as equals.

He's henpecked.

The errant ugly thought startled her. Where had that come from? Sure Beth was bossy and liked to have her own way, and Patrick let her, but only because he loved her and didn't like to cause friction. His easygoing personality had been one of the things that had attracted Nicole to him in college. He'd been her raft in a stormy sea. Ryan was more like the storm itself, blowing in and wreaking havoc in her life. Patrick calmed her. Ryan confused and agitated her.

Ryan bent over the bow to cast off a rope. Her gaze roamed over his tight backside and down the firm flex of his hamstrings. His thick biceps and the breadth of his shoulders caught her attention. Attitude wasn't the only difference between her brother-in-law and the father of her baby.

Patrick was lean and wiry and couldn't be called athletic by any stretch of the imagination. His movements were abrupt, and his clothes tended to hang on his frame rather than accentuate the shift of powerful muscles the way Ryan's T-shirt did.

Patrick reminded her of a hummingbird, all zip, dash, skittish and adorable, whereas Ryan was more like the hawk gliding purposefully over the bend in the river. Predatory. Determined. Persistent.

Ryan turned unexpectedly. Nicole yanked her eyes up to his a second too late. Her cheeks burned with guilt at being caught ogling his body.

He slowly straightened, his pupils dilating as he held her gaze. His nostrils flared. The memory of that taboo kiss made her mouth water and her pulse flutter wildly. She caught herself studying the chiseled shape of his upper lip and struggled to pull air into her tight lungs.

With tremendous effort, she pried her eyes away from

temptation and focused on the big *T* on the side of Neyland Stadium, home of the Tennessee Volunteers. But the change in scenery did nothing to alleviate the awareness unfurling inside her like a morning glory seeking the sun. She silently screamed denial, but couldn't refute the truth.

She was sexually attracted to Ryan Patrick.

This can't happen. Not with him.

She felt each step he took on the boat deck through the soles of her feet, and she saw him approach in her peripheral vision. Her spine stiffened as he stopped beside her and brushed the hair from her eyes with a feather-light touch, tucking the strands behind her ear. He removed her hair clip and tucked it into his pocket.

"Hey!"

"I hope our child has your silky hair. We're going to make a beautiful baby, Nicole."

She gulped at his rusty tone. Alarms screeched in her brain. She needed to get away from him. But her muscles ignored her frantic orders. A shiver worked down her spine and her nipples tightened. Her pulse and breathing quickened and her stomach fisted with desire. She wanted to order him to back off, but she couldn't find her voice.

His fingertips dragged down the sensitive side of her neck and rested on her collarbone. She reluctantly lifted her gaze to his and found his eyes focused on her mouth.

She wanted his kiss.

The realization shocked a gasp from her. How long had it been since she'd actually wanted to kiss someone? Not since Patrick. Sure, she'd dated in the past six years and endured dozens of mediocre good-night kisses, but she'd never craved one the way she did Ryan's. *Right now.* And that spelled disaster.

She tried to recall Patrick's face, to will his image to replace Ryan's in her mind's eye. She failed. Miserably.

One of Ryan's hands cupped her nape and gently massaged the knotted muscles. The other rested on her waist, pulling her forward. The simultaneous press of his lips and his body against hers sent shock waves of pleasure rippling through her. His mouth opened and closed, brushing hers, teasing and luring her into passion far out of her depths. He sucked her bottom lip between his, tugged gently with his teeth and then stroked her tender flesh inside with his tongue.

A current of desire crashed over her, washing away her resistance and the reasons why this shouldn't happen. His hot, slick tongue caressed hers, and his palm gently covered her breast with a blanket of heat. A whirlpool of sensation twisted deep inside her.

Trying to dam her response was a waste of time. Her hands drifted to his hips, then a rising tide of hunger carried them to his shoulders. Her fingers tangled in his short, crisp, sun-warmed hair.

His hand scorched a trail from her nape to her bottom, kneading her, cupping her and pulling her closer. The ridge of his hardening flesh against her belly exhilarated her. She leaned into him, reveling in the novel sensations swamping her.

She couldn't take enough breath through her nose to keep the dizziness at bay. Her breast tingled beneath his thumb's caress, and she hungered for more. More of his kisses. More of his touch. More of his taste. As if he'd read her thoughts, he widened his stance, pulled her between his legs and plunged deeper into her mouth. He found her tight nipple and rolled it between his fingertips. A riptide of need tugged at her core, making her ache with an unfamiliar emptiness that yearned to be filled.

Why had she never wanted like this before? Why now? Why Ryan? Besides the life they'd inadvertently created, what power did he have over her?

Her fingers flexed involuntarily in a last-ditch effort to stop the insanity, and her nails scraped across the warm skin on his neck.

He shuddered and groaned into her mouth, rocking her like a rogue wave knocking a buoy off balance, and making her crave more of whatever it was he was doing to her body, her mind, her soul. But at the same time, her response startled her enough to make her realize this was the siren's song that lured her mother into so many meaningless affairs. Passion for a man you knew and cared little about.

Panic hit like a sobering plunge into Arctic waters. Nicole shoved against Ryan's chest, jerked free and, gulping in one desperate breath after another, backed as far away as the confines of the boat would allow.

She would not become her mother. No matter what Beth said.

Nicole had spent her adulthood proving she wasn't impetuous and that she always considered the consequences before taking action.

"Nicole." Ryan reached for her again, his eyes burning with hunger, but she evaded him. She *had* to evade him. The way he made her feel was too dangerous, too out of control.

"Ryan, we can't do this. This desire, this connection between us…it isn't real. We're both caught up in the magical moment of what we shared at the doctor's office today."

His eyes narrowed. "If you believe that, then you're fooling yourself."

Maybe so. "I can't become involved with a man who is trying to take my baby and destroy my relationship with my family."

"Our baby," he corrected again and this time a yawning emptiness opened deep inside her.

Their baby. The words resurrected a dream she'd abandoned long ago. A dream of having her own home and family with a man who adored her. A dream that had died when the man she loved married her sister.

"Stop saying that."

"Not saying it won't change the facts."

"I want to go ashore."

He caught her elbow. "I'd like to show you something first."

"I don't think—"

"My favorite spot in the river is about a mile from here. Our son or daughter will be seeing a lot of it."

He'd said the one thing guaranteed to keep her on board. "Boating isn't safe for a baby."

"I've told you before I don't take unnecessary risks. They make infant life jackets. I love the water, and I intend to share that interest with my child the way my grandfather shared his with me."

Instantly, an image of a gangly dark-haired, blue-eyed boy filled her mind. She did not need that cute picture in her head.

Gazes locked, tense silence stretched between them like an anchor rope. Did she dare go with Ryan? Eager to soak up anything she might possibly miss in her baby's future, she inclined her head. It would only take a few minutes, and she'd keep her distance from Ryan and his devastating kisses.

He released her arm and bent over, breaking the connection. When he straightened all traces of desire had vanished from his face. He held a ball cap and a life jacket which he'd pulled from one of the side compartments. He thrust the flotation device in her hands and gently settled the cap on her head.

"I don't have sunscreen on board. You'll need the hat. Keep the life jacket close by."

He pivoted abruptly, crossed to the wheel and fired the engine. The strength left Nicole's legs and she sank onto the bench seat clutching the life jacket to her chest.

After casting off the stern line, Ryan returned to the controls. Seconds later the boat glided smoothly away from the dock. Nicole released a slow breath. Kiss ended. Catastrophe averted.

But strangely, her relief felt a lot like disappointment, and the hunger gnawing at her stomach had nothing to do with delicious aromas emitting from the take-out bag on the bench beside her.

Eight

Mistake. The word reverberated in Ryan's head, drowning out the roar of the boat's inboard motor.

Kissing Nicole had been a mistake. Both times.

She was the marrying kind. He was not.

She was family oriented. He was not.

She put others first. He looked out for number one.

But damn, her lips, the feel of her breast filling his hand and her slender body against his had set him on fire. Not what he needed to be thinking when lunch was the only thing on the menu this afternoon, and common sense told him to aim for contract not consummation.

He pulled into his favorite cove, killed the engine and let momentum carry the boat toward the dock.

What better way to ensure custody of your kid than to marry the mother?

He immediately tossed the idea overboard like an

anchor. He knew what a bad marriage could do to a child. Before she'd left his father, his mother had been demanding and needy and whined incessantly for more of her husband's attention. Ryan suspected he was enough like his workaholic father to guarantee he'd put his job first and his marriage last. He'd yet to find anything or anyone who interested him more than work. And he'd never found a woman he could trust.

An image of Nicole stretched out on his bed instead of the examination table infiltrated his brain. He shoved it aside, grabbed the bowline and looped the rope through the cleat, but the idea of hooking up with Nicole wouldn't let him go.

The boat rocked as she stood. "Aren't we trespassing?"

"With permission. This is one of the houses the real estate agent is going to show us." He pointed to the For Sale sign hanging on the covered, screened enclosure on one end of the dock. He'd considered it a stroke of luck when he'd spotted the sign on his last cruise upriver.

"I thought you were going to show me your favorite spot."

"This cove is it. Not a lot of current. Good fishing. Room to wakeboard."

She looked wary and a little put out as she scanned the wide offshoot of the river. "Couldn't we have driven here?"

"That wouldn't have blown away your headache."

Her eyes narrowed. "I never said I had a headache."

"You didn't have to. I could see it in your face and in the stiff way you moved your head. That's why I took your hair clip. But the headache is gone now, isn't it?"

Her frown deepened. "Yes. But I thought you were going to change the appointment."

He shrugged. "Since we needed to cruise upriver to find a picnic spot anyway, there wasn't any reason to cancel. The house is vacant. We'll eat in the gazebo. The agent will meet us in thirty minutes to give us a quick tour."

He tied the stern line then grabbed Nicole's shoes and the food bag and set both onto the dock. After climbing from the boat he turned and offered her a hand. She hesitated before placing her palm in his. Even though he braced himself, the zap hit him harder and more intensely than before, probably because now he knew how good she felt against him.

"Put on your shoes. You don't want to risk a splinter." He shifted his grip to her sun-warmed biceps to help her balance. The heat of her skin made him think of hot bodies—hot *naked* bodies. Arousal percolated through him along with a strong urge to rest his hand over her belly and his baby that was almost too strong to resist.

As soon as she'd donned her sexy heels he released her and led the way into the large screened portion of the dock and set the bag on the picnic table. It was much safer to focus on food rather than the forbidden.

"This is nice," she offered with her head tipped back to view the ceiling fan hanging from the steeply pitched tongue-and-groove ceiling. The honey-colored varnished wood had aged beautifully, but the perfectly mitered joints weren't what caught his attention. His gaze traced the line of Nicole's throat to the pulse fluttering beneath her pale skin.

The pose was purely sexual with her back and neck arched and her lips parted. She looked like a woman reaching climax. And the most surprising thing was that he'd swear her posture wasn't deliberate. He was used to women trolling their sensuality like bait, but he'd bet his bike Nicole had no idea she'd just sent him into testosterone overload.

He shook his head and resumed unpacking. Seeing a little of her skin had obviously short-circuited his brain.

She turned her attention to the two-story house sitting on the crest of a hill with the lush lawn terraced into two large, flat areas. "This property has the kind of fencing along the waterfront and the dock that I mentioned. It would be safe for a child to play in this yard."

"Fencing will keep a timid kid out of trouble, but a curious one will find a way around it."

"Is that the voice of experience speaking?" The look she cut him from under her lashes blasted him with a shot of heat below his belt. Did she have any idea how strong a punch the combination of her light eyes, sparkling with amusement, and long dark lashes packed? Probably not.

"I was an inquisitive kid. Were you?"

She bit her bottom lip and averted her face. "I found my share of scrapes to get into. Beth always helped me out of them by running interference with my parents."

That piqued his interested. "What kind of things?"

She fussed with the lid of the chicken box and shrugged. "Just dumb stuff to get my parents' attention. Nothing illegal."

"I wouldn't have pegged you as the mischievous type. Trying to get our parents' attention is something we have in common."

She stared at him for a moment then swallowed. "How old were you when your parents separated?"

"Ten. Old enough to understand most of what was going on and resent the hell out of it."

"If your parents were miserable together, it's better that they separated."

"Better than me being the bone between two fighting dogs?" Damn, he hadn't meant to say that. He wasn't a whiner. The past was over.

"Better than being forgotten." She ducked her head again as if she regretted her words.

Ryan had researched Nicole's family since the Labor Day picnic enough to know hers wasn't average. Her parents' exploits often made front page in the society section.

"You're not forgettable, Nicole."

Where had that come from? Put a lid on it, Patrick.

She stared up at him with rounded eyes. The urge to kiss her pushed him forward. Her cheeks flushed. She turned abruptly and looked at the house. "The style is reminiscent of the New Orleans French Quarter. I love the wrought iron railings and arches."

He wanted to know her story, but knowing meant caring and that wasn't part of his plan. But damned if he could stop the questions pounding his brain or the anger stirring through him. "Did your parents neglect you?"

"Neglect? No. But my mother was a firm believer in tough love and living with the consequences of your actions. I guess I wanted her to be the milk-and-cookies and kiss-your-boo-boos type." She sighed and shook her head. "Tell me about the house."

He let her change the subject because thinking of a kid needing a hug reminded him of the days he'd sat on the front steps waiting in vain for his father to come home. "The house has four thousand square feet, five bedrooms and six baths. There's a nanny apartment over the garages."

"A nanny apartment?"

"Yes."

"You're going to hire a nanny?"

"It won't be any different if the child is in day care except for the on-site convenience factor."

"HAMC's day care is just down the hall. I can log in

and watch the baby from my desk, and I can spend my lunch hour with him or her."

"When I work at home I'll be under the same roof." That hadn't been part of his original plan, but it sounded feasible—if the house were laid out right and had a decent home office setup. A hands-on dad like his had been before his mother turned the house into a battlefield every time his father came to visit. Eventually his dad had quit coming.

He yanked himself back to the present. "I'm familiar with the builder. He does quality work. The neighborhood has a pool, tennis courts and a gym in the clubhouse."

If his father didn't consider this a stable, put-down-roots address, then nothing would please him.

Nicole nodded. "Not having a pool on the property is a plus."

He finished unpacking the plastic utensils and paper plates. The delicious aromas filled his nose and his stomach growled in anticipation. He gestured to their picnic. "Help yourself."

She wasted no time filling her plate, and after he'd done the same she scooped up a spoonful of her peach cobbler and popped it between her lips.

Dessert first. His kind of girl.

None of that. No woman was his kind of girl—except the temporary ones who provided sex or an escort when a formal affair required one.

He turned his attention to an appetite he could safely satisfy. The fried chicken was crispy on the outside and juicy on the inside—just the way he liked it. Not as good as his grandmother's recipe, but close.

Nicole paused between bites, her aqua eyes finding his. "If you had an unhappy childhood, what makes you think you'll know how to be a good parent?"

He chewed and swallowed while he decided how much to share. "I never said I was unhappy. Like fifty-some percent of all marriages my parents' ended in divorce. I still had good role models in my maternal grandparents and my father when he made an appearance."

His mother had often dumped him on his grandparents when his father wasn't around, but those days with his grandparents had been some of the best of his life. Since he needed Nicole to feel secure in the child's future, he decided to volunteer some information.

"My grandfather shared his love of the water with me. My grandmother was a firm believer in the idle-hands-find-trouble theory. She taught me to cook and clean up after myself." The softening expression in Nicole's eyes set off alarm bells. "Your folks stayed together, how is that going to make you a better parent?"

Her chin tilted at a defensive angle. "We're not talking about me. Beth will be a great mom. And Patrick will be an amazing father. He's kind and patient and never raises his voice. And he's talented. He can play almost any musical instrument. He teaches music at the University of Tennessee. His family is warm, welcoming, generous and tight-knit. They have family reunions every summer and get together each Christmas. His parents are amazing. This child will be very lucky to have them as grandparents."

The flush on her cheeks when she talked about the greedy little weasel annoyed him because, without a doubt, Patrick Ryan would have taken the payout Ryan had offered if his wife hadn't intervened. He might still be convinced to take it.

"Sounds like you should have married him instead of your sister."

Nicole froze then paled. She focused on eating her cobbler.

He didn't like the vibe coming his way—especially when added to the fact that her brother-in-law had been the intended father of her child.

"Is there something going on between you and Patrick Ryan?"

She gulped down a mouthful and carefully wiped her lips with a paper napkin. "What a ridiculous question. Of course not."

"He's ten or fifteen years older than you and your degree is from UT. Did you fall for your professor, Nicole?"

She hid her face by sipping from her cup of sweet iced tea, but her red cheeks gave him his answer. For some reason the idea of her with Professor Ryan made him want to hit something.

She finally lowered the cup. "My private life is none of your business unless it pertains to the health of this baby."

Ryan leaned back against the railing, studying her and wondering how the professor could be dumb enough to have chosen the wrong sister. Anyone that stupid had no business fathering or parenting a child. "How did he end up with your sister?"

She pushed the thick vegetable stew around on her sectioned plate with her fork. "Tell me more about the house."

His lips twitched at her obvious evasion. "Were you in one of his classes?"

"That's none of your business."

"It is if he makes a habit of hooking up with his students."

She looked insulted. "Patrick has never cheated on Beth."

She seemed determined to defend the little twerp. "Are you sure of that?"

"From the moment he laid eyes on her he never wanted anyone else." She looked down. Her fingers clenched her fork. "We need to finish eating if we're going to tour the house and get me back to work."

"Answer my questions first."

She abandoned her utensils. "Why is it relevant?"

"I'm trying to understand why you would relinquish this baby when it is tearing you apart."

"Because it's the right thing to do," she almost shouted, the pain clear in her voice.

"Most women will fight to keep their kids even if they don't want them just for the power it gives them over their ex." Realization hit him like a falling concrete wall. "That's it. This baby is the linchpin. It's your connection to your brother-in-law even after he divorces your sister."

"No!"

An uglier thought occurred to him. "Or maybe he's leaving your sister for you. She's a real ball breaker, and you were supposed to be having his kid. Maybe he was going to boot your sister out of that house in the suburbs, and you're planning to take her place."

Every speck of color fled her face. "How dare you. And you're wrong. Even if Beth and Patrick did separate I would never take him back." Her eyes widened and her lips slammed shut as she regretted the slip.

Being right didn't fill him with satisfaction. "So he was yours first. Did Beth steal him?"

"Stop it."

"What happened, Nicole? You brought him home to meet the family and big sister stole him?" He could tell from her shattered expression that he'd guessed correctly, and while he regretted acting like a prick by ripping the scab off an old wound, his rage toward the weasel who'd hurt her far surpassed courtesy.

She stood, hands fisted by her side. "Take me back. Now."

"Does the truth make you uncomfortable?"

"If you won't take me, I'll hitch a ride with your real estate agent."

"Patrick Ryan is an idiot. You're better off without him."

She stalked out of the screened porch and up the dock toward the house. Ryan watched her go. What in the hell had gotten into him? He'd never been the type to torment a woman like that. But Nicole's feelings for the jackass had irritated his stomach like the burn of cheap tequila.

Best to give her time to cool off and him time to get his head back on straight because losing control with her wasn't going to get him anywhere but in trouble.

One thing was certain, he decided as he repacked the remnants of their lunch, Nicole's bastard of a brother-in-law was not getting his hands on this baby. Ryan intended to make damned sure of it—no matter how far he had to go to guarantee success.

Nicole could practically hear the sound of children's laughter echoing through the empty house, and her heart ached. She would never have a home like this or the family the bright, spacious rooms called out for. She wouldn't let herself.

She couldn't marry when her heart still belonged to Patrick. She'd seen how tying yourself to the wrong person turned out. If her mother had married the man she loved instead of the one her father had chosen for her as part of a business deal, then the Hightower family would have been filled with love instead of headed by two people miserably and grudgingly doing their duty. Two people who should have divorced long ago if the hateful words they'd shouted at each other were the truth.

Nicole visually tracked Ryan's progress across the lush

green lawn from her position in the open set of double French doors leading from the huge eat-in kitchen to the brick patio that overlooked the river and boat dock.

He approached the tree house built in one corner of the backyard. Looking up, he circled the base suspended a yard above his head. Next he examined the ladder, shook it and then tested the bottom tread with his foot.

The real estate agent chuckled beside Nicole as Ryan climbed and disappeared through the wooden floor above him. "Boys will be boys."

"I guess so." But her brothers had never had a tree house. Planes, boats, vacation homes, yes. Nicole had taken advantage of the last two, but not the first. She'd always been interested in learning to fly, but Beth had cautioned her that unless she wanted to be an absentee mother like theirs she'd better leave piloting to the men.

And now, the irony was she wouldn't be a mother at all.

The shutters of the simple wooden structure opened and Ryan's face appeared. "Come on up, Nicole."

Surprised, she startled. "I don't think so."

"It's structurally sound. Don't tell me you're chicken."

Chicken? Her spine snapped straight. He had no idea how often she'd heard that dare. Or how many times it had gotten her in trouble. As the youngest, she'd had a lot to prove.

"You know you want to see the kind of place your child will be playing in," he added.

Dirty. He'd hit her in her most vulnerable spot. She approached the structure, her heels sinking into the grass with each step. At the bottom of the ladder she kicked off her shoes and climbed. Her head cleared the opening, and she gasped in delight at the miniature home. Small scaled wooden tables, chairs and even a bunk bed filled the space.

Ryan cupped her elbow and helped her stand. Even after he released her the heat of his touch lingered on her skin. Despite the vaulted ceiling complete with skylights, Ryan dwarfed the space. She turned a slow circle. "Any child would love this hideout."

"My father and I designed a clubhouse very similar to this."

Something in the tone of his voice caught her attention. She leaned back to study his face. "Did you build it?"

The regret in his eyes gave her the answer before he shook his head. "My parents divorced before we could start."

Her heart ached for the confused child he must have been. She wanted her baby to have a father who would plan tree houses and fishing trips. A father like Ryan. Patrick would never be the type to risk looking silly by acting boyish. She couldn't picture him stooping in a kid's playhouse or scaling a homemade ladder.

Her fingers curled around Ryan's forearm in an offer of support before she realized what she was doing.

He pressed his hand overtop hers before she could pull away and his gaze drilled hers. "I was out of line earlier when I harassed you about your brother-in-law. I apologize."

Surprised, she stared at him. His words demonstrated yet another difference between the two men. Ryan regretted hurting her feelings. Patrick had never apologized for devastating her life. "Apology accepted."

Her anger toward Ryan had already dissipated, anyway. She couldn't blame him for putting the puzzle pieces of her life together, and accurately, too. It wasn't his fault that she didn't like the segment he'd chosen to highlight.

"It's his loss, Nicole." He released her hand but her reprieve was short-lived. One long finger brushed her cheek, sending a frisson of awareness over her.

She couldn't risk another one of his devastating kisses. She backed to the open window, turned and looked out over the yard, house and river below. "This house couldn't be more perfect if you'd drawn the plans yourself."

He joined her, his elbows and upper arms bumping hers as he leaned on the narrow sill beside her. "It's not bad."

"Not bad? Ryan, every safety feature that could be added has been. The home office is amazing, and this yard and tree house are wonderful. The kitchen is made for big family dinners. Everything about this property cries out for children."

Ryan scanned the property and then his eyes met hers. "Don't do it."

Confused, she frowned. "Don't do what?"

"Relinquish."

She gasped at the intrusion of real life. "We've been over this, Ryan."

"You claim Beth and Patrick want this baby, but if that were true nothing would have kept them from that appointment today. Nothing could have kept me from being there."

Nicole winced at the accuracy of his statement. In weak moments, she'd thought the same thing. She straightened and crossed the tiny space. "They were busy."

The excuse was pathetic and, she suspected, untrue.

"The kid is not theirs. They've done nothing to help you with expenses. Break the contract, Nicole. You have two valid reasons for doing so."

"But I—"

"Don't drag this kid through the hell you know is coming. I've seen enough of my friends' marriages end to recognize when there's no love left, and it's time to cut your losses. I'm sure you have, too. Beth and Patrick have reached that point. You can see it in their distance when they're together."

His words chiseled away another chunk of her confidence that giving up her baby was the right thing to do. A cold knot formed in her middle. "A baby will make them happy."

"Are you absolutely certain of that? A baby is more likely to increase their problems than erase them."

She couldn't respond. Not the way she wanted to.

"My lawyer claims breaking the contract will be almost impossible given the legal precedents already set, and changing my mind could tear my family apart."

"Or it could set your sister free from an obligation she no longer wants to keep." The certainty in his voice and in his cobalt eyes ignited a spark of hope in her heart, but she was afraid to fan the flame only to have it snuffed out.

He'd voiced her greatest fear and her greatest hope—something she hadn't even allowed herself to put into words. Was he right? Did Beth want out of their agreement now that they knew the baby wasn't Patrick's? Was that why she kept delaying the announcement? Nicole couldn't blame her sister if she'd changed her mind. Maybe Beth was sticking by her promise out of a sense of duty.

Nicole wanted to keep her baby with every fiber of her being, ached for it to have two parents who would love it, cherish it and want the best for it. For a moment in this perfect little cabin in the trees she believed she and Patrick could be those parents. Maybe not in the traditional, married sense, but parents who shared custody and love of the child they'd created.

But she'd given her word, and she would not break it

unless Beth and Patrick wanted out of their agreement. Otherwise, she could lose everything. Her job. Her family. And her baby.

And then she'd have nothing and no one.

Nine

Over. Finally.

Nicole closed her file and exhaled in relief Friday afternoon as the Patrick Architectural team of Ryan and his father exited her office.

She'd barely been able to concentrate during her first consult with them. Simple facts had been hard to retrieve. Not that anyone who didn't know her well would have noticed, but it had been a constant struggle to stick to her planned pitch because every time Ryan had made eye contact, her thoughts had scattered like fall leaves. And her mind would wander off to replay the kisses she'd shared with him and the carrot of custody he'd dangled in front of her two days ago. Two days in which Beth had avoided Nicole's calls and hadn't come into the office.

"I'll see you tonight."

Ryan's voice brought her head up. He'd stopped in her doorway instead of following his father out. "I'm sorry?"

"At the party."

"Party? What par—" Surprise made her breath catch. With all the upheaval in her life she'd completely forgotten the annual black-tie affair for Hightower Air's employees and clients was tonight. "Of course. It slipped my mind."

One dark eyebrow lifted. "Have a date?"

Trick question? Ah, but Ryan wouldn't know. "I never take a date to company affairs."

"Why?"

"Because I talk shop and it bores most men to sleep."

"It won't bore me. I'll pick you up."

Exactly what she didn't need. "Thank you, but I have to be there early to make sure everything is ready."

"Beth and Patrick should see us as a united team."

The battle resumed inside her, but she knew herself well enough to know that if Beth and Patrick truly wanted this child, then she would not deny them their hearts' desire even though it would break hers. She shifted in her pumps, afraid to commit, but very aware of what she'd lose if she did…and if she didn't.

"I haven't decided to take that route yet. I need to talk to them first."

"No point in both of us going stag. I don't mind arriving early."

He moved into her personal space, crowding her against the leather sofa where they'd concluded their meeting. Her calves pressed the cool upholstery. His heat, his tangy scent and his sheer physical presence overwhelmed her. Her brain screamed a warning. She couldn't remember ever being this aware of any other person in her life. He felt it, too. She could see the awareness in his parted lips and expanding pupils. Her pulse skipped. She swallowed the flood of moisture in her mouth.

"I have to be there at eight." She wanted to slap her hand over the errant orifice. Where had that come from? What had happened to the polite refusal she'd intended? She hadn't meant to imply an invitation with her tone.

"I'll pick you up at twenty before." Ryan held her gaze without touching her, but he might as well. Every cell in her being tap-danced with excitement.

She wished he would leave.

She wished he would kiss her.

She wished she knew what she wanted. Being wishy-washy ticked her off, and everything about their complicated situation confused her.

"Good job today. You impressed the hell out of my father when you took him through the plane and covered all the technical jargon. Brains and beauty are one hell of a potent combo. You and HAMC have certainly exceeded our expectations to this point."

His praise took her aback and warmed her cheeks. She decided to focus on the business component of his comment rather than the personal reaction she couldn't understand. "Thank you, Ryan. I hope we continue to do so."

It was her job to orient her clients to their new aircraft, to walk them through the aircraft they'd chosen and to explain the services HAMC could provide—and of course to offer more services which could be had for an additional fee. Few ever bothered to express gratitude for her hard work. Meeting their requirements was her job, one they took for granted she'd do successfully. She only heard about it when she failed to meet their expectations which, thank goodness, was a rarity.

Which brought her back to that strangely intimate

moment in the tree house. For a moment there she'd felt closer to him than to anyone ever in her life. He knew her darkest secret and didn't despise her for it.

Ryan reached into his coat pocket and pulled out a small wrapped package the size of a paperback book. "For you."

A gift? She took it with reservations and tore the glossy yellow paper. A white picture frame hand-painted with pastel-colored baby blocks held the ultrasound photograph the doctor had snapped at the moment when their baby's little fingers had wiggled almost as if he or she had been waving hello. Emotion welled inside her. Nicole pressed her fingers to her lips to stop the sob pushing its way up her throat.

"That's our son. Or daughter." His voice had a rough quality as if he were as emotionally affected as she was.

She inhaled a ragged breath. Her eyes and throat burned as she traced the shadowy outline. She suspected he'd be the kind of father who offered praise and encouragement along with his time and guidance. The kind she'd always wanted. The kind every child deserved.

"Thank you, Ryan."

"You're welcome." She jerked at the contact of his fingertip on her cheek and then he dragged a hot sweep of temptation that stopped at the corner of her mouth. Her lips parted. She tasted salt and realized he'd mapped a tear she hadn't noticed escaping.

"I'll see you tonight." He turned abruptly and strode out of her office, leaving her with a hurricane of emotion twisting through her system and an ache for…something she couldn't name.

She clutched the frame to her chest. He couldn't have given her anything more meaningful. And she didn't miss the symbolism. He wanted to give her their baby.

"Tell me you bought a killer new dress for this thing." Lea's quip jerked her out of her trance.

Nicole wasn't ready to share Ryan's paternity yet because that would lead to twenty questions—questions she didn't have the answers to yet. She turned toward her desk, surreptitiously wiping her cheeks, and slipped the photo into a drawer.

"Nicole, are you okay?"

"Yes. But I'm embarrassed to confess that with the pregnancy and all, I forgot about the gala."

"Well, now you have a hot date with a steamy guy who happens to be loaded and doesn't mind that you're pregnant with another man's baby. We have work to do, girlfriend."

She winced at Lea's misconception, but didn't have the fortitude to explain the situation at the moment.

She mentally searched her closet and discarded her entire wardrobe. What was wrong with her? Anything she had would have been suitable. Ten minutes ago.

But not anymore.

"I guess you're right. I don't have anything to wear."

Lea threw an arm around her shoulders. "We have no time to shop. We'll swing by my place. It's on your way home. Lucky for you I'm an outlet sales addict, and I buy more than I need. I have a ruby-red Calvin Klein halter dress that will look great on you."

Lea, an admitted shopaholic, had gushed about the dress for a week after she'd found it on the clearance rack. "I can't take that. You haven't worn it yet."

"Trust me, the pleated sweetheart neckline will look better on you with your…accentuated assets than it does on my flat chest. Ryan can't help but notice those babies." Lea's nod indicated Nicole's pregnancy-swollen breasts, and Nicole groaned.

"Lea, stop matchmaking."

"Who's matchmaking? I'm just stating the obvious. I need a cold shower after seeing that little exchange between you two. You're going to look hot, and he's going to notice."

That was not what Nicole needed since resisting temptation in the form of Ryan Patrick was at the top of her list.

Nicole surreptitiously glanced at her Cartier watch. Her evening had been a total failure thus far. Not by anyone else's standards, but by hers.

Her goal tonight while having her entire family in the same room was to remind herself of what she'd lose if she chose to be selfish.

Instead, as she stood on the balcony overlooking the elegant ballroom below and scanned the guests, seeking out her siblings scattered far and wide across the travertine floor, she realized how alone each of them was in the crowd.

Trent, the oldest and company CEO, stood with his babe de jour and the president of HAMC's largest client. Trent's twin, Brent, with his usual Scotch in hand, was nowhere near his pregnant wife. No surprise there.

Beth and Patrick were side by side, but at the same time miles apart. When, why and how had that happened? Had the stress of infertility caused their emotional separation or was it something more? Would the baby fix the situation or make it worse? Nicole needed to look Beth in the eye and ask if she wanted out of their agreement, but her sister had been avoiding her.

You would have thought having to rely on each other while growing up would have brought the Hightower siblings closer and made them friends as well as family. It hadn't. Other than the same parents and the same employer, they had nothing in common.

Nicole wanted a tight familial connection for her child. On her first date with Patrick he'd taken her to his family reunion. She'd seen what families should be like and craved it ever since.

Her mother sidled up to the banister beside her. Her gaze ran over Nicole. "You look quite lovely tonight. Not your usual style, but the gown works for you."

"Thank you, Mother."

A heavy silence descended between them. Nicole resumed her search for Ryan's dark hair, broad shoulders and black tux.

"Nicole, if you have a problem you can come to me."

Nicole blinked and looked at her mother in surprise, but Jacqueline sipped her champagne and focused on the guests gathered below.

The shoulder her mother offered came a little too late. They'd never had the kind of relationship where Nicole could comfortably pour out her fears—especially something of this magnitude. "I'll keep that in mind."

Jacqueline turned then and lifted a hand as if to touch Nicole's face, but dropped it without making contact. "I haven't always been there for you. I'm just now beginning to realize and regret how much I've missed." Her heavily made-up eyes echoed the sentiment of her words. "Enjoy your evening and your beau."

Her mother stalked away leaving a cloud of Armani Diamonds perfume behind.

Did her mother's regrets have something to do with the daughter she'd given up? Nicole found Lauren, the newest addition to the family. Lauren was living proof that everyone needed to be connected somehow. After her father's death she had come looking for her relatives. Unfortunately for her, that family happened to be the aloof Hightowers instead of a warm, welcoming clan like Patrick's.

Not your problem. You have more than enough on your plate.

Where was Ryan? Nicole didn't see him anywhere in the ballroom. Her heart missed a beat. Had he grown tired of her working the crowd and her clients and left? He hadn't seemed to mind her preoccupation. In fact, having him by her side while she greeted the guests tonight had felt good, and for the first time she'd felt like part of a couple. Listening to him interact with them had taught her a valuable lesson. Ryan was smart and ambitious and had a memory like a steel trap. She'd have to be careful not to underestimate him.

"You haven't danced with me."

She jumped at his voice behind her and spun around. "I haven't danced with anyone. I've been working. Parties like this are an opportunity for me to have face time with clients I only talk to via phone or e-mail the rest of the year."

"And you excel at making each client feel valued. That's an important trait in my business, as well."

More praise. It warmed her all over.

His brilliant blue gaze slid from her face to her breasts which tightened under his perusal, then on to her waist and back up again. She was used to dressing to please herself, but the instant she'd seen the approval in his eyes when he'd arrived at her home earlier, she'd been glad she'd let Lea talk her into this sexier little number.

He offered his hand, palm up. "The band is about to begin the final song of the night. Dance with me."

The excited leap of her pulse sent a warning. One she decided to ignore. What could one dance hurt? They were in a roomful of people. Nothing could happen.

She placed her hand in his and let him lead her to the

grand staircase. Heads turned as they descended to the main ballroom. She did her best to ignore the curious eyes, but she couldn't deny feeling a little like Cinderella, the belle of the ball with the handsome prince at her side.

Ryan in a tux took her breath away. The epitome of tall, dark and handsome, his shoulders filled out his black jacket and his bow tie framed his square jaw. He was easily the most attractive man present tonight, but his appeal was more than just good looks. His allure derived from the confident way he carried himself, the intelligence shining from his gorgeous blue eyes and in the way he made her feel like the most desirable woman present. And wasn't that a fairy tale? She shot him a sideway smile which he returned with knee-weakening potency.

He led her into the middle of the dance floor and pulled her into his arms. The gentle impact of his big, solid body against hers knocked the breath right out of her—not from the force of the contact, but from the sheer strength of the combustion between them.

She inhaled deeply and his tangy scent filled her lungs. One wide palm splayed across her back. His hard thigh slotted between hers, and with each step his hips brushed her tummy over the tiny life they'd created. The ruby sateen fabric of her dress did nothing to block the pooling heat his proximity created. Ryan overwhelmed and overpowered her senses, and for once she let herself be swept away instead of fighting the current of desire.

Her eyes locked with his, and as he guided her around the floor awareness of the curious gazes of her family and coworkers faded until her focus narrowed to just him and her and the bond they shared.

The sad fact of the matter was that she felt more connected to Ryan Patrick, a man she hadn't known existed three weeks ago, than she did to any of her family members. He'd understood how much the ultrasound peek at their child had meant to her, and it had apparently meant as much to him. Her own sister hadn't cared enough to show up to meet the child she planned to adopt and had promised to love.

Ryan had noticed when she had a headache and insisted on an impromptu picnic to help her de-stress. He read her in a way she couldn't remember anyone else ever doing. Patrick certainly hadn't. Ryan was in fact the only person in her life who understood the pain of losing her child.

The press of his leg against her center sent a rush of arousal through her, making her entire body come alive with awareness. Her breaths rasped audibly, and her pulse roared in her ears drowning out the music of the band behind her. Need radiated from her center.

She wanted Ryan in a way she'd never wanted anyone before. Just for tonight she needed to feel connected to someone who understood the tangle of emotions tearing her apart, someone who wanted to give instead of take. She'd handle the consequences, be what they may, tomorrow.

As if she'd telegraphed her thoughts, Ryan's pupils expanded. He leaned forward and his lips grazed her ear with spine-tingling results. "Let's get out of here."

His gruff whisper caused the hairs on her nape to lift. "Yes. Please."

Keeping possession of her hand, he strode toward the exit at a brisk pace. He didn't look left or right or pause to speak to anyone. The limo slid to a stop in front of them even before they'd reached the curb as if the driver had been waiting for them to appear. Ryan hustled her into the backseat.

"My place," he told the driver through the open window

between the front and back compartments before pushing the button to slide the tinted glass closed.

Nicole knew she should argue, knew exactly where they were headed if she didn't. Not just to Ryan's condo, but to his bed. She subdued her protests even though crossing the intimacy line was something she rarely allowed herself to do.

Ryan's arm slid around her waist. He scooped her into his lap in the darkened car and slanted his mouth across hers, capturing her gasp on his tongue. His fingers tangled in her hair, cupping her nape and holding her captive while one hungry kiss melded into another. He kissed like he did everything else: with deliberation, precision and devastating skill. The two kisses they'd shared previously had been tame compared to the way he consumed her mouth tonight.

He stroked, sucked, nipped her mouth with urgent passion that incited and invited her own. His other hand caressed her back, her lower belly and then slid toward her breast.

Her body stilled in anticipation as a response she couldn't ignore swelled within her. She wanted his touch, ached for it. Arching her back, she pressed her breast into his palm.

Her stomach fluttered like the tail of a kite in a strong wind, and a line of tension formed between her nipples and her core. Each brush of his thumb against her stretched it tighter. The burn deep inside made her shift her hips. His groan rumbled down her throat. He arched against her, pressing a thick erection to her bottom.

And then he yanked his mouth free and hissed in a breath. "If you'd rather go home alone, tell me now."

She couldn't see his eyes in the shadowy interior, but his gravelly tone and his hard body said he wanted her as much as she wanted him.

Run, the way you always do.

But she didn't want to run this time, didn't want to play it safe. She wanted to surrender instead of holding back, wanted to revel in wanting someone as much as he wanted her. It was only physical. She knew that. But she and Ryan shared so many things. A past rebellious spirit. An interest in the child she carried. And now a passion that couldn't be denied.

Being in his arms felt right. Scarily, eerily right. She couldn't believe making love with him would be a mistake. For her sake, for her baby's sake, she had to see where this would lead.

"I want to go home with you, Ryan."

Nicole wasn't the first woman Ryan had brought to his place, and she wouldn't be the last.

But this time felt different.

In the past the need for raw sex had been his primary agenda. Satisfy the hunger. Take the lady home. End of story.

With Nicole, he wanted to go slow, to linger over her subtle curves despite the urgency burning his gut. He wanted to map each inch of the body nurturing his child.

Even more, he wanted to crawl inside her head and understand why she was willing to make such a great personal sacrifice for someone she loved. Such selflessness was beyond his experience. In his world people always looked out for their own interests. Was Nicole truly that generous? Or was she using this baby to sink a hook in her brother-in-law? He wanted to believe the latter, but everything he'd learned about her pointed to the former.

Lacing his fingers through hers, he led her toward his bedroom without turning on the lights. Moonbeams from the uncurtained windows painted a glistening white path on the polished dark slate floors. His platform bed rested half in shadow, half in moonlight. He urged Nicole toward the light. He wanted to see every inch of her.

The rug surrounding his bed silenced the tap of her heels. He turned and soaked up the view. She'd left her hair down tonight. Curled strands draped over her shoulders, the ends teasing the top of her dress. The shiny red fabric hugged and lifted her breasts, tempting him, making his mouth water for a taste and his hands twitch for a touch. Her perfume, a light, floral scent, teased him. The whisper of her rapid breathing echoed his own.

"Your doctor said this was safe?" he confirmed.

"Yes. You heard her."

The fiery blush that had covered Nicole's face following the doctor's unsolicited statement returned. Twenty-eight and she still blushed. Interesting.

He cupped her warm cheek, stroked her silky soft skin. His fingers drifted down over the pulse fluttering at the base of her neck. That wild beat, combined with her parted lips and darkened eyes telegraphed her desire. His body received the signal loud and clear and multiplied it exponentially.

"You look beautiful tonight." He hadn't told her earlier because she'd been skittish. Who was he kidding? She'd taken his breath when she opened her door. He'd barely been able to think straight let alone form coherent sentences.

Her throat worked beneath his thumb as she swallowed. "Thank you."

He traced her collarbone then the narrow strap of her dress to the red material curving over the swells of her breasts. She gasped when he dipped his fingers into her warm shadowy cleavage, and then her chest shuddered on a ragged exhalation.

Nicole Hightower in full war paint was a sight to behold, and watching her work tonight had been impressive.

She'd been poised and confident and had her clients eating out of her hand. The combination was sexy as hell.

He felt a twinge of guilt for using the attraction between them against her, but shoved it aside and kissed her again, savoring the taste of her soft lips and the warmth of her body pressed against his. He outlined her waist, her hips, and then followed her spine upward to locate her zipper tab between her shoulder blades. His knuckles brushed warm skin, smoother than the satin of her dress, as he tugged the zipper down. He eased the garment from her shoulders.

She wasn't wearing a bra. Her breasts weren't large, but what she had was perfectly shaped. Round and full, the nipples hard and dusky-pink. No tan lines. He swallowed the rush of saliva filling his mouth, and pushed the fabric over her hips, leaving her in lacy red panties and her heels. He looked her up and down. Exquisite. How had he ever mistaken her subtle curves for skinny?

She braced a hand on his shoulder as she stepped free of her gown. Wanting her hands on his skin, he resented the barrier of clothing between them. As soon as she regained her balance, he shrugged out of his tux coat, tossed it toward the bench at the end of his bed and tackled his bow tie.

He hungrily drank her in with his eyes as he worked the buttons of his shirt free. She watched him, shifting on her feet and dampening her lips with her tongue. The fire building within him blazed hotter. Her skin was as pale as cream in the moonlight, her fingers fiddling nervously by her sides. He wanted those restless fingers on him. He shucked his shirt and kicked off his shoes.

"You're beautiful. Perfect." He reached for his belt, but the leather resisted him before giving way.

She covered her breasts. "I'm not usually so…pregnancy has made them larger."

He reached out and brushed her hands away, grazing her nipples in the process. Her gasp rent the air, mingling with the whistle of his indrawn breath as he dragged his knuckles over her stiff peaks again just for the pleasure of feeling the soft little beads bump over his skin.

He cupped her, thumbed the tips then bent to capture one with his lips because he couldn't wait another second to taste her. Her back arched, offering him more which he greedily took, sucking her deep into his mouth. He rolled his tongue around the tip and gently grazed her with his teeth.

She shivered in his arms and speared her fingers through his hair, holding him close as he sampled one soft mound and then the other. Grasping her waist, he backed toward the leather bench at the foot of his bed and sat. He pulled Nicole between his legs and feasted on her breasts.

Her nails dug into his scalp, and her soft moan filled the room. Fighting the urgency telling him to hurry, he smoothed a hand from her breast to her belly, reverently stroking the barely discernable sign that his child rested beneath.

His son or daughter.

His and Nicole's.

No. His. He couldn't settle for less than full custody.

His lips followed the trail his hand had blazed. He sipped and laved her skin, letting her unique flavor coat his tongue and her fragrance fill his nostrils. The scent of her arousal combined with her perfume, and his groin engorged in appreciation.

He caressed her long legs, his fingertips tracing the smooth skin covering her lean muscles, until he reached her ankles and the tiny buckles on her sandals. It took one hundred percent of his concentration to find the coordination to make his fingers work the narrow straps and remove her shoes. When he finished he hooked his thumbs in the lacy band of her panties and tugged them down her legs.

Dark curls surrounded her center, some of the tendrils already glistening with arousal. As soon as he'd discarded her lingerie he traced the damp line, finding her slick swollen flesh. She jerked and her breath hitched. He wanted more. Wanted to hear the sound she made when she came, feel her shudder and clench around him. Need drew his body up tight and hard. His pulse roared in his ears.

Recapturing a stiff dusky tip with his mouth, he matched the suckling and stroking of his tongue to the tempo of his fingers. Nicole's nails dug into his shoulders. He nudged her knees apart, widening her stance so he could pleasure her better. Within moments her legs began to quiver and her breath to quicken. Her back bowed and then, muscles tensing, she jerked as a whimper spilled from her mouth. He rose quickly to capture the remnants of her cry with his lips.

As her spasms died down, she clung to him, hung on him, her weight a delicious burden, her heat like a crackling fire. He broke the kiss and stared into her flushed face and slumberous eyes. He'd never seen a more alluring sight.

He had to have her. Now.

Grasping her hand, he backed toward the head of the bed, ripped the spread off with a yank that sent pillows flying and urged her onto the sheets.

She inched backward onto the mattress, her legs parting intermittently and giving him flashes of her damp center as she moved to the middle. That he believed the peep show unintentional made it all that more exciting. But that was Nicole. She had no idea how sensual she was.

And he had no business taking advantage of her. But the ends justified the means, and at least his desire for her was honest and intense and unlike anything he'd ever experienced before.

He shed the rest of his clothes in record time and eased over her. Bracing himself on straight arms, he slowly lowered his weight onto her until he had full body contact from ankles to lips. He didn't want to hurt her, but her skin branded him and her mouth devoured his. His erection rested against her smooth, hot stomach, and he had to grit his teeth to keep from driving against her. She felt so damned good.

He eased one knee between hers and then the other, opening her to him. It took everything he had not to ram hard and fast into her wetness. Remembering the life she cradled, he took himself in hand and stroked his rock hard flesh against her, teasing her swollen center and coating himself with her moisture to ease entry. He waited until she tensed and a flush covered her cheeks, and then he eased inside one gut-wrenching inch at a time, sliding deep into her body until he couldn't go any farther.

Her slick heat surrounded him and hunger ravaged him. He used his thumb to caress her, circling until she went over the edge. The rhythmic clenching of her internal muscles set him ablaze. A groan burst from his throat. He bore down on every cell in his being to keep from losing control. When he had a grip on his raging desire he dared to meet her aqua gaze. "You okay?"

"Yes," she all but hissed through kiss-swollen lips. "It feels good. *You* feel good, Ryan."

The breathless way she said his name made him molten hot.

"Not…too…much?" His voice was as rough as cold asphalt.

She shifted beneath him and every wiggle steamed a few brain cells. "Just right."

His control wavered. He withdrew and eased in again and again, faster each time. He tried to keep from thrusting too deep, too hard, but when she linked her ankles at the base of his spine he lost it. Instinct took over. Her nails scored his back, his butt, his chest. Her teeth nipped his lip, his shoulder, his neck. He told himself he couldn't be hurting her because she met each thrust and countered each swivel of his hips, and the sexy-as-hell noises coming from her mouth were signs of pleasure not pain.

He buried his face in her neck and quit fighting. The fire rushed from his toes and his fingertips to coalesce in his gut and consume him as his climax roasted him alive. "I'm coming, baby."

Her cry and the squeeze and release of her body told him she was with him. After the last spasm of pleasure faded, his muscles went lax. He caught himself before he crushed her. Braced on his elbows, he battled to regulate his breathing.

As the smoke slowly cleared from his skull he told himself that great sex was all they'd shared. Nothing more. It didn't matter that whatever he and Nicole had just done beat the hell out of anything he'd ever done before. He wouldn't be stupid enough to fall for another woman who could screw him over the way his ex had or the way his mother had his father.

Women were fickle and they fought dirty.

He needed to remember his relationship with Nicole was a short-term alliance. She had a product he wanted and a service he needed. If they had a pleasant interval in the process, so be it. But it would be temporary.

But as his lids grew heavy and his muscles turned to lead he decided making love with her had been a big mistake. Sex clouded the issues. But even as he acknowledged the mistake, he knew he'd repeat it. How could he not?

But he was strong enough to keep his priorities straight. He'd keep his eye on the job of getting custody of his child and never forget for one moment to look out for number one.

Ten

They hadn't used protection.

Every lax, sated muscle in Nicole's body went rigid.

What's going to happen? You're already pregnant with his child, and you know from his medical records that he doesn't have anything contagious.

Still…

She had never been careless. Never. She didn't have sex often, and when she did she didn't forget to protect herself. Physically or emotionally. Tonight she'd forgotten both.

Why had she chosen to drop her usual caution with Ryan? She eased onto her side in his bed and studied him in the dim light. His face had relaxed in sleep, softening his lips and the grooves beside his mouth. His hair was a spiky wreck from her fingers grabbing fistfuls of the thick strands. The sheet he'd pulled over them barely covered his privates.

Ohmigod. Were those scratch marks on his shoulders?

A wave of embarrassment burned over her. She'd never marked a lover before. She wasn't the type to lose control to that extent. Or she hadn't been until tonight when she'd been careless and out of control.

Just like your mother.

Alarms shrieked in her subconscious.

She had to get out of here.

She didn't want to talk to Ryan or look him in the eye until she figured out why she'd let herself go. She'd read that some women were more sensitive during pregnancy and more easily aroused. If her multiple orgasms were an indicator, she must be one of them. That had to be it. She had a case of raging pregnancy hormones, a body primed for sex, and he was her only outlet.

Are you sure it's not more than that?

It couldn't be. She and Ryan barely knew each other.

So he'd guessed she needed to de-stress after the ultrasound. Big deal. And so what if he'd realized she had a headache before she'd admitted it to herself. They had nothing in common except their baby, chemistry and a shared past of acting out to get their parents' attention. None of that meant anything. Or did it?

Was this the connection she'd always yearned for?

Couldn't be.

Her feelings for him were definitely…intense. She'd never experienced anything as powerful as what she and Ryan had shared with anyone—not even Patrick, the only man she'd ever loved and ever would love.

But she wasn't in love with Ryan. Love was soft and cuddly like a cozy fleece blanket. Her feelings for Ryan were more like coarse wool. Rough, prickly and uncomfortable.

Except making love with him had been…*amazing.*

Uneasiness wrapped around her like a spiderweb. She needed to go.

Holding her breath and trying not to shake the mattress, she inched out from under the sheet. When her feet touched the rug she exhaled in relief and then took another deep breath before carefully levering herself off the bed. She didn't breathe again until she had both feet on the floor.

She checked to make sure his eyes were still closed. The steady rise and fall of his bare chest caught her attention. The man was built like a gold medal swimmer, all defined muscles, wide shoulders and sleek bronzed skin. Just looking at him raised her temperature.

Get out before he wakes.

She scooped up her panties, shoes and dress and tiptoed out of his bedroom. She didn't stop moving until she reached a puddle of moonlight in his living room where she pulled on her clothes. The loud rustling of her dress made her wince and look over her shoulder for signs of motion in the bed. None. She struggled with the zipper but managed to get it only halfway up.

Carrying her shoes, she headed for the door. *Her purse.* Cringing, she stopped. Where had she left it? And then remembered Ryan had slipped her tiny clutch into the pocket of his tux jacket at the gala. She couldn't leave without it since her cash, credit card, house key and cell phone were inside.

Argh. She couldn't even call Lea to come and get her unless she used Ryan's phone or the one at the gatehouse. Even if she could call Lea, she wouldn't. How could she explain the situation to her friend when she didn't understand it herself? And Lea would demand an explanation.

Nicole raked her fingers through her tangled hair. Why had she slept with Ryan? Wasn't their relationship complicated enough without throwing an affair into the mix?

But it had seemed like a good idea at the time. She'd been rattled by Beth's obvious avoidance and her family's lack of a bond and she'd needed someone. Someone who understood her situation. She'd been carried away by the romance of the evening and turned on by dancing close to him. Falling into bed with him had made sense. Then. Now it felt more like she'd slept with the enemy—the one man who could cost her everything that mattered to her.

She eyed the exit and then his bedroom doorway, torn between the bad choice of calling Lea from the guardhouse for rescue and the worse one of staying. Dismay settled over her like a wet blanket. She had to go back into Ryan's bedroom to retrieve her purse.

She deposited her shoes on an end table and tiptoed back into the room. Her dress *swished* with each step, the sound echoing off the hard surfaces of his apartment. She paused just inside the threshold and scanned the space around the bed. Trying to locate his black coat in a dark room challenged her especially since his decor was all black. Black bed, comforter, sheets and even a black rug on the dark charcoal slate floor.

Where had he thrown his jacket? She spotted it draped across the corner of the bench at the end of the bed and took one careful step and then another toward it.

"Going somewhere?" Ryan's husky voice asked.

Nicole nearly jumped out of her skin. "I need my purse."

"Were you sneaking out on me?" he asked, his voice laced with disbelief as he sat up in bed and turned on a lamp.

Heat rushed her face. She ducked her chin, smoothed her hair then reached for his jacket. "I was going to let you sleep."

"I'll drive you home." He tossed off the sheet and rose from the bed, all lean muscles and masculine vitality.

She couldn't stop herself from soaking him up any more than she could stop a Boeing Business Jet bare-handed. The desire she'd thought quenched rekindled deep inside her.

"I appreciate the offer, but it's not necessary. I'll call a cab."

With his eyes locked on hers, he strolled toward her, setting her heart thumping double-time. He halted inches away, plucked his coat from her hands and tossed it on the bed out of her reach. He dragged his knuckles down her arm, raking up a trail of goose bumps. "I brought you. I'll take you home."

A tingle of unease danced over her skin. If she could react this strongly to Ryan, what did that say about her feelings for Patrick? The question rattled her. She didn't have an answer. She needed privacy to figure this out. A long hot bath…a glass of wine… No. No wine.

A very old memory seeped into her brain of her mother playing a song over and over. "Torn Between Two Lovers." Nicole couldn't have been more than five. And now she was living that life. Was she repeating her mother's mistakes?

"I—I need to go."

Ryan picked up his pants and stepped into them, pulling them over his bare buttocks. Next he reached for his shirt. Watching him put it back on was equally as heart-accelerating as watching him remove it had been. She did not need to find him any more appealing than she already did, but her palms-damp, lips-dry reaction couldn't be denied.

Pressing a cold hand to her hot chest, she turned her

back. Ryan's fingers nudged her spine. She jumped and arousal shivered over her. He pulled up her zipper.

Pregnancy hormones. That's all this is.

Or was it? At the moment she wasn't sure of anything.

Nicole awoke Saturday morning determined to make a decision one way or the other. Living in limbo was tearing her apart.

Was this her baby? Or was it Beth's?

She had to move forward and that meant confronting her sister. She lifted a hand and knocked on her sister's front door instead of walking in the way she usually did. Patrick opened the door. Surprise stole her breath. She hadn't expected to run into him. He always shot eighteen holes with his coworkers on Saturday mornings.

He looked about as happy to see her as she was to see him—which was not at all. A first for her. She blamed her strange reaction on not being ready to face him when she'd washed off Ryan's scent only a few hours ago.

She swallowed to ease her dry mouth. "Hi. Aren't you playing golf today?"

"No." The corners of Patrick's mouth had a downward, dissatisfied turn. Had he always frowned like that?

She tried to recall, but the only face in her mind was Ryan's, particularly, Ryan's face just before he'd left her at her door last night after a devastating good-night kiss. The intensity of her reciprocal need had frightened her. She'd almost invited him in.

"I need to talk to Beth."

"She's making an early-morning grocery run."

He hesitated and shifted on his bare feet. She felt as if she were seeing him for the first time. He wasn't as tall as she remembered, and his sandy-blond hair looked washed out. Wait. Were those gray roots? Had he been coloring his hair?

"Do you want to come in and wait?"

Not the most gracious invitation she'd ever heard, but what choice did she have when Beth refused to return her calls? "Yes. Thanks."

"Coffee?"

She wished she could. She probably hadn't slept more than two hours after Ryan left her. How could she sleep with her body humming and her mind churning? Not even a warm bath had helped. Her life had gone from smooth flying to extreme turbulence seemingly overnight. "I can't. I've cut out caffeine. But thanks."

"Right. So…" An awkward silence stretched between them.

Until now she'd always been comfortable with Patrick, despite him dumping her, because she'd made a tremendous effort to keep things friendly. She hadn't wanted either him or Beth to know how much his change of heart had hurt her. After all, when she'd brought him home to meet her family no words of love or promises of forever had been spoken between them.

She focused on the reason she'd come. "Patrick, do you and Beth still want to adopt my baby?"

He looked away and gulped his coffee. "A baby is all Beth wants. The only reason she keeps me around is for my sperm."

Nicole winced. Ryan was right. There was definitely trouble in paradise—trouble a baby might not fix. "I'm sure that's not true."

He eyed her with a combination of incredulity and pity. "You don't know your sister at all. You only see what she wants you to see. Beth never does anything that doesn't benefit Beth."

That didn't sound good. "Maybe the two of you should see a marriage counselor."

"For that to work she'd have to admit she might be wrong. That's not going to happen."

True. Beth was a perfectionist. If she couldn't do something right then she'd prefer not to do it at all.

The look in his eyes turned downright ugly. "You were with him last night. You left with him."

His accusatory tone raised a red flag. She hoped her cheeks weren't as flushed as they felt. "Ryan? We rode together."

"He just wants his kid. He doesn't want you."

The cruel words stabbed deeply, and as Patrick stared at her she realized she'd never seen him look this unattractive.

"You don't know that, Patrick." But was he right? Was the baby the only reason Ryan had slept with her? No. His desire had been too strong, too real.

"You were always the smarter sister. Don't be stupid over this guy."

A compliment followed by bitter, petty words. This was not the man she'd fallen in love with in college. She took a mental step back and reminded herself of the stress Patrick had been under. The visit was not going the way she'd anticipated, and she didn't like the side her former lover was showing. She had to get her answers and get out of here.

"Patrick, could you love a child that isn't yours?"

His lips twisted into a petulant line as he stared into his mug. "It's Beth's decision."

Not the enthusiastic reply she'd wanted. "That's not an answer."

"It's the only one you're going to get from me."

Nicole had a sinking feeling that whatever Beth decided Patrick would not welcome her baby with open arms. Could she blame him for not wanting to raise another man's child? Some people handled adoption beautifully. They accepted and loved the gift they were given. But some didn't.

Now that she thought about it, Patrick had always been possessive and particular about *his* things. When they'd been dating he'd never even let her drive his car although he'd driven hers often enough. He'd never shared his dessert or even let her sip from his drink. What was his, was *his*. How had she missed his selfish streak?

"I should have married you," he grumbled.

Nicole couldn't breathe. Those were the words she'd been waiting to hear for a very long time, but they didn't give her the satisfaction she'd expected. Instead, they repulsed her. How could he say or think that now? How could he do that to Beth? His family would be ashamed to hear him speak that way.

How could you have believed you loved him all these years? He's a jerk.

Sadness weighted her chest as the understanding dawned. She had been so afraid of behaving like her mother that she'd convinced herself she could only love one man in her lifetime, and she'd chosen the wrong man for the wrong reasons. She hadn't loved Patrick. She'd fallen for his family—the kind of family she'd always craved. The kind of family she wanted for her baby if she couldn't have it herself.

A hollow ache filled her belly. "When is Beth due back?"

Patrick cocked his head at the sound of a car in the driveway. "That's probably her."

He turned on his heel and stalked out of the kitchen. Seconds later she heard his feet stomping upstairs.

As much as Nicole dreaded the conversation to come, she had to get it over with. She met Beth in the garage. "Hi. Need help with the groceries?"

"It's just one bag."

Uneasiness swirled in Nicole's belly. "Can we talk?"

"I have to get ready for a lunch appointment."

Nicole had always put her family first, but it was time she put herself and her baby at the top of the list. "Beth, I need five minutes."

"Make it quick," Beth grumbled grudgingly. Nicole followed her inside. Beth went straight for the coffeepot. "What is it?"

"The baby isn't biologically yours or Patrick's. I will understand if you don't want to stick with our agreement. Just please, be honest with me. Tell me what you want."

"I don't want to have this conversation."

"It's overdue. Beth, this is not a good time for you and Patrick to add to the strain your marriage is already under with a baby. You need to focus on the two of you."

"My marriage is none of your business."

The caustic words hurt. Nicole tried a different tactic. "I don't think Patrick can love this baby."

"Patrick can't love anyone but Patrick." Beth's bitterness rang loud and clear.

Living with two parents who said ugly things about each other would not be a healthy environment for a child. Nicole wet her lips and took a deep breath. She swallowed the lump in her throat and rubbed her agitated stomach. *Say it.* "I want to keep my baby."

Beth drew herself up, her face indignant and flushed with angry color. She slammed her mug on the counter, sloshing the dark brew over the rim. "You'd betray me after all I've done for you? You never intended to go through with the adoption, did you?"

Regret settled heavily on Nicole's shoulders. "Of course I did, and I still would if I thought it was the right thing to do. But it's not. Once Ryan came on the scene you and Patrick lost interest. And who could blame you? It's not your husband's child. Beth, you avoid me. You don't return my phone calls or even my e-mails."

"I didn't call you because I couldn't stand to see you get everything I wanted once again."

Shock rocked Nicole to the soles of her shoes. "What are you talking about?"

"Everything always came easy for you, Nicole. Boyfriends. Good grades. College. Life. You even got pregnant on the first try. I had to work for everything, and I still got left on the sidelines."

She'd had no idea Beth harbored such resentment. "You chose to be on the sidelines, Beth. You like playing it safe."

As soon as Nicole said the words, she knew they were true. Why hadn't she noticed before that Beth liked to watch life rather than live it?

"Well, this time I win. I'm pregnant, too. And I don't need your damned baby to have a family. I'm having three of my own. Mine and Patrick's. Three! Top that."

Nicole staggered back not only at the news but also at Beth's over-the-top competitive and emotional response. "You're pregnant? How?"

"I've been seeing a specialist in New York for months. That's why I've missed work. He confirmed last week that I'm carrying triplets. We thought I might be pregnant before the Labor Day picnic, but we weren't sure."

"Congratulations," Nicole uttered automatically. Part of her was thrilled that her sister's dream of having a family was coming true. But another part resented Beth for putting her through this emotional wringer while she continued to try to conceive. It felt like a betrayal.

Anger licked through her. "What was I? Your insurance policy? You'd keep my baby only if you didn't conceive your own? What if the fertility clinic hadn't made a mistake? What if this had been Patrick's child?"

"Then you'd have what you've wanted all along—a piece of my husband."

Nicole recoiled. "I have never made one inappropriate move toward Patrick."

"But you wanted to. You loved him first. But don't forget, you've signed over your rights to the baby you're carrying. You can't keep it."

"You're pregnant with triplets! Why would you want my baby, too?"

"Because we need the money Ryan offered. The fertility treatments were expensive. And there will be even more money from the malpractice suit we're filing against the fertility clinic for their screwup."

Nicole stumbled backward. For a fraction of a second she hated both Beth and Patrick. She had offered them a gift that would have torn out her heart, and they were using her with no regard for her feelings whatsoever.

She reined in her anger. "Don't plan on using my baby or me as your cash cow. If I have to liquidate everything I own and take out loans to pay the legal fees, I will make absolutely certain you don't see a dime from my baby. And Ryan will side with me."

"The law is on my side. That contract is as ironclad as it can possibly be." A disgusted sound rumbled from Beth's throat. "Look at yourself, Nicole. You've become our mother."

She flinched. "What is that supposed to mean?"

"You've fallen for your lover and you think just because you're knocked up with his brat he'll marry you. Well, your Ryan is going to turn out just like Lauren's father. He's going to use you and toss you aside."

"You don't know that's what happened to our mother."

"Yes, I do. My bedroom was next to Mom and Dad's. I heard their arguments. Everybody knows they didn't love each other, that Dad married her for her money to keep Hightower Aviation afloat. What you don't know is that she fell in love with Lauren's father. But she got dumped and so will you. Once Ryan gets his hands on this kid you will be nothing to him. He'll cut you off, and you'll be lucky if you ever get to see your baby again."

Horrified, Nicole braced herself on the counter. "You're wrong."

Beth's laugh held no humor. "We'll see, won't we?"

Nicole broke out in a cold sweat. She had to talk to Ryan. He was the only one who could help her now. With the echoes of Beth's prediction ringing in her ears, she fled to her car and raced toward Ryan's condo.

Her stomach twisted with anxiety but a new realization seeped into her conscience. If she didn't love Patrick, then that left the door open for loving someone else—someone who made her feel more alive than she ever had before.

Someone who obviously wanted a family as badly as she did.

Someone who might help her keep her baby.

Ryan.

Eleven

"I need your help," Nicole blurted the second Ryan opened the door to his condo Saturday afternoon.

He took in her subtle curves outlined by a lavender cashmere cowl-neck sweater and navy slacks and hunger licked through him. He hadn't been able to get Friday night out of his head. The way she looked. The way she tasted. The way she'd shuddered in his arms and clenched him in her slick body.

The way she'd trusted him, and the guilt he'd felt after dropping her off.

The tension straining her pale face told him they wouldn't be revisiting his bed in the next few minutes for more of that stellar sex. Just as well. His conscience was giving him hell.

Even though he'd known it would be a mistake, he'd come close to asking her to stay all night. Dangerous territory. How many times had he seen a friend start thinking with his dick and lose his common sense? The only thing worse was getting emotionally involved. That left a man weak and at the whims of the woman pulling his strings.

It wasn't going to happen to him. He'd keep his eye on the goal.

But damn, the sex had been great, their chemistry unbelievable. He wanted more. But sex and the baby they shared were her only appeal. And once he had his kid, he wouldn't need Nicole. For now he needed to pull his head together and get back in the game.

He stepped away from the door. "Come in."

Nicole headed straight for his den, her sexy high-heeled boots rapping out a rhythm on his slate floors. She stopped abruptly short of the windows and turned. Her fear of heights shouldn't be endearing, but it was. Probably because she fought so hard to hide it. But the telling way she backed away from his window each time she got too near the glass gave her away.

Her bottom lip was swollen as if she'd been biting it. "I'm sorry I didn't call, but I didn't have your home or cell number."

He dug his wallet out of his pants as he followed her into the room, withdrew a business card, located a pen and wrote his personal numbers on the back. He offered the information to her. "Now you have all my numbers."

She took the card and the touch of her fingertips against his zapped him with an electric charge. Static, no doubt. Or maybe just lust.

She shoved the info into her pocket without looking at it. "Beth is pregnant with triplets."

That should have been good news, but even though she hid it well, he could feel Nicole's anxiety rolling off her in waves. Odd. He'd never been that sensitive to another woman's emotions. "I thought she couldn't get pregnant."

"She's been seeing a new fertility specialist behind my back."

"She and Patrick should be willing to cancel the surrogacy contract now." That put him head-to-head with Nicole, who'd already relinquished her parental rights. His odds of winning looked good. But the pain and panic in her eyes tugged at him. His winning meant her losing.

"You would think so, but she intends to hold me to it."

"Why would she if she's pregnant?"

"She wants the money you offered to defray the cost of her medical expenses. And she plans to sue the clinic for malpractice and make even more money."

The strength of his anger on Nicole's behalf surprised him. He rocked back on his heels. The greedy bastards. Nicole was willing to cut out her heart for them, and they were going to squeeze out every last cent at her expense.

And how is what you're doing any better? You're pitting her against her sister.

He ignored the pesky protest of his conscience. "That doesn't surprise me."

"Ryan…" Nicole's gaze dropped to the floor and her hands fisted. She took a deep breath as if gathering her courage, and then lifted her eyes again. "I'm going to try and revoke my surrogacy contract. My attorney says it's almost impossible, but as you said, Beth and Patrick are not good candidates for parenting our baby. Their marriage is in trouble. Add in her high-risk multiple pregnancy, and I think I stand at least a slim chance of succeeding. And then…we'll share custody. You and me."

His heart kicked faster. Dissension among the Hightowers had been his plan all along. It brought his goal of having a child to cinch his position at Patrick Architectural closer. But sharing custody wasn't an option.

His relationship with Nicole would be a casualty, but a long-term or permanent involvement with her had never been part of his plan. All that mattered was keeping his father from selling the company out from under him. He had to win. And for him to win somebody had to lose.

Success had never felt so lousy.

"I'll speak to my attorney." But he wouldn't be initiating the proceedings Nicole expected. He'd be doing what he did best. Looking out for number one. The only person who never let him down.

Beth stormed into Nicole's office late Monday afternoon and hurled a sheaf of papers across her desk. "I told you the bastard would screw you over. And he's taking us down with you."

Nicole reached for the scattered sheets. "What are you talking about?"

"He's trying to steal our baby."

"He who?" But she knew. Tension spiraled up her spine.

"Ryan Patrick."

The letterhead from one of Knoxville's most powerful and prestigious attorneys caught Nicole's attention. She scanned the text and ice seeped into her veins. Her arms went weak and the document slipped from her grasp. "Ryan is suing for sole custody of my baby."

"*My* baby. You promised this baby to me."

"And you don't want it. You plan to sell it like a black-market baby."

"I'm not going to sell it. I'm agreeing to settle custody out of court. The money was Ryan's idea. Remember? He came to us."

"Same difference, Beth. You're taking money for a child that isn't even yours—one I will carry and nourish and love for nine months. A baby I ache for. And you intend to rip it from my arms for money."

"You agreed to this."

"I agreed to give you and Patrick the family you so desperately wanted because it would make you happy. Now all I ask is that you be as unselfish for me."

"I've done nothing but give to you my entire life. I gave up dates to babysit you."

"We had nannies who were paid to do that."

"I was there for you. I gave you my time, my attention and my advice when our mother wouldn't give you hers," Beth continued in a righteous tone.

"And now you're taking what matters most. My child."

Beth emitted a furious hiss and stormed out of the office. Nicole let her go. She tried to gather her shattered composure and focus on the issue. She wanted to believe Ryan wasn't betraying her. Maybe he had a strategy—one that would get around the surrogacy contract she'd signed.

She rose on shaky legs and crossed to the fax machine. Within moments the pages were on their way to her attorney. Then Nicole returned to her desk and dug Ryan's business card from her purse. She had to talk to him. She punched in his office number.

"Nicole Hightower for Ryan Patrick, please," she said as soon as the receptionist answered.

"He's unavailable at the moment, Ms. Hightower. May I take a message?"

She needed him now. "No. Thank you."

She dialed his cell number. Voice mail picked up. "It's Nicole. Please call me."

She tried his house and left another message. Where was he? Was he refusing to answer because he saw her name on caller ID? Why would he avoid her unless he had something to hide? A sick feeling invaded her stomach. What if Beth was right? What if Ryan had used her to weaken Beth and Patrick's claim on the baby?

She had to find him. She bolted to her feet and raced out, barely pausing by Lea's desk. "I have to leave early."

She didn't give her assistant a chance to ask questions. Within minutes she was in her car and headed toward the glass office tower housing Patrick Architectural. She hustled inside. The elevator rocketed upward.

She stormed into the thirtieth-floor offices just before five o'clock and marched up to the receptionist's desk. "I need to see Ryan Patrick. It's urgent."

The woman took her name, called someone on the phone and then pointed. "Last door on the right."

Fear and apprehension made Nicole tremble as she made her way across the plush carpet. The door was open. An older lady rose from behind a maple desk. "Ryan will see you now."

She gestured for Nicole to go through another door. Ryan stood by a drafting table in the corner of the room. Nicole quickly scanned his office. The frosted glass, maple and chrome furnishings were just as modern as the decor of his house. But whereas his home was all dark colors, straight lines and sharp corners, his office was brightly lit and decorated in pale neutrals with furniture comprised of curves and round-edged, frosted glass.

He laid down his tools and turned. The carefully blank expression on his face made her stomach sink. "I take it you've heard from Beth."

She met his solemn gaze. "Please tell me you have a

master strategy that will allow me to co-parent my child with you. Because the petition doesn't read that way."

Ryan's jaw went rigid. "I'm sorry, Nicole. I'm suing for full custody."

A crushing sensation settled in her chest. "What about me?"

"You relinquished your rights. The waiver you signed is airtight."

She wound her arms around her middle. "Ryan, this is my baby."

"I don't have time for a lengthy custody battle. I need a child now."

"Why? Why do you have to do this?"

"My father is planning to retire next year. Like you, he equates fast cars, boats and motorcycles and a bachelor pad with an unwillingness to grow up or think ahead. He's threatening to sell Patrick Architectural out from under me. I hired a surrogate to give him a grandchild to prove I am planning for the future. Instead, I got you."

Horrified, she backed away. Ryan had encouraged her to turn against her sister, most likely irrevocably damaging her family relationship. For greed? "You don't want a baby at all. You just want this company?"

"What I want is to disabuse my father of his old-fashioned notion that a man has to be married to be mature and responsible and dedicated to his job. I'm sorry for the pain this is going to cause you, Nicole. But you're young. You'll have other children."

Her throat tightened. Her heart ached. "Was sleeping with me a way to coerce me into cutting Beth and Patrick out of the picture?"

His hesitation spoke volumes. "We have great sexual chemistry."

Sexual chemistry? Was that all they shared? She'd been telling herself the same thing. So why did it slice like a razor when he said it? "What you're telling me is that this child was merely a means to an end for you and that you want it for all the wrong reasons. A baby deserves to be loved, Ryan, not just used."

"He became more than a tool when I saw him on the ultrasound."

The pain swelled inside her until she was almost dizzy with it. "I don't believe you."

He strode behind his desk, yanked open the top drawer and pulled something out. With a flick of his wrist he slung the object across the table just like he'd tossed those letters the day they'd met. A twin to the picture he'd given her slid to a stop near the edge in front of her. Then he flipped open his wallet, revealing a smaller version of the same photo.

He shoved his wallet back into his pocket. "Believe that. This is my son or daughter, and I want it as badly as you do. I've been robbed of a child once before. I won't let it happen again."

"That's why I thought you'd understand how much being a part of my child's life means to me. But you used me. Just like you planned to use and discard your surrogate. Ryan, I would never keep you from your child. Why can't we share custody?"

"Shared custody leaves the door open for you to change your mind and use the child as a weapon against me. I won't let that happen."

Head reeling, knees weak, she needed to sit down, but she didn't dare reveal her weakness to the enemy. Beth and Patrick were right. All Ryan wanted was the baby she carried. He'd told her that from day one. So why did it hurt so much to have it verified now?

Because you were falling for him.

Correction. She'd already fallen for him like a climber slipping off the face of a glacier. There would be nothing but pain in her immediate future.

By hiding behind her old feelings for Patrick, she'd fooled herself into believing she couldn't be swept off her feet by Ryan's old-fashioned gestures, the understanding she'd seen in his eyes and the passion his touch ignited. But he'd slipped past her defenses when she'd thought herself safe.

It was like being kicked when she was already down from Beth's treachery. She backed blindly toward the door. "I will see you in court, and I promise I will fight you to my last cent. No child deserves a heartless manipulative bastard like you for a father."

She turned on her heel and fled because if she stayed, she was going to break down in front of him. Ryan's betrayal was ten times worse than Patrick's because, unlike her first love, Ryan knew he was tearing out her heart by taking her baby. But she couldn't bear to lose what was left of her pride by letting him know she'd fallen in love with him.

A heartless manipulative bastard.

The description fit like a cheap shirt.

Ryan wanted to go after Nicole. But what could he say?

She was right. He'd gone into this surrogacy plan with purely selfish motives. He hadn't intended for anyone to get hurt. But there was no denying the agony clouding Nicole's beautiful aqua eyes before she'd left.

His lungs felt tight, but not because he was afraid of her threat to take him to court. The law was on his side, and according to his attorney, Nicole had a slim-to-none chance of getting custody as a result of the waiver she'd signed. He, on the other hand, stood a very good probability of defeating Beth and Patrick who had no DNA connection to the baby whatsoever.

Divide and conquer, his attorney had suggested, and Ryan had done exactly that. But where was the satisfaction he should be feeling? He raked a hand through his hair.

His father entered without knocking. "Was that Nicole I saw getting into the elevator?"

"Yes."

"She looked upset. Is there a problem with the plane or the flight?"

HAMC had scheduled a test run for the Patrick Architectural executives to show the rest of the team how their mobile office worked. "No."

"You left the ball with her Friday night."

"Yes."

"I like her, Ryan. She's the kind of woman you should have been dating all these years instead of your brainless twits."

"Yes."

His father frowned. "What's with the monosyllabic answers? Not your usual style."

Hell, he might as well get it out in the open. Owning up to a mistake was the first step toward fixing it. And he had made a mistake—one that might not be forgivable.

He picked up the photo and offered it to his father. "Nicole is carrying my child. Your grandchild. The one you've been harping about for years."

His father stared at the picture in silence and then his gaze met Ryan's. "So you lied. You were dating her before you suggested the plane."

"No."

"Then what? You had a one-night stand? Didn't I warn you to be careful?"

"I hired a surrogate. The plan backfired."

His father went silent once more then finally said, "Explain."

"I want to be president of Patrick Architectural when you retire. I'm damned good at my job, and I have the awards to prove it. I know this company. I know this business. I shouldn't have to be married, drive a sedan, have a house in the suburbs filled with children or live *your* dream to win your approval.

"Despite the decade of sweat equity I've put in at P.A. you keep demanding more proof that I consider this firm my future. But whatever I do, it's never enough. How can I prove I've never wanted to work anywhere else? I thought a kid, another generation of Patricks to carry on, would demonstrate my…loyalty to the firm."

Hearing his plot out loud made Ryan realize he'd been an idiot. How had he ever considered this a logical plan? "Wrong move. I know that now."

His father stood the frame up on the desk. "Where does Nicole come into this? I don't see her as the type to hire out her body."

"You're right. She's the kind of woman who always puts family first and herself last. The antithesis of my mother and my ex-wife."

His father grimaced. "Your mother demanded a lot of attention. But sometimes no matter how much you give someone it's never enough because the void they're trying to fill is internal. The more your mother tried to use you, the more I backed off because you kept getting hurt. I'm sorry you were caught in the middle of our breakup.

"As for your ex, you did the honorable thing in marrying

her. Too bad she had no honor or honesty in her. But that's in the past and it can't be changed. Tell me about the present. What's Nicole's role?"

"Nicole volunteered to carry a child for her infertile sister even though relinquishing the baby would rip her heart out. But the fertility clinic made a mistake and inseminated Nicole with my sperm instead of her brother-in-law's. I'm suing for full custody."

"And the sister's claim?"

"She's pregnant with triplets and no longer needs this child."

His father clamped a hand on his shoulder. "You know I'm old-fashioned, and I won't deny I've made my desire for grandchildren clear, but I pressured you into marrying for the sake of a baby once already. I won't repeat that mistake. But is marriage out of the question? I've seen you two together, son. You and Nicole have something…something that might be worth fighting for."

"I'll never marry again. You know why."

"But is denying the woman her child the right thing to do?"

Before he'd met Nicole, Ryan could have answered in the affirmative without reservations. Now he wasn't so sure. He'd had more candidates for the surrogate position than he'd had time to interview. Women competing for the right to sell their bodies and their babies. But Nicole wasn't like them. "She signed away her rights."

"Circumstances have changed. She's not giving her sister a gift of love anymore."

"This is my child."

"And hers." His father pointed out the obvious. "Is there a reason why you think Nicole would be an unfit mother?"

Guilt stabbed him. "None whatsoever."

"However oddly your relationship began, you've created a child together. If you can't love her, then let her go and work out a solution for the child that allows it to benefit from both parents. But be aware that in the future some other man may be stepfathering your child."

The words hit Ryan like a fist to the gut, punching the air from his lungs. He hadn't thought about Nicole with another man. A woman like her had too much to offer to be alone for long. But the idea of her in someone else's bed, someone else's arms made him want to crawl out of his skin.

He wasn't feeling territorial, was he? He'd never been possessive of a woman before—not even his ex. But the idea of Nicole crying out as some other man drove into her slender body, of her shuddering as the faceless ass brought her to orgasm, ripped a hole in Ryan's stomach and spilled burning acid through his body.

"I can't risk another marriage."

"Another betrayal, you mean. I understand. We all want to avoid that kind of pain. And some of us never find the courage to try again."

The solemn statement staggered Ryan. Until now his father had never admitted that the divorce had hurt him. He'd hidden his feeling behind a gruff, no-nonsense facade.

"But, Ryan, think long and hard before you deprive a baby of its mother. No one will love the child more. That's why I let you go. It wasn't that I didn't love you or want you around. It's that you were your mother's life, her reason for being. I'm not sure what would have happened to her if I'd taken you away."

Surprised, he searched his father's face to see if he were telling the truth, and found pain and regret in his father's eyes. "I wish you'd told me that sooner, Dad."

"I didn't want to diminish your love for your mother by pointing out her weaknesses. We all have flaws. It's how we deal with them that counts. And I loved your mother despite hers."

"But you divorced her."

"She divorced me. Your mother was the love of my life. After you came along I wanted to give you both more. A bigger house. Private school. Nicer cars. A Cornell education like your grandfather and I had. I worked extra hours, probably more than I should have. Your mother became convinced I was cheating on her. I wasn't, but she wouldn't believe me, and once the trust is gone…" Sadness deepened the lines on his face.

And Ryan had just destroyed Nicole's trust.

His father shrugged. "Still, I got you out of the deal, so even though the marriage ended badly, the pain was worth it."

"Dad, I don't want my kid to be caught in a tug-of-war."

"Then you'd better work out a fair solution you and Nicole can live with. Better that than a vicious legal battle that drags on for a decade. But remember, the child's welfare always comes first. *Always.* Even if it might be the most difficult decision you'll ever make. Walking away from you was that for me."

Ryan looked at his father with a new perspective, one that allowed him a clearer view of the decisions his father had made over the years.

And now Ryan was in the same no-win situation. Did he look out for number one the way he always had? Or did he put his child first? And could he ever regain Nicole's trust? Right now that job seemed to be the most urgent.

He stared into blue eyes so similar to the ones he saw in the mirror each morning, but these eyes were older, wiser and more generous. "Dad, this is one time I wish you could tell me what to do."

His father patted his shoulder. "And this is the one time no one but you has the answer. Whatever you decide, son, I'll back you one hundred percent. But do the right thing by my grandchild."

His father had said it perfectly. No one would love this child more than Nicole. No one had a more generous heart. But granting her joint custody meant leaving the door open for another chunk of his heart to be imploded if she decided later to cut him out of her and their baby's life.

Was the risk worth it?

Twelve

Nicole stood in the boardroom early Tuesday morning staring at her siblings and her parents and listening to the hum of their conversations as she gathered her courage for what she had to do. Only Patrick and Lauren, neither of whom owned any HAMC stock, were missing.

It would be much easier to do as her mother had done and simply disappear. But life on the run really wasn't fair to a child. Besides, her baby deserved to know its aunts, uncles and grandparents even if the Hightowers weren't the warmest, fuzziest bunch. And Ryan had been robbed of a child once already. Nicole couldn't do that to him again. That meant taking the easy way out wasn't an option.

"I'm pregnant."

Her words silenced the chatter. All eyes turned to her.

Beth crossed her arms and stuck her jaw out at a belligerent angle. "Great. Make this all about you again."

Nicole realized Patrick was right. She hadn't known her sister. Otherwise, she would have recognized Beth's petty jealousy long ago.

"Who's the father?" Trent asked in a deadly calm voice.

"Ryan Patrick. That's why I asked to be excused as his CAM." Fist clenched, Trent rose looking ready to do battle. "Sit down, big brother. This situation is far more complicated than you think." He resettled uneasily in his chair.

"Let me begin at the beginning. Beth and Patrick asked me to be a surrogate for them and I agreed. I was supposed to have Patrick's child, but the fertility clinic transposed the first and last names of the donors, and I'm carrying Ryan's baby instead."

Bodies shifted around the table as they digested the information. "In the meantime, congratulations are in order. Beth has been seeing a new fertility specialist, and she and Patrick have just discovered they're expecting triplets. They'll need your support in the coming months. Being pregnant with triplets won't be easy. Neither will caring for them after the delivery."

She rested a hand over the slight swell marking her baby and gave her family time to offer Beth their good wishes while she tried to remember her practiced speech without luck.

The conversation died down and everyone's attention returned to her. "In light of Beth's pregnancy, I've decided to keep my baby, but Beth and Patrick and Ryan are also fighting for custody. The battle is likely to get ugly, and the scandal might make headlines. I don't want to turn Hightower Aviation into a battlefield where we destroy our family by choosing sides. If you'd like me to resign, I will, or I can transfer to one of our foreign operation centers."

Her mother stood and every muscle in Nicole's body tightened. Surely her mother wouldn't denounce her if she'd meant what she'd said about regretting not being there for her children in the past.

Her mother met her gaze. "Scandals come and go. Hightowers survive them. Nicole, you have my full support. And I would hope Beth and Patrick will be mature enough to stop their nonsense and give theirs, as well. Your generosity is overwhelming, and I am proud to call you my daughter."

Relief weakened Nicole and tears clogged her throat. She grasped the table's edge to stay upright. This wasn't the mother she'd known for the past twenty-eight years. "Thank you, Mom."

Beth looked none-too-happy with their mother's pronouncement. "Even if Patrick and I drop the custody battle, Ryan has a damned good chance of winning. He has a DNA link to the baby. And Nicole waived her parental rights."

Jacqueline Hightower looked down her nose at her oldest daughter. "That is my grandbaby Nicole is carrying, and Ryan Patrick has no idea how dangerous a pissed off Hightower can be."

Trent sat forward in his chair. "We'll go after him with both barrels, Nicole."

Nicole's vision blurred and tears burned hot trails on her cheeks. She might lose her baby, but she wouldn't have to go through it alone. She'd have her family beside her. And while she'd always wanted the Hightowers to be closer, this wasn't exactly what she had in mind.

"Flowers for you," Lea said from Nicole's doorway late Monday afternoon.

Nicole looked up. A large arrangement of mixed blooms in shades of peach, cream, orange and yellow completely obscured her assistant's torso. "They're beautiful."

Lea set them on the corner of Nicole's desk and turned to go without her usual fifty questions. That was odd, but Nicole let it go. Lea had been tiptoeing cautiously since Nicole had given her the full story two weeks ago.

The sweet fragrance of the blooms filled Nicole's nose as she searched for a card. Who had sent them and why? It wasn't her birthday. She hadn't done anything to warrant an extravagant thank-you from a client. Nor was she the type of woman who regularly—if ever—received flowers from an admirer.

Perhaps Beth had sent them as an apology?

She couldn't find the card. "Lea, did you take the card?"

"I have it."

Ryan's deep voice brought her head up with a jerk. Her stomach and pulse fluttered wildly. She hadn't heard from him in two weeks, but that didn't mean he hadn't been constantly in her thoughts.

He strolled in wearing a black suit, pale yellow shirt and another one of his geometric print ties, this one in greens, blacks and yellows. The man liked his lines which was not surprising since he drew buildings for a living. The small white envelope he held between his fingertips explained why Lea hadn't been pawing through the blooms. She'd known who had the card.

Nicole folded her arms. "My lawyer says I'm not supposed to talk to you."

The slow, sensual way Ryan's intense blue gaze rolled over her reminded her of the night in his bedroom. Beneath her conservative navy suit her skin flushed and dampened. She sank back into her chair, exhaling in a futile attempt to ease her tension.

"Then you must not have talked to her today." He shut her office door, enclosing them in a mouth-drying intimacy. She wasn't ready for this.

"What do you mean?"

"Your sister and brother-in-law have dropped their custody suit. This is between you and me now." He offered the card.

Nicole reluctantly accepted it. She hadn't liked anything he'd given her to read thus far. She slipped the seal and pulled out the plain white folded square. A brass key fell out and clattered onto her desk.

Your new address, he'd written in bold script, followed by a Knoxville street address.

She searched his serious face. "What does this mean?"

"You claimed the house was perfect for raising a family. I bought it. For you."

She shook her head. "Me? I don't understand."

"We both want what's best for our child. I want you to raise our baby in that house."

Raise our baby in that house. Her heart thumped harder. This sounded too good to be true. She must have misunderstood. "I still don't understand. Why are you doing this, Ryan? What's in it for you?"

"No one will love our child more than you. Consider custody and the house my gifts to the baby. To both of you. The deed will be in your name as soon as you sign the papers."

He circled her desk and leaned forward to plant his hands on the arms of her chair, trapping her with his body and those mesmerizing blue eyes. He bent his elbows until his face was level with hers.

Nicole tilted back her head. Her mouth watered. She dampened her lips, wanting his kiss. How could she still want him after what he'd done? And did she dare trust him? Was this a trick? It had to be.

His eyes tracked the sweep of her tongue, but he didn't move any closer. "There's a catch."

Her brain slowly caught gear and shifted forward. Of course there was a catch. "What kind of catch?"

"I want to live there with you."

He wanted to live with her? She shot backward, rolling the chair out of his reach and bolted to her feet. Pain and disappointment vied for supremacy. "Is this another sneaky, underhanded way to get your father to leave you Patrick Architectural? How low will you go, Ryan?"

He clenched his fists by his sides. "I screwed up. I had tunnel vision. My father has been nagging me for grandchildren for years. I decided to give him exactly what he asked for. I saw the brass ring and nothing more.

"After my ex-wife's betrayal I swore I'd never let anyone or anything matter that much again. But I was wrong. I'd never met anyone like you, Nicole. Someone who always put others first. Someone who gave even though it ripped her heart out. I didn't trust it. I didn't trust you. Now I do."

He stepped closer. She backed up.

"You're always doing for others. When was the last time someone did something for you?"

She put the chair between them. "Taking care of others is my job."

"That's professionally. I meant personally."

"I can take care of my needs."

"Then it's about time someone spoiled you. Let me be that someone. Teach me how."

She didn't dare believe that tender look in his eyes. It had to be fake, another go at hoodwinking her. "Ryan, what are you trying to pull?"

He extracted a thick business-size envelope from his

jacket and she rolled her eyes. Déjà vu. The return address from her attorney's office caught her eye. "I asked Meredith Jones to let me deliver this personally."

Her attorney would never have trusted him with anything that could hurt her. Nicole snatched the envelope from his hand and ripped it open. She recognized Meredith's handwriting on the short notepaper clipped to a thick sheaf of papers.

Nicole,
I'll go over the legalese with you later, but the gist is, Ryan Patrick has signed papers granting you sole custody of the baby you carry. He's waived all parental rights if, but only if, *you* raise the child. He would like visitation, but is not forcing the issue.
Details later, but this is legit.
Congratulations, Mommy.
Meredith

Mommy. Nicole clutched the papers to her chest and searched Ryan's face. "What about Patrick Architectural?"

He shrugged. "I'm damned good at what I do. If my father chooses to sell P.A., then I'll move on. I can join another firm or open my own."

"Why, Ryan? Why walk away from something that matters so much to you?"

He inhaled then exhaled slowly. "Because your generosity blows me away. You're the only woman I've ever met who never asked 'What's in it for me?' I've fallen in love with you, Nicole."

Her heart stuttered then lurched into a wild rhythm. She was afraid to believe the emotion thickening his voice and the love she saw in his eyes. She couldn't handle getting her heart broken again.

Her lips quivered. "Don't try to manipulate me with lies."

He flinched. A nerve in his jaw twitched. "I deserve that. But I have never lied to you except by omission. The passion we shared was real. I know I hurt you. I'd like the chance to make it right. I'm hoping you'll eventually find room in that generous heart of yours for me."

He pushed the chair aside and dropped to one knee. "I want to marry you, Nicole, raise a family with you and spoil you like you've never allowed anyone else to do. But mostly, I want the chance to love you. And I want you to teach me how to be as giving as you are."

She couldn't speak. She ached so badly for what he said to be true. When the silence stretched between them he paled, bowed his head. A few seconds later he nodded and rose stiffly.

"The house and baby are yours. No strings attached. I would like to be as involved in your life and our child's as you'll let me. But if you can't handle that, I'll accept your decision and keep my distance."

He turned and strode toward the door, and it was as if he'd taken her heart and all the oxygen in the room with him as he walked away. She'd never felt so empty. She hadn't hurt this much when she'd realized she'd lost Patrick. Like she couldn't breathe. Like her legs wouldn't support her. Like her world would end without him in it.

This body-consuming craving, the necessity to keep him close was love.

What she'd felt for Patrick had been a tepid imitation. And loving more than once didn't make her weak, like she'd always thought her mother to be. Love gave her the strength to try again until she got it right. And this time she had the right man. Ryan. If she didn't let him get away.

"Ryan, don't go."

He stopped with his hand on the doorknob and slowly pivoted. His face looked drawn and composed, as if he'd donned a mask. But hope flickered in his eyes, and it was that trace of emotion he couldn't hide that told her he wasn't lying about loving her and not just their child.

"I want everything you said. With you. Only you. I love you. And I want to raise this baby—*our* baby—with you."

Love softened his entire face and his tender smile made her eyes burn with happy tears. He quickly closed the distance between them and swept her into his arms and off her feet. He buried his face in her neck and hugged her with almost rib-cracking strength as if he never wanted to let her go.

He drew back, met her gaze and slowly eased her back onto her feet. "On one condition."

She stiffened.

"You start putting yourself first for a change, because you're the one who matters the most to me."

"I'll see what I can do, but I might need your help fulfilling that request."

* * * * *

Don't miss the next passionate story in
THE HIGHTOWER AFFAIRS
series *by Emilie Rose!*
Coming next month from
Mills & Boon® Desire™.

THE UNTAMED SHEIKH

BY
TESSA RADLEY

Dear Reader,

It was a great thrill to be asked to write *The Untamed Sheikh*. It's a very special book for me for several reasons.

Shafir, the hero, is a sheikh. An untamed, very male, very primal sheikh. Many years ago I discovered E M Hull's *The Sheikh* on my mother's bookshelves and devoured it. Mom also had black-and-white photos of Rudolph Valentino, the sheikh of the silent screen, that she'd collected. And sheikh romances have remained a firm favourite of mine.

The Untamed Sheikh also gave me a chance to write Megan Saxon's story. If you missed THE SAXON BRIDES, please visit www.tessaradley.com, for more details. I love Megan's wit and joie de vivre and it was a great pleasure to find a hero to match her.

Finally, this is the tenth book I have written for Desire™! Please celebrate with me.

See you soon,

Tessa

Tessa Radley loves travelling, reading and watching the world around her. As a teenager, Tessa wanted to be an intrepid foreign correspondent. But after completing a bachelor of arts degree and marrying her sweetheart, she became fascinated by law and ended up studying further and practising as an attorney in a city practice.

A six-month break travelling through Australia with her family reawoke the yen to write. And life as a writer suits her perfectly; travelling and reading count as research, and as for analysing the world…well, she can think "what if" all day long. When she's not reading, travelling or thinking about writing, she's spending time with her husband, her two sons or her zany and wonderful friends. You can contact Tessa through her website, www.tessaradley.com.

To Mom

One

Silence greeted Prince Shafir ibn Selim al Dhahara as, traditional robes billowing, he swept through the tall, carved wooden doors that a palace aide had flung open at his approach.

The mood inside the king's personal chamber was somber. Three men huddled over a laptop in the center of a round antique table and glanced up at Shafir's entrance. While his two brothers looked relieved to see him, his father—King Selim—was frowning.

Once seated with them at the table, Shafir leaned back, crossed his ankles and met his father's piercing gaze. The king's frown deepened at the informal pose. "You are late, Shafir."

"I was in the desert. I came as quickly as I could." Shafir gestured down to his dusty boots. "I didn't even take the time to change."

As the head of Dhahara's tourism ministry, Shafir had

spent the past week showing an international delegation the adventure tourism and trail-hiking potential of their small desert kingdom. Much time had been spent ensuring that each country's representative understood that opening Dhahara to international tourism meant putting in place measures to guarantee the desert would remain rugged and unspoiled.

"There is a problem, Father?"

"Not a problem exactly." The king's frown lines eased a little. "A challenge."

"A challenge?" Shafir exchanged a questioning glance with his older brother, Khalid—His Royal Highness Crown Prince Khalid ibn Selim al Dhahara, to give him his full title. Their father's idea of a challenge meant a situation fraught with difficulty—one of his father's own diplomats' worst nightmares.

"It is a challenge that should suit you well, Shafir."

"Me?" Shafir raised a dark eyebrow. "What about my honorable brothers? Or have you already allocated other challenges to them?"

Khalid grinned. "You arrived last—you drew the short straw."

"The most honorable straw, and a chance to be a hero." His younger brother, Rafiq, appeared wickedly amused.

"Be a hero?" Shafir eyed his brothers. Both looked like they were trying hard not to laugh.

His father, by contrast, looked grave. "Shafir, you are a man who has been forged and hardened to steel by the Dhaharan desert."

Shafir bowed his head, then lifted it to assess his father respectfully.

Black eyes set in a wise, weather-beaten face stared back at him. "My son, I don't want any scandal, so it has to be one of you three who take care of it. Rafiq is already committed, and his beloved may not understand." The king glanced to his right. "And Khalid is the crown prince. I cannot afford—"

Shafir interrupted. "So what *is* this challenge?"

"It's not that tough." Rafiq clicked open an image on the laptop on the table in front of them. "And this time I wouldn't exactly call it a challenge. All you need to do is get rid of *her.*"

An image of a woman flashed up on the monitor. Shafir got an impression of dark hair, plus eyes tilted up at the corners and brimming with laughter. The barrage of questions he'd been about to ask evaporated, leaving only one: "Who is she?"

"She is the woman who is about to derail Zara's fairy-tale wedding," said Rafiq.

"Do not mock your cousin." The king scowled. "Zara's wedding is the first in our family in almost two decades. My three sons have failed to oblige me."

"Our hopes are pinned on Rafiq," Shafir said quickly, and flags of color flared in his younger brother's cheeks. "He's in love."

"But not yet betrothed to be wed." A reproachful glance at all of them accompanied the king's words. "For now there is only Zara's wedding. With the immense media buildup, I cannot let that woman wreck the dreams of our nation."

The glare the king bestowed on *that woman's* image gave Shafir pause. This was the first he'd heard of any threat to his cousin's wedding. But it certainly explained his father's displeasure. The king had always doted on Zara, his dead brother's only child.

Shafir had met the intended bridegroom. Jacques Garnier was a French businessman whose family was enormously wealthy. Apart from other interests, like importing rugs and olives from the Middle East, the Garniers owned a château in the Loire Valley, and Jacques exported wines worldwide from the family winery. King Selim had been highly satisfied with the match, particularly since Zara was very much in love.

But now there appeared to be a glitch. Shafir suppressed a curse and stared at the screen. "What is her name?"

"Megan Saxon."

It wasn't her regular, unmistakably beautiful features that captured Shafir's attention. It was the zest for life that she radiated, her eyes sparking with the same irrepressible humor that curved her lips upward. *Joie de vivre,* the French called it.

Shafir glanced away. "How do you know she intends to sabotage Zara's wedding?"

His father sighed. "Garnier has been abstracted, so Zara knew something was wrong. Then she found missed calls from this woman on Garnier's private cell phone and recognized the name as one of his business colleagues. At first she thought the worst and cried for a whole day. Finally she confronted Garnier."

"And?"

"Ay, me." King Selim shook his head. "The woman is stalking him. Garnier hadn't told Zara because he didn't want to scare her, but the woman won't give up. And now she's coming to Dhahara."

"She's coming here?" Shafir leaned forward. That was a lot more serious than merely calling and texting.

"She called him just before her flight took off."

Shafir blew out a breath in frustration. "So when did he intend to tell us?"

The king flapped a hand. "It doesn't matter. We know now and can sort out a plan. You can call security in, though, if the woman proves to be…" He paused.

"Too much of a challenge for Shafir?" Khalid said, his eyes dancing.

"The woman hasn't been born who is too much of a challenge," Shafir said dryly. "But we need to contain this. No security forces. No police. We don't want an international incident." He thought of the delegation he'd impressed with Dhahara's marketability as a safe yet exotic tourism destination. At his invitation, two members of the delegation had extended their planned trip and were staying for Zara's wedding. Now it appeared the wedding was at risk.

And Zara's happiness.

Like his brothers, he had a soft spot for Zara, and he'd always gone out of his way to try to be the older brother she'd never had. Just as his father did his best to fill the space left by her father's death.

"Shafir, I need you to stop this woman from wrecking the wedding," said the king.

"Tell her that she's wasting her time—Jacques is marrying Zara," Rafiq suggested. "Convince her to go home."

Shaking his head, Shafir said, "If she's come all this way and has her heart set on Jacques, it won't be that easy." But if this woman thought she could hurt Zara, she'd soon learn she'd have to get through him.

"No," agreed Khalid. "She could easily turn nasty and tell Zara a lot of ass's tales."

Shafir shook his head slowly. "She won't get access to Zara. We'll tighten security." He'd see to that personally. No one was going to harm his sweet-natured cousin.

"But she might sell a pack of lies to one of those European scandal sheets." The king shuddered. "They don't peddle truth."

"She could do that." Shafir rubbed his chin, deep in thought.

"Seduce her, Shafir. Then she'll forget all about Jacques." Rafiq's dark eyes were full of humor.

Khalid roared with laughter. Even his father threw back his head and cackled.

Was Shafir the only one who didn't find it funny?

"You're confusing me with Khalid," he countered. "Women cling to him like bees to a honey pot."

"You scare them," said Rafiq. "Your reputation precedes you."

Khalid nodded. "Women want to be courted, flattered. The desert has taken you over. Look at you, covered in dust, your hair wild and sun streaked."

Shafir glowered and ran one hand through his overlong hair. "It protects my neck from the sun."

"Hmm...but that dangerous, untamed aura might appeal to the woman." Rafiq cocked his head to one side. "I dare you to seduce her."

Shafir glared at them. He didn't do seduction. It wasn't his style. He played it straight and fair with women, just the way he dealt with everyone else he met. "I'm not sinking that low."

"Scared?" ribbed Khalid.

"Of a woman?" Shafir shrugged a shoulder carelessly. "Never."

"My sons," chided the king, "there is work to be done." To Shafir he added, "Keep her from causing mischief by whatever means you choose, and Rafiq will make sure the path of true love runs smooth between Zara and Jacques." His father reached over and patted Shafir on the back. "But I want no scandal, hear? The only story I want to see on our TVs or in the Western magazines is Zara's—"

"—Fairy-tale wedding." Khalid rolled his eyes to the ornately carved ceiling.

"Given all the planning, it should be the wedding of the decade," muttered Rafiq.

"Do I hear a touch of longing, little brother? Perhaps it's time you got married, too," Khalid said slyly.

"Married?" The king straightened. "Khalid, as the crown prince it is your duty to marry first."

Khalid resumed gazing at the ceiling.

Shafir ignored the banter. As long as he was off the marriage hook, that was all that mattered. The woman hadn't been born who could compete with his love for the vastness of the Dhaharan desert.

He cast another glance at the laptop. His task was hardly a challenge. All he had to do was stop Megan Saxon from contacting Jacques Garnier long enough for Zara to marry the bridegroom of her dreams.

No problem.

As Shafir's limousine drew up outside the airport, a plane touched down on the runway. He narrowed his eyes. Megan Saxon was on that plane; he'd already received the confirmation from the airport's chief of security.

It had begun.

Jacques had wanted to meet her at the airport, determined to try to persuade her to leave Dhahara.

"I feel responsible," the Frenchman had said two hours earlier, his normally carefree expression bearing signs of strain. "Through business dealings with this madwoman I've created this unpleasantness for Zara. I need to make it clear to her that I love my fiancée."

But though he admired the other man for taking responsibility for the whole unsavory matter, Shafir had shaken his head. "I can't allow that. It's too risky. The woman is clearly obsessed with you. She might make a public scene." Which was what the king dreaded. "Or try hurting you. And what would Zara say then?"

He'd assured the anxious Jacques that he would deal

with this Megan personally, and finally the Frenchman had relented.

"It must be my fault," Jacques had said as he prepared to leave the palace, "yet I keep going over my business encounters with this woman, and I can't figure out what I did to attract this."

"Don't blame yourself. She's a lunatic."

At the relief on Jacques's face Shafir was seized by a surge of fury at the unknown Megan Saxon. Jacques didn't deserve this persecution—no man did. The woman had also caused Zara a great deal of unhappiness and put a huge strain on the bridal couple's relationship.

Now as he alighted from the limousine, he vowed to sort Megan Saxon out. He'd slicked back his hair and taken great care to dress European-style in a dark made-to-measure suit and immaculate white shirt. The last thing he wanted was for her to be spooked.

But his fashionable exterior was deceiving. As the king's second son, Shafir had been allowed an amount of freedom that Khalid hadn't. While Khalid had been schooled to succeed their father, Shafir had spent several years growing up with his grandmother in the desert, attending the local village school and later visiting *bedu* tribes. It was no secret that the people of Dhahara called him the untamed one.

Shafir was anything but a meek, by-the-book prince.

His jaw firming, Shafir nodded to the chauffeur and gestured to his bodyguards in the accompanying car to await his return. He moved with sleek grace as he entered the international terminal. Ignoring the sideways glances of recognition he attracted, he strode across the marble expanse, confident that his determined demeanor would ensure that people kept their distance.

He would meet Megan Saxon alone. She was going to rue the day she'd decided to threaten Zara's happiness.

* * *

The vast space of Dhahara's international arrivals hall struck Megan first. Its high vaulted ceilings were inset with skylights that let bright light filter in and made the air sparkle. Then there were the acres of white marble floors. If she hadn't already known, the airport would have announced the desert country's breathtaking riches.

A little way ahead behind a brass railing, a knot of people—most of them men wearing the traditional white thobes and holding up signs in Arabic script—waited for flight-weary passengers.

Jacques would be there, too.

His text just before she'd taken off at LAX on the final leg of this long haul—"See u tomorrow. Can't wait" followed by hugs and kisses—had promised that.

Megan picked up her pace, hauling her suitcase behind her. Excitement started to thrum in her belly. It had been over three months since she'd last seen him, too briefly, in Paris, where they'd seen the New Year in together before each jetting off in separate directions. He to pursue business interests in the desert kingdom and she back to New Zealand.

Telephone calls and frequent texts were no substitute for face-to-face contact. Then Jacques had suggested they spend some time together. Megan had jumped at the opportunity to get to know such a romantic, caring man better. Fired up by his stories about the exoticism of Dhahara, she'd booked their accommodation in Katar, the capital.

Unexpectedly, Jacques had objected, suggesting they visit nearby Oman instead. But Megan had her heart set on Dhahara. And finally Jacques had agreed to the luxurious villa in the desert she'd discovered. Megan hoped that this brief escape would give her a chance to get to know him properly…to discover whether the interest that had shimmered between them at international wine shows where they'd met intermittently during the past year was the real thing.

This time there would be no rush and bustle of work to distract them. This time they had six whole days to devote to getting to know each other.

Megan scanned the sea of faces as she approached.

A hard, hawkish face stood out from the rest. Their eyes clashed, his a dark, implacable bronze. His expression was tight and unwelcoming.

Nothing like Jacques's easy French charm.

A shiver ran down her spine and she looked quickly away, her gaze moving along the row. A crease formed between her brows as, decidedly uneasy now, she searched again for Jacques. Nothing.

Unbidden, her gaze flitted back to the unwelcoming stranger. He wore a beautifully tailored suit. Expensive—her fashion-conscious eye pegged it as Dior. He wore no tie. A crisp white shirt with the top button undone provided a startling contrast to his honeyed skin.

Megan lifted her eyes to his face and felt the sear of his inspection as his gaze traveled over her. The lightweight gray pantsuit that had seemed a perfect compromise between circumspect covering for an Arabian country and suitable for the hot desert climate now felt incredibly filmy. She should've worn her black linen business suit, the one with the high mandarin collar and the long skirt. Sure she would have boiled. But perhaps then she wouldn't have felt so terribly exposed under his relentless gaze. When his eyes met hers there was a slight curl to his lip as if he hadn't been impressed by what he had seen.

Megan was shaken by the sense of rejection that ripped through her. She wasn't vain, but she knew she was attractive. Outgoing and friendly, men liked her. She didn't usually inspire this kind of reaction.

Thankfully he was destined to remain a stranger.

She tossed her head and stared dismissively past him, renewing her search for Jacques. Never before had his idiosyncratic lack of punctuality irritated her this much. She felt exposed, naked, and she wished he'd been on time for once in his charming life. This time the effusive apologies that always made her laugh weren't going to be enough. More than anything she wanted to hurry to Jacques's car and escape that disconcerting bronze gaze.

Megan sighed, impatient with herself. She was granting a stranger too much importance. Her gaze swept the arrivals hall, hoping for a glimpse of Jacques's lean body tearing toward her, his hair flopping around his face.

No sign of merry green eyes, no laughing mouth.

"Megan Saxon."

At the sound of her name murmured in a deep, unfamiliar voice, Megan whipped around to find the stranger beside her.

"What do you want?" She glared at him, acutely aware of every exaggerated tale she'd ever heard about Middle Eastern males—their chauvinism, and their assumption that any Western woman was theirs for the taking.

Not that he'd struggle to find female companionship. He was handsome in a hard-edged way. Pretty gorgeous actually, if you liked your men fierce and frowning, which Megan did not.

And he knew her name.

"Come with me."

"Most certainly not." Surely white-slavers, however well-dressed, didn't frequent such public places, Megan speculated with acerbic humor. But despite her bravado she took a quick glance around. Reassuringly there were lots of people in the airport. Men. Groups of veiled women. Families. Even a sprinkling of guards in official-looking uniforms. Several people were looking their way with curious interest in their eyes, but they maintained a respectful distance.

No cause for concern.

At least, not yet.

A hand landed on her arm.

"Don't touch me." She used her most freezing tone—the one that made even her brothers back off.

"Forgive me," he said smoothly, removing his hand. "I startled you. My name is Shafir." A brief hesitation, then he added, "I am a friend of Jacques's."

Her anger fizzled away under a tide of embarrassment.

"Why didn't you say so?" The memory of the disdainful inspection he'd given her flitted through her mind, and she hesitated. No hint of criticism remained in those piercing eyes. Had she imagined it? Or had it just been the standard inspection of an Arabian man for an unaccompanied woman?

He gave her a smile, and it lit up his face. Wow. He'd been handsome enough before, but with the darkness banished he was simply devastating.

"Uh…where is Jacques?" Megan stuttered, unable to take her eyes off him, stunned by how much difference a smile could make. He should smile all the time. Or maybe not. He'd be a danger to the ability of any susceptible female to think straight. Although she wasn't about to forget that unsettling once-over he'd given her. "When will he get here?"

"Jacques is not coming."

She tensed again, her eyes searching his face, scared to voice the sudden fear that struck black ice into her heart.

But he must have seen something in her expression, because he said quickly, "Nothing has happened to him."

Relief flooded her. "You must think I'm neurotic. My brother died in a car accident and for a moment I thought…" Her voice trailed away and she gave a small shrug. Nothing could describe the bewilderment, the sense of loss that had followed Roland's death. And she didn't owe this man any explanation anyway.

"Jacques is fine—he's not hurt. He simply asked me to meet you in his place." His voice deepened further, and Megan thought she detected sympathy in his eyes.

"Oh, maybe he left me a message." Megan reached into the tote slung over her shoulder for her cell phone. She had yet to switch it on; the No Cell Phones signs in the customs hall had been quite clear.

"You haven't been to Dhahara before, have you?"

Megan gave the imposing stranger an abstracted glance.

"If you don't have a local SIM card it will take some time for your phone's roaming system to register the Dhaharan network."

Megan glanced down at her phone, noting the turning hourglass on the backlit screen. Seemed he was right.

With a sigh she dropped the phone back into her tote. "Why isn't Jacques here, then?"

"He had a meeting—"

"—With a Persian rug merchant. I remember." Megan nodded. Jacques had mentioned it when they'd spoken while she'd been waiting to board in Auckland two days ago.

His eyes narrowed a little. "Their meeting is dragging on longer than expected. He asked me to fetch you and take you to your hotel."

Instantly her suspicions seemed foolish. If it hadn't been for that initial inspection he'd given her, Megan would have relaxed completely. "Thank you for meeting me."

"It is my pleasure."

Megan allowed him to relieve her of the retractable pull handle of her suitcase. Conscious of his strength and the muscular bulk of his body under the exquisitely tailored suit, she trotted beside him as they headed for the airport's glass exit doors.

Outside, a host of unfamiliar scents assailed her. Spices. Heat. Dust. The hot, dry fragrance of the Dhaharan desert.

A frisson of delight shook her. This was a wild untamed world such that she, a New Zealand country girl at heart, had never experienced. Nomads. Caravans. She couldn't wait to explore it further with Jacques at her side.

"This way." The command uttered in a throaty growl brought her back to earth.

This way revealed a shiny white limousine with a second car waiting behind. A uniformed man built like a barn door leaned against the front passenger door while a chauffeur stood attentively beside the open rear door. Except this chauffeur wore flowing robes and a white headdress that was secured with the black cords that the guidebook she'd read on the plane said were called *agal*. A far cry from the black uniform and peaked cap she was accustomed to. Bemused, Megan ducked into the silent interior.

The cool air-conditioning was disappointing after the hot air redolent with Arabian fragrances. Megan leaned back against plush black velvet cushions and spared a glance for the man who had followed her in.

He dominated the enclosed space, giving Megan the sense of a wild animal that had been temporarily caged. A wolf perhaps. She met those bronze eyes. No, not a wolf—this was no animal that ran in packs. A panther. Or a jaguar. Wild and very, very dangerous.

She stilled, her pulse quickening with sudden apprehension. Then he smiled and the mood of danger evaporated. He was urbane, smooth, a civilized twenty-first-century man. Except for the reflected gleam of those magnetic eyes in the dimness.

Okay, maybe not completely civilized.

Megan shook off the strange fancy. Civilized or not, he wasn't her problem. Thank God.

A need to fill the prickling silence forced her into conversation. "You said you and Jacques are friends?"

A nod. But he didn't bother to expand.

Megan swallowed. She needed to see Jacques again. Despite his family's wealth, Jacques was predictable… easygoing…charming.

Civilized.

Everything this man wasn't.

After drawing in a deep breath, she exhaled. "It was a long flight," she said as his head turned toward her. "How long will it take to get to the hotel?" It would be a relief to freshen up the room she had booked for the night. She and Jacques planned to leave for the desert villa early tomorrow morning.

The man who had introduced himself only as Shafir leaned forward and opened the door of a well-concealed fridge. "Forgive me. I have been remiss. Would you like a drink? Champagne, perhaps?"

So he could produce manners when he had to. For the first time Megan realized her throat was parched. "A drink would be lovely, but I'd prefer mineral water, please."

She'd barely eaten on the flight, and there was no point getting light-headed. There would be time enough for that tomorrow. No doubt she and Jacques would share a bottle of champagne on the terrace overlooking the desert and toast each other…and their hopes of discovering something meaningful.

A small green bottle and a glass appeared with a flourish. The sound of gurgling water filled the space between them. Then Megan found herself holding a cold, smooth glass. A crack sounded as he pulled the tab off a Coca-Cola and lifted the can to his lips.

The dimmed ceiling lights reflected off his hair. It hung to just below his collar, longer than she would've expected given his carefully conservative attire. Below his chin she could see his throat moving as he drank thirstily, his sleek skin gleaming as the light caught it.

Wrenching her gaze away, Megan took a hurried sip of the water. The dryness in her throat eased. Resolutely she turned her head as the limousine crested a rise and stared out through the tinted windows to where the concrete highway uncurled through the desert like a silver ribbon. In the distance the sands undulated in mounds. Dunes. Again a sense of anticipation stirred her.

It was all so wonderfully alien.

And so different from the lush green of the Hawkes Bay where she'd grown up and where—aside from the frequent business trips abroad to wine shows—she'd lived all her life.

She leaned forward, absorbing the view, the exoticism of it all. "That's the Dhaharan desert, right?" She couldn't suppress the lilt in her voice. "Almost four thousand square miles of dry sand that comparatively few people inhabit."

"That's correct. But it's not as bleak as people think."

Scanning the stark, golden dunes that sloped dramatically away from the highway, concealing the city of Katar that lay beyond, she said, "I read that tourism in Dhahara will be expanding in the near future."

"You're well informed." He sounded surprised.

"I was interested."

"Why?"

There was an edge to his voice. Yanked from her study of the dunes, Megan looked away from the gold-shaded landscape. "Why not?" She shrugged. "I also read that while Dhahara does import some products from the United States and the European Union, it's pretty self-sufficient and does very well on exports like oil, olives and handmade rugs." Suddenly conscious of sounding like she'd swallowed a guidebook, Megan abruptly stopped talking.

"What do you hope to find here in Dhahara?"

Definitely an edge and a glint of suspicion in those strange eyes.

"What do I hope to find?" she echoed his question. "What does anyone hope for when they visit a place they've never been? Excitement…adventure…romance." His expression darkened at her flippant reply. "Okay, more than anything I want to relax. It's been a long time since I've had a holiday." *And I badly want to fall in love with Jacques.* But she didn't say that. Instead she asked, "How long until we reach Katar? I can't wait to freshen up."

He blinked.

Unease coiled coldly in the pit of her stomach. She glanced out the window. The dunes had receded, giving the impression that the desert had expanded. "Shouldn't there be buildings…high-rises out there?"

"There are no high-rises in Dhahara. We pride ourselves on preserving our desert heritage—even in our cities."

Of course. She'd read about the determination of the Dhaharans to keep their traditional architecture. But where was the urban sprawl of industrial buildings that lay on the outskirts of most big cities?

She fell silent and scanned the landscape beyond the glass. Surely the highway should be packed with vehicles? After all, according to the guidebook she'd devoured on the plane, millions lived in Katar. Yet there was little sign of human activity, just the odd dot far ahead of them on the highway and even fewer in their wake. Even the car that had been waiting behind them at the airport had disappeared.

Megan's unease deepened.

He'd never answered her question about how long it would take to reach the capital. Apart from what looked like tracks, no major roads branched off the highway, which cut straight through the desert.

The first shard of real fear spiked through her. Polite inquiry had gotten her nowhere, and she'd never been one to avoid an issue. "You're not taking me to my hotel, are you?"

He stared at her from inscrutable eyes.

The fear spread. "Answer me! Where are you taking me?" Stupid! Why had she ever gotten into this limousine with him at all? He'd said his name was Shafir. No surname. And that he was a friend of Jacques. That was the sum total she knew about the man.

What had she done?

"I want to talk to Jacques. Now." Her voice shook just a little. Inside, her heart was hammering against her rib cage.

"He's in a meeting."

The pitch of his voice didn't change, but Megan no longer believed him. "You're lying! Where is Jacques? I don't think you're a friend of his at all. What have you done to him?"

"Calm down." The icy whiplash of his voice steadied her. "I have done nothing to Jacques."

"Who the hell are you?" She thought desperately about everything she'd devoured about Dhahara. It was a wealthy kingdom ruled by King Selim al Dhahara. She couldn't recall reading about any political unrest. Or kidnappings. But then, she'd been excited at the prospect of seeing Jacques again. Her focus had been on the exotic and romantic aspect of the country. Beyond assuring herself that the country was safe and tourist friendly, she hadn't done a lot to find out about the political subtleties. Another mistake. Was he some crazed politico? Or a bandit out for ransom? Or, heaven help her, a terrorist?

Oh, God.

She stared at him, her eyes stretched wide, her pulse pounding in her ears.

"Don't look at me like that. I'm not going to hurt you." In one swift movement he crumpled the can and slotted it into a concealed rubbish holder.

Megan's gaze fixed on the mangled red-and-white remains of metal. "I'm supposed to believe that?" she muttered.

He growled something that she barely heard, too focused on the ruthless strength he'd revealed by crushing that can as if it were no more than a wad of tissue paper.

The frantic vibration of her cell phone diverted her attention from the crumpled metal between his fingers. Her messages had come through—the roaming service must have kicked in, and not a minute too soon! Feeling like the cavalry had arrived, Megan reached for her bag, but as she extracted the phone, a hard hand closed over hers.

"I'll take that."

No way! Disregarding his power, his size, Megan grabbed his wrist and wrestled with him, determined not to let him commandeer her last link to the outside world.

In one simple move he seized the phone and transferred it to his other hand and held it away from her. Driven by desperation, Megan dove across his lap, intent on claiming back the phone—*her* phone, dammit.

The hard thighs that tightened to rocklike firmness beneath his elegant trousers was the first warning that she had made a colossal mistake. She jerked her gaze upward.

Oh, no.

Bare inches separated their faces. Megan was aware of muscle shifting under her. He surrounded her. And he was big—much bigger than she'd realized.

Her breath came in ragged fits, yet he didn't appear to be breathing at all. She gulped in air, but she could do nothing about her pounding heart.

A stillness fell between them.

Danger. Her senses shrieked the warning. It struck Megan

exactly how vulnerable her position was. Scrambling off his lap, she abandoned all attempts to retrieve her phone.

"Sorry," she muttered, unsettled by her rash stupidity.

"Don't be sorry." But he didn't smile. His cheekbones stood out starkly under the tight mask of tawny skin. "Be careful."

Two

Was that a threat?

How could she have put herself at risk in this way?

Thoughts tumbling through Megan's head made it ache as she watched him open the window a crack and calmly dispose of her phone through the gap. She started to protest—then thought better of it. He'd said he wouldn't hurt her. But that had been before she'd clambered all over him fighting him for her phone.

Now she was heart-stoppingly conscious of the hard strength of his body. How could he not be equally aware of hers? Her eyes darted around. They were alone in the dimly lit limousine. What if he decided to…

Not that!

Her mind blanked out.

Megan pulled herself together. Think! She picked up her water to buy herself time and took an unsteady sip.

"Your phone is of no use deep in the desert. There are no cell phone towers."

Of course he'd say that.

Bastard.

Megan didn't deign to look at him. She took another sip of water and started to count silently and a little shakily to herself. One. Two. She wasn't going to respond to anything he said. Three.

"I hate it when women sulk."

Megan forgot she wasn't going to look at him, that she intended to starve him of her responses. Instead she blurted out, "I never sulk."

"Your lips are pursed, and your hands are clenched around that glass so hard it's going to shatter between your fingers." He sighed. "I recognize the signs."

Feminine fury rose into her throat in a hot ball.

Next he'd be accusing her of suffering from PMS.

She turned her head and gave him her most haughty glare. "First you kidnap me. And then you rob me. And now you've become an article in a women's magazine. I don't see that I have to talk to you. You're a lowlife. A thief. Someone should cut your right hand off."

For a moment he sat perfectly still, his eyes turning incandescent with spectacular rage.

Then he moved.

Megan's instincts for survival took over. She flung the contents of her glass straight into his face.

The instant she'd done it she regretted it. He'd abducted her, and yet instead of playing along, she'd antagonized him.

Now he was surely going to kill her.

She shrank away into the corner of the seat, her hands shielding herself from his approach. He was so big, so overwhelming. And she had no idea who the devil he was.

Or what he intended to do with her out here in this ominously bleak, empty desert.

The shock of cold water against his skin registered. Shafir wiped his hand across his eyes and stared in disbelief at the droplets wetting his fingers. Outrage added to the moisture already misting his vision. No woman had ever *dared* do anything like that to him, a prince of the royal household of Dhahara, before.

He moved swiftly, swept up on a tide of anger and affronted male pride that demanded reprisal. At once. Her defiance, her insulting reference to him as a thief, her insistent demands to be taken to Jacques, all added to the emotions that churned inside him. Somewhere in the maelstrom desire was building momentum. The curve of her buttocks in his lap had been firm but unmistakably feminine; she had smelled of flowers and amber, all woman.

A desire to yank her up against him—to kiss her into submission—rushed through him. Until he caught a glimpse of the glistening sloe eyes between the hands raised to fend him off.

Megan Saxon was scared. No, petrified.

Of him. Shafir discovered he didn't like that notion at all.

How had he gotten stuck in this situation? By the devil, he didn't care for the challenge his father had given him. He didn't care for terrorizing a lone woman.

Shafir paused. No, that wasn't quite true. His motives hadn't been so heroic. He'd intended to scare her a little—teach her a lesson for threatening Zara's happiness. But he'd never meant to terrify her out of her wits.

He reached out a still-damp hand.

"Stay away from me, or you'll regret it."

At the sound of her desperation his anger subsided as

quickly as it had risen. Desperate. But brave too. Shafir admired that.

Dropping his hand to his side, he deliberately softened his voice. "I've already told you that I don't hurt women."

"Really?"

The sarcasm caught him on the raw. "Really," he bit out. It was true some women feared him and gave him a wide berth, but there were plenty who were drawn to the danger, the legend that he'd become. He was a sheik of the desert. He was wealthy. And he was a royal prince.

Of course there would always be women.

But he'd never found what he sought.

He'd decided the love his parents shared had disappeared with their generation. Though they'd been fortunate. It could have been a disastrous union—after all, they'd been promised to each other from birth. *Insha'allah.*

He'd managed to avoid such a bargain.

Instead he took what women offered him. Willingly. And then returned to his desert lair without a backward glance when the affair was over.

But Megan Saxon was beautiful.

And spirited.

Shafir examined her through narrowed eyes. Long, silky, dark hair, lovely eyes, and skin so pale it looked like the delicate petals of almond blossom. He'd known she was attractive—the computer images had revealed that, though it had also shown a dazzling smile he had yet to experience. But no image could reveal the full extent of her beauty, or the bold, unfettered spirit that went with it. From the first moment her truculent gaze had met his in the airport she'd taken his breath away.

Fire and ice.

"Stop looking at me like that!"

"How am I looking at you?"

"With calculation. I don't like it."

She was perceptive. And still frightened. The rise and fall of her breasts revealed her agitation. Shafir couldn't help noticing that the top button of her jacket was missing—almost certainly lost in her scuffle with him over her phone—and that in the valley between her breasts her skin was pale and creamy. He tore his gaze away and met a pair of furious feminine eyes.

"Take me back to Jacques."

That was impossible. "Would it help if I gave you my solemn word that I won't harm you?" he offered instead. "That you are perfectly safe?"

For a moment she didn't say anything. Then she muttered, "Why should I accept your word? You told me Jacques had asked you to pick me up from the airport and take me to the hotel. But you're not taking me to Jacques or to the hotel, are you?"

Shafir hesitated for a split second, weighing the possible responses. Soon enough she'd know for sure anyway.

"No, I'm not taking you to Jacques."

Surprise flared briefly in her eyes. She'd expected him to lie again.

"So where are you taking me?" She controlled her fear admirably.

A sudden pang of sympathy for her surprised him. "You won't want for comfort. It's better than any hotel."

Her chin went up. "I don't care about comfort—"

"You'll be safe. I promise."

He ignored her snort of disbelief as the limousine slowed to a crawl and the wheels crunched on gravel. Without giving her a chance to argue, or question his promise, he said, "We are here. You can freshen up and judge the comfort for yourself."

Megan turned away from him and bent forward to peer

through the darkened windows. He knew what she'd see. High castellated walls, curved domes and turrets.

"Good grief, it's a castle."

Before he could respond, the limo door opened. A hand appeared and the cuff of a uniform embroidered with gold braid followed.

"Welcome, Your—"

"Thank you, Hanif." Shafir cut off the aide's welcome before Hanif could give away more than Shafir wanted.

Immediately Megan turned her head to glare at him, and he could tell she'd added yet another black mark against him, this time for inconsiderate rudeness. Even his scrupulously polite "After you" received no softening in her disapproving eyes.

He followed her out into the relentless late afternoon heat. Conscious that the beating sun must be draining to someone unaccustomed to it, he put a guiding arm around her to lead her inside. Megan shifted sideways, hitching her tote higher on her shoulder, and his hand fell away.

"Where are we? What is this place?"

"Qasr Al-Ward. The Palace of the Roses."

Megan balked. "My God, it looks like a cliff face. I've never seen anything that less resembles a rose. Who lives here?"

He did. This was the home of his heart. But he had no intention of revealing that to her. "It's been in my family for generations."

He could see her thinking that if she went in she might never escape. At least it would take her mind off the identity of his family. Not for the first time, he wondered if it had been a mistake bringing her here. Rafiq had thought it a much better idea than taking her to a remote Bedouin settlement. She was less likely to escape…to wander off into the desert.

"Is your family here now?"

"Everyone—except for me and my staff—is in the capital." Preparing for Zara's wedding, as she well knew. He pressed his lips together and waited for her response.

"That's where I should be, too."

She hadn't even blinked at the allusion to Zara's wedding.

His mouth tightened further. All she cared about was getting to Katar to stop Zara's wedding to Jacques. Anger balled in his chest. With every mile that had passed his hopes had been growing that his family had gotten it wrong, that Megan was not the self-centered somewhat crazy woman they'd all described. Now it appeared their reports had been all too accurate.

She was set on returning to the city come hell or high water to disrupt Zara's wedding.

But she'd reckoned without him! He was not going to give her any opportunity to wreak the havoc she'd planned.

"Come," he said, impatient now to have this farce over.

She dug her high-heeled shoes into the gravel driveway and stared belligerently at him. "I'm not going in there. I want you to take me back to the capital. At once."

Evidently no longer caring that she was thirsty and tired, Megan had edged back to the limousine and was trying to open the door.

Shafir folded his arms, rocked back on his heels and waited. "It is locked."

"Give me the keys."

"I can't." He shrugged. "Malik has them."

"Malik?"

"My chauffeur."

"Then order him to unlock it." There was immense frustration in her voice as her eyes frantically searched their surroundings for the missing Malik. "Where has he gone?"

"Most probably—" Shafir allowed himself a smile "—to find his wife."

She stared at him, clearly disconcerted. "What?"

"My chauffeur has gone to find Aniya, his wife. He hasn't seen her for two weeks." Shafir didn't bother suppressing the unholy surge of humor. "He misses her when he is away."

The look that Megan Saxon gave him warned him that she'd like nothing better than to see him burn in the flames of hell.

Megan followed slowly as Shafir mounted stairs cut out of desert stone that led up to the imposing facade of the palace. Entering the antechamber, she caught her breath at the riot of color that confronted her.

Her ire at Shafir temporarily forgotten, she gazed around in stunned amazement. Arches met overhead in a glorious celebration of an ancient stonecutter's skill, with the walls between painted a deep, rich red. Persian carpets in jewel hues covered dark clay tiles.

"This is like something out of *The Arabian Nights,*" she murmured, overawed by the patina of ancient opulence. "It couldn't be a bigger contrast to the arid desert outside."

"Wait until you see the gardens."

"Gardens?" Megan turned her head to see if he was joking. But there was no sign of humor in the implacable features. "There are gardens? In the desert?"

His head inclined in the smallest of nods. "Oh, yes. Lush, fragrant gardens with fountains and pools. There's even a palmerie."

He sounded convincing—not like he was ridiculing her. Finally she said, "I'd like to see them."

"You will. But I'm sure you'd like to freshen up first."

A slender young woman appeared. Megan hadn't noticed her before. Nor had she seen Shafir beckon to her. The leather slippers she wore trod soundlessly on the floor even though the robe that covered her from head to foot rustled softly.

"Go with Naema."

"But—"

He was already striding away. Swallowing her thousand and one questions, Megan followed Naema through a doorway set unobtrusively in the farthest wall of the antechamber.

She found herself standing in what had to be a powder room. But what a room. Rugs covered the floor, and the walls were hung with fabric that looked suspiciously like silk shot through with gold thread.

A large, sunken white-marble tub took up most of the center of the room. One wall was covered from floor to ceiling with smoky mirrors that reflected the mass of ferns spilling from ornate wrought iron baskets suspended above the tub. Along the opposite wall was a marble slab set with two basins, folded towels piled on one end.

Naema pulled open the doors of a cupboard set above the marble slab to reveal a blow-dryer, toiletries, toothbrushes and paste, lotions and designer makeup, all still wrapped and sealed. Every frippery a twenty-first-century woman might desire.

"If you'd like a massage after you have bathed—" Naema pushed open a door to reveal a raised bed "—I will do that here."

Megan was sorely tempted. But she suspected that once she allowed herself to be indulged her guard might drop, and that she couldn't allow.

Dumping her tote on the marble slab, she answered, "I'll just wash my face and do something with my hair."

"I can do your hair. Very pretty." Naema sounded eager.

"No, thank you, I'll be all right."

"I can fetch clothes, if you desire."

Her own clothes? Megan realized she hadn't seen her suitcase brought in. "My suitcase…?"

"It has been taken to your room."

Her room? The first surge of relief that she wouldn't lose her familiar things vanished as she made the connection. Her room. She'd been expected here.

The anxiety that had ebbed away was back in full force. What did Shafir want with her? Why had he taken her?

"I can go and get it if you desire."

"What?" Megan didn't know what Naema was talking about.

"Your suitcase. I will fetch it."

"Oh, no, don't worry." But Megan found herself speaking to empty air. Naema had already darted out.

The young woman's eagerness to please was bewildering, given that Megan was here as Shafir's captive.

As she splashed cool water onto her face it crossed her mind that Shafir's reasons for bringing her here might be about sex. There was a moment of wild, raw fear, but then, her stomach sinking in embarrassment, she remembered those moments in the limousine when she'd straddled his lap. He'd had every opportunity to make a move on her then, to grope her, to force himself on her.

Yet he'd chosen not to.

Instead he'd efficiently disposed of her phone, radiating tension and danger. Even when she'd hurled water in his face he hadn't retaliated, even though she'd seen the blatant male rage in those fierce eyes. Instead he'd assured her that she was safe. And later he'd talked about gardens. The man who'd kidnapped her had offered to show her gardens, for heaven's sake!

He was as enigmatic as the Sphinx. With a confused sigh Megan turned the faucet off and reached for one of the thick, soft towels. Whatever he wanted, she doubted it was a sex slave. And she should thank the heavens for that.

So what was left?

Ransom? Could he know her family was wealthy? Maybe he meant to sell her back to Jacques Garnier at an extortionate rate. Did he need money? She touched the veined marble slab. It certainly didn't look like it. Not if his family owned this magnificent palace.

Who was this man who called himself Shafir?

Shafir narrowed his gaze as the door closed and Megan Saxon sauntered into the panelled salon that was very much his territory.

She'd brushed her hair until it shone like the wing of a blackbird. But she hadn't changed out of the gray suit.

Perhaps she considered that that would be admitting defeat. He braced himself to expect another demand to take her to Jacques. Hadn't she yet realized the futility of that? Or perhaps the suit was the only appropriate garment she had to wear, and the remaining clothes she'd packed were chosen for a tryst with Garnier.

He didn't care for that thought, and his eyes hardened as they swept her face with its glowing skin from which all artifice had been washed, making her look more radiant—and less capable of deceit—than ever.

Her gaze tangled with his as she halted in front of the divan where he reclined, his suit jacket abandoned, his legs stretched out and crossed at the ankles.

"So who are you, Shafir? You don't dress like a bandit," said Megan.

"A bandit?" Irritation filled Shafir even as good manners impelled him to rise to his feet. "You believe I am a bandit?"

She tilted her head to one side and examined him through critical eyes. "I'm considering it."

He knew what she would see. Most days he dressed for comfort—usually in a thobe. Today's suit had been in her honor. He'd figured she would be more likely to accompany a man in an expensive suit. And he'd been right. He knew what he looked like. Wealthy. Distinguished. Powerful.

Nothing like a bandit.

"Of course, I have no personal experience of how bandits dress. I suppose some dress very well."

Her up-down glance dismissed him in a manner that left him intensely annoyed.

"Then what makes you think I am a bandit?" Shafir's soft tone would have warned his enemies that he was at his most lethal.

But she appeared oblivious to the danger as she turned away and examined the collection of antique scimitars hanging on the wall. Her back to him, she said, "Your behavior suggests that you must be a bandit, though I'm not sure what you think kidnapping me will gain you."

"Will gain *me?*" He found himself repeating the ludicrous words. He, a prince of Dhahara, didn't need anything that she could bring him. Shaking his head in disbelief, he said, "Come, tell me what you believe I will gain."

She faced him, her eyes watchful. "Money. I think you plan to hold me for ransom."

He almost laughed, until he realized she was serious. And if she believed that she must be more scared than she was letting on. A twinge of remorse pricked him.

"But that would be an awful mistake. I'm just an ordinary tourist."

At that Shafir did laugh, though without humor, and all feelings of remorse evaporated. Did she think he was such a gullible fool? "Hardly ordinary," he mocked, drawing close enough to smell the hint of mint from toothpaste on her breath. "You're Garnier's girlfriend, and his family is worth millions."

"So this *is* about ransom." Disappointment clouded her expressive features. "He won't pay, I assure you. You're wasting your time. I mean nothing to him. I'm not even his girlfriend."

Now there was an interesting strategy. "You shouldn't tell me that." Didn't the woman have any sense of self-preservation? "You should be ensuring that the blackmailer keeps you alive by telling me how important you are to Jacques."

She eased away from him without giving the impression that she was backing off. "Thanks for the advice. Are you after a ransom or not?"

"Of course not. I told you—I'm a friend of Jacques's."

"That could've been nothing more than another convenient lie, told to persuade me to leave the airport with you." She inspected him again. Apart from the fancy suit, he didn't look like he had anything in common with Jacques. "So what's your connection with Jacques? Business?"

He inclined his head. "And family."

"You're related?" That surprised her. "Jacques never mentioned having family in Dhahara."

"Jacques and I will be family soon. By marriage," he added, giving her a brooding stare.

Megan pitied Shafir's prospective bride. The poor woman would be stuck with this fierce, arrogant man for life—or at least until he decided he'd had enough of her and divorced her at a whim. No doubt the laws of Dhahara favored men and the cast-off ex-wives were left high and dry.

Did Jacques know how risky it would be to allow Shafir to marry his relation? Did he have any concept of how dangerous Shafir was? If so, maybe he could talk sense into whatever relation of his was going to marry Shafir. A cousin? A stepsister? Megan couldn't remember Jacques mentioning a sister, but she vaguely recalled talk of a brother. Just went to prove that they had a lot to learn about each other—and Shafir was thwarting their plans of a relaxed, romantic get-to-know-each-other interlude.

"The prenuptial contract has already been drawn up," he said, interrupting her musings, his eyes fierce and restless as they swept over her.

Megan shivered in reaction. He looked driven, and she shook off the cold tingles that rippled up and down her spine. Surely Shafir must love his bride-to-be? Or perhaps not. It might be an arranged marriage. For all she knew such weddings were the norm in Dhahara. Her pity for his prospective bride increased, but she pushed it away. She didn't want to think about her. Their nuptials were none of her business.

All she cared about was getting to the bottom of whatever mad idea had caused him to carry her off and bring her here. And then she should be able to convince him to let her go.

She studied the scimitars on the wall again. They looked real enough. If he didn't release her, one of those might come in handy—and that way his bride would be spared, too, from a fate worse than death.

Her lips quirked.

The sound of the door opening halted her murderous thoughts. Megan caught a glimpse of the aide from earlier.

"Dinner is served, Your Highness."

Megan's mouth dropped open. "*Your Highness*?"

"*Your Highness?*" Megan repeated incredulously minutes later, when they were seated at a polished table that seemed to stretch for miles down the formal dining room. Portraits of fierce-eyed sheiks stared down at her from the walls. His royal ancestors? She shook her head, trying to dislodge the feeling of disbelief.

He raised one eyebrow and carried on eating.

After picking up a fork, she tasted a morsel and then speared what looked like a meatball. No point going on a hunger strike.

Sure, she'd read about the royal family in the guidebook that had kept her occupied during the series of long flights from Auckland; but what had she done to merit being kidnapped by a royal sheik? This was the twenty-first century, and it wasn't as if he'd glimpsed her in the desert and been so enthralled by her beauty…that he'd felt compelled to snatch her away to keep for himself.

A shiver ran through her at that crazy thought.

Darn.

What kind of naive fantasy was that?

No, he'd known before they'd even met what he planned to do. It had been coldly calculated, not the act of a man driven by passion.

But he was still a member of the royal family, and that must mean he had certain responsibilities. "Are you totally out of your mind?"

"Do not insult me." Shafir's fork landed on his empty plate. His eyes flashed and again that sense of danger was all around her. "I am no *majnum,* no madman."

But she would not be silenced. "How dare you, a member of the royal family, kidnap me!"

His mouth hardened. "I wasn't dared. And I did not kidnap you."

"Really? Then *I* must be delusional." She raised her chin a notch. "Because it certainly feels like I was abducted."

"No chloroform. No hood over your head. No force. Not even a bruise on your arm." He reached out to touch the skin beneath her elbow and fresh shivers danced in the wake of what was almost a caress. "You came without a murmur."

She swallowed. She should have kicked and screamed.

Instead she'd suppressed the twinges of misgiving, more fool her. "You misled me…lied to me."

"But I never forced you. And I've promised I won't harm you, haven't I?"

She couldn't deny that and gave a reluctant nod. Falling silent, she thought furiously about what she knew of the family. King Selim had no daughters, only sons. Three, she seemed to remember. There was a crown prince, a son who was involved in Dhahara's finance sector and a third who ran the country's tourism ministry, from what she could recall. Past that sketchy information, she drew a blank.

"So which son are you? The heir apparent, the money man or the spin doctor?"

"Spin doctor?" Something that might have been amusement glinted in his eyes.

"Yes—spinning a web of elaborate deceit, convincing gullible tourists to visit Dhahara."

"That would make me the spin doctor, then."

"You're in charge of the country's tourism?" Megan gave a breathy laugh of disbelief. "Well, you're going to have your work cut out for you."

"I am?"

Megan nodded emphatically. "Once people—especially women—hear there's a very real threat of abduction in Dhahara your visitor figures will plummet. Goodbye, tourism."

All traces of amusement vanished. "Are you threatening me?"

Megan widened her eyes. "Threatening you? Of course not."

"Good," he growled. "Then we understand one another. Because no one is going to hear about this kidnapping from you, are they?"

Megan tilted her head to one side. Above his jaw, a

muscle tightened. Fascinated, she watched the ripple of movement under his smooth skin. "Well, my family will have been waiting to hear from me, to know that I've arrived safely. When they don't, they'll start asking questions, and until she started helping me with the PR for the winery, Alyssa, my sister-in-law, was a damned good investigative journalist."

Megan lifted her shoulders and carelessly let them fall again, doing her best to project an image of being relaxed and being totally in control. Perhaps, then, this devil in front of her would never realize how shaky she felt inside.

His face darkened. "You *are* threatening me!"

"It's not a threat."

"But you said—"

"It's a certainty." With satisfaction she watched the way his eyes turned to a flat, dull bronze. Perhaps Prince Shafir would now realize he'd bitten off more than he could chew.

His harsh features came closer, so close she could see every sun-beaten line around his eyes. "You are very fortunate," he murmured through barely parted lips.

Her heart started to thud as apprehension flooded her. "Fortunate? I've been abducted, taken to a remote area of some godforsaken desert, and you call that fortunate?"

"Yes. If you'd threatened another man with exposure, he might feel compelled to kill you."

"You're a member of the royal family, so you wouldn't dare. You couldn't afford the scandal."

His eyes narrowed to slits. "Who would ever know?"

Three

Megan awoke, blinking against the beams of golden sunlight that filtered through the fine fabric of the bed hangings surrounding the four-poster bed.

She'd tossed and turned all night long after that final exchange with Shafir, until a combination of jet lag and a plump feather mattress had lulled her churning concerns to sleep just before dawn.

But this morning her disquiet returned, and despite the sunlight her arms prickled with gooseflesh.

"You wouldn't dare," she'd hurled at Shafir last night. But Megan had a sinking feeling that her bronze-eyed abductor wasn't constrained by the rules of civilized society. He would dare whatever he desired.

As he'd said, who would ever know?

Yet, despite the shiver that had trembled through her at the low words uttered with throaty menace, Megan had felt even then that it hadn't been a threat, but rather a demonstration of Shafir's brand of humor. A not-so-funny, rather bleak, very black humor, but humor nonetheless. Megan was still trying to remember every nuance of his expression as he'd uttered the words when a knock sounded on the door.

"One minute," she called, kicking the covers off. She clambered out of bed and pulled a pair of lightweight track pants over her short nightgown before padding over to the door and unlocking it. She then pulled it open a crack to reveal a short, plump woman with friendly eyes.

Relieved, Megan opened the heavily carved door fully.

"Sabah ala-kheir. Good morning. I am Aniya."

This then must be Malik's wife.

Aniya bowed, her head covered by a *hijab,* her hands pressed together in front against a tunic of woven blue fabric. "His Highness sent me to invite you for breakfast."

"So I'm not to be starved."

Aniya looked horrified, her hands coming up to cover her mouth. "Oh, never. His Highness—"

"It was a joke." A bad one perhaps—maybe black humor was contagious. Although she'd always been prone to saying the wrong thing at the wrong time. Foot-in-mouth disease, her family called it. But Aniya certainly looked shocked at the idea of His Highness starving a kidnap victim. And Megan remembered Naema's eagerness to carry out her every wish yesterday.

Could it be possible that the staff didn't know His Highness had abducted her?

"I'm sorry. Tell Prince Shafir I'll be down in ten minutes."

Aniya hovered in the doorway. "Would you like I ask Naema to iron your clothes?"

"No!" At the other woman's crestfallen expression Megan said kindly, "I didn't pack anything that might crease."

"It is the first time that Prince Shafir has brought a

woman here. We are very—" Aniya broke off, clearly searching for the right word "—excited."

Megan gave the other woman a startled look. Did no one think it was peculiar that His Highness had brought a woman to stay who wasn't his fiancée? She shook the thought off. It wasn't her concern. The only thing that mattered to her was correcting the staff's wrong impression about her relationship with Shafir.

She started to assure Aniya, intending to assure her that there was no need for excitement, but then she stopped as dark amusement filled her.

So the staff thought her appearance here was about romance.

It would serve Shafir right if everyone thought she was his love. After what he'd done to her—kidnapping her, terrifying her—the prospect of seeing him writhe with discomfort was too good to miss.

Maybe his prospective bride would find out, too, and have second thoughts about their wedding. Yes, it would serve him right to be dumped! Megan wasn't usually given to vengeance, but his actions yesterday had roused a fiery indignation she'd never experienced before. Besides, the poor woman he was marrying deserved to know she was getting a knight in very tarnished armor.

So Megan smiled, a white, vengeful smile. "I'm so very fortunate."

"Yes." Aniya's features grew animated. "Prince Shafir is so handsome, and so wise."

"Wise?" In Megan's opinion, a man who kidnapped a foreign tourist—a man who happened to be part of the royal family and head of the country's tourism—exhibited little evidence of wisdom.

"Oh, yes. People come from far over the desert to consult with the sheik…and he listens to everyone."

Aniya's version of Shafir certainly didn't mesh with her own. And Megan would take wicked delight in scoring points off him. She wasn't scared of him. She would make him regret kidnapping her and bringing her here to keep her captive against her wishes.

Aniya's voice interrupted her planning. "I will tell His Highness his beautiful guest will be with him soon."

Downstairs, Megan came to an abrupt stop.

Shafir was standing at the edge of a covered balcony that opened off a large dining room to the east of the palace. And he was magnificent, every inch the powerful sheik in a snowy thobe that contrasted with his ebony hair. He hadn't seen her yet. He stood, his hands braced against the stone balustrade, his forearms corded with ridges of muscle as he stared out over the high walls that surrounded the palace gardens he'd told her about, to the unrelenting desert that stretched to the horizon.

Beyond the palms in the garden there were no trees to be seen, no hint of green…nor life.

Hard, brutal terrain.

Already a haze of heat shimmered over the golden expanse.

Megan looked away to where breakfast had been laid out buffet-style on a side table butted against the wall. The loyal Hanif hovered near a tall copper coffeepot, and Aniya appeared at that moment, carrying a platter on which sliced peaches, plump dates and shavings of white cheese were arranged. She set it down on the table between a bowl of creamy yogurt and a basket overflowing with exotic breads.

Shafir turned away from the view at the disturbance and Megan found herself impaled by that fierce gaze.

He took a step toward her, and Megan's nerve almost gave out.

Almost.

She rallied herself. He'd promised not to harm her, hadn't he? A quick glance revealed that Aniya was right behind her. And Hanif was pouring the fragrant coffee into little cups. Good. An audience.

Her lashes fluttered. "Oh, honey, you're already here."

Shafir froze.

Gotcha!

Before she could savor her triumph, he lifted his head like an animal scenting trouble and his metallic eyes glinted. He took another step toward her. Alarm filled Megan and she skittered back.

"Sorry," she mumbled as she bumped into Aniya. But her nerves steadied at the contact. There was safety in numbers, she thought with grim humor.

Shafir prowled closer. "Good morning, Megan Saxon."

Megan searched her memory. *"Sabah ala-kheir."* She dredged up sounds that she hoped resembled the words Aniya had greeted her with earlier.

For a split second something that might have been approval lit his eyes. He inclined his head and Megan relaxed infinitesimally.

"Did you sleep well?"

"What do you think?" she challenged him.

The chair beside her scraped out. He leaned close. Instantly her stomach tightened and butterflies started to flutter.

"Conscience bothering you?" he murmured into her ear.

She stilled, willing herself not to quiver as ripples of sensation rushed down her spine. "What do you mean?"

At this range she could feel the heat of his body, could smell the scent of soap and sandalwood and a hint of some elusive spice that clung to his skin. In her peripheral vision she glimpsed Aniya pressing her hands together, a smile of indulgent delight brightening her round face. No doubt she thought they were whispering sweet nothings to each other.

Keeping her voice low, Megan hissed, "There's nothing wrong with *my* conscience. I'm the victim here. Don't try to make this my fault and blame me for your unspeakable behavior!"

"Be seated."

It was an order. No doubt about that. A reminder of who he was and the power he held here in this vast world. Coming back to reality with a thud, Megan curbed the retort that sprang to her tongue and slid into the chair he held. He'd rue that arrogant tone, she promised herself.

Once he'd seated himself at the head of the table beside her, Megan placed her hand on his arm and said softly, "Could you pass me some juice?"

Muscles tightened under her fingertips. Megan flinched and almost whipped her hand back, but by sheer force of will she kept her fingers still.

Hanif deserted the coffeepot and materialized beside her. "Madam would like orange juice?"

Leaving her hand on Shafir's forearm, she turned her head and gave him a quick smile. "Please."

When Hanif had tended to her, Megan took a sip of the juice before giving Shafir a beaming smile. "I can't wait to meet your family."

His eyes narrowed to chinks of fire, and underneath her fingertips the muscle and sinew tensed again. "Indeed?"

"Oh, yes." She gave a little breathy laugh and hoped it didn't sound as fake to everyone else's ears as it did to her own. "I have so much to tell them."

The man opposite her might have been carved from stone.

Except that his flesh was hot and all too human beneath her fingers.

Daunted, Megan looked away from the unwavering stare—only to meet Aniya's enraptured gaze. From where she was standing the maid wouldn't be able to see Shafir's sphinx-like expression. Aniya looked ecstatic, as if the romance of the decade were being played out in front of her eyes.

Megan's mouth grew dry. Well, she'd taken pains to sow the seeds to create that impression. She couldn't back down now.

Forcing herself to meet Shafir's inscrutable gaze, she said, "I will ask your family what you were like as a little boy." Her lips curved up in a smile to hide the fact that her heart was pounding in her throat. "I'm sure you were a *charming* child."

Once upon a time. Before he became the harsh, arrogant bastard he was now.

The ironic emphasis on *charming* together with the pointed look had conveyed her meaning—though it was quite lost on Aniya, judging from the soft sigh that drifted from behind Megan.

A hand landed on top of her own, trapping her fingers between his palm and the taut skin that covered his arm. The gaze that imprisoned hers was brooding and a flash of awareness bottomed out her stomach.

No!

How could he arouse such feelings in her?

He'd stolen her away in broad daylight, brought her to this desert palace and still hadn't told her what he wanted with her. How could she respond to him like this?

She swallowed.

His eyes followed the movement. "Your throat is dry? Some more juice perhaps?"

"Yes," she croaked, trying surreptitiously to pull her hand free of his. His grip tightened.

He was too strong.

Reluctant to make a scene after she'd gone to so much effort to build this into a misleading tête-à-tête, Megan raised the half-empty glass of fruit juice with her other hand and took a quick sip. The sweetness of freshly squeezed oranges filled her mouth and slid down her grateful throat.

"So you want to meet my family?"

What had possessed her to start this? But darn it, she wasn't letting him intimidate her. The glass hit the table. Thankfully no juice spilled onto the starched white linen tablecloth.

"Yes," she deliberately babbled, "I'd love to meet your brothers, your father…even your mother, to see what kind of woman gave birth to such a man."

His brows jerked together. "You want me to arrange a meeting to satisfy your…curiosity?" Every word fell like a stone into the palpitating silence.

"Why not, honey? Especially since as it looks like I'm here to stay. You're not going to let me go anytime soon, are you?"

Megan could hear Aniya and Hanif adding it all up and coming up with goodness knew what.

Love?

Marriage?

A baby in a pretty pink carriage?

But the absolute lack of emotion in Shafir's expression made her wonder if she'd started something she wouldn't be able to stop. She'd tugged the tiger's tail this time.

And discovered a dangerous beast who didn't appreciate being provoked.

"So how is the babysitting going?"

Shafir had just returned to his father's palace in Katar after hosting the tourism representatives at their final meal before all except the two remaining behind for

Zara's wedding flew out of Dhahara at midnight. The dinner, which had taken place at a fine restaurant in one of the luxury seven-star hotels in the city, had gone well, with all the officials eager to set up ecotourism ventures in Dhahara.

What Shafir didn't need now was his older brother reminding him about the woman he'd tried all day not to think about. He wouldn't have been human if he hadn't wondered what Megan had said at lunch when she'd discovered him gone.

Vixen!

So he slanted a long look at Khalid before saying, "The babe is going to drive me crazy."

Khalid laughed. "We all knew she was a lunatic."

Even his father nodded in agreement from where he relaxed in a leather La-Z-Boy recliner positioned beneath a medley of paintings that included a Botticelli angel and a Picasso clown.

"I'm no longer so sure about that," Shafir said, shedding his suit jacket before dropping down onto the brown leather sofa alongside Khalid.

Crown prince Khalid leaned forward. "Then why is she driving you crazy?"

Pushing his hands through his hair, Shafir said, "I've been thinking that perhaps we couldn't beat the donkey so we beat the saddle instead."

"What makes you think we've missed the real problem?" asked Khalid.

"Megan knew Garnier was having a meeting with a rug merchant just before her plane was due in."

"That's easily explained," said the king with a dismissive wave of his hand. "Jacques says she is a trusted colleague. He must have mentioned it in passing."

The lessons of a lifetime were ingrained, so Shafir didn't argue with his father, but he wasn't convinced.

"And you haven't told us yet what she's doing to drive you crazy," said Khalid.

Shafir refused to admit, even to himself, that the passion that had arced through him this morning had caused him to flee from the palace before he did something he might regret. Like yank Megan into his arms and kiss her until the teasing glimpse in her eyes darkened into the same desire that burned in his soul.

Too many times today images of her seductive smile had flashed through his head at the most inopportune moments, causing him to wonder if he was indeed quietly going insane. Returning to the city was intended to banish her from his thoughts.

But he had absolutely no intention of confessing this to his brother. So he grinned disarmingly and said, "You know how women are."

Of course Rafiq, the romantic, had to choose that moment to return from *majlis,* the evening counsel for citizens. "Ah, so you have noticed she is a woman."

"I'd have to be blind not to notice. No man ever had curves or long hair like that."

But Shafir's biting sarcasm didn't disconcert Rafiq, who chortled. "I did say you should seduce her…make her forget all about Jacques."

If Rafiq only knew. It had been Megan who'd been intent on seducing *him* this morning.

Loosening his tie at the sudden surge of heat that took him by surprise, Shafir unbuttoned the top button of his shirt.

"You shouldn't be here. You need to keep up the pressure if you want the seduction to be effective," Khalid added to the unwanted advice.

"Perhaps it is a good thing for him to be away a while." The king rocked forward onto the edge of his recliner. "Absence might make the heart grow fonder."

Shafir almost laughed. She wouldn't miss him—it was a crazy idea. Megan hated him. And how could he blame her? She was his prisoner. And he'd ensured that escape was impossible.

His too-sexy, too-distracting captive would have to await his return…at his convenience.

"Talking of absence, I haven't seen Zara yet. How are the wedding plans going?" Shafir changed the subject before he got tangled up into a knot he couldn't unravel.

Rafiq grinned. "No problems there. Zara is very much in love."

"And very much oblivious to the trouble this woman tried to cause by coming to Dhahara," added Khalid.

"I want it to stay that way." King Selim fixed his dark gaze on his middle son. "That is understood, Shafir?"

Shafir nodded. "Absolutely." He might be the second son, he might have been given more freedom from duty than Khalid, but he would never disobey an order from the man who was both father and king to him.

Turning his attention back to Rafiq, Shafir asked, "And the bridegroom?"

"What about Jacques?" Rafiq gave him a curious look.

"Is he as eager for the wedding to happen?"

"Why shouldn't he be?"

"He's been a wealthy and eligible bachelor for many years." Shafir raised an eyebrow in a man-to-man way. "You know, perhaps he regrets losing his freedom. Last-minute jitters. Maybe he thinks this matter with Megan Saxon will give him a way out."

"Oh, no." Rafiq shook his head. "He had a lot to say about how very relieved he was that you were taking care of this woman…that the wedding hasn't been jeopardized. He'll take good care of Zara."

"Hmm." Shafir crossed his legs and studied his highly

polished Italian loafers. He'd been poised to give Megan Saxon the benefit of the doubt, planning to corner Jacques and ask him a few questions of his own….

Until this morning.

Because there'd been no mistaking Megan's intentions, except that this time it hadn't been Garnier who was her quarry, but him. It had reinforced that she was nothing but a girl after a good time and a rich man.

The sound of his father asking Rafiq a question about the bridal festivities faded in the background as Shafir recalled the honeyed pitch of Megan's voice—clearly fake—and the silken touch of her fingers against his skin. It had all been carefully orchestrated, but hell, she'd been impossible to resist. The muscles in his thighs had clenched to steel-like rigidity, even though he'd known she was putting it all on.

Though for what purpose, he didn't know.

But her behavior had been the first indication he'd had that the seductress mold his family had cast her in might be correct. And he'd felt a wrenching disappointment because until that point he'd been starting to doubt what he'd been told.

He flicked a glance to Khalid as his brother threw back his head and laughed, his father joining in.

These men were his family and he'd never doubted their wisdom before. The years he'd spent growing up in the desert had underlined the respect warring tribes had for his father.

Yet he'd almost been convinced that his father and brothers had misjudged Megan Saxon.

And why? Because she had spontaneity, a candid way of saying the first thing that came into her head that made her seem so transparently honest.

And a way of arousing his protective instincts so that he'd found himself promising her she would be safe… even from him.

Four

Megan's first reaction to learning that Shafir had departed to tend to business in Katar was euphoria. She had no intention of still being around when he returned, and her initial plan was to commandeer one of the vehicles she'd seen on arrival.

Hanif had smiled when she glibly told him that after lunch she wanted to take a drive into the desert. "The sheik said you might want to go for a drive, but the desert is dangerous. There are many perils for someone not familiar with it, so he said you must not go alone."

Oh, he'd been clever!

"I'll be fine," she said airily. "I won't go far, and if I have a good map I won't get lost."

"The vehicles have GPS systems," Hanif supplied helpfully, "but Prince Shafir was quite clear about ensuring your safety. I will be happy to accompany you on your exploration. And Naema will come along as a chaperone."

Megan gave in. Escape didn't need a tour guide—or a chaperone. "I will await the sheik's return."

Hanif bowed respectfully while Megan seethed quietly. She would have to find another way out.

Her next quest was to locate a computer. Trying her best to look casual and inconspicuous, she sauntered into Shafir's study. A sharp contrast to the rich ambience of rest of the rooms in the palace, this room was clinically tidy. No computers lay conveniently around. And the sight of a power outlet made Megan wish she'd brought her laptop along to Dhahara.

There was no sign of a phone, only an empty jack that indicated he'd cleverly removed it. Yanking open the drawers to his desk revealed nothing more exciting than paper, notebooks and pens, and the mahogany cupboards that ran the length of one wall were all locked.

Megan cursed silently. There *had* to be a phone somewhere in a place this size.

The next day she started to search the palace systematically with no success.

Finally she sneaked into Shafir's bedroom, having put his suite off until last. As she crossed the threshold, Megan was instantly overwhelmed by the stamp of his personality. Feeling like an intruder, she closed the door behind her.

An immense carved bed dominated the space, while rich brocade curtains in deep blues and warm tones of gold framed huge arches that opened onto a secluded balcony. At night there would be a stunning view of the desert stars from the bed.

Megan ripped her gaze away.

Beside the bed a bank of state-of-the-art stereo equipment revealed an unexpected love for music, and a pile of books sat on his bedside table beside a phone.

A phone.

Her heart sang. Despite her curiosity, Megan didn't waste time glancing at the titles on his bed stand. She could already taste her freedom.

Jacques's cell-phone number, securely captured in her phone, was lost to her. Unfortunately she'd never thought to memorize it. But she would call his company—track him down and ask him to come and get her. Then, with her escape route in place, she would call her parents and fill them in on the horrible situation she'd landed in.

But her exhilaration was short-lived.

Although the directory operator was able to give her a number for Garnier International, she discovered a toll call block prevented her from using it. Once again Shafir had anticipated her.

The trapped feeling closed around her again.

It appeared she was doomed to stay.

It took the sight of Naema talking into a cell phone the following day to jerk Megan out of her despondency.

She hadn't even thought of asking the staff if she could borrow a cell phone. Shafir had said there were no cell phone towers and no reception here in the desert and she'd never questioned it.

Damn him.

"Can I borrow your phone?"

"Sure." Naema smiled, but she looked puzzled. "There is not very much credit left."

Just her luck. But it was better than nothing.

A few steps took her out of Naema's earshot. A call to Garnier International in Paris got her Jacques's office number. And that landed her a frosty personal assistant who refused to divulge his cell-phone number, despite Megan's pleas—and her hasty invention of a meeting with Jacques the next day.

Naema looked increasingly curious with every passing moment. Megan lowered her voice further.

At last the PA agreed to get a message to Jacques.

"Staying with Prince Shafir at Qasr Al-Ward—please fetch me urgently," Megan dictated.

The PA sounded even frostier, and Megan was quite sure she'd been dismissed as a total loon. To top it all, as she was in the midst of telling the PA how critical the message was, the cell phone's credit ran out.

"I'm sorry," she said to Naema. "I'll give you money for another card." All was not lost. She'd simply call again once Naema had funded her phone card again.

"Malik will bring me a card when he returns from Katar. He always does," said Naema.

"Malik? The sheik's chauffeur?"

"Yes, he's with Prince Shafir."

"That's the only way to get a card?"

Naema nodded.

Megan eyed the useless cell phone. "Does Aniya have a phone?"

The young woman laughed. "Oh, no. She says she is too old for such a toy. And Hanif refuses to use them—he's superstitious."

Megan thought of the pools, the gardens, the many rooms in the palace that would need maintenance. But she'd only seen Aniya, Hanif and Naema over the past few days. The wide-as-a-barn-door bodyguard must have gone with Shafir. "Does any one else stay here?"

Naema shook her head. "Only Malik and the sheik's personal guards. He's been talking of bringing a new man to help Hanif, but Prince Shafir likes peace."

"What about the gardens? The pools? Who looks after them?"

"There are cleaners and workmen who come—they will be here again at the end of the week."

And that would be too late for her. Shafir would have long returned by then.

Megan waited, but Jacques never arrived to rescue her. His icy PA had probably tossed the message in the trash the instant she'd set the phone down.

To burn off her frustration she had explored the palace, the walled orchard and a hidden garden with its masses of fragrant blooms. Yesterday she had lounged beside a mosaic-tiled pool that was surrounded by high walls shrouded in creepers heavy with exotic blooms. Yet, despite the beauty, despite being waited on hand and foot in the height of luxury, the feeling of being caged had intensified.

Not that she could reveal it.

The first sign of pacing had elicited smug smiles from Aniya and waggling eyebrows from Hanif. It hadn't taken Megan long to realize that they assumed her restlessness stemmed from the fact that she must be missing His Highness. She'd given them a sickly smile—which they'd interpreted as lovesick.

At least, any residual fear at being kidnapped had long since vanished, along with His Highness's disappearance. Now, as Megan strode back to the palace, her body cooled by a late afternoon swim, she was just plain mad at Shafir's desertion.

Yet underneath her simmering anger lay a nagging anxiety that wouldn't abate.

Back in New Zealand her family would be worrying about her, their concern increasing with each passing day. They would have expected her to call and let them know she'd arrived safely—what must they be thinking? One of these days they'd expect her home, and when she didn't arrive, her mother would be going out of her mind with worry.

It was all *his* fault.

And what about Jacques? It was obvious that the message she'd left with his PA hadn't gotten to him. In which case he'd be worried sick, too. She cursed the icy woman.

About to mount the steps, Megan paused. Or had her message gotten through? Had Jacques contacted Shafir and been fed a bunch of lies? She didn't know. And that was driving her crazy, too.

And in the meantime she was trapped in a deception of her own creation. Shc had to keep up the pretense that she'd started: that she was totally besotted with His Royal Highness.

To Shafir's immense disgust, his strategic retreat to Katar had failed to achieve its objective. He still hadn't managed to dislodge Megan from his mind.

Each evening, along with his brothers, he attended *majlis*—the counsel where citizens sought the help of the royal family—in the great rooms that opened off the entrance to the king's palace. He'd hoped fervently that listening to the problems of others would take his mind off his own.

It didn't.

When a citizen reported that his brother had taken his television without permission and broken it, Shafir thought of Megan's rage after he'd seized her cell phone. Thief, she'd called him. The fate of Megan's phone weighed heavily on his conscience.

Then a villager who had traveled a whole day to Katar for an audience told of how his betrothed had run off with a neighbor. The man confessed to wanting to kill the man who'd stolen her, and Shafir thought instantly of Megan, whom he'd taken against her will and angered in doing so.

Yet he could not condone murder. He counseled the

man out of taking such a path, pointing out that it would not be worth risking his freedom—even his life—for vengeance. Better to let the woman go.

Yet the knowledge that he would not be following his own advice and freeing Megan, that her anger would increase day by day, caused an unfamiliar emotion to flare in his chest. He was not accustomed to feeling guilt or shame.

Even as the last petitioner finished, he had no respite because Zara and her mother swept in with Jacques trailing in their wake. Zara's normally tranquil expression was marred by faint worry lines around her eyes, and even the debonair Jacques looked a little rattled.

Was he wondering what Shafir had done with Megan?

Enough! Shafir blocked out all thoughts of his vixen.

As Zara and her mother, an Australian who had fallen in love with Shafir's now-deceased uncle, each embraced the king, Jacques edged toward the tables that had been used for *majlis.* Shafir studied the Frenchman from beneath lowered eyelids.

"I hope you don't have a problem." Shafir glanced meaningfully toward Zara. "If it is a problem of the heart, we should call Rafiq. He is an expert on such matters."

"Oh, no, no. Nothing like that." Jacques grinned, his teeth even, but the laughter did not reach his eyes. He turned to Khalid. "I understand that I owe you my humble thanks for relieving me from a terrible situation."

Khalid said, "You owe Shafir. The king told us you've been having trouble with this Saxon woman for a while."

"Oh, yes!" An emphatic nod.

Shafir pounced. "Why didn't you tell us sooner?"

Jacques stilled. A beat of time passed, and then he spread his hands. "I didn't want it to come out. I was worried about Zara." He flicked a glance to where his fiancée was still conversing with the king.

Had it been another man Shafir might have suspected the groom didn't want to lose his wealthy bride. But this was Jacques Garnier, son of Pierre Garnier and heir to a fortune. And supposedly in love with Zara.

"You should have trusted us," Khalid scolded. "We wouldn't have told Zara anything that would distress her. My father adores her. He would never allow her to be upset."

The Frenchman shifted his feet and his gaze moved from Khalid to Shafir.

"Perhaps I should have told you, but to be frank it's so—" Jacques looked uncomfortable "—humiliating to be pursued by a woman to this extent."

Humiliating?

Shafir thought of Megan, of her bright sparkling eyes, of the softness of her derriere when she'd landed in his lap in the limousine. "I don't know about that," he objected. "I think any man would be wildly flattered to be pursued by such a desirable woman."

An odd expression flitted across Garnier's face. "You think so?"

"Oh, yes," said Shafir, driven by demons he couldn't name. "When she lays her hand over yours her skin is like silk, her voice drops…" He let his voice trail away.

Both Khalid and Jacques were staring at him. Jacques stuttered, "She has done this?"

Shafir allowed a slow smile to curve his mouth as if recalling a memory of intense sensual pleasure. "She has indeed."

Jacques looked positively displeased—and not nearly as relieved as Shafir would have expected, given his protests.

"But then it is to be expected." Shafir tossed the bomb into the sudden electric silence.

"What do you mean?"

"It is her modus operandi, is it not? She has simply

transferred her unwelcome attentions from you to me." Shafir leaned back, stretching his arms above him, every bit the satisfied male. "I have become the target of her obsession."

He smiled. A tiger's smile.

And waited.

Khalid looked stunned, while Jacques stared at him, bug-eyed.

After the silence had stretched to breaking point, Shafir said with all the pretence of civility, "It is good that I am keeping her otherwise occupied. It will allow you to be married without any interference from a woman who humiliates with her passion for you, *n'est ce pas?*"

"You are, of course, correct," Jacques said stiffly.

Shafir widened his smile further. "Good. Then we are all satisfied."

"Your Highness."

Megan swayed toward him, and Shafir froze.

The journey back to Qasr Al-Ward had passed in record time—he'd promised Malik a bonus—and with every mile his anticipation at seeing her again had increased tenfold.

But this greeting surpassed even his fantasies. He couldn't help staring at her like a hungry, oversexed boy. She wore a dress that covered her arms and fell to her ankles in the most exquisite rich turquoise, which brought out raven-blue highlights in her hair. Her sloe-shaped eyes were outlined with kohl, giving her a sultry sensuality that stopped his heart.

And when her hands landed on his shoulders, he stiffened as the essence of her surrounded him.

Soft. Scented. All woman.

He hauled in a deep breath and inhaled more of her. A pulse started to pound, resounding through his head…his chest…his groin.

"Megan," he acknowledged, surprised that he still sounded coherent.

"Shafir, I…*we* are pleased you have returned." Her fingers trailed along his sleeve, and the gaze that met his was limpid.

Some inkling of sanity, of self-preservation, remained. What the hell was she playing at?

Her lashes sank, dark crescents against her fine translucent skin. He glanced around. Hanif was smiling indulgently, while Aniya wore the same expression she did when she watched the soap operas she adored. A twinge of foreboding filled Shafir as he turned his attention back to Megan.

Her lashes flicked up. Shafir's stomach, already tightened by the dangerous game she was playing, clenched further as the slanted gaze collided with his.

"You have kept yourself busy?" Some imp of the devil caused him to needle her, to remind her that he'd been so confident of keeping her under his control that he hadn't even bothered to advise her he was leaving.

But she didn't react. Instead she said, "I have only one longing." Her fingers walked up the arm of his white thobe, leaving a trail of fire in their wake.

At the wistful tone Shafir found himself conjuring up X-rated images of what Megan's longings might be…and a terrifying desire to fulfil every one of them in slow motion.

In the privacy of his bedroom.

Certainly not while Hanif and Aniya looked on, enthralled at the drama being played out. And it *was* a masterful performance. He must not forget that.

His brows jerked together and he dragged his gaze away from the seductress, fixing it on Hanif. "I'd like coffee please…and for Ms. Saxon, too."

"Of course, Your Highness." Hanif bowed respectfully and retreated, as loyal and obedient as ever.

So why did he get the feeling he'd lost control of his staff?

"I have a yen to find out more about your longings," he told Megan, aware only she would hear the threat of retribution behind his words. He could've sworn he heard Aniya sigh. But when he glanced over his shoulder she was already trudging down the long corridor.

Manacling Megan's impudent finger-walking hand in his, Shafir led her to the small salon and closed the door firmly behind them. "What do you want?"

With grim amusement he watched as she tugged her arm free and scooted three quick steps back. Not so confident without an audience then.

"I'd like to use a phone."

Was there no end to the woman's effrontery? "You want to use a phone?"

She nodded, her eyes wide.

Good, she was starting to realize there would be a price to pay for her provocation. "That's your deepest longing?"

She nodded.

"You disappoint me." He stretched forward and touched her cheek. "I thought your deepest longing might have something to do with this." As his thumb stroked down her cheek and across her lips she gasped, the warmth of her breath misting his skin.

"Or this." He ran his thumb across the soft flesh of her bottom lip.

Her breath caught.

"Or perhaps this." Bending forward, he replaced his thumb with his tongue and slid it over the moist tissue of her inner lip. For a moment she softened at the bold intimacy, her lips parting, and then he felt her body stiffen.

"No!" Two hands came up and pushed hard at his chest. "I don't want that at all… I want a phone."

He resisted her shove. "To call your French lover."

"If you mean Jacques—" she gave him a quick glance

from under long, dark lashes "—then yes. He will be worried."

Shafir thought of Jacques as he'd last seen him, his arm resting around Zara's shoulders. "You think so?"

"Of course. Wouldn't you be if the light of your life disappeared?"

Taking a step back, Shafir said softly, "You are the light of Jacques's life?"

"Yes." But she looked away.

"You assured me you weren't his girlfriend, that he wouldn't pay ransom for you because you meant nothing to him."

"I lied. I am his girlfriend."

Was she lying now? Or had she lied in the past? Either way, he now had proof that she couldn't be trusted. So what else had she lied about?

Jacques had always maintained she'd come onto him. Could it be true after all? Was his family right? Was this bright, sparkling woman nothing more than a manipulative female out to grab a wealthy man, even if it screwed up Zara's life in the process?

Shafir rubbed his hand over his jaw and wondered if Megan had any idea that Zara's name meant light. Or if she even cared that Jacques was the light of Zara's life.

Suddenly he was tired of it all.

To hell with it.

Coming to a decision, he walked across the room and extracted the hi-tech satellite phone from his briefcase. Let her call Jacques. Then he'd see for himself who was telling the truth. Megan or Jacques…or both of them.

He handed her the phone and watched her eyes widen in astonishment. "Call then…see if he comes running."

"Thank God he will come. Not every man is quite the savage you are."

That lit his fuse. "Perhaps if I whistled, you would come," he said softly.

"In your dreams."

"No, *honey*—" he used the endearment she'd flung at him "—it would be both our dreams."

Her eyes sizzled with sheer, consuming rage. Her passion burned him. But he ignored it, his arm extended as he offered her the satellite handset. "It's different from a cell phone—better in the patchy reception in the desert. You'll need to stand by the window or it won't work."

After a second she snatched the phone from his hand, her fingers brushing his, the brief contact causing heat to flare hot and uncontrolled within him.

It startled him, this raw, unrestrained response to her. He wasn't a boy anymore. He'd had more lovers than he could remember, and he'd learned about pleasure from women who treated lovemaking as an art, practiced to perfection... yet he couldn't remember when last a simple, accidental touch had roused so much awareness.

By the time he came back to the present she was already talking, her back to him as she faced the wide panes of glass.

"Mum? I just wanted to let you know that I'm in Dhahara."

He stared at the back of Megan's head in disbelief. She was talking to her mother!

She hadn't called Jacques at all.

Megan's free hand was waving as she talked...telling her mother about the shade of gold the dawn turned the desert sands, making mundane enquiries about her father, the weather, the harvest. All things that mattered in the fabric of life.

Then every muscle in his body tensed in disbelief as she said, "Love you, too, Mum. Can I talk to Alyssa now?"

Her sister-in-law. The journalist. Shafir stalked forward and grabbed the phone out of her hand, clicking the off switch. "Oh, no, you don't!"

Five

"You can't do that!" Megan swung around and glared at him. "My mother will worry herself to death."

"You'd already said your farewells. She'll assume it's a connection problem." Shafir waved her concerns away with a dismissive hand, and the gesture caused his thobe to swirl around him.

"She's expecting me home soon."

"You told her you're still in Dhahara. You're a grown woman. She'll assume you'll contact her when you're ready to leave."

Megan sucked her cheeks in and counted to ten. He had an answer for everything. And dammit, he sounded so reasonable.

"Your Highness, dinner is served." Aniya's singsong voice interrupted Megan's intention of telling him exactly what she thought of him and his high-handed, unbelievably arrogant behavior.

"I'm not hungry." The last thing she felt like right now was food.

Especially if it meant sharing a room with *him.*

Shafir raised an eyebrow in an infuriatingly arrogant manner. "And add credence to the rumor that I starve you?"

Aniya must have told him what she'd said. "So your staff spies for you?"

"Amongst other things. I pay them well." His teeth flashed. "Aniya even acts the jailer on my request."

He was laughing at her, damn him.

Yet the thought of the plump, kind Aniya being a jailer made even Megan's lips twitch. And the sight of Aniya's anxious expression made her surrender. "Okay, I'll join you for dinner."

Aniya's expression eased then broke into a smile when Megan cast what she hoped could be construed as an adoring look in Shafir's direction. But she was only doing it because she didn't want the kind, motherly woman to be upset, Megan told herself. Aniya had probably spent hours preparing the food.

Megan tripped behind Shafir to where a table was laid for two in an alcove tucked cozily under a deep Moorish arch.

Wooden latticed casements had been flung open to let in the evening air, and from up here Megan could see the magnificent gardens she'd spent the past few days exploring. From the perfume garden, the rich scent of gardenia mingled with jasmine wafted upward, along with other exotic fragrances that she couldn't identify.

A manservant, not Hanif—a younger man, who must've returned from the city with Shafir—padded in and placed a hand-painted steaming dish alongside smaller dishes of assorted vegetables. Despite claiming not to be hungry, her stomach gave a plaintive grumble.

Then the young man retreated in even greater silence, leaving Megan and Shafir alone.

It was a departure from the previous nights when Megan had been seated in the great dining hall and tended to by Aniya and Hanif, who had leapt to serve her every time she lifted a hand. She had all but begged them to leave her in peace. After her own riotous family—who gabbled incessantly at mealtimes while poor Ivy, the family housekeeper, tried to keep everyone in line—all the expectant silence and hovering attention had been a bit much. But her pleas had fallen on deaf ears.

Now, contrarily, she wished for their presence.

But at least their absense freed her from the pretense that she'd begun. There was no need to flirt with Shafir… and watch his eyes narrow alarmingly as she touched him.

Shafir passed her a dish, breaking into her thoughts.

"What is that?"

"*Bamia,* a stew of baby okra and lamb in a tomato base."

"Sounds delicious." Megan served herself and started to dig in and found that it was. The okra was tender and there was a hint of coriander, too.

"This is *fattoush.*"

She glanced at the mix of chopped cucumber, tomato and shredded mint topped with golden toasted croutons that he offered. "Yes, I had it last night."

"I am surprised Aniya prepared it again so soon."

"I told Hanif I liked it." It touched her that his staff had gone to the trouble of preparing a dish for which she had expressed appreciation.

"Oh." He examined her.

How she wished she could read the thoughts behind Shafir's narrowed bronze gaze. Would he appreciate Aniya and Hanif's consideration for his guest? Or would he berate them for trying to make her comfortable?

That led her back to the question that had dominated her thoughts while he was gone. "Don't you think it's time you told me why you're keeping me here?"

He gazed at her without blinking.

She gave an impatient sigh and set down her fork. "Oh, come on, Shafir, this has gone on too long now. Don't I deserve to know?"

More silence.

Finally Megan threw up her hands. "Don't answer, then. I'll talk…tell you what I think. I had a lot of spare time to puzzle on it while you were gone."

Shafir had stopped eating, so at least she had his undivided attention.

"You don't intend to harm me."

"What has convinced you of that?"

Megan lifted her eyes to the ceiling. "Praise be to Allah, His Highness speaks."

"Don't blaspheme." But his mouth had softened and she could swear there was a twinkle in his eyes.

"Your staff convinced me. Aniya, Naema and Hanif treat me with great respect," she elaborated. "They behave as though I'm an honored guest in a five-star hotel, granting my every whim."

He inclined his head. "I am pleased to hear you have been satisfactorily looked after."

"That's just the point."

"You haven't been well looked after?"

"No, not that." Megan glared at him in exasperation. Thanks to her machinations, his staff thought her a very special female "friend" of the sheik's.

It made her wonder about the woman Shafir was supposed to be marrying. The woman who would link him by marriage to Jacques.

Over the past few days Megan had come to the conclusion that the marriage had to be an arranged one, since his staff had clearly never met—perhaps didn't even know about the existence of—his fiancée.

Which meant Shafir couldn't possibly love her.

And that was a tragedy in the making.

"What are you thinking?"

Megan blinked. "Nothing."

She couldn't possibly admit she'd been thinking how awful it would be for him to be trapped in a loveless relationship. It probably wouldn't worry him—he could marry as many wives as he wanted, couldn't he? And why was she wasting her emotions fretting about his love life anyway? It wasn't as if he was a friend, or someone she cared about.

Dragging her mind back to the important issue, she said, "The only explanation that makes sense is that you kidnapped me to extort ransom from Jacques."

"That makes sense?" His mouth slanted. "I'm a member of the royal household, and the royal coffers have plenty of gold. Why would I need to ransom you?"

His mockery irked her. "It makes perfect sense if you need money but your family doesn't know that."

The twist to his mouth flattened. Her theory hadn't pleased him. She could see that in those very unamused eyes.

She decided to nudge him a little more. "Maybe you have a habit you need money for."

"A habit?"

She nodded. "Not the garment, like a nun wears," she explained, the ridiculous picture of Shafir in a black habit making her suppress a smile. "It means something you do that has become a problem. Do you gamble? Are you in debt?"

"I know what a habit is. I can't believe—"

"What? That someone found out the truth? Is that why you disappeared for the past few days? To gamble 24/7?"

The look he blasted at her was just plain furious. Uh-oh.

Maybe she should've kept her mouth shut. Maybe he was a drug addict. Or an arms dealer.

She shivered.

"I do not need money. Understand?"

She nodded, rapidly, and didn't say a word.

Keep your mouth shut, Megan, she told herself.

But that didn't seem to appease him, either.

He glowered at her. "So?"

So? What did he mean *so?* She hesitated. "Could I have some of that, please?" She pointed to a bowl containing *muhammar,* a mixture of sweet rice and dates.

For a moment his eyes smoldered. Then he shook his head. "You accuse me of…" Words seemed to desert him. "And now you want more food?"

He pressed his lips together as if he were fighting an unexpected urge to laugh, and his eyes turned to a bright burnished bronze.

"Please."

Megan felt a lot better. He wasn't angry anymore. He hadn't even flung in her face her initial stand that she wasn't hungry. And suddenly she was quite, quite sure that Shafir would never harm her.

And that he wasn't an arms dealer or a gunrunner, either.

He might be hard, but she'd stake her life on it that he was honorable. He couldn't possibly make money out of human misery.

After that Megan relaxed. It was easy to ask him about the kind of music he enjoyed, to talk about the latest novels they'd read, and from there the conversation shifted to a photographic exhibition they'd both seen. When he talked his eyes glowed and he forgot to be reserved and arrogant, and he gestured with his beautiful hands to make a point.

He fascinated her.

He was such a complex mix of seemingly irreconcilable

opposites. The desert sheik, the man who could wear a designer suit with panache yet seemed much happier wearing traditional robes—which Megan had to concede suited him to perfection.

By the time Hanif arrived with a copper pot and small cups to serve coffee, Megan was replete…and strangely content. For once she didn't manufacture an opportunity to flirtatiously brush his hand and act the lover. She simply relaxed.

"Oh, I couldn't eat another thing," she protested after Hanif had gone and Shafir held out a bowl filled with slices of halva.

"Try it. It's delicious."

"I know." She gave the sweet a longing look. "But I'm too full."

He picked a small piece up in his fingers and popped it into his mouth. "Mmm…"

She watched, wishing she hadn't declined. He must've read her thoughts because he picked up another piece and lifted it to her lips. "One taste."

Megan suppressed a moan. She opened her mouth and the halva melted against her tongue.

His eyes held hers as she savored the sweet taste, the crumbly texture. She saw his pupils darken and his whole body stilled.

"That was delicious." She strove for matter-of-factness but the words sounded husky…and far too sexy.

Sexy? Oh, God.

She closed her eyes in despair. What was she doing?

"Would you like to join me for a walk in the gardens?"

Her eyes shot open. Why was he asking? Did he think she'd be more…susceptible to seduction out in the dusk?

Then she mentally shook herself. They were alone in an intimate alcove yet he hadn't tried anything. Even though he must've read…whatever in her eyes while she'd eaten that damned halva.

"Yes." Suddenly desperate to get out of the cozy, confined space, Megan pushed her chair back and stood.

Once they'd stepped outside into the golden glow of the evening, Megan found she could breathe again.

A serene stillness settled like gossamer silk around them. Overhead the sky was shaded in hues of deep rose, fading to amber beyond the high stone walls where the last fingers of sunlight beckoned.

"It's beautiful." Megan sighed. "It makes one forget how harsh the desert can be."

"And how dangerous to the unwary."

Megan shot him a quick look. Was that a warning? His harsh features could have been hewn out of the same rock from which the palace had been built. No hint of softness, as harsh and dangerous as the land that surrounded the high walls.

Wrenching her gaze away, Megan walked forward into a walled garden where honeysuckle spilled down the walls, giving the evening air an exotic, pungent scent. She'd spent many hours in here, reading and thinking, while he'd been gone.

"Not all of it is like that." She stopped beside a fountain where water bubbled, the spray moistening her skin, blissful in the dry heat. "There's no danger or harshness here."

"I would've thought that you'd considered this particular garden the cruelest and harshest place of all."

"What do you mean?"

There was a peculiar expression in his eyes. "It's walled for a reason."

"What reason?" Even as she asked a sinking sensation dropped through the pit of her stomach.

"It was to this palace that my ancestors brought the women they had captured."

"Sex slaves?"

He cocked his head. "And this walled perfume garden and the adjoining orchard—"

"—Was part of the harem!"

She'd spent so much time here. If she'd imagined…

"How did you guess?"

"The walls," she said simply. "And the fact that I could wander here when so many other areas I could see from upstairs are closed off and clearly off-limits."

"The best parts are in the harem, though—like the Garden of Pools that's been there for hundreds of years."

"The Palace of Roses…shouldn't it be called the Pleasure Palace?"

"That is exactly what it was originally."

Her stomach turned. "And the women? The ones your ancestors kept imprisoned here? What happened to them?"

"Many of them lived long and happy lives."

"I don't believe it!"

He shrugged. "There are journals that survived. One or two have been translated into English if you care to read them."

"No." She recoiled.

"Strange." He pinned her with the gaze she'd once considered so fierce. "I hadn't realized you were narrow-minded."

"I am not narrow-minded." She forced the words through tight lips until his gaze dropped to her mouth and studied it with careful deliberation.

Instantly prickles of bewildering sensation filled her.

"Then why do you withdraw when you have the chance to discover more?"

Was that what she was doing? Megan examined her reactions. He hadn't threatened her. Their surroundings were gorgeous, and he could have left her in ignorance. Yet he'd chosen to tell her the truth about their origins.

She wasn't one of those poor women. That was in the past. She was very much her own woman. Strong. Determined. Independent. And reading about the lives those long-dead women had led would be interesting. It certainly couldn't threaten her.

"I'm sure the women were brainwashed," she retorted with a shrug. "But you can send a book up with Naema later if you like. I might read it."

He nodded and hooded that penetrating gaze.

To her annoyance Megan felt cheated. Cheated that he hadn't reacted with smug glee to her concession, that he hadn't insisted she must read the memoir she'd said he could send up. If he'd done either it would have been easy to dismiss him as a controlling jerk.

Instead he led her away from the fountain and stopped beneath an ancient, wizened tree with a thick, knotted trunk. "Legend has it that this olive tree was brought to Dhahara by Phoenician traders."

"That would make it…" Megan tried to calculate the age of the tree.

"Over 1,500 years old."

"Goodness." She stared at the tree. "Has it been carbon-tested…or whatever they do to work out the age of a tree?"

He shook his head. "No. We've spoken about it, but my grandmother told me her mother never wanted the legend debunked." He spread his hands. "And what does it matter how old the tree turns out to be? It's the idea that matters—that it has survived here in this place through centuries and watched untold generations come and go."

"That's amazing."

"There are other more amazing stories about the gardens, too," Shafir said as he led her past a row of almond trees, crowned with pretty pink-and-white blossoms.

"They're a work of art. Who started them?"

"One of my ancestors, King Aziz, for his new wife. It is said that she was Persian and she missed the lushly planted terraces, the hanging gardens, where she'd grown up."

"So this was all done for one woman?"

"Yes." He led her deep into the heart of the perfumed garden. "Tell me what you see."

"Rosebushes. Lots of them."

"What kind of roses?"

Walking around the nearest bush with its crimson roses, Megan studied it carefully. The throats of the roses were a dark, rich pink while the outer edges of the petals were the deepest red. The blooms on the next bush were identical. A sweet scent hung in the air, and in the stillness of the dusk she could still hear the hum of bees.

"It's not a trick question. Just tell me what you see."

"All the roses look the same to me."

"Exactly." Shafir gave her a satisfied smile that turned her stomach to liquid. "They're all descendants of the original bush that was brought by the bride, Farrin, when she traveled from Persia to Dhahara to marry King Aziz. This was his favorite palace. He spent most of his life in the surrounding desert. He used to take his new wife with him on his trips out to the nomadic tribes, and when they returned he would help her to design, expand and plant a new piece of garden."

"Qasr Al-Ward. The Palace of Roses, you said on the first day. And these must be the roses for which it is named."

Shafir nodded and leaned forward to pick a bloom. Straightening, he held it out to her. "Smell."

She took it from him and sniffed deeply. "It's glorious."

"The sight and scent of the rose reminded Farrin of

home. But it was also a symbol of love and commitment… a pledge of what she felt for the man she'd given up her family and homeland for."

"Yes, but she wouldn't have had much choice. Surely it was an arranged marriage?"

"That is true. But sometimes such marriages are best."

An alien ache settled in the vicinity of her heart. Would Shafir grow to love his wife?

Megan raised an eyebrow at him. "Did he feel the same way about Farrin as she did about him?"

Shafir's gaze was fixed on the rose she held. "Oh, yes," he said softly. "He wrote that she was the wife of his desert heart. She was his *ain*—the spring that feeds the desert."

The words stroked her like a soft, warm wind and Megan quivered. "That's so romantic."

"Sometimes there is just pure beauty."

"And no harsh and terrible cruelty?"

"Exactly."

"I suppose he died soon after she arrived…or she died in childbirth? Such stories always seem to have a bitter-sweet ending."

A gleam of appreciation lit his eyes. "No, they both lived long and happy lives."

"While she shared him with all the occupants of the harem." Megan gestured to the space around them.

"It is said that one woman gave him the pleasure thousands could not. She was the woman who made him forsake all others."

"Now that is impressive."

Shafir's lips curved up. "Finally you're impressed."

There was a charged silence as her eyes held his. "Will you be able to do that?"

"Forsake all women for one?"

"Yes."

"The day I marry, my wife will know she is the only one." There was an intensity in his gaze. "And you? Could you forsake all men for only one, Megan?"

She paused before responding, unable to prevent a flutter of envy for his bride. Then she said, "If I loved him enough, yes—with ease."

"Have you ever loved enough?"

Megan wanted to laugh dismissively, to tell him to mind his own darn business. But she couldn't bring herself to break the invisible bond between them.

"Well?"

"I'm thinking." No one came close. She thought about her brothers. None of them would hesitate for a moment. They'd all found that forsake-all-others kind of love. But she hadn't.

Not yet.

Jacques…

The moment seemed wrong to think of Jacques, of her determination to fall in love with him. Yet he'd seemed so right. He was courteous; he strove so hard to please her. And, like her, his family was devoted to their vineyards. It should've been the perfect match.

But confronted by Shafir's question she wondered whether loving Jacques would ever be enough.

"And?"

Megan gave a sigh. "No, I haven't found that person yet."

She slid her gaze to him. He was fierce and uncompromising. A savage. A desert sheik. A kidnapper. She should have had nothing in common with him.

But beneath all the differences dividing them lay a thread of empathy that united them…and that bewildered her.

Which made her hugely curious about the woman he was engaged to. Megan had spent the evening with him, talking about everything under the sun, yet not once had he mentioned his impending marriage.

"Where will this marriage take place?"

Darkness had fallen like a velvet cloak over them. Megan could smell orange blossoms and an unidentifiable exotic fragrance that was growing stronger. The desert air whispered against her bare arms as she waited for him to say something, anything, that would break the tension that expanded within her until she could barely breathe.

And he felt it, too.

It was there in the way the last glimmer of light shifted in his bronze eyes, the way he held himself very, very upright.

"Well?" She echoed his earlier comment. But it came out breathy rather than slightly mocking as she'd intended.

"All the marriages of the royal family are solemnized in Katar." Then he moved sleekly, like the big dangerous cats he so often reminded her of, his body solid and compact.

She backed up, but branches of an orange tree stopped her from retreating farther. Something in his eyes warned her of his intention. "I don't think—"

"Don't think." His head came closer. There was a split second where she knew she could have stopped him if she'd wanted to. But she didn't.

And he kissed her.

It was incredibly erotic. His mouth moved on hers and heat streaked through her. Lust. Or was it desire? She'd just started to kiss him back when he lifted his head.

The emotions that swirled through her then were even more confusing. She hadn't wanted him to stop. She'd loved the headlong rush of excitement.

As his head descended a second time her heart thudded in her throat. His warm breath whispered against her lips, and Megan knew he was about to kiss her again.

One hand cupped the back of her head, holding her in

place. The other stroked down her back until it paused at the indent at the base of her spine. He pressed her closer.

Megan moaned as his hard body imprinted itself on hers, the silk of her long dress forming a thin veil to the heat of his body under the thobe. She craved the kiss that was coming.

But it was wrong.

And as their lips connected, her guilt won out.

Shuddering, she put two hands against his chest and shoved him back. Hard. Then she ripped herself out of his arms, out of the tangled hold of the orange tree. "How could you do that?"

"Do what?"

"Kiss me!" An anger fueled by disappointment, betrayal, by a torrent of complex emotions she couldn't identify ripped through her. A burning, scalding anger.

It was then that Megan realized why she was so mad. It was either that or cry, dammit.

And she refused to cry. Not because of him. And certainly not in front of him.

"What's wrong?"

She was going to hit him. "You're such a chauvinist. You don't even know that?"

How could she ever have kissed such a jerk back?

He stared at her as if she'd gone crazy. Maybe she had. What other explanation was there for kissing him back?

"Why are you so upset?"

"You can ask that?" She wiped the back of her hand across her eyes and glared at him, wishing she'd denied she was upset. That implied this mattered.

"You never shed a tear when you discovered I had no intention of taking you to your city hotel—not even when you were terrified. So, yes, of course I'm asking."

"You kissed me!"

"So?"

He appeared gloriously unconcerned by her accusation. Megan wanted to murder him. If one of those scimitars had been handy, he wouldn't have stood a chance. "You shouldn't have."

"Why not? We both wanted it."

She didn't dare touch the second part of his statement, confining herself to, "I don't mess around with other women's men, so since you're getting married that makes you pretty much off-limits. And I don't care if it's an arranged match."

As the long silence stretched out Megan found herself getting more and more worked up.

She despised herself for participating in that kiss. She'd never done anything like that before. Thankfully she didn't know his wretched fiancée, otherwise she'd feel even worse—if that were possible. Though she'd like to be able to tell the unsuspecting woman what a skunk he was and save her from a life of misery.

Finally he said, "I'm getting *what?*"

"Married. To your bride. The woman you should be forsaking all others for—even before your marriage is solemnized in Katar."

"Shouldn't I know about this marriage?"

"Oh, please. You're saying you don't know you're getting married?"

He shook his head. "Who told you this?"

"You did." Now she did feel as if she'd lost her mind.

"*I* did?" He stared. "When exactly did I say such a thing?"

"You told me that…" She searched her memory for the exact words. "You said you and Jacques will be family soon. By marriage."

He gave her a very strange look. "So you believed that meant I was getting married?"

"Well, yes, of course. What else could you have meant?"

"I was speaking of Jacques's marriage," he said very quietly into the stillness of the night.

Six

"Jacques?"

Standing dead still in the middle of the garden surrounded by the tantalizing scent of orange and almond blossoms, Shafir watched her struggle to put it all together.

"*My* Jacques?" she said at last.

A wave of sheer masculine possessiveness swept him. "Not your Jacques," he bit out, reeling from the edgy resentment. "Garnier is to marry *my* cousin, Zara."

She looked shaken.

I don't mess around with other women's men, so since you're getting married, that makes you off-limits. The implication of that was that Megan hadn't known Garnier was engaged when she came to Dhahara, that she hadn't come to cold-bloodedly wreck the wedding. He badly wanted to believe that she bore Zara no malice. But he couldn't afford to be wrong, not with Zara's happiness at stake. How could he blacken Jacques in Zara's eyes until he was certain

Megan was telling the truth? This might simply be another very accomplished piece of acting designed to take him in.

"Jacques can't—" She broke off.

Then her head came up and her eyes glinted with some emotion he could not read in the dimness. "Why should I believe a word you say, Shafir? Your behavior up till now has hardly been exemplary." But her voice was thin.

In the half light he saw the movement as her hands came up and brushed her hair back off her face. A spray of white blossoms stood out against her midnight hair. He reached out to remove the trapped blooms, but she flinched away and the twig fell to the ground.

"Jacques wouldn't do this to me." Her hands dropped to her sides and curled into fists.

If this was an act, it was a damn good one. He squashed the urge to take those hands, to hold and rub them until they relaxed. Her shock had to be real…or she deserved a solid-gold Oscar. Yet he couldn't set aside his lingering doubts, based on her falsely loving behavior when he'd arrived home—a performance his staff had lapped up. By Allah, he almost had, too.

No, this, too, had to be an act. Shafir couldn't stop his lip curling as he said, "You know Garnier so well that you can predict what he would or wouldn't do?" It came out with an edge.

Her eyes glittered in the darkness of the desert night. "I know that Jacques is a gentleman. He would never steal—or kidnap a woman."

Anger rose quickly at the personal attack. "I'll tell you what I think. I think you saw Jacques Garnier as a great opportunity to land yourself a wealthy man."

"That's rubbish! Jacques and I had something special. He was courting me."

Shafir forced himself to calm down, to think through

what she was telling him. It wasn't true, of course… What was he missing?

"Courting you?" Shafir started to shake his head in denial. But even as he did another possibility struck him. Perhaps it was not an act at all. Perhaps Megan had misinterpreted Jacques's gallant manner and good manners to mean something more and had built a romantic dream from a few flowery phrases. He gave a short laugh. "You've misinterpreted his intentions."

"Don't patronize me! I know when a man is interested in me. I don't need your opinions. You're nothing but a savage."

Shafir's eyes narrowed dangerously. It was a look that anyone who knew him well would have taken as a warning. Even under the cover of darkness Megan seemed to realize that she'd said too much, for she instantly said, "I've had enough. I want to go to my room."

He grabbed her arm as she swung away. "I have not dismissed you yet."

"I don't need your permission to leave." Her voice was tight with displeasure.

"Yes, you do." She had riled him. He would have to watch that. He could not allow her to weaken him in any way. He pulled her to him. Her feet trampled the spray of orange blossoms that had fallen and a burst of incongruous sweetness filled the air.

Shafir dug into the pocket of his robe, searching for his satellite phone, then held it out to her. In a softer, no less lethal tone he added, "Here, call Jacques."

Had he been a betting man, Shafir would've put money on it that Garnier was not going to be pleased to hear from Megan. He considered the woman a menace.

She snatched the phone out of his hand, then hesitated.

"I don't know his number by rote—and you threw away my phone."

With a growl of impatience, Shafir took back his phone and located the number before handing it back.

Turning away from him, Megan bent over the backlit keypad before hitting the dial button.

"Jacques? Listen, I need your help."

There was silence. Every muscle in Shafir's body went taut as he waited.

After a long tense moment she thrust the phone at him and walked rapidly away. It appeared she really had believed that Garnier had been courting her. But that belief was clearly false and founded on a womanly need for love. Shafir watched her go, troubled by the notion that for Megan something priceless had just been destroyed.

In the breaking dawn Megan stood on the quaint balcony of her bedroom, her hands gripping the intricately carved railing as she stared blindly over the palace gardens as the first light from the east bathed them in a rosy glow.

How could she have gotten it so wrong?

Last night Jacques had been desperate to get off the phone and had told her never to call him again. It was obvious he'd answered only because he'd thought it was His Highness Prince Shafir al Dhahara calling, his fiancée's cousin. If he'd known it was her, she realized, he would've ignored her call.

As he must have ignored the message of distress she'd left for him days ago.

Despair filled her.

Oh, she'd come to Dhahara with such high hopes….

Jacques had seemed so right in every way. With his laughing green eyes and floppy hair, he was handsome in a dashing kind of way. He'd made her laugh…and his grand romantic gestures had threatened to sweep her off her feet. The bouquet of a hundred long-stemmed red roses, the huge box of Godiva chocolates, the crystal flagon of perfume. Sure, the sweet, drenching scent had been too overpowering, but she'd appreciated it. Only Jacques could have gotten away with such extravagant clichés. Somehow it made him even more endearing to her.

He'd made her feel so special.

So womanly and delicate, something that a female growing up with three brothers on a vineyard rarely felt. Femininity hadn't been a valued trait. Growing up, her brothers had preferred that she could ride and swim with them, and catch a cricket ball without dropping it, and survive an overzealous rugby tackle without dissolving into tears.

And, to be truthful, it wasn't just the over-the-top gifts, or even the fact that Jacques had seemed perfect. She'd been ready to fall headlong into love. Back home, her brothers had been falling like flies…looking starry-eyed and happy. And she'd wanted her turn, too.

Blowing out a hard breath, she admitted to herself that maybe she'd been in too much of a rush to love. Like an overripe peach, she'd been waiting for Jacques to come along and consume her.

Never again.

She'd reached that decision during the long hours of wakefulness through the night.

It was too humiliating.

She hadn't even realized that Jacques had been toying with her, though in hindsight all the signs had been there.

Sometimes his voice had lowered while they were talking. She'd thought it was sexy, but now she realized he hadn't wanted to be overheard. Not so sexy at all. The rat!

Often he hadn't been available to take her calls. She'd put that down to the fact that he was busy…a committed businessman, a wealthy high-profile entrepreneur. She'd been dazzled by his success, his suave good looks, his sexy talk.

How dumb could a woman get?

While she'd been hoping to find love, Jacques had been after a last fling before getting married. No wonder he hadn't been keen on her insistence on Dhahara as a holiday destination. No wonder he had wanted to stay as deep in the desert as possible.

Romance had nothing to do with it. He'd been leery of Zara's family uncovering the sordid truth.

They knew part of it. But thanks to Jacques they thought the worst of her. A gold digger, after a wealthy man.

How awful.

She heard a door close in the bedchamber behind her, and her hands tightened on the wooden railing. She didn't need to turn to know who had just entered her suite. And it wasn't Naema.

She didn't even wonder what he was doing here at this unspeakable time of the morning. She hadn't slept a wink last night—she'd been too upset, too ashamed by her bad judgment.

Stiffening, Megan waited for him to accuse her of further stupidity.

"See those palms?"

Relieved that she'd been granted a reprieve, Megan's eyes followed the path of his graceful hand to where a row of palms led to an arch set in a wall. Through the arch she glimpsed sunbeams reflecting off the surface of the largest pool, transforming it to a sheet of pure gold.

"I see them."

"They were planted by my father when he was a boy."

"King Selim planted them?" She knew she sounded disbelieving. "With his own hands?"

"He had some help, but he did a large part of the work himself."

Shafir moved up beside her and leaned forward to rest his elbows on the railing. The fresh scents of soap, sandalwood and that elusive spice were all too familiar. A sideways glance revealed that he wore a track suit, his feet bare and his hair damp. He must've come straight from a shower. The dawn light turned his skin to a warm bronze and added a sheen to his cheekbones. His amazing eyes were fiercely alive.

Megan looked away.

"My grandmother was a great believer in the power of gardens."

Tilting her face toward the rising sun, she said, "That's not surprising, given what you told me about your ancestor's Persian bride."

At the edge of her vision, she saw movement as Shafir nodded, and the bleak dull pain beneath her breast started to ease.

"She said the art of tending the gardens is a part of our heritage. She believed that they gave us spaces of stillness where we could reflect, that they brought great pleasure to life and that every child should experience the satisfaction of designing and building a piece of garden art."

She glanced at him again, a quick furtive look. "Did you build one?"

"Yes, a palmerie. It lies to the east of the palace."

"I haven't seen it."

"It's not part of the women's gardens."

The idea of that fierce segregation worried her. Her brows drew together. "So I'll never be allowed to see it then?"

"I will take you."

"You will?" She turned her head and stared at him in disbelief. Why would he grant her anything when he must despise her dreadfully. Damn Jacques!

"I will."

At his response, hope surged in her. "When?"

Perhaps time spent with him would give her a chance to show him the real Megan Saxon.

The side of his mouth kicked up. "You are always full of questions. What? Why? When? You need to learn patience."

For the first time since last night she felt her spirits lift. "Now you sound like my mother."

He looked intrigued. "Tell me about her."

"She's very elegant. Cultured. And she loves us all to death. The past year has been very hard for her—for all of us."

He didn't prompt her and Megan found herself wanting to tell him about it all. Perhaps then he might understand why she'd yearned for love and happiness.

"My brother died—Roland was killed in a car accident. Then we—that's me and my brothers Joshua and Heath—found out that my parents had adopted Roland before we were born."

"It was a shock?"

"Well, yes. It felt like a betrayal."

Shafir fell silent for a moment. In the distance the dark shapes of crows circled in the pale sky.

"I can understand that. I would have felt the same way."

"It was so hard to understand why they'd never told us. Mum said at first they thought we were all too young to deal with it, and later it became too hard to tell Roland. She was afraid it would've made him an outsider in his own family."

"I can understand that, too."

"But we loved him. It didn't matter that he was adopted. He was still our brother."

His hand closed over her fists where they clenched the railing. "Then you are fortunate to have shared his life for so many years."

The warmth from his fingers seeped into her skin.

"Yes, we were." What Shafir said was true. She was incredibly lucky to have grown up with Roland…and the rest of her tight-knit family. "But it was a difficult time. Before we'd had time to grieve for my brother, Rafaelo arrived."

"Rafaelo?" There was an odd note in his voice. "You met a man?"

Shafir lifted his hand away and she was conscious of a nagging sense of loss.

"No, no, nothing like that. Rafaelo is my father's illegitimate son, conceived not long after my parents adopted Roland. To make it worse, my mother knew nothing about his existence—or my father's affair. Nor did we."

He raised a dark, finely arched eyebrow. "That must have been another shock."

A breath of warm desert wind caught at her hair and Megan brushed the inky tendrils off her face. With a sense of shame she remembered the hostile reception they'd given Rafaelo. Megan was conscious of telling Shafir stuff she never shared. She wasn't normally given to confessing her life story to strangers. Yet oddly Shafir no longer seemed to be a stranger. And nor did she want him to continue to hold the impression that he already held. "I don't expect that you would understand how awful it was for us."

"Why shouldn't I?" His brows jerked together.

"Having half-brothers is a normal part of your society. There isn't the same expectation of fidelity of a married man."

"Only about seven percent of Dhaharans take a second wife." Shafir's bronze gaze was unrelenting. "But even then there is an expectation of honesty. Each wife knows where she stands in her husband's life. The number-one wife has more power than any other—and under Dhaharan law she must consent to her husband's taking a new wife before the wedding takes place, otherwise the marriage is void. And she would certainly know when one of her husband's other wives was pregnant."

"I would never agree to my husband marrying a second wife. I can't understand any woman putting herself in a position where such a thing might happen." Megan found such acceptance of a second wife impossible to understand.

Shafir lifted a shoulder and dropped it in a shrug. "The old ways are changing. Many modern Dhaharan women stipulate in a prenuptial agreement that their husband may not take another wife, and that they do not wish to reside with their in-laws. That is their right."

"They'd be silly not to do so." Megan considered him. "My mother thought she'd married Dad for better or worse, and she was shattered by the discovery of Dad's deception. For a while we all thought she was going to divorce him. She went to stay with her family. After a while she came back. Dad missed her terribly. And she forgave him."

Shafir held her gaze. "Your mother must love your father to forgive him. And if he loves her, he must regret his actions."

"He does! And he's doing everything he can to make it up to her." Megan couldn't bring herself to break the bond by looking away. A familiar frisson of awareness quivered through her. "But I could never forgive a man for that kind of betrayal. I hate Jacques."

It spilled out of her.

She clapped a hand over her mouth and drew a shuddering breath. "I didn't mean to say that. You're too easy to confide in."

He made a dismissive gesture with his hand. "I was taught to listen. And I never tell."

"Taught to listen?"

"It is part of our role as royalty. Every evening there

is *majlis*—people come from far and wide to tell us of their problems."

"I thought I knew him."

For a moment the abrupt change of subject confused Shafir. Then he realized Megan was talking about Jacques. He gave her a pitying look.

Her shoulders drooped. "I credited him with qualities he never had."

There was disillusionment in her voice and an air of dejection about her—the slump of her body, the hopelessness that flickered for a moment in her eyes. Shafir suppressed the first flare of doubt. Jacques couldn't have—would never have—double-crossed Zara. His fervent avowals of love aside, there was too much riding on the merger the wedding would bring—connections, increased wealth and trading opportunities. No man would risk such riches for an affair.

But having heard of her family's suffering, he couldn't help the wave of sympathy that swept him.

Averting his gaze from her, he stared over the desert, noticing that the group of crows had grown in size.

Did Megan still believe Jacques would be the man to make her forsake all others?

His gut tightened, and he came to a decision.

Swiveling on his heel, he placed his hands on her shoulders and drew her to face him. "I'm sorry."

Her eyes sparkled with the gloss of unshed tears. "Are you? Really sorry? I'm sorry," she parroted, "but I don't believe you."

Her bitterness knifed him. Shafir wanted to see the sparkle of joy back in her eyes. "I am very sorry that you feel you were deceived."

She made a sound of disgust. "I *was* deceived."

"I will accept that you didn't know Jacques was getting married."

"Gee, that's big of you."

He ignored that and continued, "But you read too much into a male business colleague's good manners, and you misinterpreted his intentions." Shafir gave a careless shrug. "It happens to men all the time."

Megan looked as though she was about to explode. Words appeared to fail her. Then he thought he heard the word *"arrogant"* and *"chauvinist"* but the rest disappeared in a hiss as her teeth snapped shut.

"We will agree to disagree about this," he said hastily.

"I suppose I misinterpreted the fact that you kidnapped me, too?" Megan glared at him, her hair gleaming as the sunlight danced across the black silk. "Is this the reason you abducted me? Because you thought that I knew about your cousin's wedding? Because you thought I'd come to Dhahara to stop it?"

What the devil was he supposed to say? He couldn't deny that. Shafir lifted his hand from her upper arm and cupped the soft skin of her cheek. "Megan, you must understand that—"

"Oh, I understand," Megan interrupted, her tone growing acid. "I understand that Jacques is a bastard."

Shafir blinked.

"As for you, Your Royal Highness, you're not much better." She slid out of his arms and sidled along the balcony.

"Hey, wait a minute—"

"You scared me nearly to death. Then you left me here to cool my heels—"

"In absolute luxury, with servants at your beck and call."

"I am not finished!"

Her back had straightened, and the dejection in her eyes had vanished. Fury and indignation came off her in waves, scorching Shafir.

"You never bothered to tell me what crime I'd been accused of. If I'd known what Jacques was like, I would've gladly left him for your cousin. Gift-wrapped, if she'd been dumb enough to still want him once she'd learned that he'd been two-timing both of us."

Shafir didn't bother to correct her that Jacques had done nothing wrong—the mistake had all been on her side.

Choosing his words carefully, he said, "I didn't tell you because in the beginning I didn't think it would make any difference." And once he'd taken her from the airport against her will, it had been too late to tell her—or to let her go. The papers would've been all over the story just as she'd threatened, and that would have wrecked the wedding anyway.

Tipping her head to one side, she scrutinized him through the slanting eyes that drove him wild. "Wouldn't make any difference? You thought that even if you told me, I wouldn't care? That I was after Jacques because he was rich? Because I'm the stereotypical little gold digger?"

His expression must've given him away, because she gave a derogatory laugh. "Now why doesn't that surprise me?"

"Megan—"

"You are rude, overbearing and incredibly arrogant. Do not interrupt me until I am finished," she warned as he started to protest. "You are every bit as much of a bastard as Jacques. You have no honor—"

That was too much. No one had ever dared make such accusations. Shafir descended on her. She continued to berate him, too far gone to realize that she'd gone past the boundaries that he would tolerate.

"Enough," he growled, his hands closing over her shoulders.

She was so soft. He eased his hold, but not his intent. Pulling her into his arms he slanted his mouth across hers, shutting off the tide of turbulent words.

He kissed her with hunger.

After a moment of stiff surprise, her lips softened and she kissed him back. She tasted sweet…so sweet.

She whimpered, a soft keening sound in the back of her throat.

Want overwhelmed him.

His hands trembled as they stroked along her back, finding the furrow of her spine under her wrap. He caressed the subtle valley, the firm flesh tempting him to touch more.

Silk bunched beneath his fingers as he cupped her buttocks and lifted her onto her tiptoes. The cradle of her hips rocked against his thighs, and desire exploded through him.

At last he lifted his head. "I should not have done that."

Shafir knew he should not be taking advantage of her while she was so vulnerable, so sure that she'd been betrayed by Garnier. But it was difficult to let her go, to step away from her and put the distance between them that his heart told him he needed to give her.

She was breathing fast, but the glazed look vanished quickly. "You're right. You should not."

Her tongue tip flicked over her bottom lip, moistening the soft pad of flesh.

He groaned at the provocative gesture. "How am I supposed to resist you?"

Lifting her easily, he strode through the doors off the balcony into the bedchamber, to the ancient, carved bed. He let her slide slowly down his body, aware of every delectable inch of her womanly body.

But instead of subsiding onto the bed behind her, Megan struggled out of his arms. "No, I don't want this. I don't even want to be here."

"After kissing me like you'd discovered paradise, where else would you like to be?"

"I want to go home."

* * *

"You want me to take you back to Jacques?" Shafir shook his head as if to clear it of confusion. "Even though you believe he two-timed you and know he is about to marry another woman?"

Megan stared at him in disappointment. Clearly he'd thought by kissing her he'd silence her into submission. No chance.

"If I never see bloody Jacques again this side of eternity, that would be too soon." She brushed her hair back from her face with shaking hands.

"Then…" Hc took a step forward.

Dropping her hands, she scrambled away from him. "Stay away from me!"

She didn't want him kissing her again. Despite her bravado, she had to admit his kisses caused her head to spin. And they made her crave all sorts of things she'd never considered—how much she wanted to kiss him and see where it would lead. How could she have mistaken the liking she felt for Jacques for passion? And how could any man, however courtly, ever be more desirable than this savage sheik?

Ah, hell.

"I never want to see you again, either. Or anyone else from this blighted country." She flung the words at him from the opposite side of the four-poster bed to prevent herself from caving in and letting him take her all the way to paradise. "I want to go home."

Edging around the giant bed, she glanced desperately toward the door.

And in case there should be any further misunderstanding, she held his gaze and said as firmly as she could manage, "I want to go home to New Zealand, back to my family."

Shafir didn't react. He just stood there looking unmoved by her plea.

She drew a ragged breath. "No need to worry that I'm a threat to Jacques's wedding to your cousin. I don't want him." But to her horror he was already shaking his head. "You can't refuse!"

"You can't go home yet."

Tears of frustration and thwarted rage thickened her throat. In a tight, hoarse voice, she said, "*Why?* You have no reason to imprison me any longer."

"Oh, yes, I do."

"What do you mean?"

"If I let you go home, you will tell your family that you were kidnapped—"

"So?" He was dreaming if he thought she was going to agree to say nothing. "Last time I heard, freedom of speech still existed—or doesn't Dhahara go in for that?"

"My country is very enlightened."

Megan couldn't help herself—she laughed. All the empathy she'd felt with him not so long ago evaporated. He was back to being the hard-assed, arrogant jerk she hated. "Sure," she scoffed. "And you're a very liberated man."

"It is for this reason that I cannot let you go."

Megan laughed more loudly and hoped he didn't hear the edge of hysteria that underpinned it. "Because I have a great sense of humor? Or because I'm not afraid to stand up and tell you what you are? A kidnapper, a thief and a liar."

She heard the breath he sucked in.

Good! Let him count to ten for a change.

"Because you have a sister-in-law who is a journalist."

"You should have thought of the likely fallout that would happen before kidnapping me. People deserve to know what you did. You might be a member of the royal family, you might control the tourism ministry in Dhahara, but your actions are inexcusable." Immediately after her outburst Megan wished, for once in her life, that she'd kept her overzealous mouth shut. Why, oh, why had she allowed him to push her buttons? Now he had even less reason to let her go.

For the first time in days apprehension quaked through her. She was in a remote region, far from help, and under his absolute control. She'd convinced herself he wasn't going to hurt her…but when would he let her go? Or did he plan to keep her incarcerated indefinitely?

At last she voiced her fear. "What if I promise never to say anything? Then will you release me?"

"Yes, I will let you go—after the wedding."

Relief surged through her. He didn't intend to lock her up and throw away the key. Then caution kicked in. "How long away is that?"

"Two weeks."

"Two weeks?"

Her relief evaporated. Right now fourteen days of living in proximity with Shafir seemed like a life sentence. In the bright morning light she scanned his face. The chinks of bronze, the bladed nose and the chiseled mouth that had not so long ago kissed her with such passion. She dared not let herself even think about that.

She couldn't stay. He was too dangerous to her peace of mind. "Please Shafir, let me go."

He shook his head, his eyes filled with an emotion akin to regret. "Not until Zara is married. Nothing is going to derail the wedding."

A wave of frustration swept through her at his utter intransigence. She wished she had the courage to yell at him and beat her fists against the wall of his chest. Instead she said, "I can't believe you'd let a rat like Jacques marry the cousin you must dearly love."

Seven

I can't believe you'd let a rat like Jacques marry the cousin you must dearly love.

Megan's parting words nagged at the edges of Shafir's mind as he strode through the palmerie he'd planted years ago. He told himself they were the angry words of an angry woman who believed she'd been scorned. The words held no truth. Right now Megan was intent on getting back at Jacques.

She'd do whatever she could to convince Shafir to call off the wedding.

And Shafir had no intention of being manipulated just because of a kiss that had offered him a glimpse of heaven.

He stopped abruptly, staring unseeingly at palm trees and rocks that had been landscaped to look wild and natural. Yet he couldn't forget the feel of her skin under the filmy wrap she'd worn, or the curves of her body as she'd arched against him….

He shook off the memory.

It had been over too damn quickly.

But it wouldn't change his mind. Megan had misread her business relationship with Jacques and misconstrued his courtesy. Zara and Jacques would get married as planned. It would be a good union, with benefits to both families, and leading to improved trade opportunities for the Garnier corporation and increased distribution channels for Dhahara's exports. Being a Garnier would catapult Zara into the top echelons of European society, a world where she would thrive.

He certainly wasn't about to be swayed by a lush, womanly body—or even by a bewildered expression and a pair of hurt eyes.

Yet Shafir couldn't deny that Megan's desperation to go home made him feel curiously guilty. Her unhappiness was a marked contrast to the sexy, seductive woman who had welcomed him back from Katar. And, despite now knowing that the flirtatious looks and soft touches had all been an act aimed at putting him in an uncomfortable position with his imagined fiancée, he was male enough to want that desirable woman back.

He tipped his head back and stared at the clear blue sky.

Nor did he like the notion that Megan viewed him with the same contempt and dislike that she now felt toward Jacques. She'd branded them both with the same harsh label. He didn't care for that at all.

And Dhahara didn't deserve to be dismissed as a blighted country.

He was sure that once Megan had a chance to reflect, she would realize that she'd been unfair to Jacques. But he suspected he'd have to work harder to change her low opinion of himself. She considered him a thief and a kidnapper. It would take some work to convince her he was not the ruthless bastard she believed him to be. And that Dhahara was the most special place in the world.

And he had only fourteen days in which to change her mind.

"There is another reason I can't let you go," Shafir told Megan later that day when they encountered each other in the small salon.

Still enraged by his assumption that she'd misread Jacques's very clear intentions, Megan had retreated inside to get out of the sweltering late afternoon heat and had been hoping for a quiet cup of mint tea to help her calm down. Now she hesitated on the threshold at the sight of Shafir ensconced in an armchair reading a newspaper.

"Oh, and why is that?" She'd successfully avoided him all day. Now she entered the room with reluctance.

"I want to change your mind."

Megan raised her eyebrows. "You think you can change my opinion about you?"

Folding the newspaper and dropping it on the floor beside him, Shafir said, "I don't care that you think I'm a bastard, a thief or a liar."

Yet Megan noticed that his fist curled into his lap. Clearly her opinion had rankled.

"But I want the chance to give you a better impression of Dhahara, of its people," he continued.

So he hadn't appreciated her dismissal, her reference to his homeland as a blighted place.

"I don't think you can." She perched herself on the edge of the sofa nearest the door, the better to make a quick escape. "The perceptions I have of Dhahara are not good. It would take dynamite to change them."

"But you love the palace and gardens."

"That's true," she conceded. "And the stories you told me about your ancestors were fascinating, too."

"It's not all the people of Dhahara you detest—you're fond of Aniya and Naema. I've seen the way you talk to them."

"That is true, too." She drew a deep breath. "You know, it's weird. I really wanted to visit Dhahara. Ever since I first heard that Jacques had business with the kingdom I've been fascinated. Coming here was a supposed to be the fulfilment of a fantasy."

"It can still be," said Shafir.

But Megan was shaking her head. "It's too late. I'm no longer the same person I was when I arrived in Dhahara. I've given up on the fantasy."

Stretching folded arms above his head, Shafir admired the picture she made with her dark hair and eyes against the deep red sofa before saying, "So you still believe this nonsense that Jacques was trying to seduce you?"

Her chin came up a notch. "It's not nonsense. And I never said he was trying to seduce me—he convinced me that it was possible for us to fall in love with each other."

Shafir clicked his tongue dismissively. "Women fall in love at the inflection of a man's voice, at the sight of a handsome face."

"Not me."

Something tightened in Shafir's chest at the idea of Megan falling for Jacques. "So you can prove this?"

"Prove it?" Megan's puzzled gaze met his.

Shafir forced himself not to be drawn into the dark, sultry depths. "Prove that Jacques was pursuing you."

She leaned forward. "Oh, yes. He sent me roses and chocolate. And there's the fact that I wanted to stay in a hotel in the medina of Katar—but Jacques thought the desert might be more romantic."

"Jacques made accommodation bookings?"

Megan slowly shook her head. "No, I did. I booked a night in Katar and for the rest of my time here I booked a remote villa in the desert." She made a sound of disgust. "Obviously Jacques was afraid of being seen with me in the capital."

Shafir ignored the last. "The chocolates and flowers are gone, and Jacques never made the booking. So you have no proof of these things you accuse Jacques of?"

"There was my cell phone—I'd kept the texts he'd sent. But, of course, you got rid of that."

"How convenient for you."

Her eyes took on a militant glint. "Are you accusing me of lying? Of making up stories about Jacques? Why would I do that?"

He considered that. Then dismissed it. He was quite sure that Megan wasn't a liar. But she was a woman. And women were prone to flights of fancy—especially where love was concerned. Perhaps Jacques had sent her flowers and chocolates. Nothing wrong with that. Why, he's sent those to staff and colleagues, too. In appreciation. Or as a marketing strategy. In which case, Megan had misconstrued a gesture that meant nothing more than "Thank you." "You told me yourself you came to Dhahara seeking adventure, excitement and romance."

"Because of Jacques."

Impatience rose in him. Clearly she was still determined to make Jacques out to be a villain. The truth of the matter was that she had simply misconstrued Jacques's behavior as a result of a typically feminine desire to be loved.

"Jacques was nothing more than a work colleague. The romance is all in your own mind. There's not a shred of evidence that Jacques did anything wrong."

* * *

"There is something I want to show you today, Megan."

They had finished breakfast. Megan had eaten in silence, not once lifting her eyes to meet his. Knowing it was her way of conveying her displeasure, Shafir remained unruffled. The day was clear, promising to be dry and hot. He rose to his feet, impatient to be gone before the real heat set in. "Put on something comfortable—sweats or jeans."

Megan remained seated, but her lashes flicked up to reveal expressionless eyes. "Is this part of your campaign to change my mind about Dhahara?"

He only smiled.

Although Shafir had claimed he didn't care what she thought about him, he knew he did. Now he examined the short-sleeved T-shirt she wore. "Don't forget to wear a long-sleeved shirt for the sun." He didn't want that exquisite creamy skin burned.

Finally she pushed back her chair and asked, "Where are we going?"

At least she hadn't refused to come. "You will see."

When he met Megan at the door to the courtyard twenty minutes later, jeans peeked out from under the loose abaya he'd sent up, and he could see the collar of a white shirt at her neckline and white cuffs jutting out where the robe fell back to expose her lower arms.

"Are we going riding?" she asked.

"There's a village not far from here, with an *ain.* A spring," he clarified. "I thought you might enjoy a camel ride."

Excitement lit up her face. "A camel ride. That would be—" The excitement dimmed as she broke off.

She was still angry at him for speaking the truth yesterday, Shafir realized.

But she would come around. Sooner or later she would have to admit that he was right.

* * *

The *ain* was surrounded by clumps of leafy tamarisk and carob trees that guarded the entrance to the village. The scent of wild mint filled the air as the camels lumbered under the branches. After being exposed to the hot sun in the desert, Megan found the cool greenness a welcome relief.

Ahead, Shafir pulled his camel to a halt and Megan came up beside him.

"Legend has it that this is where my ancestor brought his Farrin to drink from the healing water of this spring. The village is named *Ain Farrin* after the spring and his Persian bride."

Megan forgot that she'd meant to be silent and reserved to remind Shafir of her ire at his arrogant dismissal of her grievances against Jacques. Bursting into speech, she asked, "Did they build the well, too?" She pointed to the stone structure that looked like it had stood there for a long time.

He shook his head. "That is the labor of later generations. It still operates."

He'd barely finished when a gaggle of children came running, drawn like magnets to the visitors. Shafir grinned and waved. The group grew bigger and louder as they proceeded into the heart of the village. Megan couldn't help thinking they must look like a Pied Piper procession.

She was laughing by the time the camels sank down and they finally dismounted.

Several of men came to embrace Shafir, and back-slappings and greetings were exchanged. He drew Megan forward and the babble subsided. "Come," he said, "Ahmed and Mona have invited us to their home for a cup of coffee."

He led her to where a couple waited.

Deep laugh lines were carved into Ahmed's face under the checked black-and-white *ghutrah* he wore on his head.

He gently drew the woman who had been waiting beside him forward. "This is my wife, Mona."

There was pride in his voice, and Mona gave him a secret little smile that revealed their love without a word.

Their home was a simple dwelling constructed of blocks of stone and baked earth. Inside, it was spotless. The kitchen was dominated by an open-fire oven set in one wall. There were several trays of dough already in the oven and the warm smell of baking filled the room.

Megan was soon sipping *gahwa,* the strong bitter coffee that left a tang in her mouth. Mona produced triangles of baklava that melted on her tongue. Ahmed had cornered Shafir and the two men sat with their heads together, as Ahmed fired off what was clearly a string of questions.

"I'm sorry," Mona said to Megan. "My husband is rude talking in our language. But he can't resist the chance to get the sheik's view on the new school we are building."

Not for the first time Megan wished she could speak a smattering of Arabic, and she mentioned that to Mona. Mona instantly offered to teach her what she could, and the next half hour passed in gales of laughter that drew smiles of indulgence from both men.

A young girl carrying a tray with balls of dough entered the house and Mona took the tray from her, exchanging a few words in Arabic. And this time Megan understood a few of the pleasantries and thank-yous that followed.

"Ahmed is the village baker," Shafir murmured to Megan as they departed. "People bring the breads they have prepared and he bakes them."

"Oh."

"I'm sorry that I left you to your own devices."

She gave him a smile and watched as his concern for her eased from his eyes. "No need to apologize, Mona is very sweet, and I understand that Ahmed wanted your advice on a matter that is important to the community."

Shafir hoped that the day had given Megan fresh insight into Dhahara. On the ride back, her face was thoughtful, and, despite that fact that she must be sore from the camel's uncomfortable gait, she made no complaint. The coolness that she'd exhibited at the start of the day had evaporated, and he was glad. He resolved not to be drawn into any discussions about Jacques; it only created unpleasant tension between them.

Back at the palace they dismounted and Megan stroked the nose of her camel.

"Thank you."

The camel harrumphed.

Shafir couldn't help it—he laughed at the expression on her face.

Megan glanced over and poked a pink tongue out at him. "The nose is so soft. Like velvet." She stroked again and Shafir felt his smile start to slip. He wished her hands were stroking him like that.

"Did you enjoy the ride?" he asked abruptly.

"Oh, yes." Her face lit up. "I loved the desert…it's so wide and open. I've never felt anything like it. The *ain* was such a contrast, so cool and green. And Mona and Ahmed were so welcoming."

Shafir hesitated. "I heard you tell Mona that you would like to learn to speak Arabic. Is that true?"

She frowned at him. "Of course it was true. Why should I lie about something like that?"

"Perhaps you were being polite."

She fell silent. Then she said, "I want to learn. It's frustrating not being able to follow the conversation around me."

"It won't be easy," he warned.

"I know." She lifted her chin. "But I think I'll catch on quickly. I speak tolerable French and I found that easy to learn."

Jacques. A flare of emotion dangerously akin to envy spread through Shafir. Had she learned to speak French to impress her business connection?

"Arabic is not French," he growled, relinquishing the reins of his camel to a groom and following her up the stairs that led to the palace. "It is far more complex and has nuances it can take years to understand."

She stopped at the top of the stairway. "Hey, I don't intend to get a doctorate in the language. I only want to gain some insight into the people and the land during the time that I am here."

He pounced on that. "So you will not fight me with demands to go home?"

There was astonishment as her eyes met his. "Yes, I want to stay. I had a wonderful day. I hope that the next thirteen days will be as good."

Pleasure warmed Shafir. "I am pleased," he said simply.

"That's what you intended, wasn't it?" Awareness dawned in her slanted eyes. "You're incredibly sneaky." But she was smiling and there was no barb to the words.

Shafir grinned back. "I will have to make sure that every day is better than the day before. You are generous to give Dhahara a chance." But what he really meant was that she'd given him another chance. A chance to prove he wasn't the criminal jerk she considered him to be.

"Put like that, how can I possibly refuse? If I do, I lose the quality of generosity."

"If you leave and go home you will never know what you missed out on."

A shadow crossed her face. "I've already missed out on what I came for."

She was talking about romance…excitement… adventure. His gut tightened. "Sometimes what you think you want is not what you really need," he said enigmatically.

"That sounds like a riddle."

"Perhaps it is." To him Megan was the most complex riddle of them all. One that he was trying his best to figure out and understand. Not once today had she shown any flighty feminine traits. Not once had she misconstrued anything anyone had said. So why had she been so desperate to fall for Jacques?

The next few days passed in a whirl of activity. Megan had to admit that Shafir was doing a marvelous job at showing her a side of Dhahara she would never have discovered on her own and making sure that each day surpassed the one before.

As long as she didn't discuss Jacques and stayed away from contentious topics like Jacques chasing her while he was engaged to Zara—which Shafir simply refused to accept—or her belief that Shafir should put a stop to the wedding, they got along just fine.

For a royal prince, he'd proved to be an enthusiastic guide. Penance, she decided. He was doing penance for the wrong he'd done by bringing her here against her will.

The souk they'd visited that day had been an eye-opener. Located at the crossroads of two ancient desert routes, the stalls had been crammed together and people seemed to have come from all corners of the earth to sell their goods. There were caftans, carpets, baskets, jewelry and even goats for sale.

From the instant she'd stepped out of the vehicle, Megan was astounded by the explosion of color. Red. Turquoise.

Gold. Ochre. While the backdrop of the bleached gold of the desert made her reach for her sunglasses.

Then she became aware of the babble of noise. Slowly it separated into discernable sounds. The croaking of three black crows perched on a railing nearby. The *mah-mah* of goats bleating. Vendors chanting to attract buyers.

There were big bins full of spices. A jumble of rugs, copper pots, porcelain and fabrics in all the colors of the rainbow filled the stalls.

Megan hurried forward and touched the brightly hued silks with reverent fingers. "These are beautiful," she murmured as Shafir came up behind her.

A merchant appeared from nowhere and almost bowed to the ground when he recognized his illustrious visitor.

"Look at this." She drew a bolt of deep-pink silk off the rail. "The color, it's amazing."

She held it up against herself. A breath of mischievous wind blew off the headscarf she'd tied in a makeshift *hijab* around her hair.

Shafir's breath caught in his throat.

"It suits you." Against her windswept dark hair and pale skin the color glowed like a rich jewel, throwing her coloring into sharp relief. With the slope of her eyes, she looked exotic. Beautiful. Infinitely desirable. Shafir felt heat stir in his groin.

"We will take it." He shot a glance at the merchant, knowing it was folly to announce his intention before the barter started. But to his surprise the merchant was shaking his head.

"A gift. It is an honor to supply a garment for your lady."

Megan cast a quick glance at Shafir before turning to bestow a dazzling smile on the merchant. "Thank you. I'll treasure it always."

"The pleasure belongs to me." The merchant bowed to Shafir. "You have chosen well, Your Highness."

Shafir wanted to explain. Then he decided it was better to keep silent. News traveled with the speed of a sandstorm in the desert. Yet right now he couldn't even define their relationship himself, and he certainly didn't want the entire population of Dhahara speculating about it.

"I want to buy some things for my brothers…my sisters-in-law." Her face alight, she darted in and out between the stalls, her enthusiasm boundless.

Shafir didn't need to warn her about paying unrealistic prices. It was clear that she knew exactly what the items she selected were worth—and how much she was prepared to pay for the fabrics and jewelry she bought.

He stood by, conscious of the smiles she attracted—and the curious glances cast in his direction. He cursed himself for not giving a thought to how she might stand out here, how memorable she might be.

"Oh, look, Shafir."

He turned his head to see what had drawn her attention. A camel was tied to a post near where the trio of crows had settled earlier.

"Isn't he sweet?"

"Be careful." He hastened to warn her. "Camels can be exceedingly bad-tempered."

"Not this one. Are you, my sweetie?" she crooned in a tone that sent vibrations down Shafir's spine.

"You don't need a camel."

"I wish I could take him home. But how could I put you in my luggage, gorgeous?" She glanced up. "What about you, Shafir? Couldn't you use another?"

"I have sufficient camels."

"That camel is already sold, but I have another madam might like."

Megan started as the wizened camel trader appeared. "Oh, I'm sorry. I hope you don't mind me patting him." She apologized and threw him a smile that had Shafir gnashing his teeth. Why couldn't she smile at him with that carefree joy?

He resisted the impulse to tell her to cover up. Except for her loose hair, she was already quite respectable. It wasn't her fault that her smile, her *joie de vivre,* drew attention—it had attracted him from the first, too.

As he watched Megan charm the weary camel trader, Shafir decided Jacques must be made of steel to have resisted the temptation Megan offered. Idly he wondered how Jacques had failed to notice that Megan was building hopes of a romance around their business meetings. Why had Jacques not put a stop to it? Had he been flattered?

Brooding now, Shafir decided he needed to have a word with the man and warn him to tone down his Gallic charm so that there could be no more misunderstandings.

But the unease that had settled in the pit of his stomach would not relent. Still watching Megan chatting, Shafir cast his mind over the time he'd spent with Megan during the past days—and could remember no hint of flirtatious behavior.

Not even with him. And he found himself missing the seductive smiles and soft touches that had clearly been nothing more than a ploy to punish him for kidnapping her. It had worked—it had made him sweat.

Yet Megan had not followed up on her advantage.

Shafir knew he was extremely eligible. If it had been a wealthy man Megan was after, she would have wasted no time pursuing him. But she hadn't.

Instead they'd spent evenings listening to music together and the days out exploring—and talking about everything under the sun. Except the tense triangle between Megan, Jacques and Zara.

And every hour in her company had confirmed that Megan was funny and smart.

Now she was laughing at something the camel trader had

said. The man smiled, too, a gummy grin where he no longer possessed teeth. He heard her try out an Arabic phrase, saw the surprised pleasure that lit the trader's face.

What if Megan had not been misguided? What if Jacques had flirted with her, romanced her and had deliberately led her to believe he was falling in love with her?

Shafir didn't want to believe it. If that was true then he couldn't possibly allow Zara to marry Jacques. And he'd have to break the awkward news to Zara that Jacques had been two-timing her. He shuddered at the thought of bringing pain to a young woman he had protected from hardship since she was a child.

It was the thought of Zara's pain that gave him pause. Although there wasn't a lot of time left before the wedding, he had no intention of acting recklessly or breaking Zara's heart unless he was very certain.

He'd take a few days to consider carefully what needed to be done. And the place he thought most clearly was in the empty space of the desert.

Making the decision gave him a sense of relief. They would leave in the morning.

"Your woman is like fire. She crackles with energy."

Shafir bit back the retort that Megan was not his woman. He turned from where he was busy filling his horse's saddle bag with provisions for the return trip to Qasr Al-Ward to see what the *Bedu* elder, who had come quietly up behind him, was referring to.

He discovered Megan surrounded by a group of women and children and, in typical Megan fashion, he could see that she was talking, using a scattering of Arabic words and waving her hands in the air to help convey her meaning. Her wide smile flashed as one of the other women said something.

Shafir felt himself start to smile, too.

It was easy to see why the tribal elder compared her to leaping flames.

"Yes," he agreed. "And like a fire, she warms everyone around her." It was true, he realized. His life had changed since the day he'd taken Megan from the airport. Every day seemed brighter, filled with more. His staff were fond of her, and here at a Bedouin camp in the desert, again she charmed people.

"She will always be of fire—do not seek to change her, Prince Shafir."

The old tribesman's words were cryptic. Last night Megan had sat with the same group of women beside the great communal fire while men clad in pristine white robes performed dances with sticks. Her face had reflected excitement and pleasure, and Shafir had wondered if this was the adventure that she had sought by coming to Dhahara.

"Like fire, she has strength," he replied. "I do not think the man has been born who can change her."

"You are wise not to want to change such a woman. Bring her to visit us again. She will be welcomed."

"I will." Shafir moved away from the saddlebags to embrace the old man.

"Prince Shafir," the elder tapped Shafir's arm. "Remember to dance with the flame, too. You are still young for the burdens that have been placed on your shoulders. You must remember to enjoy yourself—to laugh sometimes."

Shafir inclined his head.

For the first time in his life the desert had brought him no peace—and he was no nearer to a decision than when they'd arrived. Was it any wonder he didn't feel like laughing?

As he went to tell Megan that it was almost time to leave, he knew that the choice he had to make was simple: to tell Zara it was possible that Jacques had not been faithful, or to remain silent and let the wedding proceed because, as yet, he had no proof. It was only that his unease had grown with every day he got to know Megan better, until he was prepared to admit that she probably had not been mistaken. His gaze lingered on her, and she looked up and threw him a quick smile that lit up her eyes and caused his heart to contract in his chest. Then a toddler tugged at her skirt and she glanced away. The moment of connection was past.

Megan wasn't flighty or flirty or any of the other ridiculous things women could be.

But it wasn't his life that would lie in tatters if Megan was proved right. It would be Zara's life that would be shattered.

The only other course of action was to confront Jacques. But if the Frenchman had been mucking around, he was hardly going to admit it.

Shafir knew that speaking to his father and brothers would bring him no closer to a solution. They'd all believed that Megan was here in Dhahara to force Zara and Jacques apart. No one was going to believe her without proof.

Except perhaps him.

Eight

It was four days after they had set off into the desert. They were riding the same stocky horses along the same route through a craggy wadi when danger struck.

Over the course of the days spent at the Bedouin encampment, Megan had come to realize that Shafir was wildly popular out here in the desert—that everyone knew him. He listened to the goatherd's father's complaint that his son was missing too much of the village school, laughed at the village elders' observation that it was time for him to get married and agreed to an old woman's request for a new loom.

He listened. And more than that, he cared.

The man she'd thought little more than a savage was turning out to have depths that she would never have guessed. Megan was still musing about how wrong she'd been in her initial estimation of Shafir's character when Hanif came riding hard across the desert and spoke to Shafir in a volley of Arabic.

Megan turned her head.

One glance showed her all she needed to know. Bandits. Red headscarfs wound around their heads, faces covered in black beards, scruffy ponies.

"Oh, no."

"Don't worry." Shafir rode closer to her.

"But they don't look like Dhaharans."

"Some might be. And the rest will come from Marulla, which lies behind the mountain ranges. There is no oil in their country…infighting amongst their sheiks and the ravages of war on their far border have taken their toll."

The group kept coming toward them.

Shafir wheeled his horse around.

"Stay here," he commanded. "Hanif, take care of her."

He rode forward.

Megan watched him go, feeling helpless. How could she ever have suspected him of being a bandit? The difference was marked. He sat proud in the saddle, centuries of Dhaharan pride showing.

The untamed one. What a catch a royal prince would be for this ragged group.

This time the dangers of kidnap and ransom were not aimed at her, but at Shafir.

The fool!

Why had he put himself at risk?

The scrape of metal caught her attention. A sideways glance revealed that the guard now riding beside her held a rifle low across his leg, out of sight to the approaching riders.

The other guard had moved up behind Shafir's mount. For the first time she realized that their escort was heavily armed. No doubt Shafir carried a weapon in the bag strapped across the front of his saddle, too. For all his fierceness, the aura of raw power that he carried with him, Shafir was not reckless.

He was no fool, this desert prince.

But she did not want to see him hurt.

Strangely she gave no thought to her own safety, about what might happen if these rough men captured her. All her thoughts were of him. He was the person of consequence, and he would be the greatest prize.

She urged her horse forward.

"Madam," Hanif spoke, "don't go. You will only distract His Highness from the task at hand."

"But he is in danger."

Hanif gave her a sun-beaten smile. "Not today. He will be fine. Wait and you will see. Insha'allah."

The inevitability of it all made her want to scream. Instead she reined back the mare and watched as Shafir raised a hand and called out a greeting. Two men from the other group trotted out. The three horses and their riders stood bunched together, Shafir's guard hanging back.

Anxiety filled her. "Why's he letting them get so close?"

"They are talking to him," said Hanif peaceably.

"I can see that," she snapped, growing edgier by the minute.

"They have a problem."

She stared at the older man with suspicion. "How do you know that? Do you know these men?"

He lost his air of insouciance. "I would never lead His Highness into an ambush. I have been with him since he was a boy." He pointed. "But if you look, you will see that he is listening. These men are men with something weighing on their minds. The sheik will fix it. It is what he does best."

Megan followed the line of the bent finger. Shafir's head was tilted to one side—as it had been when she'd told him about her brother's death. Even as she watched, he gave that slight nod, that small incline of his head that she'd come to know so well.

He was not going to be abducted…or worse, killed.

She would have another chance to meet those bronze eyes, to touch him, to talk to him.

Megan didn't want to put a name to the emotions that careened through her when he finally swung his horse away from the other men and rode back to where she and Hanif waited.

But she knew that she would never again believe that she hated him.

Megan stepped onto the top step of the largest pool in the Garden of Pools and the silken water rippled around her legs. Slowly she lowered herself into the deliciously soothing water that sparkled in the slanting light of the sinking sun.

Despite the fright the encounter with the bandits had given her, Megan still couldn't bring herself to regret the trip into the desert, which had shown her a different side of the man who aroused such complex emotions within her.

Shafir had kept her safe.

Her fear for him earlier had been very real. She'd *cared* about what might happen to him out in the sun-bleached desert. She'd been terrified that something might happen to him.

And it wasn't a fear for herself.

It was all for him.

Crazily, somehow he'd started to become important to her.

Stockholm syndrome, she thought cynically. The captive starting to become dependent on the captor.

Diving deep into the still water to escape the disturbing notion, she stroked for the other side of the pool, the cerulean blue and ochre patterns of the mosaics vivid beneath her. Ten minutes later, lungs bursting from plowing up and down, Megan exploded to the surface, only to find the man who had hijacked her thoughts sitting on the edge of a lounger, a towel wrapped around his waist as he toed off a pair of docksiders.

She stood, uncertain of protocol when she was so scantily dressed in only a bikini. She'd always been alone at the pools, with only Naema coming to see if she required anything. Should she leave?

"I won't be long."

"Take your time. There's enough space for both of us." He rose to his full height and loosened the towel.

Megan caught a glimpse of a narrow black Speedo, narrow hips and wide muscled shoulders turned bronze by the sun, before she whipped her eyes away and sank back under the water to where the patterned mosaics created an exotic underwater world.

There was a dull splash behind her. She swam faster. She wasn't ready to confront what she felt about him.

Not yet.

A moment later the water beside her moved and she knew Shafir had caught up with her.

She closed her eyes and waited for a surge of water to tell her he had passed. But he stayed with her. Opening her eyes, she lifted her head and took a breath. His strokes were lazy, just enough to keep up with her. When she reached the other end she grabbed the side and trod water.

He stopped, too.

"Go ahead," she said. "Do your laps, I don't need entertaining."

His eyes crinkled and the sides of his mouth curled up. "Maybe I do."

Her heart stopped at the impact of his smile. He'd been so serious over the past few days—somber, almost reserved. She'd forgotten the *wow* feeling when he beamed that full wattage at her.

Megan scrambled to collect her thoughts and find her

voice. Play it cool. No need for him to know about the turmoil churning inside her. "Uh…so now I'm entertainment, am I?"

"I like watching you."

What the hell was that supposed to mean? Was it a line? "Really?"

He nodded. "Really. You have an amazingly expressive face."

Oh, no. She rolled her eyes and hoped he didn't see what a mess she was in. "Not that again!"

"What do you mean?"

"That's what my family says. My mother says, when I was a little girl, she could tell with one look whether I was lying to her. And I'm always in trouble for putting my foot in it." She laughed, lightly, almost convincing herself that her world hadn't turned upside down out there in the desert today when she'd thought she might lose him to a bunch of bandits. Glancing away from his piercing gaze, she said with deliberate irony, "I can't keep a secret to save my life."

"Well, then, I know never to tell you my secrets."

"You have secrets?"

"Plenty," he said in a husky voice that made her tingle.

"If-I-tell-you-then-I'll-have-to-kill-you kind of secrets?"

He burst into laughter. "That's why you entertain me."

"Thanks. I think."

He drifted closer.

"It's a pleasure." There was definitely a light in his eyes now.

"Are you flirting with me?" The words erupted before she'd thought about them, and Megan found herself blushing furiously. "Sorry, ignore that, I shouldn't have said it. Of course you're not flirting with me."

"You want to know my intentions?" His eyes were half closed, concealing the fierce predatory eyes.

"Yes," she said boldly.

"I don't know." He looked surprised at the admission. After a beat, he said, "Maybe I am flirting with you."

Well, the man had faced possible death today. Hardly surprising he was doing things he would normally never contemplate.

He drifted closer still and his legs brushed hers. A bolt of electricity surged through Megan followed by a rush of excitement.

"That's entertainment, right?" There should have been a slight snap to the comment, instead it came out breathless.

"This is entertainment."

He kissed her. His mouth sleek and knowing and very, very experienced.

Megan didn't find it entertaining. It was overwhelming, scary. Anything but entertaining.

When it ended she almost said "wow." But she managed to bite it back. She wasn't going to let him know how much the kiss had shaken her.

So she decided to amuse him—she might as well give him the entertainment he sought. "If you kiss me, do you have to kill me?"

He didn't laugh. Instead he looked offended. "What kind of man do you think I am? An animal?"

She stared into those bronze eyes, thought about the power in his shoulders, the wild grace with which he moved.

"Well?" He was frowning now.

"You're not an animal."

"That—" his gaze scanned her face "—was not convincing."

She was conscious of how close he was, of how little clothes they wore. And against all odds a frisson of excitement shivered through her.

"Well, you're hardly a pussycat." She dropped her

lashes, reluctant for him to read the strange awareness that was pulsing through her, tightening her skin and the tips of her breasts. Signs she was sure he would read without hesitation.

"A pussycat? What kind of man wants to be a pussycat?" He sounded disgusted.

Megan glanced up, and their gazes meshed.

"Megan!"

Her name was a hoarse groan. And she knew that he'd seen exactly how she felt.

This time he trapped her against the wall, the full length of his body plastered against hers. Shafir's mouth opened on hers, ravenous, demanding. And she gave him everything he wanted.

When the kiss ended, her breath was coming in shallow pants. "You could've been killed today."

She could have bitten her tongue out the moment the words escaped.

"But I wasn't."

His legs brushed hers under the water and she felt his arousal. Passion and fury surged through her. "It was stupid to ride out to meet them."

"I recognized one of them…he is the son of a cousin of Ahmed's neighbor. His family worries about him. I told him I will carry news back to them about him. He knows I couldn't do that if they killed me. And the men wanted my help. I can't help them if I'm dead."

It sounded so reasonable, almost prosaic, but it did nothing to soothe the terrible cold fear that still lingered in the aftermath.

"You were worried about me."

There was an intensity in the fierce eyes.

Her eyelashes fell. "No."

He put a finger under her chin and lifted it. "Yes."

She met his eyes in the waning light and found herself searching them frantically. Earlier there'd been that awful moment when she'd wondered if she'd ever have the chance to do this again. Or touch him.

Her hand reached out almost against her will, and she touched him, there…at his core. It was real, it was life affirming.

"*Megan.*"

Nine

Passion ripped through his taut form, scorching him with fire, filling him with a yearning need that he'd never known.

Shafir couldn't have stopped himself kissing Megan if a hurricane had arrived.

He licked at her soft, moist lips. Heard her groan and felt her body arch against him. And that set off another explosion of heat.

He went rigid.

"I suppose you're going to tell me I should not be doing this. If you are, stop me now."

"Do it again," she said hoarsely.

His hands stroked up her arms and over her naked shoulders in long, slow sweeps that roused shivers of endless pleasure. His fingers played a game of erotic tag against her spine.

Her hand clenched around his hard length, making him

convulse with pleasure, the black swimsuit offering little protection.

Water lapped against his sleek, naked skin. His legs, corded with muscle, brushed against hers. The contrast of male and female, hard and soft, the sensual whisper of the water all conspired to make him harden against her fingers.

She brought him out of the swimsuit. "I want you," she murmured as he gasped against her mouth. "Now."

"It will be over in a minute if you carry on."

"I don't care."

Her fingers drove him insane. He threw back his head and squeezed his eyes shut and, holding his breath, waited for the starbursts.

It came too suddenly, a wild moment of sharp, escalating pleasure that left him aching for more.

Before she could move away, he clasped his hands around her hips and hoisted her onto the edge of the poolside.

"Put your hands behind you and brace yourself."

"Shafir! What are you doing?"

"Your turn now."

Her breath caught, the sound loud in the stillness of the Garden of Pools. "I've already had my turn."

"The pleasure was all mine…none belonged to you."

Her dark eyes were wild with emotion. "But the satisfaction was mine. I needed to know that you are functioning. That you are safe."

"Oh, Megan."

Driven to desperation by the words that tugged at his heart, he rose up out of the water and his mouth closed over the tight nipples covered by the clinging, wet Lycra bikini.

It was her turn to gasp, and the hoarse sound filled him with soaring pleasure. One hand slid under the bottom of edge of the suit, sliding over the base of the breast his mouth sucked.

Cupping the heavy warmth of her breast, he massaged the voluptuous flesh while his tongue played across the rigid tip, separated from her skin only by a barrier of thin cloth.

Megan flung her head back, sounds of ecstasy escaping her.

It was time.

Sliding back into the pool, freeing his hand, Shafir dropped lower. The curve of her mons under the swimsuit drew his eye. She was exquisite. Pressing open-mouthed kisses over the mound that her bikini bottoms concealed, he stroked the firm flesh of her belly until she moaned with delight.

Lifting his head, he hooked his thumbs over the edges of her bikini bottoms and pulled them off.

She was so sweet. He tasted her, kissed her, until she spasmed beneath his mouth, her thighs trembling around him.

When he raised his head, her gaze met his, dark and slumberous in the twilight. "And don't you dare tell me tomorrow that I imagined this," she said, "that it's nothing more than a fantasy fueled by my feminine mind."

That night, lying alone in the darkness of bedchamber, Shafir thought about the softness of her skin, the silky hair, the scent of her and tried to make sense of what the hell had happened out there in the Garden of Pools.

Don't you dare tell me tomorrow that I imagined this.

Oh, hell.

He hadn't lost control and spilled himself like that since he'd taken his first woman. What power did Megan Saxon hold over him?

A fantasy fueled by my feminine mind.

Her biting words had shaken him. As, no doubt, she'd meant them to. He saw with utter clarity that Megan had told him the truth about Jacques—the man had been two-timing Zara and Megan. He'd arrogantly chosen to disregard it—had attributed it to frivolity—and now he had to deal with the fallout.

He couldn't bear to think of her performing such intimacies with Jacques…or any man. This woman had been made for him.

His brain must be heat crazed. He was going mad!

It was almost possible to believe she was a *houri* who promised him all the pleasures of paradise. The sound choked out of him didn't resemble humor.

Surrounded by darkness, he remembered his grandmother telling him of how Sheherazade had spun tales that had saved her from certain death and mesmerized the hapless sultan each night. Megan reduced him to being her captive with ease.

Entertain me.

But he hadn't meant for her to turn him to putty in her hands. Hell, he couldn't think straight.

For the first time in his life Shafir found himself in a situation where sensual pleasure ruled. In the past, he'd been driven by clear, cold intellect. Yet now all he could think of was Megan. Making love to Megan. Talking to Megan. Filling his life with Megan.

In the past few hours he'd even started to have traitorous thoughts about asking her to stay with him in Dhahara, to be his lover. If he did what his senses craved, his family would think she'd made him as crazy as they believed her to be.

What a mess!

At last, after much tossing and turning, a little after midnight, he came to a decision.

Tomorrow he would return to the city. He would confront Garnier—and then he would face the difficult task of telling Zara the unpalatable truth.

And then he would need to find the strength to apologize to Megan for misjudging her.

She would have every right to call him a bastard.

The limousine cut a straight track through the desert as though the hounds of hell were on their tail.

"Why the hurry?" asked Megan, slanting a glance to the man beside her.

Shafir had been silent, brooding, since they'd parted last night.

Last night…

Megan didn't want to think about last night. The shivery pleasure. The heat that had scorched her. The cool silkiness of the water and the heat of his mouth.

Oh, dear God, how would she ever forget it?

"I am needed in the capital. For a meeting," he said abruptly.

She yanked herself back to the present. "Today?"

"Tomorrow."

She wouldn't be surprised if the meeting had been hurriedly set up this morning—if it existed at all. She didn't believe for a moment that a meeting was the reason for their return to Katar.

She considered, and abandoned, the idea that the events in the pool last night might be responsible for this rush from Qasr Al-Ward. Shafir was not a man governed by passion. He was much too hard and fierce. No, this must have to do with his family, with his cousin's wedding.

She was shaken by how little she'd wanted to leave the palace, the surrounding desert, and venture back into the city. Her memories of Dhahara would be colored by the world Shafir had shown her. She would treasure those.

"If you only need to attend a meeting tomorrow, then surely we can slow down to ensure Your Highness makes it back in one piece?"

He glowered at her sarcasm.

The limousine swerved. Megan clutched the edge of her seat. "There. See, that's what I mean."

Shafir bent forward and yanked open the window to the driver's compartment and spoke in rapid-fire Arabic. Megan caught *"shway shway."* Slowly. She relaxed a little.

"It was a camel."

"A camel?"

"A wild camel in the road."

"Oh, no. Did we hit it?" She hadn't felt any impact.

"No, no. There are lots of wild camels. The desert is full of them."

"I've fallen in love with your camels. I think it's their eyes…and those beautiful eyelashes."

"I thought you said it was their soft noses that appealed to you."

"Oh, it's everything about them."

Shafir couldn't believe that he was being sucked into a discussion about the appeal of camels, of all creatures.

At last he said, "There is a camel stud farm not far from here where they breed racing camels."

"Oh, please, can we go look?"

Shafir's lips compressed.

"Don't worry," Megan said, and sank back against the plush seat, closing her eyes to shut him out. "I know, you have a meeting."

An hour later the limousine slowed and Shafir watched as Megan's eyelashes fluttered up.

She stretched her arms up and the curve of her breasts rose against the shirt she wore.

He stifled a moan.

"You're awake."

Catching his gaze on her, she paused in midstretch. Her arms fell to her sides and Shafir sighed with regret.

"How far are we from Katar? Why are we slowing?"

"We're at the camel stud farm."

"But I thought—" Midsentence she stopped. "Thank you, Shafir."

Her face lit up, and for a moment he thought she was going to hurl herself across the seat at him. He tensed in anticipation. But at the last moment she cast him an uncertain smile. "I can't wait."

"Be careful," he warned. "Camels are moody animals, they can be fierce and troublesome."

"I know all about fierce and troublesome animals." And she shot him a look that was full of wicked humor.

Shafir couldn't decide whether he should shout with laughter or scold her severely. Or simply kiss her.

There were more camels at the stud farm than Shafir had ever seen in one place before, and Megan seemed to want to examine each one.

The wealthy, fleshy Arab who owned the farm was examining Megan with lazy approval. "You like what you see," he tossed out.

"I am not certain," Shafir bit out.

The breeder caught Shafir's dangerous glare and froze. Making a hasty excuse, he took himself off in a hurry.

"Jerk," murmured Shafir.

"Who? The breeder?" Megan turned to him. "I thought he was very helpful."

"Too damned helpful," he muttered.

But her gaze was on the camels. "Oh, Shafir, look at the young camel there. The pale one."

"He is too pale for the desert. He will suffer in the sun."

"Oh, the poor thing." Megan looked worried.

He rapped out an instruction to a man by the fence. Minutes later the camel stood before Megan, a groom at its head.

"Oh, look at the tufts of hair on its head, and its nose feels like velvet. Shafir, it's gorgeous."

"He."

"He?" A furrow appeared between her eyes.

"He, not *it*."

"Oh…am I insulting your manhood, boy?" she murmured to the camel.

The camel buried his head against her shirt and Shafir decided that the camel was a male after his own heart.

Afterward while Megan returned to the limousine, despite his raised hackles, Shafir had a few surreptitious words with the breeder to secure a price for the camel and arrange to have it delivered. Not that he needed another camel.

Not that Megan would ever know he'd bought it…or even see the animal she had fallen in love with.

It was highly unlikely that she would be visiting Qasr Al-Ward again. But he would have a concrete symbol to remind him of her. And he knew that this camel would be the most spoiled animal that had ever wandered the Dhaharan desert.

Two days later Shafir threw his pen down and stared out the window of the spacious library that doubled as a study in his city home and sighed.

He was running out of time. Jacques Garnier appeared

to have vanished off the face of the earth, and Shafir was having a devil of a time tracking him down. Instead of confronting Garnier, all he seemed to be doing was thinking of Megan every waking moment. Wondering what she was doing when he was out, if she was bored, if she was missing the gardens of Qasr Al-Ward. And when he would manage to screw up the guts to apologize to her…

She'd assured him that she wasn't bored. He knew she'd discovered his library and had spent hours hidden away, reading memoirs and books about Dhahara, as well of some of the Jack Reacher novels he possessed.

A rap on the door interrupted his thoughts and he sat up in anticipation.

Megan.

To his disappointment, Zara swept in, followed by his aunt Lily. Quashing the feeling of anticlimax, he rose to his feet with a welcoming smile.

"I'm sorry, Your Highness." His city aide's worried face appeared around the doorjamb. "They didn't wait to be announced."

Shafir waved the aide away. But his smile faded as he took in his cousin's pale face.

Shock? Had Zara encountered Megan in the house? Had she known who Megan was? Dear Allah, he hoped not.

"What brings you here, Zara?" he asked, rapidly deciding that he couldn't tell her the truth before he'd confronted Garnier. "Are you not caught up in the throes of last-minute arrangements for the wedding?"

"There is going to be no wedding," Zara declared dramatically.

Aunt Lily closed her eyes in resignation. Clearly she'd heard this already.

Shafir froze. "What do you mean?"

"Jacques is going to jilt me."

His first thought was of Megan. Was it possible that she'd made contact with Jacques Garnier in the two days since they'd arrived in the city? Had she threatened Garnier if he didn't call the wedding off? His first reaction was denial. Megan had been quite definite that she never wanted to see Garnier again.

But it was possible that she might have relished threatening this man. A heaviness settled in his stomach at the very thought. He would discuss it with her later.

What if she had seen Jacques?

What if Jacques tried to convince her she meant something to him? He hoped she would not be swayed.

He pushed it out his mind. For now he had to get to the bottom of the immediate crisis.

"Garnier has told you he's jilting you?"

"Not in so many words."

Tapping his fingers against his thigh, he studied Zara through contemplative eyes. "So what makes you so certain he intends to call it off?"

"He has another woman."

His fingers stilled. "You have proof of this?"

"I have heard that he has a woman." She gave a sob. "I asked him if it was true. He says he loves only me."

So Zara knew where the Frenchman was. "But you don't believe him?"

"I no longer know what to believe."

Focussing all his attention on his cousin, he asked, "What do you mean?"

"There was that other woman who was stalking him…now there is this hussy who I hear he is having an affair with. I don't like it."

Shafir didn't like it, either. But at least it meant Megan

hadn't been to see Garnier. Zara was talking of someone else. The relief that swept over Shafir was overwhelming.

Not that he'd ever believed Megan would take up with Garnier again…but she was quite capable of threatening him.

"Zara," her mother interjected, "Jacques is a wealthy man, and he is going to be pursued by women. There will always be rumors. You will have to get used to it. You must trust him—you are to be married."

"I don't know if I do anymore. What if these women are the same person? What if he was never being stalked at all and Jacques is making a fool of me? Lying to me for the sake of his whore?"

"Zara!" Shafir thundered. "I do not want to hear such talk." A fierce protective emotion swamped him. He would allow no one—not even his dearest cousin—to talk about Megan in such a manner.

"But who else will listen to me?"

Pity for Zara filled him. "Cousin, do you love this man?"

"Yes!"

"You want to spend your life with him, grow old with him?"

She looked at him as though he'd grown horns. "Why else would I marry him?"

"There are lots of reasons people get married, and they are not always the right ones."

"I love Jacques."

"Then he is a lucky man. And before you jump to conclusions about another woman, consider whether he would do such a thing if he loves you." But Shafir knew there was no conviction in his words. He knew that the gossip was probably correct. He would be making discreet inquiries about exactly whom Jacques had been meeting.

If Zara still wanted to marry the man knowing what he'd

done, then by Allah he'd make Garnier understand there would be no more affairs or flirtations. Ever. Not unless he wanted to end his chances of begetting sons.

Shafir had just seen Zara and his aunt Lily off when the king arrived with his phalanx of security guards. Leaving the guards patrolling the perimeter of the property, the king entered the house and demanded to know why Shafir was back in the city.

"Business, Father."

"And the woman? Where is she?" His father looked around the entrance hall and up and down the staircase as if expecting Megan to emerge at any second.

It struck Shafir that he hadn't seen Megan for a while.

"Do not concern yourself with the woman, Father." A note of irony crept into his voice as he echoed his father's "the woman."

His father frowned, his astute eyes examining Shafir with fierce attention.

It was a standing joke that the king knew what would happen in Dhahara before perpetrators had even decided to commit a crime. Now Shafir wondered if the king knew something he didn't. Had Megan indeed been in contact with Garnier, and had the king's force of aides and guards discovered it?

"You have changed."

"No, Father, I am still your son."

The king harrumped. "I hear from my guards that this woman is living with you in your house here in the city."

That was it.

Shafir bowed his head in assent, relieved that his apprehensions that Megan had been seen meeting with Jacques had been unfounded.

"Come, Father, let us sit in comfort."

"It is dangerous for her to be here in the city. Zara could find out—"

"Zara will discover nothing!"

"It will be easier for this woman to contact Zara, to make trouble."

Shafir's patience snapped. "Do not refer to her as 'this woman.' She has a name—Megan." He held his father's gaze. "She will not make trouble. She is not the type."

"She is a lunatic."

"She is far from crazy."

"You disagree with me to defend this woman?"

"She wasn't stalking Jacques—he made that up."

"Why would he lie?"

Shafir gave his father a very male look. "Why do you think?"

"You mean—"

Shafir nodded and ushered his father into the library.

"Oh." The king appeared at a loss for words. He walked across the Persian rug and settled himself on a chair with an upright back. "But such a woman shouldn't be living in your house."

He'd found something to say soon enough, Shafir thought with grim humor as he leaned against the desk and crossed one ankle over the other. He refrained from pointing out that the reason Megan was staying in his house at all was because the king had ordered him to keep her from making mischief in any way he chose. Which he had done.

"People will think—"

"I don't care what people think."

"You think it doesn't matter what people think, my son?" King Selim gave a sigh.

"They call me the untamed one. I have more freedom than Khalid."

"You know they call you that? You think it is a good thing?" His father shook his head. "I am not sure. I wish your mother were alive. I could do with her counsel now."

For the first time Shafir realized that his father was getting older. There were lines across his forehead that he was certain hadn't been there only months ago.

"If your mother were here she would've known what to do about this woman—"

"Megan!"

"About this Megan." His father pinched the bridge of his nose. "Khalid and you would both have been married by now. She would have arranged it."

With difficulty Shafir stopped himself from rolling his eyes. Instead he folded his arms, and said defensively, "I can find my own wife."

"But you are tardy in doing so, my son. And having this woman staying in your home is not going to help find you a wife." Another heavy sigh accompanied this observation. "And it might come to Zara's attention—she would be upset. You know how fond she is of you."

"There's no reason for her to link Megan to Jacques Garnier, unless someone tells her. And I have done everything possible to keep her out of the way so that nothing can endanger Zara's marriage to Garnier." He didn't add that he'd had an awful moment when he thought that Zara had bumped into Megan earlier. Nor did he add that he would be taking care of Jacques. No point in alarming his father further.

"But—"

"Megan is a nice woman, Father."

"I don't think—"

"You should meet her." He steamrolled over his father's objections. "Perhaps we can all dine together one night?"

The king looked horrified. "I don't want to meet this woman who causes such misery."

"Megan. Her name is Megan. Say it."

"Megan," said the king with utter reluctance.

"Our family has done her a grave wrong. The very least we can do is acknowledge her."

"A grave wrong?" The king grew more horrified. "Oh, no. You did what Rafiq suggested! You seduced this woman to keep her mind off Jacques."

Shafir raised his hand. "Enough."

"Ay, me." The king threw his hands into the air. "I can listen no more. I told you to keep this woman out of the way until the wedding was over. You have disobeyed me."

In all his life he had never deliberately disobeyed the king. But he had brought Megan back to the city against his father's dictates.

Because he had wanted to deal with Garnier.

"Father, I did not seduce her—"

King Selim was on his feet. "I can see from your face that there is something between you. You cannot lie to me, my son. She is your mistress."

He hesitated too long before denying it. "No, I have not asked her to be my mistress."

And suddenly he was fiercely glad that he had not done so.

Megan deserved better.

His father stalked closer and, putting his face close to Shafir's, he said, "You have chosen to bring her to the city, to live unchaperoned with her in your home, to bring shame on your family."

"Father—"

"But you will obey me in this, my son. You will keep her away from the wedding, even if that means you do not attend yourself."

Before he could draw a breath and tell his father that there might not be a wedding—unless Zara demanded it—the king had turned on his heel and stormed out of the library. Anger rising, Shafir strode after him.

"Father, her name has been dragged through the mud by a—"

The front door slammed. The entrance hall was empty.

The king had gone.

Ten

Framed in the doorway of the library, Shafir halted mid-step as Megan spoke into the prickling silence: "So you planned to seduce me to keep me away from Jacques?"

Hampered by her long skirt, she clambered down from the little suspended loft where she'd been curled up reading when Zara and Lily had entered the room. Once they'd started speaking, she'd been trapped.

Facing a fiercely frowning Shafir, she refused to be intimated by the grandeur he radiated in his sparkling white thobe, his swathe of overlong hair brushing past his collar. "Am I to understand that you planned everything that happened beside the pool at the Palace of Roses?" The extent of the hurt and betrayal that rolled inside her took Megan by surprise.

"Have you been here all the time?"

She could see him rapidly trying to recall all that had been said, everything damaging she might have heard.

"Oh, yes. I heard about your brother's idea for you to seduce me so that I would forget all about Jacques and wouldn't threaten Zara's wedding."

Glowering at her, clearly hating being caught in the wrong, he walked slowly into the room. "You should've made your presence known."

"And spoil the fun? I didn't get the chance. How could I emerge when Zara had just announced that Jacques was jilting her? How do you think she would've felt to know that a stranger had witnessed her humiliation? But it's just as well I stayed, because I learned so much." The searing hurt was awful. So much worse than when she'd discovered the truth about how Jacques had been jerking her around. What had happened in the Garden of Pools had been special.

Or so she'd thought.

"I hope you found it entertaining," she spat out.

Four long strides brought him to a halt in front of her. He stretched out a conciliatory hand. "Megan—"

She slapped his hand away and retreated to stand beside the couch. "Don't 'Megan' me."

Drawing a deep breath, she raked her fingers through her long hair and fought for composure. She would not let him see her fall apart. She could cry later.

When she was alone.

"You planned with your brother how you were going to seduce me."

"I di—"

"How dare you do such a thing?"

She let the rage that had been festering for weeks loose. His abduction of her. Jacques's betrayal of her. It all erupted.

"You didn't know me, had never seen me." Something flared in his eyes. "You knew what I looked like," she said slowly.

"I saw photos."

"Photos? Where did you get photos of me?"

Shafir shrugged. "My father has security resources—"

"You *spied* on me?"

"Not me."

"Your family spied on me. Oh, God, I'm going to be sick."

"Sit down, before you fall down. You look like you're going to faint," he said with brutal frankness.

Megan sank onto the sofa. She did feel ill; her stomach was churning. It would serve him right if she vomited all over the Persian rug that she suspected was worth a fortune. "You are despicable. You're all despicable."

"I never planned to seduce you." Shafir leaned back against the desk and folded his arms across his chest. "In fact, when Rafiq suggested it, I told him that I would never sink that low."

"Well, you appear to have forgotten your good intentions!" She was too fired up to acknowledge that she'd played a big part in what had happened at the pool.

"Megan, what you and I did—"

She bent her head and stared at the flat gold leather sandals she wore. "I don't want to talk about it."

"We have to."

She shook her head, "No, I want to talk about what your father believes. He said—"

"A lot of things. All of them based on incorrect assumptions. And I defended you."

That brought her gaze back to his face. She searched his features, looking for the truth. "Not that I heard."

"You must have heard me say that you were a nice woman. We weren't in the library for the rest."

"How convenient."

Shafir had given her exquisite pleasure, without feeling a shred of any softer emotion for her. She felt used. Even though she knew she was probably overreacting, given that she'd started the chain of events that had culminated in this.

But she'd been so scared for him that day.

Terrified by what might have happened out there in the desert. The bandits might have killed him.

It mattered. Because somehow she'd grown to care for him.

And that made her feel even sicker. Heartsick.

Oh, Lord, please not heartsick.

She clamped her arms across her stomach. How could she have been such a fool? For a second time? *Fool me once, shame on you, fool me twice, shame on me.* But this time she hadn't been in love with the idea of being in love; this time the emotion that twisted her heart was so much more powerful.

And this time she'd picked a man who could marry up to four wives if he chose. A man who lived in a country a world away from her own, where most of the inhabitants couldn't speak English.

A man who described her only as *nice.*

She was asking for heartbreak.

"And your cousin—" she forced herself to look at him without revealing the shuddering shock of realization "—she shares some of these misapprehensions about me?"

Shafir's sigh said it all.

"So she does. Tell me what I'm supposed to have done to merit such antagonism. I have a right to know."

So he told her how his father had discovered her impending arrival and had feared that she planned to stop the wedding between Jacques and Zara.

Megan perched on the edge of the sofa. "He just assumed I would do that?"

"Garnier confirmed it."

"Jacques did?"

How many shocks was she going to have to bear?

"You mean, he was asked about me right in the beginning, before you abducted me?"

Shafir nodded, and she glimpsed distaste in his eyes. Despite his casual posture against the desk, his folded arms, she could detect his tension. "Zara found missed calls from you on his phone. She confronted him. He told her you were a business colleague who'd turned into a crazy stalker."

"Me? Stalking him?" She thought about his smooth approach the first time they'd met, his offer to buy her a drink, his intent gaze as he'd spun her a line about how she had to be his soul mate.

She'd swallowed it hook, line and sinker.

The rat!

A clever rat, because in ten minutes flat he'd discerned what she'd been seeking. A soul mate. She hadn't even known it herself…

If Jacques hadn't lied, Shafir would never have kidnapped her. She might never have met him.

Megan shot Shafir a sideways look. Despite his ruthlessness, she knew he would *never* prey on a woman's most secret needs like that.

"You know, if I were Zara, I'd want to know that Jacques lied about those calls without blinking. I'd want to know that he is a two-timing rat."

"Zara has already heard rumors of a woman, you heard that. Yet she says she loves Jacques. If he hurts her after their marriage he will pay—Rafiq and I will make sure he understands that."

"Would you care if your woman had another man?"

Dark heat flared in his eyes. "Of course I'd care. I'd want her to be mine, only mine."

"Would you grant her the same courtesy?" Megan held her breath.

"I've told you before that when I find a woman special enough, I would forsake all others."

"Forever?"

He tilted his head in that familiar half-nod and stared at her from narrowed, inscrutable eyes. "Forever."

The breath Megan had been holding escaped in a rush.

"And, believe me, it will be forever. For both of us." His expression was fierce, his mouth passionate. "My woman will not need to seek love elsewhere."

Megan believed him.

Lucky woman.

But that woman could never be her.

He thought she was nice. Nothing more. She fixed her gaze on her sandals again. He was nothing like Jacques. He would be more true than her father had been.

Even though Shafir had kidnapped her, taken her to his palace, it had been done for his family. Because it was what his father wanted. Because he loved his cousin and didn't want to see her hurt.

Megan could see it all so clearly now.

But she needed to know more. Lifting her head, she asked, "When I said I wanted to go home, you refused to let me. At first you believed I might generate adverse publicity and jeopardise Zara's wedding. Then you came up with another ploy."

"It wasn't a ploy."

"Wasn't it?" She waited a beat, then asked softly, "So why did you keep me here?"

"I told you, I wanted to change your mind about Dhahara. I couldn't let you leave with the impression you'd gained of the country and people." But he glanced away and flicked nonexistent dust from the front of his thobe. "Okay, maybe I wasn't…" His voice trailed away.

"Honest? You're not telling me everything. I think you

wanted an excuse to keep me close. I think you wanted to keep me under observation."

She waited for a long moment.

"Nothing more to say? Well then, I suppose that's it then."

She got to her feet.

"It's all been about Zara's precious wedding, making sure that nothing happens to undo that. I hope she appreciates the lengths you've gone to for her. Kidnapping—"

"Megan—"

"—Seducing the enemy—"

"Megan!"

He'd straightened and was no longer leaning idly against the desk.

"It's true." She shook her head and her long hair, unconstrained by a *hijab,* whipped against her face. "I'm so sick of all the doublespeak, all the lies."

She walked to where he stood.

"Shafir, I've had enough. I want to go home. And this time nothing is going to stop me."

She wanted to leave.

As Megan's words sank in, something tore deep inside Shafir's chest. He was not losing her. Megan was not walking out on him; he would not allow it.

A dark emotion swarmed over him. "So you think I'm the enemy? You think I set out to deliberately seduce you?"

She shrugged. "Seduce…make love…what's the difference?"

Her attitude sparked the first real flare of anger. "There's a world of difference between what happened in the Garden of Pools and a calculated seduction."

"You think?" She swung away and headed for the door. But he leaped across the room and got there first.

Slamming the heavy door shut, he locked it and said, "I'll show you the difference."

She glared up at him. "Get out of my way."

He didn't answer. Instead, he cupped his hand beneath her jaw and stroked the soft, sensitive skin behind her ears. Using every ounce of sensual skill he possessed he worked on making her aware of him in a deeply primal way. He knew he'd won when she quivered under his fingertips.

"See? Your body betrays you," he said roughly. "I knew you would respond if I touched you like this…and this."

"Shafir!" She leaned weakly against the door, horrified by the breathiness in her own voice, hating herself for responding so readily to his high-handedness.

His hands slid up under the T-shirt she wore and stripped it over her head in one quick move. She wore no bra. Excitement surged through her. He cupped her breast and, before she could think of objecting, his head dropped. He teased the hard pebble of her nipple with light flicks of his tongue.

Waves of delight pulsed through her. The heavy wood of the door was cool and hard against her naked back. Her knees had gone weak and her body had acquired a disturbing will of its own.

When he lifted his head, Megan saw that his hair was rumpled and his fierce bronze eyes burned.

His fingers pushed down the elastic waistband of her swirling skirt. A twist of the panties she wore and the lace snapped.

Before she could murmur more than a half-hearted objection he stroked her intimately, his fingers finding the secret furrow and sliding back and forth to create a delicious friction. Closing her eyes, she moaned as those knowing fingers slid into her, stroking her, heating her, until her hips arched away from the door.

She was breathing heavily.

He moved away from her and her eyes cracked open in time to see him shuck off the thobe, the white T-shirt beneath and the long, soft, white cotton pants he wore. The last item to land on the heap were his boxers.

He stood before her, naked, virile and one hundred percent male.

Shafir stepped forward, his thigh pushing between hers. Meeting with the obstruction of her silky skirt, he eased the garment further down over her legs. Bare legs tangled.

Hers soft and feminine, his hard and muscled.

Circling her hips with his hands, he lifted her, holding her in place against the door. Megan moved, rocked against him, and his erection settled against the junction of her thighs.

Shafir groaned out loud.

Holding her tightly, he slid forward into her heat. Deep. Dark. And incredibly dangerous…

He hadn't used protection.

Hell. The instant he thought it, he tried to pull out. She wound her legs around his hips. His brain melted as she started to move. The hot friction. The pure, passionate pleasure. The explosive heat. It all swirled around him like the bright, bold colors of a kaleidoscope.

Bending his head, he covered her mouth with his and tasted her.

The peaks of pleasure built rapidly. He cried out as she shuddered around him, and he came into her in a series of short, sharp bursts.

Afterward, Shafir turned away from her, filled with soul-destroying guilt.

He couldn't bring himself to meet her eyes, so hot with passion. He'd used the simmering attraction between them to seduce her. Seduce her in icy anger to underscore his point.

He'd set out to show her what it felt like to be seduced.

He had taken her uncaring of their surroundings, uncaring of her comfort, and he had striven only for the quick pleasure of immediate gratification. He had played her body expertly, tempting her with sensation, and Megan had never stood a chance of resisting him.

How could he have neglected to use protection?

He'd never taken such a risk before.

Shame swept him.

Picking her T-shirt up off the floor, he handed it to her. Her lashes veiled her eyes as she scooped up her skirt and tugged it on. He glanced away from the scraps of devastated lace that had been her briefs.

"I told my father that you had been wronged by our family," he said lamely.

"I heard something to that effect."

"I have wronged you, too. Both in the past by thinking you'd misinterpreted Jacques's manners for something more, and just now."

"Shafir—"

With difficulty he met her eyes. There was none of the fury he expected. She looked bewildered—and vulnerable.

His heart contracted. "Megan, I am sorry. I don't expect you to forgive me for what just happened—"

"I could have said no," she pointed out.

The first stirring of hope awakened. Passion so perfect could not end like this. Perhaps he hadn't lost her yet. Then he remembered that she wanted to go home. He had lost her.

But first, his family owed her an apology.

"Before you leave, I am going to arrange for you to meet my family." Shafir made the announcement that following morning after breakfast as they sipped the Arabian coffee that Hanif had prepared.

It was the remorse Shafir exhibited that triggered the realization of how much she loved him. But Megan gave a laugh that was half groan. "Oh, Shafir. It's far from that easy."

He set down his cup. "What's hard about it?"

"Your father thinks that associating with me will ruin you. I'm not the kind of woman he wants you to marry."

Then she flushed, because marriage had never even been mentioned.

Keep your mouth shut, she told herself. Megan had no illusions about the chances of survival of a relationship between herself and Shafir.

He was a desert prince.

She wasn't exactly a pauper—her family was extremely wealthy in their own right—but his father was a king with the wealth of Croesus and they lived in palaces and jetted around in private jets.

The woman whom Shafir married would need to have been groomed for the position from birth.

But instead of laughing at her, he said, "Well, he's certainly never managed to produce the kind of woman that I do want to marry."

She'd overheard something along those lines yesterday. "In the library your father wished your mother was here." She paused, searching for the right words. Aniya had said something weeks ago in passing that had suggested Shafir and his brothers had no mother.

"She's dead," he said abruptly.

"I'm sorry." He'd listened to her talk about the problems between her parents, her grief at the death of her brother. But she'd never asked him about his mother. Suddenly Megan felt very small. "I'm so sorry."

"It was a long time ago."

She suspected he needed time, that this was not an easy subject for him. She took a quick sip of the strong, dark Arabian coffee and returned to the subject that was clear-cut. “I need to move out of your home. I heard your father saying you wouldn’t be welcome at your cousin’s wedding. If I go, that will change.”

He held her gaze. “In case you’ve forgotten, the reason you’re with me in the first place is because I kidnapped you because of that damned wedding. My father can’t change the tune now. And the wedding might not even happen. If Zara has any sense, she will agree to call it off after I’ve dealt with Jacques.”

“Still, if the wedding goes forward, I’m the last woman in the world your family will want to meet.”

“They will love you once they get to know you.” An aura of absolute certainty surrounded him. Once she’d called it arrogance. “You will see.”

She wished she could share his confidence. Instead she sighed and pushed the empty cup away. “There’s no point to all this, Shafir. I am leaving. You’re making waves with your family for no reason.”

She wasn’t ready to face the thought of leaving.

But she had to.

She’d come starry-eyed to Dhahara on a quest to find excitement, adventure and romance. Yet instead of love, Jacques had betrayed her. She’d been so gullible, and had vowed never again. Her trust in her own judgment had been shattered.

And now that it was time to leave, she’d fallen in love—real love—with the sheik she’d so scornfully dismissed as a savage.

The irony.

“You need to meet my family.” His dark eyebrows formed a formidable frown. “I’d say that Jacques’s muddying your name and my family all believing it is reason enough.”

So this had to do with his concept of honor.

It made her love him even more.

But she couldn't help wishing he'd been doing all this because he loved her in return, rather than because he felt obliged to right a wrong.

But however much she valued the gesture, she couldn't let him alienate himself from his family only for the sake of a nice woman's tarnished reputation.

"And the sooner my family realizes that I will not miss Zara's wedding—and you will be attending with me—the better."

The flat gaze warned her that he was deadly serious. He would put her ahead of his family's and Zara's wishes.

Oh, but she was tempted….

She drew a shuddering breath. "I will refuse."

There was no other choice.

His eyes narrowed to metallic chinks. "Because of Jacques?"

Annoyance flared. "How many times do I need to tell you I don't care about Jacques anymore? I won't go because of *you.* Your father is right. Our association will do you no good."

Her stomach rolled over as their eyes remained locked.

It would be so easy to say yes, so easy to admit her love and never leave….

But she owed him more.

Later that day Megan had been told by an excited Naema, who had arrived in Katar a few days after she had, that the sheik was taking her out to dinner.

Megan wondered if taking her out on the town was an attempt to flaunt her presence in the city. Despite his father's orders, it certainly looked like Shafir had no intention of keeping her hidden. She'd considered refusing—for his own good. But in the end, she'd been too weak to resist what would have to be the first and final night out with him.

She'd soaked in the tub and Naema had rubbed scented oils into her skin afterward. Megan was feeling gloriously relaxed by the time Naema laid out her clothes.

"Don't you think that is too ornate?" She eyed the yellow caftan with gold thread on the bed. It had arrived in a box tied with gold ribbons.

"No. It's perfect, and it comes with this." Naema held up a fine piece of silk. "For your head," she explained.

By the time Megan was dressed, she was sure it was all too much. But Naema wouldn't hear a word of it. "This is what His Highness wanted you to wear tonight."

"Prince Shafir chose my clothes?"

The young woman looked apprehensive. "Yes."

But once she got downstairs, she was glad she'd let Naema sway her. Shafir looked magnificent in a richly embroidered thobe that made him appear…princely…and emphasized the gulf that yawned between them.

Shafir wasn't terribly forthcoming about where they were going when he led her out to the waiting limousine. The first inkling she had that this was more than a dinner date was when the car drew up outside an elaborate white marble building that glowed like a pearl in the evening light.

Megan did a double take. "I've seen photos of this—it's the official state palace of King Selim."

"Yes, it is."

It was the lack of inflection in his voice that caused reality to penetrate. She turned to him. "Tell me we're not about to visit your father."

"Don't worry, we won't be alone. My brothers will be there, too. We're going to dinner."

"Oh, no." She raised a hand to cover her mouth. "Shafir, you should've warned me."

"And have you refuse to come? It's easier this way."

"Easier?" Her voice rose. "Easier for whom?"

"For you. Otherwise you would have fretted."

"Are you surprised? It's not every day that I get to meet a king. You could've given me time to prepare."

"What's to prepare? He's just a man."

"A very powerful man," she corrected. And he was Shafir's father. A father who already disapproved of her.

"Relax," Shafir urged.

She resisted the impulse to snort. And then there was no more time for talk because the vehicle had pulled up beside a grand set of stairs and the chauffeur had opened the door.

Megan focused on slow, deep breaths as she passed through the arched doorway. The entrance lobby was lit with hundreds of candles, and the corridor they took seemed to go on for miles before they reached a salon.

Noise and a blur of color bombarded her, before it separated itself into a group of people. An older man, two tall men, one accompanied by a tiny, beautiful, delicate creature with cat-green eyes and a pouting mouth.

Megan hesitated. Then she squared her shoulders and strode forward. Dammit, she'd done nothing wrong.

At the last moment she realized that she'd forgotten to ask Shafir if she was supposed to curtsy, or what, when introduced to the king. Her stomach balled with nerves.

Be yourself, she decided.

So she smiled as the king stepped forward.

He inspected her with sharp eyes that she guessed missed very little.

"My father, His Royal Highness, King Selim al Dhahara." Megan found she was shaking, and her hand trembled as the king lifted it and bowed over it in an old-fashioned courtly gesture.

She was relieved when Shafir finally led her over and introduced her to his brothers and Rafiq's girlfriend.

The ribbing and jokes surprised her. The family was tight-knit.

Everywhere Megan went she was aware of the King's gaze following her. She knew he wished to protect his son. Yet the tension between the king and Shafir was palpable.

And despite everyone's smiles and well-mannered small talk, misery overwhelmed Megan.

She was the cause of this rift between father and son.

And everyone here knew it.

Eleven

Dinner passed in a haze of careful politeness. The food was beautifully prepared, but it could've been sawdust for all Megan knew. She barely tasted it.

Once coffee had been served and the robed manservant had retreated, Megan comforted herself with the promise that the evening would soon be over. But even as her anxiety finally began to settle, a commotion behind her caused her to look to the doorway.

Two women entered the long dining hall. The younger was striking. Of medium height, she was slender and moved with easy grace. A gauzy chiffon scarf was draped around her neck, and the lights of the chandeliers picked out gold highlights in her tawny hair. The second woman was older. But the high cheekbones and delicate bone structure marked her as the younger woman's mother.

Megan's heart sank.

Beside her she felt Shafir stiffen.

This must be Zara, and the older woman would be her mother, Lily.

There was an awkward silence as the women came toward them, and Megan pretended not to see the glances that were flashed her way.

"I have something to tell you all." Zara's announcement broke the taut stillness.

"We have a visitor with us tonight," said Shafir interrupting.

"Oh." She paused, and her curious brown eyes fell on Megan. Then she smiled. "I am Zara."

Megan smiled back. Zara was lovely, with a delicate gazelle-like femininity that made it easy to see why Shafir was so protective of her.

"It's nice to meet you, Zara. I'm Megan."

"Megan?" Zara's eyes grew curious. Then she stepped forward.

The silence that followed pressed against Megan's eardrums. Zara *must* know, she thought.

"I'm sorry for interrupting your dinner."

The whole room seemed to let out a collective sigh of relief.

Megan wanted to laugh at the absurdity of Zara's apology. She was hardly an honored guest. "We've already finished. And I think it's probably time for me to leave." She glanced a little desperately at Shafir.

But he didn't move.

"Oh, I don't want to break up the party."

Did Zara know who she was? Apparently not. But this uncomfortable situation could hardly be described as a party. And Megan was relieved when Shafir said, "You haven't crashed a party."

"Good." Zara moved over to where the King sat at the

head of the table. "Because I didn't want you to have another reason to be angry with me, Uncle Selim."

"What is it, child?" Concern filled his wrinkled face. "What can be so terrible that it brings shadows to your eyes?"

Zara gave her uncle a grateful look. "I have broken my engagement to Jacques, and the wedding is only three days away. What are we going to do?"

Megan heard Shafir's breath catch—it echoed her own shock. He rose to his feet, saying, "It doesn't matter. We will cancel it."

"But what about the celebrations, the concerts?" Zara glanced back at the king. "And what will we say to the people of Dhahara who have been looking forward to the wedding? I feel so terrible about letting everyone down."

Megan didn't envy Zara the anxiety and misery she was going through. But she couldn't help thinking that she'd had a lucky escape.

"Are you sure of this, Zara?" Rafiq asked. "Or is this nothing more than a squabble of lovebirds?"

"I am certain." Zara's voice rang out with conviction. "I do not want to marry a man who has another woman."

Megan felt the weight of Shafir's troubled gaze. Then he turned his attention back to Zara. "There may not be another woman, cousin."

"Oh, there is." Certainty sparked in her eyes. "Jacques has been seeing her every afternoon. He comes to visit me reeking of her."

There was a nasty silence.

The color drained out Megan's cheeks and she experienced a sinking sensation in the pit of her stomach.

They must think Zara was referring to *her.* But what

concerned her most was whether Shafir suspected her of sneaking out behind his back to meet with Jacques.

She wished she could see his eyes and assess for herself what he believed.

It took all her self-restraint to stop herself from leaping to her feet and yelling out, "It wasn't me."

Instead she sat and stared at her nails, awfully conscious of the undercurrents in the room, while of course Zara appeared blissfully oblivious.

"Zara, you might be mistaken," Khalid said half-heartedly.

"I am not! Jacques admitted everything. Her name is Rosie Smith, and she's an English tourist. And she's not the business colleague who's been stalking him. Jacques told me he met this woman less than a week ago."

Despite being aware of the discomfort of all the men, and despite Zara's misery, an indescribable relief swept through Megan.

At least Shafir now knew she hadn't being seeing Jacques on the sly.

"He told me he's found his soul mate." Zara sounded so bewildered that Megan's heart went out to her. "I always thought that was me."

A burst of annoyance caused Megan to say, "I wouldn't worry about it. There's no value in being his soul mate. It's an overused position."

All eyes turned to her.

Now she'd put her foot in it. For a brief space in time Megan wished she'd kept her mouth shut.

"He's a dog," said Shafir in a voice like steel. "You are well rid of him."

She glanced up and met his eyes and saw the summation was for her, as well as Zara. Shafir was right: Jacques was a dog. No doubt about it. And Zara had been saved much unhappiness. "I couldn't agree more."

He didn't smile, but his eyes were warm as they met hers. It gave her the strength she needed.

"There is something I have to say." She drew a ragged breath. "Zara, I came to Dhahara because of Jacques."

"You mean, Jacques invited you?"

"I'm the crazed colleague he told you was stalking him."

"You're that Megan?" The other woman's eyes went wide. "But—"

"He never told me he was engaged to you, that you were getting married in three weeks' time." Megan knew if she didn't get it all out now, she never would. Aware of Shafir standing tall and proud beside her, she focused on Zara.

"When he first told me he had business dealings with Dhahara, he kindled my interest in the country. When he suggested a short vacation together to get to know each other better—I insisted on going to Dhahara." Megan couldn't stop her lips curving upward. "Boy, he must have sweated about that."

"No, he thought he could get away with it. The arrogance of it!" Zara gave a snort of disgust. "He must think all women are stupid."

"He promised we would explore Dhahara and see if we had feelings for each other," Megan said. "No pressure."

"He said similar things to me, too. He was so romantic. I thought it was all for me."

"I know." Megan nodded. "And he's probably used the same script with this Rosie, too."

"I am so glad you told me that. I thought it was something that I'd done that made him stop loving me. My fault. That I wasn't woman enough for him."

"He's a serial adulterer," said Shafir with anger. "What woman would want such a man?"

"Not me," said Zara.

"Nor me," said Megan with a smile at the other woman.

"He's a rat," said Zara, warming to the theme.

"*Kalb*—a dog," growled Shafir.

"A rat-eating dog," said Zara with relish.

Mirth filled Megan. "A flea-infested, rat-eating dog."

The king laughed first, and everyone else followed suit.

When the hilarity was over, Rafiq said, "We will have to run the vermin out of town. And someone is going to have to let the people and the media know that there will be no wedding."

"I will," said Shafir. "And I must remember to tell the two tourism delegates I invited, too."

"That can all wait until tomorrow," said the king. "For tonight we will celebrate Zara's narrow escape. Ay me, when I think of how Zara might have suffered in the years to come…" He broke off and rubbed the bridge of his nose. Then his sharp black eyes rested on Megan. "I make my apologies to you, too, Megan, for any unhappiness you have endured. I can only say I am pleased that both you and Zara discovered what a weak character this man has."

"You see, that wasn't so bad," Shafir said, once they were back in the comfort of his home, as he poured Megan a cup of mint tea. Though it was nearly midnight, he'd made the offer of tea because she looked so wired he suspected the hot drink would help her to sleep.

She took the cup from him, cradling it between her hands and sank into the dark crimson sofa. "It was worse than bad, it was terrible. When Zara arrived…" Her voice trailed away and she shook her head at the memory.

"It saved me from the horns of a dilemma," said Shafir,

perching himself on the arm of the sofa. "Whether to tell Zara the truth, or to threaten Jacques with castration if he ever screwed around on Zara."

"Shafir, you savage!" But Megan couldn't stop the gurgle of laughter at the mental picture of his threatening Jacques.

"What do women see in him?" Shafir sounded driven.

She lifted one shoulder in a shrug and dropped it. "He's easy on the eyes."

Shafir snorted. "You and Zara are both intelligent women. The man must have something more than good looks."

It was not easy exposing her dreams. But Shafir was not the brute his reputation suggested. He listened. He understood. Most of the time. Perhaps he'd understand this, too.

She searched for the right words. "Jacques has a talent for homing in on what a woman most wants and saying what she most wants to hear. I wanted love—I suspect Zara was looking for that, too. The soul mate line worked. Jacques is charming. He courted me as if I were the only woman in the world for him. I started to believe it. Zara probably did, too."

It left a bitter taste in her mouth to realize how easily she'd been duped. "He was very convincing."

"I'm sure he was," he said abruptly.

"I wanted to fall in love. And he looked like he had all the right qualifications. He even knew about wine—and that's important to my family."

"And to you?" he asked quietly. "Is that essential?"

"All I want is someone who loves me more than anyone, anything in the world. You should see how my brothers look at the women they love. It's got nothing to do with what they do for a living. It's about who they are. Beloved."

Shafir slowly let out the breath he'd been holding.

Megan took another sip of tea. "Now that I've met your parents like you wanted, and now that Zara's not getting married, that means I'm free to go home, doesn't it?"

Her words resounded within him like the hollow knell of a heavy brass bell. "You don't have to go yet. You once said you'd come here seeking excitement, adventure, romance. Have you found all those?"

She shook her head slowly. "I was being flippant when I said that. Shafir, I can't stay. I need to get back home. There'll be tons of work to be done."

"You could come work here."

As he spoke, Shafir realized it offered a possible solution. A temporary solution until he convinced her how necessary she had become to him. But this way would buy him time, and he wouldn't lose her. Yet.

"I could do with someone like you."

"You don't grow wine," Megan pointed out, her pulse starting to pound at the thought of working with Shafir all day, every day.

"Don't be smart." He grinned at her, a glorious breathtaking grin, and her heart rolled over. "Your skills are easily transferable. There are aspects of my business I don't enjoy."

"So pay someone else to do it." He was a control freak, and she couldn't readily see him delegating stuff he considered important.

"I already do. But I find that they are not up to my expectations. I want you."

Her heart leaped at that. But he didn't mean it. Not in the way she wanted him to mean it.

"And you think I would be up to your expectations?" It was flattering that he wanted to hire her, and Megan found herself smiling across at him.

"Oh, yes, I'm quite sure of it. It's that boundless energy you have. Your enthusiasm for everything and everyone. Already you are catching on to Arabic. I heard the exchange you had with Naema early this morning."

Megan discovered she was actually considering his proposal. Don't, she told herself, it will only lead to heartache. She would always want more than he would ever be able to offer her.

She shifted under his intense stare. Time to be entertaining and lighten the mood. "Don't even think about it, Shafir."

"What?"

"Refusing to let me leave the country."

"Now there's a tempting thought." But he didn't look away, and Megan could feel the temperature rising.

She shouldn't even be considering staying…she really shouldn't.

"I can't," she said.

"I've gotten used to having you around." Shafir tried to make a joke of it. "Who's going to live in my harem at Qasr Al-Ward?"

Her expression was indeterminable. "I'm sure you'll have no difficulty filling the walled perfumed garden with throngs of women."

"I've never wanted throngs of women."

After a taut moment, she said, "What do you want?"

You. The truth of that was as fundamental to him as breathing. He wanted Megan forever. But after everything she'd been subjected to, he was quite sure she couldn't wait to get out of Dhahara.

As she was leaving regardless, it was worth one shot of honesty. "You want to know what I want right now? I want to carry you to my bed and forget all about tomorrow." About the wedding celebrations that needed to be cancelled, about booking Megan a ticket to the place she called home.

"Shafir—"

She was wavering.

"Please…" He held out his hand.

She set down the tiny cup she held and came to him.

He embraced her. She was soft and warm in his arms and a surge of protective strength filled him. Mine, he thought. My woman.

My wife…

A sense of rightness filled him. Megan was his. He wouldn't ask her to stay as his mistress, and she'd already refused his offer of employment. He had tonight to convince her that they belonged together as man and woman.

Shafir carried her up the empty stairs and down the corridor to his bedchamber. Once inside, he placed Megan gently on the bedcover of rich reds and purples.

But this time it wasn't about seduction; this time it was about infinitely more.

Leaning over, he kissed her neck, her cheeks, her lips. He worshipped her with his touch. She was silent. But her fingers stroked down his back, her touch telling him what words couldn't.

From there on everything moved quickly. Her clothes, his clothes, landed on the floor in a heap.

Her naked skin glowed like lustrous pearl in the pale glow of his bedside lamp. He stroked it, loving the silken softness. She undulated, and his hand repeated the movement starting at her shoulder, sliding over the sides of her breasts, across her belly, over her thighs, and retracing the path.

His lips followed where his fingers led. Megan arched up as his mouth explored the scented valley between her breasts. Moving lower, he tasted the sweetness of her inner thigh, and she moaned.

She was moist, ready. This time he was prepared. A moment's delay as he reached for the bed stand, then he moved over her and slid home. She was hot and wet and her arms came around him, pulling him into her. It was his turn to groan out loud.

He pressed forward, sinking down, then retreating. Her hips lifted slightly in response to each thrust, increasing the pleasure as their bodies moved as one.

The friction built, sensation spiraled upward, and Shafir shut his eyes as the heat took him. As he came, Megan gasped. He felt her contractions against him, and he fell through the veils of pleasure.

Megan lay back, gasping, blood pounding through her head. *Wow.* She tipped back her head to meet the eyes of the man balanced above her, who had taken her places she'd never been before.

Her soul mate.

The burnt bronze eyes were unexpectedly solemn. He reached out a hand and stroked her hair, his touch gentle, his fingers trembling.

He'd felt it, too.

Emotion washed through her, turning her limbs to water. "I don't think I'll be able to stand. I feel so weak." She tried to make light of the moment.

His lips curved into a smile, but his eyes remained intent. Her heart skipped a beat. What now?

"Megan, will you marry me?"

When it came, it shook her world. Her first thought was that she must have misheard him.

"What?"

"Will you do me the honor of becoming my wife, living with me at Qasr Al-Ward for all of our lives?"

"Shafir!"

He couldn't be serious. But there was no humor in his face, only implacable purpose.

He meant it.

He wanted her to marry him.

Oh, God.

"I can't."

The bronze dulled a little, but the determination in the set of his chin increased. "You can…if you choose to."

He slid over to the other side of the bed and she felt a shuddering sense of loss.

He pulled a sheet up over both of them and the loneliness eased.

Temptation tugged at her. It would be easy, so easy to give in, to be with him. "It's not about what I want. Surely you know that?"

He turned onto his side and propped his head up on his hand. "That's all it is about."

He was a desert prince. And even though her family was successful and wealthy, she was still a country girl at heart. His father had clear ideas of the kind of wife he needed, and she fell far short. How could she ever say yes?

"Your father is the king of Dhahara."

His mouth kinked and the laugh lines around his eyes deepened. "You won't be marrying my father. You'll be marrying me."

She played with the edge of the sheet. "But don't you see? You should marry someone suitable."

"I see someone who is eminently suitable. I see a woman who can inspire loyalty in a household, who can talk with a baker's wife and bargain in a busy *souk.* I see a woman who is not afraid to learn a complex, foreign language, or ride a camel, or make love in a life-affirming way. The woman I see is brave and talented and passionate. What more could I ever want?"

Her breath caught. "I say the wrong things… I open my mouth when I should keep it shut… I lose my temper. None of those are qualities you need in a wife. I'm not suitable."

But her heart was hammering in her chest, and Megan realized that she wanted more than anything in the world to say yes. The look in Shafir's eyes, his gravity, the tenderness in his touch when he'd made love to her, all of it made her believe that he loved her. It was almost more than she could bear.

He reached out a hand and touched her lips. "You tell the truth. There is not a sliver of deceit in you. That is a fine quality, one that I would be proud to have in my wife, not something to be ashamed about."

"I'm not a virgin."

He gave a dismissive shrug. "Nor am I."

Megan knew there was one more thing she needed to get out the way. But how would he react?

She took a deep breath. "I came to Dhahara to—"

He interrupted her. "Megan, I don't—"

"Don't." She held up a hand. "Please don't stop me. I need to say this. If there is ever to be a way clear for us, we need to talk about Jacques. I came here to fall in love with him. Will you be able to live all our lives with the knowledge that even though I was never his lover, I came here to do my best to fall in love with another man?"

His breath caught at the admission that she and Jacques had never been lovers. She knew then that he would never have asked, and the softening in his mouth told her of his relief.

"And I had the task of keeping you away from him. I abducted you, locked you away. Will you be able to live with that?"

She took the hand that lay on the sheets and held it between both of hers. "I will thank you every day of our lives that you saved me from a horrible mistake."

"I don't believe you would have fallen in love with him."

"No, because I love you."

His eyes blazed. "That is all that matters." He swept her into his arms and kissed her until she had no breath left.

When he finally released her, she said, "We both need time."

He shook his head. "If you agree, I want to be married as soon as possible."

"Be reasonable," she pleaded.

"I am being reasonable. I don't give a fig about Garnier. About what my family thinks. All I care about is you. Haven't you realized that yet?" The intensity of his regard caused something to splinter deep in her heart. "In fact, if I had more grace I would thank Garnier for bringing you to Dhahara, for bringing us together, woman for whom I shall forsake all others."

Moved beyond measure, Megan burrowed deeper into him. "We would have met," she said at last. "You are my destiny."

"So you will marry me?"

"If you insist."

"I do."

I do.

The words had become a steady refrain over the past three days, Shafir realized with some satisfaction.

There had been the press conference. "You want to get married, Your Highness?" That had come from a stunned news reporter.

"I do."

Then her family had arrived in full force. There had been the interrogation by her three brothers, Joshua, Rafaelo and Heath, which had ended in one question: "Do you love Megan?"

"I do," he had replied.

Her mother and father had beamed with relief. Her

brothers had shaken Shafir's hand, their grip warning him that they would be expecting him to take excellent care of their baby sister.

Shafir had no intention of doing anything else.

Finally their women had hugged Megan and wished her every happiness.

And now there was the wedding. The most important "I do" moment of them all.

He'd wanted to get married immediately. But first he'd had to convince Megan.

It had taken some doing.

He'd argued that there was no need to wait—a wedding was ready to roll. What was the point of wasting a state wedding that had already been arranged?

She'd paled. "It's too grand."

"I am a royal prince. The people of Dhahara can't wait for a wedding."

"There's not enough time," she'd wailed.

"For what? We've already made all the important decisions." Like that he loved her. And she loved him.

"For a dress."

He'd laughed then. "That can be done in a day."

"To make a guest list."

"The invites went out months ago for Zara and Jacques. Sure, some of those people will drop off and you'll have some of your own guests, but it can be done." Fortunately her family and closest friends had dropped everything and flown here.

"I need time to study that list, to familiarize myself with the names so I can talk sense to your guests. It's a state occasion."

"I don't care about anyone else. You'll be talking to me. It's our wedding day."

"I need time to think."

That was the one thing he wasn't giving her. And now as she stood beside him in a stunning white silk wedding dress he was very pleased that he hadn't.

The dazed look that she'd worn over the past two days had at last subsided. He couldn't wait for the wedding to be over and to see her laugh again. Joie de vivre. He gave her hand a gentle squeeze as he prepared himself to say the words that had become the cornerstone of his life over the past few days.

I do.

I do love you.

I do cherish you.

I do forsake all others.

Forever.

His eyes met Megan's as he spoke the vows of his heart.

He forgot about the people watching—his family, her family. He forgot about the fact that the wedding was being televised for the people of his land. He forgot about everything except the woman who stood beside him.

His bride.

It was late.

The fireworks were over. Katar rested as Malik drove the limousine back to King Selim's palace where the reception had been hosted.

Shafir pulled his wife across the long seat of the limousine into his arms. "Happy?"

She tilted her head up. "Oh, yes."

Tomorrow they would return to Qasr Al-Ward. Shafir planned to take Megan deep into the desert for a few nights of time alone. But tonight they would spend in his city residence.

"I was surprised by how many people congratulated me today." She glanced up at him through her lashes. "There seemed to be a view that you were too wild for any woman to wed."

Shafir started to laugh.

"Several people expressed pity and told me that I'd have to get used to living in the desert. I told them that I came to Dhahara in search of excitement, adventure and romance."

The laughter faded from his face, and a gleam of concern lit his eyes. "Does that worry you? If it does, we can spend more time in the city."

"That would be like caging a tiger." She paused, examining her husband. "The first time I met you I decided you were untamed. Wild. A man who could never be civilized."

"A savage." His teeth flashed in the dimness.

"My savage. And it's that raw male strength that's exactly what I love. My soul mate. You're everything I ever wanted."

"You are the wife of my desert heart—my *ain.*My only one."

Megan's breath caught at his whispered words. He bent his head to kiss her, and for a few minutes there was silence.

When he raised his head, he said, "I have a wedding gift waiting for you at Qasr Al-Ward."

"A wedding gift?"

"It's not the usual jewels—although I'll buy you those, too," he added hastily. "This is something that I think no other woman would value as much as you will."

Megan tipped her head to one side. "What is it?"

"I should make you wait and see so that it's a surprise."

"Tell me!"

"It's a camel."

He watched in amusement as her eyes grew bright, her face filled with joy and she started to laugh.

"You bought the little white camel from the breeder you called a jerk, didn't you?"

He inclined his head. "You know me better than I know myself."

She threw herself against his chest and tilted her face up to his, her eyes dancing. "Now I know you love me. And I also know that you always intended for me to return to Qasr Al-Ward."

"Well, I never did show you the palmerie I planted."

She gave him a slow, secret smile. "No, I was going to remind you about that before I left."

"But now you're not leaving." There was a wealth of satisfaction in the statement.

Megan snuggled up to him. "My home is where you are."

"Tonight, home will be in Katar, and tomorrow let us go to Qasr Al-Wadi." Shafir smiled and closed his arms around her.

He'd waited too long for this joy. Now it was his.

* * * * *

Don't miss Tessa Radley's next Desire™ novel, Millionaire Under the Mistletoe, *published in November 2010 from Mills & Boon.*